PARADISE LOST AND PARADISE REGAINED

John Milton

COLLINS
CLASSICS

Harper Press
An imprint of HarperCollins*Publishers*
77–85 Fulham Palace Road
Hammersmith
London W6 8JB

This Harper Press paperback edition published 2013

A catalogue record for this book is available from the British Library

ISBN: 978-0-00-790210-1

Printed and bound in Great Britain by Clays Ltd, St Ives plc

MIX
Paper from
responsible sources
FSC™ C007454

FSC™ is a non-profit international organisation established to promote
the responsible management of the world's forests. Products carrying the
FSC label are independently certified to assure consumers that they come
from forests that are managed to meet the social, economic and
ecological needs of present and future generations,
and other controlled sources.

Find out more about HarperCollins and the environment at
www.harpercollins.co.uk/green

Life & Times section © HarperCollins*Publishers* Ltd
Gerard Cheshire asserts his moral rights as author of the Life & Times section
Classic Literature: Words and Phrases adapted from
Collins English Dictionary

Typesetting in Kalix by Palimpsest Book Production Limited,
Falkirk, Stirlingshire

All rights reserved. No part of this publication may be reproduced,
stored in a retrieval system, or transmitted, in any form or by any means,
electronic, mechanical, photocopying, recording or otherwise,
without the prior permission of the publishers.

This book is sold subject to the condition that it shall not, by way of trade
or otherwise, be lent, re-sold, hired out or otherwise circulated without the
publisher's prior consent in any form of binding or cover other than that
in which it is published and without a similar condition including
this condition being imposed on the subsequent purchaser.

History of Collins

In 1819, millworker William Collins from Glasgow, Scotland, set up a company for printing and publishing pamphlets, sermons, hymn books and prayer books. That company was Collins and was to mark the birth of HarperCollins Publishers as we know it today. The long tradition of Collins dictionary publishing can be traced back to the first dictionary William published in 1824, *Greek and English Lexicon*. Indeed, from 1840 onwards, he began to produce illustrated dictionaries and even obtained a licence to print and publish the Bible.

Soon after, William published the first Collins novel, *Ready Reckoner*, however it was the time of the Long Depression, where harvests were poor, prices were high, potato crops had failed and violence was erupting in Europe. As a result, many factories across the country were forced to close down and William chose to retire in 1846, partly due to the hardships he was facing.

Aged 30, William's son, William II took over the business. A keen humanitarian with a warm heart and a generous spirit, William II was truly 'Victorian' in his outlook. He introduced new, up-to-date steam presses and published affordable editions of Shakespeare's works and *Pilgrim's Progress*, making them available to the masses for the first time. A new demand for educational books meant that success came with the publication of travel books, scientific books, encyclopaedias and dictionaries. This demand to be educated led to the later publication of atlases and Collins also held the monopoly on scripture writing at the time.

In the 1860s Collins began to expand and diversify

and the idea of 'books for the millions' was developed. Affordable editions of classical literature were published and in 1903 Collins introduced 10 titles in their Collins Handy Illustrated Pocket Novels. These proved so popular that a few years later this had increased to an output of 50 volumes, selling nearly half a million in their year of publication. In the same year, The Everyman's Library was also instituted, with the idea of publishing an affordable library of the most important classical works, biographies, religious and philosophical treatments, plays, poems, travel and adventure. This series eclipsed all competition at the time and the introduction of paperback books in the 1950s helped to open that market and marked a high point in the industry.

HarperCollins is and has always been a champion of the classics and the current Collins Classics series follows in this tradition – publishing classical literature that is affordable and available to all. Beautifully packaged, highly collectible and intended to be reread and enjoyed at every opportunity.

Life & Times

Milton and England

In understanding works of literature it often pays to consider the context in which they were written. John Milton's poems *Paradise Lost* and *Paradise Regained* were influenced by the political landscape in England. John Milton (1608–74) was aged 34 at the outbreak of the English Civil War (1642–51), which lasted for nine years and saw tremendous suffering and upheaval visited upon the English people.

King Charles I had reigned since 1625 and generated enormous resentment throughout the country by levying heavy taxes without parliamentary consent and allying himself with the Catholic church in a Puritan Protestant country. He felt he had a divine right to absolute power and his persistence in this view eventually led to warfare and his execution in 1649. Those in support of the king were the Royalists, aka Cavaliers, and those in support of parliament were the Parliamentarians, aka the Roundheads or New Model Army.

Milton supported the latter and began writing prose in reaction to the Bellum Episcopale (Episcopal War) or Bishop's War (1639–40), which was a precursor to the civil war. As a Presbyterian, Milton favoured a church without hierarchical structure and was therefore fundamentally opposed to the monarch's favouring of episcopacy, whereby bishops controlled the church in the manner of Catholicism. Despite both being Christian faiths, such differences led to deep-seated resentment and sectarianism between groups. Within two years a divided nation would be ready to brandish arms and fight to the death.

In addition to his talent as a writer, Milton was a scholar and politician and he was in direct contact with Oliver Cromwell and the rest of the Parliamentarian leadership. Much of his writing was therefore propaganda against King Charles and the

Royalists. Following the civil war and the death of the king, the victorious Cromwell made himself Lord Protector and ruled England between 1653–58. He died of a urinary infection and was briefly succeeded by his son Richard, who resigned in 1659. By 1660 the dead king's son was reinstated as King Charles II and England's chapter as a republic was over.

In 1661 Oliver Cromwell's decomposing cadaver was exhumed from Westminster Abbey and he was posthumously executed in celebration of the restored monarchy. His body was eventually reinterred in a pit at Tyburn, while his head was displayed on a pole outside Westminster Hall for 24 years. It was eventually buried in Cambridge in 1960.

The Poems

Around the time of Cromwell's death, Milton began writing his epic poem *Paradise Lost*, which he eventually published in 1667. The core theme of the poem is the Fall of Man, which is a fundamental component in the doctrine of Christianity, as illustrated by the temptation of Adam and Eve in the Garden of Eden. In essence, humanity begins in innocence and obedience to the Christian god, but soon falls into a state of guilt and disobedience through an inability to resist temptation. Their downfall occurs when they eat the fruit of the Tree of Knowledge of Good and Evil, which causes them to act shamefully. Their god then banishes them from the garden where humanity is left perpetually attempting to return to a state of godliness.

Before this event, there is a war over heaven, which sees Satan and his followers beaten and banished to hell by the Messiah (the son of the Christian god). There is evidently a parallel in Milton's mind between this Angelic War and the English Civil War. He sees King Charles I as Satan incarnate and Oliver Cromwell as the Messiah, come to purge the nation of those with a sense of entitlement. Milton had the wisdom to realize that the population, although relieved of the king's tyranny, still had a lot to learn about following the path to divine redemption, which is why he reminded England through his poetry that humanity remained banished from paradise.

Paradise Lost comprises in excess of ten thousand lines of blank verse, which means that the poetry is non-rhyming and that each line is structured in iambic pentameter. It is divided into 12 books and most of it was written while Milton's sight was failing and he had become almost blind, which meant that he had to have it transcribed from his dictation.

In 1671 Milton published *Paradise Regained*. It is described as a mini-epic poem, as it comprises only four books. In this work Milton is focused on the theme of duality and reversal, with the central story being that of the Temptation of Christ, as opposed to the Temptation of Adam and Eve in *Paradise Lost*. The resilience and determination of Christ in the face of temptation is Milton's way of saying that paradise can be found on Earth if only people could learn the discipline of Christ. Moreover, Milton was being slightly smug about his own attainment of godliness in that regard.

Domestically, Milton had had a pretty rough time of it during the period he was writing *Paradise Lost*. He had already lost his first wife and son in 1652 and then he lost his second wife and daughter in 1658. These events undoubtedly gave Milton a more morose and morbid view on life, which must have influenced his forlorn and even vitriolic attitude at the time. By 1662 however he had married for a third time and was a far happier man. It seems that, despite his being blind, his newly found contentment had a marked effect on his temperament leading to the writing of *Paradise Regained*. He went to his grave three years later, as fulfilled and satisfied as he could hope to be.

Like William Shakespeare two generations before him, Milton made a significant contribution to the evolution of English literature. Both of them enjoyed the process of writing and finding the perfect phrase, thereby turning the prosaic into the poetic. It was this transformation of plain spoken English into an art form that brought their stories and allegories to life in the imagination of the population and turned their work into a legacy.

Milton demonstrated that he possessed considerable intelligence combined with strong opinions, which compelled him to write regardless of the reception of his work by others. In his own lifetime he was a controversial figure because he was a partisan, a propagandist and a polemicist, happily standing in the line of fire to have his voice heard. As a result he had plenty of political enemies, but as an intellect he was highly respected. Fundamentally, his critics could not argue with the achievement of *Paradise Lost*, both as a creative masterpiece and as an allegorical commentary on the human condition following the civil war.

Milton's Influence

Milton's literary influence was particularly marked in the nineteenth century when novelists, including Thomas Hardy, sought to attain a high level of literary craft in their poetry and looked to Milton's work. This disciplinarian awareness of the chosen word also found its way into their prose, so that Hardy's novels have a quasi-poetic quality to them, lending them a considered quality that he might otherwise not have achieved.

Moving into the twentieth century, Milton's influence waned because genres in prose and poetry had evolved beyond looking for direct inspiration from Renaissance writers. However, Milton is still highly regarded as a major player in the story of English literature, with *Paradise Lost* taking its place in the pantheon of all-time great works. Like Shakespeare's plays, it holds some of the literary DNA that forms the basis for modern English literature and one cannot form a lineage of English literature without including Milton.

PARADISE
LOST

BOOK I

Of Man's first disobedience, and the fruit
Of that forbidden tree whose mortal taste
Brought death into the World, and all our woe,
With loss of Eden, till one greater Man
Restore us, and regain the blissful seat,
Sing, Heavenly Muse, that, on the secret top
Of Oreb, or of Sinai, didst inspire
That shepherd who first taught the chosen seed
In the beginning how the heavens and earth
Rose out of Chaos: or, if Sion hill
Delight thee more, and Siloa's brook that flowed
Fast by the oracle of God, I thence
Invoke thy aid to my adventurous song,
That with no middle flight intends to soar
Above th' Aonian mount, while it pursues
Things unattempted yet in prose or rhyme.
And chiefly thou, O Spirit, that dost prefer
Before all temples th' upright heart and pure,
Instruct me, for thou know'st; thou from the first
Wast present, and, with mighty wings outspread,
Dove-like sat'st brooding on the vast Abyss,
And mad'st it pregnant: what in me is dark

Illumine, what is low raise and support;
That, to the height of this great argument,
I may assert Eternal Providence,
And justify the ways of God to men.
Say first—for Heaven hides nothing from thy view,
Nor the deep tract of Hell—say first what cause
Moved our grand parents, in that happy state,
Favoured of Heaven so highly, to fall off
From their Creator, and transgress his will
For one restraint, lords of the World besides.
Who first seduced them to that foul revolt?
Th' infernal Serpent; he it was whose guile,
Stirred up with envy and revenge, deceived
The mother of mankind, what time his pride
Had cast him out from Heaven, with all his host
Of rebel Angels, by whose aid, aspiring
To set himself in glory above his peers,
He trusted to have equalled the Most High,
If he opposed, and with ambitious aim
Against the throne and monarchy of God,
Raised impious war in Heaven and battle proud,
With vain attempt. Him the Almighty Power
Hurled headlong flaming from th' ethereal sky,
With hideous ruin and combustion, down
To bottomless perdition, there to dwell
In adamantine chains and penal fire,
Who durst defy th' Omnipotent to arms.
Nine times the space that measures day and night
To mortal men, he, with his horrid crew,
Lay vanquished, rolling in the fiery gulf,
Confounded, though immortal. But his doom
Reserved him to more wrath; for now the thought
Both of lost happiness and lasting pain
Torments him: round he throws his baleful eyes,
That witnessed huge affliction and dismay,

Mixed with obdurate pride and steadfast hate.
At once, as far as Angels ken, he views
The dismal situation waste and wild.
A dungeon horrible, on all sides round,
As one great furnace flamed; yet from those flames
No light; but rather darkness visible
Served only to discover sights of woe,
Regions of sorrow, doleful shades, where peace
And rest can never dwell, hope never comes
That comes to all, but torture without end
Still urges, and a fiery deluge, fed
With ever-burning sulphur unconsumed.
Such place Eternal Justice has prepared
For those rebellious; here their prison ordained
In utter darkness, and their portion set,
As far removed from God and light of Heaven
As from the centre thrice to th' utmost pole.
Oh how unlike the place from whence they fell!
There the companions of his fall, o'erwhelmed
With floods and whirlwinds of tempestuous fire,
He soon discerns; and, weltering by his side,
One next himself in power, and next in crime,
Long after known in Palestine, and named
Beelzebub. To whom th' Arch-Enemy,
And thence in Heaven called Satan, with bold words
Breaking the horrid silence, thus began:—
"If thou beest he—but O how fallen! how changed
From him who, in the happy realms of light
Clothed with transcendent brightness, didst outshine
Myriads, though bright!—if he whom mutual league,
United thoughts and counsels, equal hope
And hazard in the glorious enterprise
Joined with me once, now misery hath joined
In equal ruin; into what pit thou seest
From what height fallen: so much the stronger proved

He with his thunder; and till then who knew
The force of those dire arms? Yet not for those,
Nor what the potent Victor in his rage
Can else inflict, do I repent, or change,
Though changed in outward lustre, that fixed mind,
And high disdain from sense of injured merit,
That with the Mightiest raised me to contend,
And to the fierce contentions brought along
Innumerable force of Spirits armed,
That durst dislike his reign, and, me preferring,
His utmost power with adverse power opposed
In dubious battle on the plains of Heaven,
And shook his throne. What though the field be lost?
All is not lost—the unconquerable will,
And study of revenge, immortal hate,
And courage never to submit or yield:
And what is else not to be overcome?
That glory never shall his wrath or might
Extort from me. To bow and sue for grace
With suppliant knee, and deify his power
Who, from the terror of this arm, so late
Doubted his empire—that were low indeed;
That were an ignominy and shame beneath
This downfall; since, by fate, the strength of Gods,
And this empyreal sybstance, cannot fail;
Since, through experience of this great event,
In arms not worse, in foresight much advanced,
We may with more successful hope resolve
To wage by force or guile eternal war,
Irreconcilable to our grand Foe,
Who now triumphs, and in th' excess of joy
Sole reigning holds the tyranny of Heaven."
So spake th' apostate Angel, though in pain,
Vaunting aloud, but racked with deep despair;
And him thus answered soon his bold compeer:—

"O Prince, O Chief of many throned Powers
That led th' embattled Seraphim to war
Under thy conduct, and, in dreadful deeds
Fearless, endangered Heaven's perpetual King,
And put to proof his high supremacy,
Whether upheld by strength, or chance, or fate,
Too well I see and rue the dire event
That, with sad overthrow and foul defeat,
Hath lost us Heaven, and all this mighty host
In horrible destruction laid thus low,
As far as Gods and heavenly Essences
Can perish: for the mind and spirit remains
Invincible, and vigour soon returns,
Though all our glory extinct, and happy state
Here swallowed up in endless misery.
But what if he our Conqueror (whom I now
Of force believe almighty, since no less
Than such could have o'erpowered such force as ours)
Have left us this our spirit and strength entire,
Strongly to suffer and support our pains,
That we may so suffice his vengeful ire,
Or do him mightier service as his thralls
By right of war, whate'er his business be,
Here in the heart of Hell to work in fire,
Or do his errands in the gloomy Deep?
What can it the avail though yet we feel
Strength undiminished, or eternal being
To undergo eternal punishment?"
Whereto with speedy words th' Arch-Fiend replied:—
"Fallen Cherub, to be weak is miserable,
Doing or suffering: but of this be sure—
To do aught good never will be our task,
But ever to do ill our sole delight,
As being the contrary to his high will
Whom we resist. If then his providence

Out of our evil seek to bring forth good,
Our labour must be to pervert that end,
And out of good still to find means of evil;
Which ofttimes may succeed so as perhaps
Shall grieve him, if I fail not, and disturb
His inmost counsels from their destined aim.
But see! the angry Victor hath recalled
His ministers of vengeance and pursuit
Back to the gates of Heaven: the sulphurous hail,
Shot after us in storm, o'erblown hath laid
The fiery surge that from the precipice
Of Heaven received us falling; and the thunder,
Winged with red lightning and impetuous rage,
Perhaps hath spent his shafts, and ceases now
To bellow through the vast and boundless Deep.
Let us not slip th' occasion, whether scorn
Or satiate fury yield it from our Foe.
Seest thou yon dreary plain, forlorn and wild,
The seat of desolation, void of light,
Save what the glimmering of these livid flames
Casts pale and dreadful? Thither let us tend
From off the tossing of these fiery waves;
There rest, if any rest can harbour there;
And, re-assembling our afflicted powers,
Consult how we may henceforth most offend
Our enemy, our own loss how repair,
How overcome this dire calamity,
What reinforcement we may gain from hope,
If not, what resolution from despair."
Thus Satan, talking to his nearest mate,
With head uplift above the wave, and eyes
That sparkling blazed; his other parts besides
Prone on the flood, extended long and large,
Lay floating many a rood, in bulk as huge
As whom the fables name of monstrous size,

Titanian or Earth-born, that warred on Jove,
Briareos or Typhon, whom the den
By ancient Tarsus held, or that sea-beast
Leviathan, which God of all his works
Created hugest that swim th' ocean-stream.
Him, haply slumbering on the Norway foam,
The pilot of some small night-foundered skiff,
Deeming some island, oft, as seamen tell,
With fixed anchor in his scaly rind,
Moors by his side under the lee, while night
Invests the sea, and wished morn delays.
So stretched out huge in length the Arch-fiend lay,
Chained on the burning lake; nor ever thence
Had risen, or heaved his head, but that the will
And high permission of all-ruling Heaven
Left him at large to his own dark designs,
That with reiterated crimes he might
Heap on himself damnation, while he sought
Evil to others, and enraged might see
How all his malice served but to bring forth
Infinite goodness, grace, and mercy, shewn
On Man by him seduced, but on himself
Treble confusion, wrath, and vengeance poured.
Forthwith upright he rears from off the pool
His mighty stature; on each hand the flames
Driven backward slope their pointing spires, and rolled
In billows, leave i' th' midst a horrid vale.
Then with expanded wings he steers his flight
Aloft, incumbent on the dusky air,
That felt unusual weight; till on dry land
He lights—if it were land that ever burned
With solid, as the lake with liquid fire,
And such appeared in hue as when the force
Of subterranean wind transports a hill
Torn from Pelorus, or the shattered side

Of thundering Etna, whose combustible
And fuelled entrails, thence conceiving fire,
Sublimed with mineral fury, aid the winds,
And leave a singed bottom all involved
With stench and smoke. Such resting found the sole
Of unblest feet. Him followed his next mate;
Both glorying to have scaped the Stygian flood
As gods, and by their own recovered strength,
Not by the sufferance of supernal Power.
"Is this the region, this the soil, the clime,"
Said then the lost Archangel, "this the seat
That we must change for Heaven?—this mournful gloom
For that celestial light? Be it so, since he
Who now is sovereign can dispose and bid
What shall be right: farthest from him is best
Whom reason hath equalled, force hath made supreme
Above his equals. Farewell, happy fields,
Where joy for ever dwells! Hail, horrors! hail,
Infernal world! and thou, profoundest Hell,
Receive thy new possessor—one who brings
A mind not to be changed by place or time.
The mind is its own place, and in itself
Can make a Heaven of Hell, a Hell of Heaven.
What matter where, if I be still the same,
And what I should be, all but less than he
Whom thunder hath made greater? Here at least
We shall be free; th' Almighty hath not built
Here for his envy, will not drive us hence:
Here we may reign secure; and, in my choice,
To reign is worth ambition, though in Hell:
Better to reign in Hell than serve in Heaven.
But wherefore let we then our faithful friends,
Th' associates and co-partners of our loss,
Lie thus astonished on th' oblivious pool,
And call them not to share with us their part

In this unhappy mansion, or once more
With rallied arms to try what may be yet
Regained in Heaven, or what more lost in Hell?"
So Satan spake; and him Beelzebub
Thus answered:—"Leader of those armies bright
Which, but th' Omnipotent, none could have foiled!
If once they hear that voice, their liveliest pledge
Of hope in fears and dangers—heard so oft
In worst extremes, and on the perilous edge
Of battle, when it raged, in all assaults
Their surest signal—they will soon resume
New courage and revive, though now they lie
Grovelling and prostrate on yon lake of fire,
As we erewhile, astounded and amazed;
No wonder, fallen such a pernicious height!"
He scare had ceased when the superior Fiend
Was moving toward the shore; his ponderous shield,
Ethereal temper, massy, large, and round,
Behind him cast. The broad circumference
Hung on his shoulders like the moon, whose orb
Through optic glass the Tuscan artist views
At evening, from the top of Fesole,
Or in Valdarno, to descry new lands,
Rivers, or mountains, in her spotty globe.
His spear—to equal which the tallest pine
Hewn on Norwegian hills, to be the mast
Of some great ammiral, were but a wand—
He walked with, to support uneasy steps
Over the burning marl, not like those steps
On Heaven's azure; and the torrid clime
Smote on him sore besides, vaulted with fire.
Nathless he so endured, till on the beach
Of that inflamed sea he stood, and called
His legions—Angel Forms, who lay entranced
Thick as autumnal leaves that strow the brooks

In Vallombrosa, where th' Etrurian shades
High over-arched embower; or scattered sedge
Afloat, when with fierce winds Orion armed
Hath vexed the Red-Sea coast, whose waves o'erthrew
Busiris and his Memphian chivalry,
While with perfidious hatred they pursued
The sojourners of Goshen, who beheld
From the safe shore their floating carcases
And broken chariot-wheels. So thick bestrown,
Abject and lost, lay these, covering the flood,
Under amazement of their hideous change.
He called so loud that all the hollow deep
Of Hell resounded:—"Princes, Potentates,
Warriors, the Flower of Heaven—once yours; now lost,
If such astonishment as this can seize
Eternal Spirits! Or have ye chosen this place
After the toil of battle to repose
Your wearied virtue, for the ease you find
To slumber here, as in the vales of Heaven?
Or in this abject posture have ye sworn
To adore the Conqueror, who now beholds
Cherub and Seraph rolling in the flood
With scattered arms and ensigns, till anon
His swift pursuers from Heaven-gates discern
Th' advantage, and, descending, tread us down
Thus drooping, or with linked thunderbolts
Transfix us to the bottom of this gulf?
Awake, arise, or be for ever fallen!"
They heard, and were abashed, and up they sprung
Upon the wing, as when men wont to watch
On duty, sleeping found by whom they dread,
Rouse and bestir themselves ere well awake.
Nor did they not perceive the evil plight
In which they were, or the fierce pains not feel;
Yet to their General's voice they soon obeyed

Innumerable. As when the potent rod
Of Amram's son, in Egypt's evil day,
Waved round the coast, up-called a pitchy cloud
Of locusts, warping on the eastern wind,
That o'er the realm of impious Pharaoh hung
Like Night, and darkened all the land of Nile;
So numberless were those bad Angels seen
Hovering on wing under the cope of Hell,
'Twixt upper, nether, and surrounding fires;
Till, as a signal given, th' uplifted spear
Of their great Sultan waving to direct
Their course, in even balance down they light
On the firm brimstone, and fill all the plain:
A multitude like which the populous North
Poured never from her frozen loins to pass
Rhene or the Danaw, when her barbarous sons
Came like a deluge on the South, and spread
Beneath Gibraltar to the Libyan sands.
Forthwith, form every squadron and each band,
The heads and leaders thither haste where stood
Their great Commander—godlike Shapes, and Forms
Excelling human; princely Dignities;
And Powers that erst in Heaven sat on thrones,
Though on their names in Heavenly records now
Be no memorial, blotted out and rased
By their rebellion from the Books of Life.
Nor had they yet among the sons of Eve
Got them new names, till, wandering o'er the earth,
Through God's high sufferance for the trial of man,
By falsities and lies the greatest part
Of mankind they corrupted to forsake
God their Creator, and th' invisible
Glory of him that made them to transform
Oft to the image of a brute, adorned
With gay religions full of pomp and gold,

And devils to adore for deities:
Then were they known to men by various names,
And various idols through the heathen world.
Say, Muse, their names then known, who first, who last,
Roused from the slumber on that fiery couch,
At their great Emperor's call, as next in worth
Came singly where he stood on the bare strand,
While the promiscuous crowd stood yet aloof?
The chief were those who, from the pit of Hell
Roaming to seek their prey on Earth, durst fix
Their seats, long after, next the seat of God,
Their altars by his altar, gods adored
Among the nations round, and durst abide
Jehovah thundering out of Sion, throned
Between the Cherubim; yea, often placed
Within his sanctuary itself their shrines,
Abominations; and with cursed things
His holy rites and solemn feasts profaned,
And with their darkness durst affront his light.
First, Moloch, horrid king, besmeared with blood
Of human sacrifice, and parents' tears;
Though, for the noise of drums and timbrels loud,
Their children's cries unheard that passed through fire
To his grim idol. Him the Ammonite
Worshiped in Rabba and her watery plain,
In Argob and in Basan, to the stream
Of utmost Arnon. Nor content with such
Audacious neighbourhood, the wisest heart
Of Solomon he led by fraud to build
His temple right against the temple of God
On that opprobrious hill, and made his grove
The pleasant valley of Hinnom, Tophet thence
And black Gehenna called, the type of Hell.
Next Chemos, th' obscene dread of Moab's sons,
From Aroer to Nebo and the wild

Of southmost Abarim; in Hesebon
And Horonaim, Seon's realm, beyond
The flowery dale of Sibma clad with vines,
And Elealè to th' Asphaltic Pool:
Peor his other name, when he enticed
Israel in Sittim, on their march from Nile,
To do him wanton rites, which cost them woe.
Yet thence his lustful orgies he enlarged
Even to that hill of scandal, by the grove
Of Moloch homicide, lust hard by hate,
Till good Josiah drove them thence to Hell.
With these came they who, from the bordering flood
Of old Euphrates to the brook that parts
Egypt from Syrian ground, had general names
Of Baalim and Ashtaroth—those male,
These feminine. For Spirits, when they please,
Can either sex assume, or both; so soft
And uncompounded is their essence pure,
Not tried or manacled with joint or limb,
Nor founded on the brittle strength of bones,
Like cumbrous flesh; but, in what shape they choose,
Dilated or condensed, bright or obscure,
Can execute their airy purposes,
And works of love or enmity fulfil.
For those the race of Israel oft forsook
Their Living Strength, and unfrequented left
His righteous altar, bowing lowly down
To bestial gods; for which their heads as low
Bowed down in battle, sunk before the spear
Of despicable foes. With these in troop
Came Astoreth, whom the Phoenicians called
Astartè, queen of heaven, with crescent horns;
To whose bright image nightly by the moon
Sidonian virgins paid their vows and songs;
In Sion also not unsung, where stood

Her temple on th' offensive mountain, built
By that uxorious king whose heart, though large,
Beguiled by fair idolatresses, fell
To idols foul. Thammuz came next behind,
Whose annual wound in Lebanon allured
The Syrian damsels to lament his fate
In amorous ditties all a summer's day,
While smooth Adonis from his native rock
Ran purple to the sea, supposed with blood
Of Thammuz yearly wounded: the love-tale
Infected Sion's daughters with like heat,
Whose wanton passions in the sacred porch
Ezekiel saw, when, by the vision led,
His eye surveyed the dark idolatries
Of alienated Judah. Next came one
Who mourned in earnest, when the captive ark
Maimed his brute image, head and hands lopt off,
In his own temple, on the grunsel-edge,
Where he fell flat and shamed his worshippers:
Dagon his name, sea-monster, upward man
And downward fish; yet had his temple high
Reared in Azotus, dreaded through the coast
Of Palestine, in Gath and Ascalon,
And Accaron and Gaza's frontier bounds.
Him followed Rimmon, whose delightful seat
Was fair Damascus, on the fertile banks
Of Abbana and Pharphar, lucid streams.
He also against the house of God was bold:
A leper once he lost, and gained a king—
Ahaz, his sottish conqueror, whom he drew
God's altar to disparage and displace
For one of Syrian mode, whereon to burn
His odious offerings, and adore the gods
Whom he had vanquished. After these appeared
A crew who, under names of old renown—

Osiris, Isis, Orus, and their train—
With monstrous shapes and sorceries abused
Fanatic Egypt and her priests to seek
Their wandering gods disguised in brutish forms
Rather than human. Nor did Israel scape
Th' infection, when their borrowed gold composed
The calf in Oreb; and the rebel king
Doubled that sin in Bethel and in Dan,
Likening his Maker to the grazed ox—
Jehovah, who, in one night, when he passed
From Egypt marching, equalled with one stroke
Both her first-born and all her bleating gods.
Belial came last; than whom a Spirit more lewd
Fell not from Heaven, or more gross to love
Vice for itself. To him no temple stood
Or altar smoked; yet who more oft than he
In temples and at altars, when the priest
Turns atheist, as did Eli's sons, who filled
With lust and violence the house of God?
In courts and palaces he also reigns,
And in luxurious cities, where the noise
Of riot ascends above their loftiest towers,
And injury and outrage; and, when night
Darkens the streets, then wander forth the sons
Of Belial, flown with insolence and wine.
Witness the streets of Sodom, and that night
In Gibeah, when the hospitable door
Exposed a matron, to avoid worse rape.
These were the prime in order and in might:
The rest were long to tell; though far renowned
Th' Ionian gods—of Javan's issue held
Gods, yet confessed later than Heaven and Earth,
Their boasted parents;—Titan, Heaven's first-born,
With his enormous brood, and birthright seized
By younger Saturn: he from mightier Jove,

His own and Rhea's son, like measure found;
So Jove usurping reigned. These, first in Crete
And Ida known, thence on the snowy top
Of cold Olympus ruled the middle air,
Their highest heaven; or on the Delphian cliff,
Or in Dodona, and through all the bounds
Of Doric land; or who with Saturn old
Fled over Adria to th' Hesperian fields,
And o'er the Celtic roamed the utmost Isles.
All these and more came flocking; but with looks
Downcast and damp; yet such wherein appeared
Obscure some glimpse of joy to have found their Chief
Not in despair, to have found themselves not lost
In loss itself; which on his countenance cast
Like doubtful hue. But he, his wonted pride
Soon recollecting, with high words, that bore
Semblance of worth, not substance, gently raised
Their fainting courage, and dispelled their fears.
Then straight commands that, at the warlike sound
Of trumpets loud and clarions, be upreared
His mighty standard. That proud honour claimed
Azazel as his right, a Cherub tall:
Who forthwith from the glittering staff unfurled
Th' imperial ensign; which, full high advanced,
Shone like a meteor streaming to the wind,
With gems and golden lustre rich emblazed,
Seraphic arms and trophies; all the while
Sonorous metal blowing martial sounds:
At which the universal host up-sent
A shout that tore Hell's concave, and beyond
Frighted the reign of Chaos and old Night.
All in a moment through the gloom were seen
Ten thousand banners rise into the air,
With orient colours waving: with them rose
A forest huge of spears; and thronging helms

Appeared, and serried shields in thick array
Of depth immeasurable. Anon they move
In perfect phalanx to the Dorian mood
Of flutes and soft recorders—such as raised
To height of noblest temper heroes old
Arming to battle, and instead of rage
Deliberate valour breathed, firm, and unmoved
With dread of death to flight or foul retreat;
Nor wanting power to mitigate and swage
With solemn touches troubled thoughts, and chase
Anguish and doubt and fear and sorrow and pain
From mortal or immortal minds. Thus they,
Breathing united force with fixed thought,
Moved on in silence to soft pipes that charmed
Their painful steps o'er the burnt soil. And now
Advanced in view they stand—a horrid front
Of dreadful length and dazzling arms, in guise
Of warriors old, with ordered spear and shield,
Awaiting what command their mighty Chief
Had to impose. He through the armed files
Darts his experienced eye, and soon traverse
The whole battalion views—their order due,
Their visages and stature as of gods;
Their number last he sums. And now his heart
Distends with pride, and, hardening in his strength,
Glories: for never, since created Man,
Met such embodied force as, named with these,
Could merit more than that small infantry
Warred on by cranes—though all the giant brood
Of Phlegra with th' heroic race were joined
That fought at Thebes and Ilium, on each side
Mixed with auxiliar gods; and what resounds
In fable or romance of Uther's son,
Begirt with British and Armoric knights;
And all who since, baptized or infidel,

Jousted in Aspramont, or Montalban,
Damasco, or Marocco, or Trebisond,
Or whom Biserta sent from Afric shore
When Charlemain with all his peerage fell
By Fontarabbia. Thus far these beyond
Compare of mortal prowess, yet observed
Their dread Commander. He, above the rest
In shape and gesture proudly eminent,
Stood like a tower. His form had yet not lost
All her original brightness, nor appeared
Less than Archangel ruined, and th' excess
Of glory obscured: as when the sun new-risen
Looks through the horizontal misty air
Shorn of his beams, or, from behind the moon,
In dim eclipse, disastrous twilight sheds
On half the nations, and with fear of change
Perplexes monarchs. Darkened so, yet shone
Above them all th' Archangel: but his face
Deep scars of thunder had intrenched, and care
Sat on his faded cheek, but under brows
Of dauntless courage, and considerate pride
Waiting revenge. Cruel his eye, but cast
Signs of remorse and passion, to behold
The fellows of his crime, the followers rather
(Far other once beheld in bliss), condemned
For ever now to have their lot in pain—
Millions of Spirits for his fault amerced
Of Heaven, and from eternal splendours flung
For his revolt—yet faithful how they stood,
Their glory withered; as, when heaven's fire
Hath scathed the forest oaks or mountain pines,
With singed top their stately growth, though bare,
Stands on the blasted heath. He now prepared
To speak; whereat their doubled ranks they bend
From wing to wing, and half enclose him round

With all his peers: attention held them mute.
Thrice he assayed, and thrice, in spite of scorn,
Tears, such as Angels weep, burst forth: at last
Words interwove with sighs found out their way:—
"O myriads of immortal Spirits! O Powers
Matchless, but with th' Almighty!—and that strife
Was not inglorious, though th' event was dire,
As this place testifies, and this dire change,
Hateful to utter. But what power of mind,
Forseeing or presaging, from the depth
Of knowledge past or present, could have feared
How such united force of gods, how such
As stood like these, could ever know repulse?
For who can yet believe, though after loss,
That all these puissant legions, whose exile
Hath emptied Heaven, shall fail to re-ascend,
Self-raised, and repossess their native seat?
For me, be witness all the host of Heaven,
If counsels different, or danger shunned
By me, have lost our hopes. But he who reigns
Monarch in Heaven till then as one secure
Sat on his throne, upheld by old repute,
Consent or custom, and his regal state
Put forth at full, but still his strength concealed—
Which tempted our attempt, and wrought our fall.
Henceforth his might we know, and know our own,
So as not either to provoke, or dread
New war provoked: our better part remains
To work in close design, by fraud or guile,
What force effected not; that he no less
At length from us may find, who overcomes
By force hath overcome but half his foe.
Space may produce new Worlds; whereof so rife
There went a fame in Heaven that he ere long
Intended to create, and therein plant

A generation whom his choice regard
Should favour equal to the Sons of Heaven.
Thither, if but to pry, shall be perhaps
Our first eruption—thither, or elsewhere;
For this infernal pit shall never hold
Celestial Spirits in bondage, nor th' Abyss
Long under darkness cover. But these thoughts
Full counsel must mature. Peace is despaired;
For who can think submission? War, then, war
Open or understood, must be resolved."
He spake; and, to confirm his words, outflew
Millions of flaming swords, drawn from the thighs
Of mighty Cherubim; the sudden blaze
Far round illumined Hell. Highly they raged
Against the Highest, and fierce with grasped arms
Clashed on their sounding shields the din of war,
Hurling defiance toward the vault of Heaven.
There stood a hill not far, whose grisly top
Belched fire and rolling smoke; the rest entire
Shone with a glossy scurf—undoubted sign
That in his womb was hid metallic ore,
The work of sulphur. Thither, winged with speed,
A numerous brigade hastened: as when bands
Of pioneers, with spade and pickaxe armed,
Forerun the royal camp, to trench a field,
Or cast a rampart. Mammon led them on—
Mammon, the least erected Spirit that fell
From Heaven; for even in Heaven his looks and thoughts
Were always downward bent, admiring more
The riches of heaven's pavement, trodden gold,
Than aught divine or holy else enjoyed
In vision beatific. By him first
Men also, and by his suggestion taught,
Ransacked the centre, and with impious hands
Rifled the bowels of their mother Earth

For treasures better hid. Soon had his crew
Opened into the hill a spacious wound,
And digged out ribs of gold. Let none admire
That riches grow in Hell; that soil may best
Deserve the precious bane. And here let those
Who boast in mortal things, and wondering tell
Of Babel, and the works of Memphian kings,
Learn how their greatest monuments of fame
And strength, and art, are easily outdone
By Spirits reprobate, and in an hour
What in an age they, with incessant toil
And hands innumerable, scarce perform.
Nigh on the plain, in many cells prepared,
That underneath had veins of liquid fire
Sluiced from the lake, a second multitude
With wondrous art founded the massy ore,
Severing each kind, and scummed the bullion-dross.
A third as soon had formed within the ground
A various mould, and from the boiling cells
By strange conveyance filled each hollow nook;
As in an organ, from one blast of wind,
To many a row of pipes the sound-board breathes.
Anon out of the earth a fabric huge
Rose like an exhalation, with the sound
Of dulcet symphonies and voices sweet—
Built like a temple, where pilasters round
Were set, and Doric pillars overlaid
With golden architrave; nor did there want
Cornice or frieze, with bossy sculptures graven;
The roof was fretted gold. Not Babylon
Nor great Alcairo such magnificence
Equalled in all their glories, to enshrine
Belus or Serapis their gods, or seat
Their kings, when Egypt with Assyria strove
In wealth and luxury. Th' ascending pile

Stood fixed her stately height, and straight the doors,
Opening their brazen folds, discover, wide
Within, her ample spaces o'er the smooth
And level pavement: from the arched roof,
Pendent by subtle magic, many a row
Of starry lamps and blazing cressets, fed
With naptha and asphaltus, yielded light
As from a sky. The hasty multitude
Admiring entered; and the work some praise,
And some the architect. His hand was known
In Heaven by many a towered structure high,
Where sceptred Angels held their residence,
And sat as Princes, whom the supreme King
Exalted to such power, and gave to rule,
Each in his Hierarchy, the Orders bright.
Nor was his name unheard or unadored
In ancient Greece; and in Ausonian land
Men called him Mulciber; and how he fell
From Heaven they fabled, thrown by angry Jove
Sheer o'er the crystal battlements: from morn
To noon he fell, from noon to dewy eve,
A summer's day, and with the setting sun
Dropt from the zenith, like a falling star,
On Lemnos, th' Aegaean isle. Thus they relate,
Erring; for he with this rebellious rout
Fell long before; nor aught availed him now
To have built in Heaven high towers; nor did he scape
By all his engines, but was headlong sent,
With his industrious crew, to build in Hell.
Meanwhile the winged Heralds, by command
Of sovereign power, with awful ceremony
And trumpet's sound, throughout the host proclaim
A solemn council forthwith to be held
At Pandemonium, the high capital
Of Satan and his peers. Their summons called

From every band and squared regiment
By place or choice the worthiest: they anon
With hundreds and with thousands trooping came
Attended. All access was thronged; the gates
And porches wide, but chief the spacious hall
(Though like a covered field, where champions bold
Wont ride in armed, and at the Soldan's chair
Defied the best of Paynim chivalry
To mortal combat, or career with lance),
Thick swarmed, both on the ground and in the air,
Brushed with the hiss of rustling wings. As bees
In spring-time, when the Sun with Taurus rides.
Pour forth their populous youth about the hive
In clusters; they among fresh dews and flowers
Fly to and fro, or on the smoothed plank,
The suburb of their straw-built citadel,
New rubbed with balm, expatiate, and confer
Their state-affairs: so thick the airy crowd
Swarmed and were straitened; till, the signal given,
Behold a wonder! They but now who seemed
In bigness to surpass Earth's giant sons,
Now less than smallest dwarfs, in narrow room
Throng numberless—like that pygmean race
Beyond the Indian mount; or faery elves,
Whose midnight revels, by a forest-side
Or fountain, some belated peasant sees,
Or dreams he sees, while overhead the Moon
Sits arbitress, and nearer to the Earth
Wheels her pale course: they, on their mirth and dance
Intent, with jocund music charm his ear;
At once with joy and fear his heart rebounds.
Thus incorporeal Spirits to smallest forms
Reduced their shapes immense, and were at large,
Though without number still, amidst the hall
Of that infernal court. But far within,

And in their own dimensions like themselves,
The great Seraphic Lords and Cherubim
In close recess and secret conclave sat,
A thousand demi-gods on golden seats,
Frequent and full. After short silence then,
And summons read, the great consult began.

BOOK II

High on a throne of royal state, which far
Outshone the wealth or Ormus and of Ind,
Or where the gorgeous East with richest hand
Showers on her kings barbaric pearl and gold,
Satan exalted sat, by merit raised
To that bad eminence; and, from despair
Thus high uplifted beyond hope, aspires
Beyond thus high, insatiate to pursue
Vain war with Heaven; and, by success untaught,
His proud imaginations thus displayed:—
"Powers and Dominions, Deities of Heaven!—
For, since no deep within her gulf can hold
Immortal vigour, though oppressed and fallen,
I give not Heaven for lost: from this descent
Celestial Virtues rising will appear
More glorious and more dread than from no fall,
And trust themselves to fear no second fate!—
Me though just right, and the fixed laws of Heaven,
Did first create your leader—next, free choice
With what besides in council or in fight
Hath been achieved of merit—yet this loss,
Thus far at least recovered, hath much more

Established in a safe, unenvied throne,
Yielded with full consent. The happier state
In Heaven, which follows dignity, might draw
Envy from each inferior; but who here
Will envy whom the highest place exposes
Foremost to stand against the Thunderer's aim
Your bulwark, and condemns to greatest share
Of endless pain? Where there is, then, no good
For which to strive, no strife can grow up there
From faction: for none sure will claim in Hell
Precedence; none whose portion is so small
Of present pain that with ambitious mind
Will covet more! With this advantage, then,
To union, and firm faith, and firm accord,
More than can be in Heaven, we now return
To claim our just inheritance of old,
Surer to prosper than prosperity
Could have assured us; and by what best way,
Whether of open war or covert guile,
We now debate. Who can advise may speak."
He ceased; and next him Moloch, sceptred king,
Stood up—the strongest and the fiercest Spirit
That fought in Heaven, now fiercer by despair.
His trust was with th' Eternal to be deemed
Equal in strength, and rather than be less
Cared not to be at all; with that care lost
Went all his fear: of God, or Hell, or worse,
He recked not, and these words thereafter spake:—
"My sentence is for open war. Of wiles,
More unexpert, I boast not: them let those
Contrive who need, or when they need; not now.
For, while they sit contriving, shall the rest—
Millions that stand in arms, and longing wait
The signal to ascend—sit lingering here,
Heaven's fugitives, and for their dwelling-place

Accept this dark opprobrious den of shame,
The prison of his tyranny who reigns
By our delay? No! let us rather choose,
Armed with Hell-flames and fury, all at once
O'er Heaven's high towers to force resistless way,
Turning our tortures into horrid arms
Against the Torturer; when, to meet the noise
Of his almighty engine, he shall hear
Infernal thunder, and, for lightning, see
Black fire and horror shot with equal rage
Among his Angels, and his throne itself
Mixed with Tartarean sulphur and strange fire,
His own invented torments. But perhaps
The way seems difficult, and steep to scale
With upright wing against a higher foe!
Let such bethink them, if the sleepy drench
Of that forgetful lake benumb not still,
That in our proper motion we ascend
Up to our native seat; descent and fall
To us is adverse. Who but felt of late,
When the fierce foe hung on our broken rear
Insulting, and pursued us through the Deep,
With what compulsion and laborious flight
We sunk thus low? Th' ascent is easy, then;
Th' event is feared! Should we again provoke
Our stronger, some worse way his wrath may find
To our destruction, if there be in Hell
Fear to be worse destroyed! What can be worse
Than to dwell here, driven out from bliss, condemned
In this abhorred deep to utter woe!
Where pain of unextinguishable fire
Must exercise us without hope of end
The vassals of his anger, when the scourge
Inexorably, and the torturing hour,
Calls us to penance? More destroyed than thus,

27

We should be quite abolished, and expire.
What fear we then? what doubt we to incense
His utmost ire? which, to the height enraged,
Will either quite consume us, and reduce
To nothing this essential—happier far
Than miserable to have eternal being!—
Or, if our substance be indeed divine,
And cannot cease to be, we are at worst
On this side nothing; and by proof we feel
Our power sufficient to disturb his Heaven,
And with perpetual inroads to alarm,
Though inaccessible, his fatal throne:
Which, if not victory, is yet revenge."
He ended frowning, and his look denounced
Desperate revenge, and battle dangerous
To less than gods. On th' other side up rose
Belial, in act more graceful and humane.
A fairer person lost not Heaven; he seemed
For dignity composed, and high exploit.
But all was false and hollow; though his tongue
Dropped manna, and could make the worse appear
The better reason, to perplex and dash
Maturest counsels: for his thoughts were low—
To vice industrious, but to nobler deeds
Timorous and slothful. Yet he pleased the ear,
And with persuasive accent thus began:—
"I should be much for open war, O Peers,
As not behind in hate, if what was urged
Main reason to persuade immediate war
Did not dissuade me most, and seem to cast
Ominous conjecture on the whole success;
When he who most excels in fact of arms,
In what he counsels and in what excels
Mistrustful, grounds his courage on despair
And utter dissolution, as the scope

Of all his aim, after some dire revenge.
First, what revenge? The towers of Heaven are filled
With armed watch, that render all access
Impregnable: oft on the bordering Deep
Encamp their legions, or with obscure wing
Scout far and wide into the realm of Night,
Scorning surprise. Or, could we break our way
By force, and at our heels all Hell should rise
With blackest insurrection to confound
Heaven's purest light, yet our great Enemy,
All incorruptible, would on his throne
Sit unpolluted, and th' ethereal mould,
Incapable of stain, would soon expel
Her mischief, and purge off the baser fire,
Victorious. Thus repulsed, our final hope
Is flat despair: we must exasperate
Th' Almighty Victor to spend all his rage;
And that must end us; that must be our cure—
To be no more. Sad cure! for who would lose,
Though full of pain, this intellectual being,
Those thoughts that wander through eternity,
To perish rather, swallowed up and lost
In the wide womb of uncreated Night,
Devoid of sense and motion? And who knows,
Let this be good, whether our angry Foe
Can give it, or will ever? How he can
Is doubtful; that he never will is sure.
Will he, so wise, let loose at once his ire,
Belike through impotence or unaware,
To give his enemies their wish, and end
Them in his anger whom his anger saves
To punish endless? 'Wherefore cease we, then?'
Say they who counsel war; 'we are decreed,
Reserved, and destined to eternal woe;
Whatever doing, what can we suffer more,

What can we suffer worse?' Is this, then, worst—
Thus sitting, thus consulting, thus in arms?
What when we fled amain, pursued and struck
With Heaven's afflicting thunder, and besought
The Deep to shelter us? This Hell then seemed
A refuge from those wounds. Or when we lay
Chained on the burning lake? That sure was worse.
What if the breath that kindled those grim fires,
Awaked, should blow them into sevenfold rage,
And plunge us in the flames; or from above
Should intermitted vengeance arm again
His red right hand to plague us? What if all
Her stores were opened, and this firmament
Of Hell should spout her cataracts of fire,
Impendent horrors, threatening hideous fall
One day upon our heads; while we perhaps,
Designing or exhorting glorious war,
Caught in a fiery tempest, shall be hurled,
Each on his rock transfixed, the sport and prey
Or racking whirlwinds, or for ever sunk
Under yon boiling ocean, wrapt in chains,
There to converse with everlasting groans,
Unrespited, unpitied, unreprieved,
Ages of hopeless end? This would be worse.
War, therefore, open or concealed, alike
My voice dissuades; for what can force or guile
With him, or who deceive his mind, whose eye
Views all things at one view? He from Heaven's height
All these our motions vain sees and derides,
Not more almighty to resist our might
Than wise to frustrate all our plots and wiles.
Shall we, then, live thus vile—the race of Heaven
Thus trampled, thus expelled, to suffer here
Chains and these torments? Better these than worse,
By my advice; since fate inevitable

Subdues us, and omnipotent decree,
The Victor's will. To suffer, as to do,
Our strength is equal; nor the law unjust
That so ordains. This was at first resolved,
If we were wise, against so great a foe
Contending, and so doubtful what might fall.
I laugh when those who at the spear are bold
And venturous, if that fail them, shrink, and fear
What yet they know must follow—to endure
Exile, or igominy, or bonds, or pain,
The sentence of their Conqueror. This is now
Our doom; which if we can sustain and bear,
Our Supreme Foe in time may much remit
His anger, and perhaps, thus far removed,
Not mind us not offending, satisfied
With what is punished; whence these raging fires
Will slacken, if his breath stir not their flames.
Our purer essence then will overcome
Their noxious vapour; or, inured, not feel;
Or, changed at length, and to the place conformed
In temper and in nature, will receive
Familiar the fierce heat; and, void of pain,
This horror will grow mild, this darkness light;
Besides what hope the never-ending flight
Of future days may bring, what chance, what change
Worth waiting—since our present lot appears
For happy though but ill, for ill not worst,
If we procure not to ourselves more woe."
Thus Belial, with words clothed in reason's garb,
Counselled ignoble ease and peaceful sloth,
Not peace; and after him thus Mammon spake:—
"Either to disenthrone the King of Heaven
We war, if war be best, or to regain
Our own right lost. Him to unthrone we then
May hope, when everlasting Fate shall yield

To fickle Chance, and Chaos judge the strife.
The former, vain to hope, argues as vain
The latter; for what place can be for us
Within Heaven's bound, unless Heaven's Lord supreme
We overpower? Suppose he should relent
And publish grace to all, on promise made
Of new subjection; with what eyes could we
Stand in his presence humble, and receive
Strict laws imposed, to celebrate his throne
With warbled hymns, and to his Godhead sing
Forced hallelujahs, while he lordly sits
Our envied sovereign, and his altar breathes
Ambrosial odours and ambrosial flowers,
Our servile offerings? This must be our task
In Heaven, this our delight. How wearisome
Eternity so spent in worship paid
To whom we hate! Let us not then pursue,
By force impossible, by leave obtained
Unacceptable, though in Heaven, our state
Of splendid vassalage; but rather seek
Our own good from ourselves, and from our own
Live to ourselves, though in this vast recess,
Free and to none accountable, preferring
Hard liberty before the easy yoke
Of servile pomp. Our greatness will appear
Then most conspicuous when great things of small,
Useful of hurtful, prosperous of adverse,
We can create, and in what place soe'er
Thrive under evil, and work ease out of pain
Through labour and endurance. This deep world
Of darkness do we dread? How oft amidst
Thick clouds and dark doth Heaven's all-ruling Sire
Choose to reside, his glory unobscured,
And with the majesty of darkness round
Covers his throne, from whence deep thunders roar.

Mustering their rage, and Heaven resembles Hell!
As he our darkness, cannot we his light
Imitate when we please? This desert soil
Wants not her hidden lustre, gems and gold;
Nor want we skill or art from whence to raise
Magnificence; and what can Heaven show more?
Our torments also may, in length of time,
Become our elements, these piercing fires
As soft as now severe, our temper changed
Into their temper; which must needs remove
The sensible of pain. All things invite
To peaceful counsels, and the settled state
Of order, how in safety best we may
Compose our present evils, with regard
Of what we are and where, dismissing quite
All thoughts of war. Ye have what I advise."
He scarce had finished, when such murmur filled
Th' assembly as when hollow rocks retain
The sound of blustering winds, which all night long
Had roused the sea, now with hoarse cadence lull
Seafaring men o'erwatched, whose bark by chance
Or pinnace, anchors in a craggy bay
After the tempest. Such applause was heard
As Mammon ended, and his sentence pleased,
Advising peace: for such another field
They dreaded worse than Hell; so much the fear
Of thunder and the sword of Michael
Wrought still within them; and no less desire
To found this nether empire, which might rise,
By policy and long process of time,
In emulation opposite to Heaven.
Which when Beelzebub perceived—than whom,
Satan except, none higher sat—with grave
Aspect he rose, and in his rising seemed
A pillar of state. Deep on his front engraven

Deliberation sat, and public care;
And princely counsel in his face yet shone,
Majestic, though in ruin. Sage he stood
With Atlantean shoulders, fit to bear
The weight of mightiest monarchies; his look
Drew audience and attention still as night
Or summer's noontide air, while thus he spake:—
"Thrones and Imperial Powers, Offspring of Heaven,
Ethereal Virtues! or these titles now
Must we renounce, and, changing style, be called
Princes of Hell? for so the popular vote
Inclines—here to continue, and build up here
A growing empire; doubtless! while we dream,
And know not that the King of Heaven hath doomed
This place our dungeon, not our safe retreat
Beyond his potent arm, to live exempt
From Heaven's high jurisdiction, in new league
Banded against his throne, but to remain
In strictest bondage, though thus far removed,
Under th' inevitable curb, reserved
His captive multitude. For he, to be sure,
In height or depth, still first and last will reign
Sole king, and of his kingdom lose no part
By our revolt, but over Hell extend
His empire, and with iron sceptre rule
Us here, as with his golden those in Heaven.
What sit we then projecting peace and war?
War hath determined us and foiled with loss
Irreparable; terms of peace yet none
Vouchsafed or sought; for what peace will be given
To us enslaved, but custody severe,
And stripes and arbitrary punishment
Inflicted? and what peace can we return,
But, to our power, hostility and hate,
Untamed reluctance, and revenge, though slow,

Yet ever plotting how the Conqueror least
May reap his conquest, and may least rejoice
In doing what we most in suffering feel?
Nor will occasion want, nor shall we need
With dangerous expedition to invade
Heaven, whose high walls fear no assault or siege,
Or ambush from the Deep. What if we find
Some easier enterprise? There is a place
(If ancient and prophetic fame in Heaven
Err not)—another World, the happy seat
Of some new race, called Man, about this time
To be created like to us, though less
In power and excellence, but favoured more
Of him who rules above; so was his will
Pronounced among the Gods, and by an oath
That shook Heaven's whole circumference confirmed.
Thither let us bend all our thoughts, to learn
What creatures there inhabit, of what mould
Or substance, how endued, and what their power
And where their weakness: how attempted best,
By force of subtlety. Though Heaven be shut,
And Heaven's high Arbitrator sit secure
In his own strength, this place may lie exposed,
The utmost border of his kingdom, left
To their defence who hold it: here, perhaps,
Some advantageous act may be achieved
By sudden onset—either with Hell-fire
To waste his whole creation, or possess
All as our own, and drive, as we were driven,
The puny habitants; or, if not drive,
Seduce them to our party, that their God
May prove their foe, and with repenting hand
Abolish his own works. This would surpass
Common revenge, and interrupt his joy
In our confusion, and our joy upraise

In his disturbance; when his darling sons,
Hurled headlong to partake with us, shall curse
Their frail original, and faded bliss—
Faded so soon! Advise if this be worth
Attempting, or to sit in darkness here
Hatching vain empires." Thus Beelzebub
Pleaded his devilish counsel—first devised
By Satan, and in part proposed: for whence,
But from the author of all ill, could spring
So deep a malice, to confound the race
Of mankind in one root, and Earth with Hell
To mingle and involve, done all to spite
The great Creator? But their spite still serves
His glory to augment. The bold design
Pleased highly those infernal States, and joy
Sparkled in all their eyes: with full assent
They vote: whereat his speech he thus renews:—
"Well have ye judged, well ended long debate,
Synod of Gods, and, like to what ye are,
Great things resolved, which from the lowest deep
Will once more lift us up, in spite of fate,
Nearer our ancient seat—perhaps in view
Of those bright confines, whence, with neighbouring arms,
And opportune excursion, we may chance
Re-enter Heaven; or else in some mild zone
Dwell, not unvisited of Heaven's fair light,
Secure, and at the brightening orient beam
Purge off this gloom: the soft delicious air,
To heal the scar of these corrosive fires,
Shall breathe her balm. But, first, whom shall we send
In search of this new World? whom shall we find
Sufficient? who shall tempt with wandering feet
The dark, unbottomed, infinite Abyss,
And through the palpable obscure find out
His uncouth way, or spread his airy flight,

Upborne with indefatigable wings
Over the vast abrupt, ere he arrive
The happy Isle? What strength, what art, can then
Suffice, or what evasion bear him safe,
Through the strict senteries and stations thick
Of Angels watching round? Here he had need
All circumspection: and we now no less
Choice in our suffrage; for on whom we send
The weight of all, and our last hope, relies."
This said, he sat; and expectation held
His look suspense, awaiting who appeared
To second, or oppose, or undertake
The perilous attempt. But all sat mute,
Pondering the danger with deep thoughts; and each
In other's countenance read his own dismay,
Astonished. None among the choice and prime
Of those Heaven-warring champions could be found
So hardy as to proffer or accept,
Alone, the dreadful voyage; till, at last,
Satan, whom now transcendent glory raised
Above his fellows, with monarchal pride
Conscious of highest worth, unmoved thus spake:—
"O Progeny of Heaven! Empyreal Thrones!
With reason hath deep silence and demur
Seized us, though undismayed. Long is the way
And hard, that out of Hell leads up to light.
Our prison strong, this huge convex of fire,
Outrageous to devour, immures us round
Ninefold; and gates of burning adamant,
Barred over us, prohibit all egress.
These passed, if any pass, the void profound
Of unessential Night receives him next,
Wide-gaping, and with utter loss of being
Threatens him, plunged in that abortive gulf.
If thence he scape, into whatever world,

Or unknown region, what remains him less
Than unknown dangers, and as hard escape?
But I should ill become this throne, O Peers,
And this imperial sovereignty, adorned
With splendour, armed with power, if aught proposed
And judged of public moment in the shape
Of difficulty or danger, could deter
Me from attempting. Wherefore do I assume
These royalties, and not refuse to reign,
Refusing to accept as great a share
Of hazard as of honour, due alike
To him who reigns, and so much to him due
Of hazard more as he above the rest
High honoured sits? Go, therefore, mighty Powers,
Terror of Heaven, though fallen; intend at home,
While here shall be our home, what best may ease
The present misery, and render Hell
More tolerable; if there be cure or charm
To respite, or deceive, or slack the pain
Of this ill mansion: intermit no watch
Against a wakeful foe, while I abroad
Through all the coasts of dark destruction seek
Deliverance for us all. This enterprise
None shall partake with me." Thus saying, rose
The Monarch, and prevented all reply;
Prudent lest, from his resolution raised,
Others among the chief might offer now,
Certain to be refused, what erst they feared,
And, so refused, might in opinion stand
His rivals, winning cheap the high repute
Which he through hazard huge must earn. But they
Dreaded not more th' adventure than his voice
Forbidding; and at once with him they rose.
Their rising all at once was as the sound
Of thunder heard remote. Towards him they bend

With awful reverence prone, and as a God
Extol him equal to the Highest in Heaven.
Nor failed they to express how much they praised
That for the general safety he despised
His own: for neither do the Spirits damned
Lose all their virtue; lest bad men should boast
Their specious deeds on earth, which glory excites,
Or close ambition varnished o'er with zeal.
Thus they their doubtful consultations dark
Ended, rejoicing in their matchless Chief:
As, when from mountain-tops the dusky clouds
Ascending, while the north wind sleeps, o'erspread
Heaven's cheerful face, the louring element
Scowls o'er the darkened landscape snow or shower,
If chance the radiant sun, with farewell sweet,
Extend his evening beam, the fields revive,
The birds their notes renew, and bleating herds
Attest their joy, that hill and valley rings.
O shame to men! Devil with devil damned
Firm concord holds; men only disagree
Of creatures rational, though under hope
Of heavenly grace, and, God proclaiming peace,
Yet live in hatred, enmity, and strife
Among themselves, and levy cruel wars
Wasting the earth, each other to destroy:
As if (which might induce us to accord)
Man had not hellish foes enow besides,
That day and night for his destruction wait!
The Stygian council thus dissolved; and forth
In order came the grand infernal Peers:
Midst came their mighty Paramount, and seemed
Alone th' antagonist of Heaven, nor less
Than Hell's dread Emperor, with pomp supreme,
And god-like imitated state: him round
A globe of fiery Seraphim enclosed

With bright emblazonry, and horrent arms.
Then of their session ended they bid cry
With trumpet's regal sound the great result:
Toward the four winds four speedy Cherubim
Put to their mouths the sounding alchemy,
By herald's voice explained; the hollow Abyss
Heard far and wide, and all the host of Hell
With deafening shout returned them loud acclaim.
Thence more at ease their minds, and somewhat raised
By false presumptuous hope, the ranged Powers
Disband; and, wandering, each his several way
Pursues, as inclination or sad choice
Leads him perplexed, where he may likeliest find
Truce to his restless thoughts, and entertain
The irksome hours, till his great Chief return.
Part on the plain, or in the air sublime,
Upon the wing or in swift race contend,
As at th' Olympian games or Pythian fields;
Part curb their fiery steeds, or shun the goal
With rapid wheels, or fronted brigades form:
As when, to warn proud cities, war appears
Waged in the troubled sky, and armies rush
To battle in the clouds; before each van
Prick forth the airy knights, and couch their spears,
Till thickest legions close; with feats of arms
From either end of heaven the welkin burns.
Others, with vast Typhoean rage, more fell,
Rend up both rocks and hills, and ride the air
In whirlwind; Hell scarce holds the wild uproar:—
As when Alcides, from Oechalia crowned
With conquest, felt th' envenomed robe, and tore
Through pain up by the roots Thessalian pines,
And Lichas from the top of Oeta threw
Into th' Euboic sea. Others, more mild,
Retreated in a silent valley, sing

With notes angelical to many a harp
Their own heroic deeds, and hapless fall
By doom of battle, and complain that Fate
Free Virtue should enthrall to Force or Chance.
Their song was partial; but the harmony
(What could it less when Spirits immortal sing?)
Suspended Hell, and took with ravishment
The thronging audience. In discourse more sweet
(For Eloquence the Soul, Song charms the Sense)
Others apart sat on a hill retired,
In thoughts more elevate, and reasoned high
Of Providence, Foreknowledge, Will, and Fate—
Fixed fate, free will, foreknowledge absolute,
And found no end, in wandering mazes lost.
Of good and evil much they argued then,
Of happiness and final misery,
Passion and apathy, and glory and shame:
Vain wisdom all, and false philosophy!—
Yet, with a pleasing sorcery, could charm
Pain for a while or anguish, and excite
Fallacious hope, or arm th' obdured breast
With stubborn patience as with triple steel.
Another part, in squadrons and gross bands,
On bold adventure to discover wide
That dismal world, if any clime perhaps
Might yield them easier habitation, bend
Four ways their flying march, along the banks
Of four infernal rivers, that disgorge
Into the burning lake their baleful streams—
Abhorred Styx, the flood of deadly hate;
Sad Acheron of sorrow, black and deep;
Cocytus, named of lamentation loud
Heard on the rueful stream; fierce Phlegethon,
Whose waves of torrent fire inflame with rage.
Far off from these, a slow and silent stream,

Lethe, the river of oblivion, rolls
Her watery labyrinth, whereof who drinks
Forthwith his former state and being forgets—
Forgets both joy and grief, pleasure and pain.
Beyond this flood a frozen continent
Lies dark and wild, beat with perpetual storms
Of whirlwind and dire hail, which on firm land
Thaws not, but gathers heap, and ruin seems
Of ancient pile; all else deep snow and ice,
A gulf profound as that Serbonian bog
Betwixt Damiata and Mount Casius old,
Where armies whole have sunk: the parching air
Burns frore, and cold performs th' effect of fire.
Thither, by harpy-footed Furies haled,
At certain revolutions all the damned
Are brought; and feel by turns the bitter change
Of fierce extremes, extremes by change more fierce,
From beds of raging fire to starve in ice
Their soft ethereal warmth, and there to pine
Immovable, infixed, and frozen round
Periods of time,—thence hurried back to fire.
They ferry over this Lethean sound
Both to and fro, their sorrow to augment,
And wish and struggle, as they pass, to reach
The tempting stream, with one small drop to lose
In sweet forgetfulness all pain and woe,
All in one moment, and so near the brink;
But Fate withstands, and, to oppose th' attempt,
Medusa with Gorgonian terror guards
The ford, and of itself the water flies
All taste of living wight, as once it fled
The lip of Tantalus. Thus roving on
In confused march forlorn, th' adventurous bands,
With shuddering horror pale, and eyes aghast,
Viewed first their lamentable lot, and found

No rest. Through many a dark and dreary vale
They passed, and many a region dolorous,
O'er many a frozen, many a fiery alp,
Rocks, caves, lakes, fens, bogs, dens, and shades of death—
A universe of death, which God by curse
Created evil, for evil only good;
Where all life dies, death lives, and Nature breeds,
Perverse, all monstrous, all prodigious things,
Abominable, inutterable, and worse
Than fables yet have feigned or fear conceived,
Gorgons, and Hydras, and Chimeras dire.
Meanwhile the Adversary of God and Man,
Satan, with thoughts inflamed of highest design,
Puts on swift wings, and toward the gates of Hell
Explores his solitary flight: sometimes
He scours the right hand coast, sometimes the left;
Now shaves with level wing the deep, then soars
Up to the fiery concave towering high.
As when far off at sea a fleet descried
Hangs in the clouds, by equinoctial winds
Close sailing from Bengala, or the isles
Of Ternate and Tidore, whence merchants bring
Their spicy drugs; they on the trading flood,
Through the wide Ethiopian to the Cape,
Ply stemming nightly toward the pole: so seemed
Far off the flying Fiend. At last appear
Hell-bounds, high reaching to the horrid roof,
And thrice threefold the gates; three folds were brass,
Three iron, three of adamantine rock,
Impenetrable, impaled with circling fire,
Yet unconsumed. Before the gates there sat
On either side a formidable Shape.
The one seemed woman to the waist, and fair,
But ended foul in many a scaly fold,
Voluminous and vast—a serpent armed

With mortal sting. About her middle round
A cry of Hell-hounds never ceasing barked
With wide Cerberean mouths full loud, and rung
A hideous peal; yet, when they list, would creep,
If aught disturbed their noise, into her womb,
And kennel there; yet there still barked and howled
Within unseen. Far less abhorred than these
Vexed Scylla, bathing in the sea that parts
Calabria from the hoarse Trinacrian shore;
Nor uglier follow the night-hag, when, called
In secret, riding through the air she comes,
Lured with the smell of infant blood, to dance
With Lapland witches, while the labouring moon
Eclipses at their charms. The other Shape—
If shape it might be called that shape had none
Distinguishable in member, joint, or limb;
Or substance might be called that shadow seemed,
For each seemed either—black it stood as Night,
Fierce as ten Furies, terrible as Hell,
And shook a dreadful dart: what seemed his head
The likeness of a kingly crown had on.
Satan was now at hand, and from his seat
The monster moving onward came as fast
With horrid strides; Hell trembled as he strode.
Th' undaunted Fiend what this might be admired—
Admired, not feared (God and his Son except,
Created thing naught valued he nor shunned),
And with disdainful look thus first began:—
"Whence and what art thou, execrable Shape,
That dar'st, though grim and terrible, advance
Thy miscreated front athwart my way
To yonder gates? Through them I mean to pass,
That be assured, without leave asked of thee.
Retire; or taste thy folly, and learn by proof,
Hell-born, not to contend with Spirits of Heaven."

To whom the Goblin, full of wrath, replied:—
"Art thou that traitor Angel? art thou he,
Who first broke peace in Heaven and faith, till then
Unbroken, and in proud rebellious arms
Drew after him the third part of Heaven's sons,
Conjured against the Highest—for which both thou
And they, outcast from God, are here condemned
To waste eternal days in woe and pain?
And reckon'st thou thyself with Spirits of Heaven
Hell-doomed, and breath'st defiance here and scorn,
Where I reign king, and, to enrage thee more,
Thy king and lord? Back to thy punishment,
False fugitive; and to thy speed add wings,
Lest with a whip of scorpions I pursue
Thy lingering, or with one stroke of this dart
Strange horror seize thee, and pangs unfelt before."
So spake the grisly Terror, and in shape,
So speaking and so threatening, grew tenfold,
More dreadful and deform. On th' other side,
Incensed with indignation, Satan stood
Unterrified, and like a comet burned,
That fires the length of Ophiuchus huge
In th' arctic sky, and from his horrid hair
Shakes pestilence and war. Each at the head
Levelled his deadly aim; their fatal hands
No second stroke intend; and such a frown
Each cast at th' other as when two black clouds,
With heaven's artillery fraught, came rattling on
Over the Caspian,—then stand front to front
Hovering a space, till winds the signal blow
To join their dark encounter in mid-air.
So frowned the mighty combatants that Hell
Grew darker at their frown; so matched they stood;
For never but once more was wither like
To meet so great a foe. And now great deeds

Had been achieved, whereof all Hell had rung,
Had not the snaky Sorceress, that sat
Fast by Hell-gate and kept the fatal key,
Risen, and with hideous outcry rushed between.
"O father, what intends thy hand," she cried,
"Against thy only son? What fury, O son,
Possesses thee to bend that mortal dart
Against thy father's head? And know'st for whom?
For him who sits above, and laughs the while
At thee, ordained his drudge to execute
Whate'er his wrath, which he calls justice, bids—
His wrath, which one day will destroy ye both!"
She spake, and at her words the hellish Pest
Forbore: then these to her Satan returned:—
"So strange thy outcry, and thy words so strange
Thou interposest, that my sudden hand,
Prevented, spares to tell thee yet by deeds
What it intends, till first I know of thee
What thing thou art, thus double-formed, and why,
In this infernal vale first met, thou call'st
Me father, and that phantasm call'st my son.
I know thee not, nor ever saw till now
Sight more detestable than him and thee."
T' whom thus the Portress of Hell-gate replied:—
"Hast thou forgot me, then; and do I seem
Now in thine eye so foul?—once deemed so fair
In Heaven, when at th' assembly, and in sight
Of all the Seraphim with thee combined
In bold conspiracy against Heaven's King,
All on a sudden miserable pain
Surprised thee, dim thine eyes and dizzy swum
In darkness, while thy head flames thick and fast
Threw forth, till on the left side opening wide,
Likest to thee in shape and countenance bright,
Then shining heavenly fair, a goddess armed,

Out of thy head I sprung. Amazement seized
All th' host of Heaven; back they recoiled afraid
At first, and called me Sin, and for a sign
Portentous held me; but, familiar grown,
I pleased, and with attractive graces won
The most averse—thee chiefly, who, full oft
Thyself in me thy perfect image viewing,
Becam'st enamoured; and such joy thou took'st
With me in secret that my womb conceived
A growing burden. Meanwhile war arose,
And fields were fought in Heaven: wherein remained
(For what could else?) to our Almighty Foe
Clear victory; to our part loss and rout
Through all the Empyrean. Down they fell,
Driven headlong from the pitch of Heaven, down
Into this Deep; and in the general fall
I also: at which time this powerful key
Into my hands was given, with charge to keep
These gates for ever shut, which none can pass
Without my opening. Pensive here I sat
Alone; but long I sat not, till my womb,
Pregnant by thee, and now excessive grown,
Prodigious motion felt and rueful throes.
At last this odious offspring whom thou seest,
Thine own begotten, breaking violent way,
Tore through my entrails, that, with fear and pain
Distorted, all my nether shape thus grew
Transformed: but he my inbred enemy
Forth issued, brandishing his fatal dart,
Made to destroy. I fled, and cried out Death!
Hell trembled at the hideous name, and sighed
From all her caves, and back resounded Death!
I fled; but he pursued (though more, it seems,
Inflamed with lust than rage), and, swifter far,
Me overtook, his mother, all dismayed,

And, in embraces forcible and foul
Engendering with me, of that rape begot
These yelling monsters, that with ceaseless cry
Surround me, as thou saw'st—hourly conceived
And hourly born, with sorrow infinite
To me; for, when they list, into the womb
That bred them they return, and howl, and gnaw
My bowels, their repast; then, bursting forth
Afresh, with conscious terrors vex me round,
That rest or intermission none I find.
Before mine eyes in opposition sits
Grim Death, my son and foe, who set them on,
And me, his parent, would full soon devour
For want of other prey, but that he knows
His end with mine involved, and knows that I
Should prove a bitter morsel, and his bane,
Whenever that shall be: so Fate pronounced.
But thou, O father, I forewarn thee, shun
His deadly arrow; neither vainly hope
To be invulnerable in those bright arms,
Through tempered heavenly; for that mortal dint,
Save he who reigns above, none can resist."
She finished; and the subtle Fiend his lore
Soon learned, now milder, and thus answered smooth:—
"Dear daughter—since thou claim'st me for thy sire,
And my fair son here show'st me, the dear pledge
Of dalliance had with thee in Heaven, and joys
Then sweet, now sad to mention, through dire change
Befallen us unforeseen, unthought of, know
I come no enemy, but to set free
From out this dark and dismal house of pain
Both him and thee, and all the heavenly host
Of Spirits that, in our just pretences armed,
Fell with us from on high. From them I go
This uncouth errand sole, and one for all

Myself expose, with lonely steps to tread
Th' unfounded Deep, and through the void immense
To search, with wandering quest, a place foretold
Should be—and, by concurring signs, ere now
Created vast and round—a place of bliss
In the purlieus of Heaven; and therein placed
A race of upstart creatures, to supply
Perhaps our vacant room, though more removed,
Lest Heaven, surcharged with potent multitude,
Might hap to move new broils. Be this, or aught
Than this more secret, now designed, I haste
To know; and, this once known, shall soon return,
And bring ye to the place where thou and Death
Shall dwell at ease, and up and down unseen
Wing silently the buxom air, embalmed
With odours. There ye shall be fed and filled
Immeasurably; all things shall be your prey."
He ceased; for both seemed highly pleased, and Death
Grinned horrible a ghastly smile, to hear
His famine should be filled, and blessed his maw
Destined to that good hour. No less rejoiced
His mother bad, and thus bespake her sire:—
"The key of this infernal Pit, by due
And by command of Heaven's all-powerful King,
I keep, by him forbidden to unlock
These adamantine gates; against all force
Death ready stands to interpose his dart,
Fearless to be o'ermatched by living might.
But what owe I to his commands above,
Who hates me, and hath hither thrust me down
Into this gloom of Tartarus profound,
To sit in hateful office here confined,
Inhabitant of Heaven and heavenly born—
Here in perpetual agony and pain,
With terrors and with clamours compassed round

Of mine own brood, that on my bowels feed?
Thou art my father, thou my author, thou
My being gav'st me; whom should I obey
But thee? whom follow? Thou wilt bring me soon
To that new world of light and bliss, among
The gods who live at ease, where I shall reign
At thy right hand voluptuous, as beseems
Thy daughter and thy darling, without end."
Thus saying, from her side the fatal key,
Sad instrument of all our woe, she took;
And, towards the gate rolling her bestial train,
Forthwith the huge portcullis high up-drew,
Which, but herself, not all the Stygian Powers
Could once have moved; then in the key-hole turns
Th' intricate wards, and every bolt and bar
Of massy iron or solid rock with ease
Unfastens. On a sudden open fly,
With impetuous recoil and jarring sound,
Th' infernal doors, and on their hinges grate
Harsh thunder, that the lowest bottom shook
Of Erebus. She opened; but to shut
Excelled her power: the gates wide open stood,
That with extended wings a bannered host,
Under spread ensigns marching, might pass through
With horse and chariots ranked in loose array;
So wide they stood, and like a furnace-mouth
Cast forth redounding smoke and ruddy flame.
Before their eyes in sudden view appear
The secrets of the hoary Deep—a dark
Illimitable ocean, without bound,
Without dimension; where length, breadth, and height,
And time, and place, are lost; where eldest Night
And Chaos, ancestors of Nature, hold
Eternal anarchy, amidst the noise
Of endless wars, and by confusion stand.

For Hot, Cold, Moist, and Dry, four champions fierce,
Strive here for mastery, and to battle bring
Their embryon atoms: they around the flag
Of each his faction, in their several clans,
Light-armed or heavy, sharp, smooth, swift, or slow,
Swarm populous, unnumbered as the sands
Of Barca or Cyrene's torrid soil,
Levied to side with warring winds, and poise
Their lighter wings. To whom these most adhere
He rules a moment: Chaos umpire sits,
And by decision more embroils the fray
By which he reigns: next him, high arbiter,
Chance governs all. Into this wild Abyss,
The womb of Nature, and perhaps her grave,
Of neither sea, nor shore, nor air, nor fire,
But all these in their pregnant causes mixed
Confusedly, and which thus must ever fight,
Unless th' Almighty Maker them ordain
His dark materials to create more worlds—
Into this wild Abyss the wary Fiend
Stood on the brink of Hell and looked a while,
Pondering his voyage; for no narrow frith
He had to cross. Nor was his ear less pealed
With noises loud and ruinous (to compare
Great things with small) than when Bellona storms
With all her battering engines, bent to raze
Some capital city; or less than if this frame
Of Heaven were falling, and these elements
In mutiny had from her axle torn
The steadfast Earth. At last his sail-broad vans
He spread for flight, and, in the surging smoke
Uplifted, spurns the ground; thence many a league,
As in a cloudy chair, ascending rides
Audacious; but, that seat soon failing, meets
A vast vacuity. All unawares,

Fluttering his pennons vain, plumb-down he drops
Ten thousand fathom deep, and to this hour
Down had been falling, had not, by ill chance,
The strong rebuff of some tumultuous cloud,
Instinct with fire and nitre, hurried him
As many miles aloft. That fury stayed—
Quenched in a boggy Syrtis, neither sea,
Nor good dry land—nigh foundered, on he fares,
Treading the crude consistence, half on foot,
Half flying; behoves him now both oar and sail.
As when a gryphon through the wilderness
With winged course, o'er hill or moory dale,
Pursues the Arimaspian, who by stealth
Had from his wakeful custody purloined
The guarded gold; so eagerly the Fiend
O'er bog or steep, through strait, rough, dense, or rare,
With head, hands, wings, or feet, pursues his way,
And swims, or sinks, or wades, or creeps, or flies.
At length a universal hubbub wild
Of stunning sounds, and voices all confused,
Borne through the hollow dark, assaults his ear
With loudest vehemence. Thither he plies
Undaunted, to meet there whatever Power
Or Spirit of the nethermost Abyss
Might in that noise reside, of whom to ask
Which way the nearest coast of darkness lies
Bordering on light; when straight behold the throne
Of Chaos, and his dark pavilion spread
Wide on the wasteful Deep! With him enthroned
Sat sable-vested Night, eldest of things,
The consort of his reign; and by them stood
Orcus and Ades, and the dreaded name
Of Demogorgon; Rumour next, and Chance,
And Tumult, and Confusion, all embroiled,
And Discord with a thousand various mouths.

T' whom Satan, turning boldly, thus:—"Ye Powers
And Spirits of this nethermost Abyss,
Chaos and ancient Night, I come no spy
With purpose to explore or to disturb
The secrets of your realm; but, by constraint
Wandering this darksome desert, as my way
Lies through your spacious empire up to light,
Alone and without guide, half lost, I seek,
What readiest path leads where your gloomy bounds
Confine with Heaven; or, if some other place,
From your dominion won, th' Ethereal King
Possesses lately, thither to arrive
I travel this profound. Direct my course:
Directed, no mean recompense it brings
To your behoof, if I that region lost,
All usurpation thence expelled, reduce
To her original darkness and your sway
(Which is my present journey), and once more
Erect the standard there of ancient Night.
Yours be th' advantage all, mine the revenge!"
Thus Satan; and him thus the Anarch old,
With faltering speech and visage incomposed,
Answered: "I know thee, stranger, who thou art—
That mighty leading Angel, who of late
Made head against Heaven's King, though overthrown.
I saw and heard; for such a numerous host
Fled not in silence through the frighted Deep,
With ruin upon ruin, rout on rout,
Confusion worse confounded; and Heaven-gates
Poured out by millions her victorious bands,
Pursuing. I upon my frontiers here
Keep residence; if all I can will serve
That little which is left so to defend,
Encroached on still through our intestine broils
Weakening the sceptre of old Night: first, Hell,

Your dungeon, stretching far and wide beneath;
Now lately Heaven and Earth, another world
Hung o'er my realm, linked in a golden chain
To that side Heaven from whence your legions fell!
If that way be your walk, you have not far;
So much the nearer danger. Go, and speed;
Havoc, and spoil, and ruin, are my gain."
He ceased; and Satan stayed not to reply,
But, glad that now his sea should find a shore,
With fresh alacrity and force renewed
Springs upward, like a pyramid of fire,
Into the wild expanse, and through the shock
Of fighting elements, on all sides round
Environed, wins his way; harder beset
And more endangered than when Argo passed
Through Bosporus betwixt the justling rocks,
Or when Ulysses on the larboard shunned
Charybdis, and by th' other whirlpool steered.
So he with difficulty and labour hard
Moved on, with difficulty and labour he;
But, he once passed, soon after, when Man fell,
Strange alteration! Sin and Death amain,
Following his track (such was the will of Heaven)
Paved after him a broad and beaten way
Over the dark Abyss, whose boiling gulf
Tamely endured a bridge of wondrous length,
From Hell continued, reaching th' utmost orb
Of this frail World; by which the Spirits perverse
With easy intercourse pass to and fro
To tempt or punish mortals, except whom
God and good Angels guard by special grace.
But now at last the sacred influence
Of light appears, and from the walls of Heaven
Shoots far into the bosom of dim Night
A glimmering dawn. Here Nature first begins

Her farthest verge, and Chaos to retire,
As from her outmost works, a broken foe,
With tumult less and with less hostile din;
That Satan with less toil, and now with ease,
Wafts on the calmer wave by dubious light,
And, like a weather-beaten vessel, holds
Gladly the port, though shrouds and tackle torn;
Or in the emptier waste, resembling air,
Weighs his spread wings, at leisure to behold
Far off th' empyreal Heaven, extended wide
In circuit, undetermined square or round,
With opal towers and battlements adorned
Of living sapphire, once his native seat;
And, fast by, hanging in a golden chain,
This pendent World, in bigness as a star
Of smallest magnitude close by the moon.
Thither, full fraught with mischievous revenge,
Accursed, and in a cursed hour, he hies.

BOOK III

Hail, holy Light, offspring of Heaven firstborn,
Or of the Eternal coeternal beam
May I express thee unblam'd? since God is light,
And never but in unapproached light
Dwelt from eternity, dwelt then in thee
Bright effluence of bright essence increate.
Or hear'st thou rather pure ethereal stream,
Whose fountain who shall tell? before the sun,
Before the Heavens thou wert, and at the voice
Of God, as with a mantle, didst invest
The rising world of waters dark and deep,
Won from the void and formless infinite.
Thee I re-visit now with bolder wing,
Escap'd the Stygian pool, though long detain'd
In that obscure sojourn, while in my flight
Through utter and through middle darkness borne,
With other notes than to the Orphean lyre
I sung of Chaos and eternal Night;
Taught by the heavenly Muse to venture down
The dark descent, and up to re-ascend,
Though hard and rare: Thee I revisit safe,
And feel thy sovran vital lamp; but thou

Revisit'st not these eyes, that roll in vain
To find thy piercing ray, and find no dawn;
So thick a drop serene hath quench'd their orbs,
Or dim suffusion veil'd. Yet not the more
Cease I to wander, where the Muses haunt,
Clear spring, or shady grove, or sunny hill,
Smit with the love of sacred song; but chief
Thee, Sion, and the flowery brooks beneath,
That wash thy hallow'd feet, and warbling flow,
Nightly I visit: nor sometimes forget
So were I equall'd with them in renown,
Thy sovran command, that Man should find grace;
Blind Thamyris, and blind Maeonides,
And Tiresias, and Phineus, prophets old:
Then feed on thoughts, that voluntary move
Harmonious numbers; as the wakeful bird
Sings darkling, and in shadiest covert hid
Tunes her nocturnal note. Thus with the year
Seasons return; but not to me returns
Day, or the sweet approach of even or morn,
Or sight of vernal bloom, or summer's rose,
Or flocks, or herds, or human face divine;
But cloud instead, and ever-during dark
Surrounds me, from the cheerful ways of men
Cut off, and for the book of knowledge fair
Presented with a universal blank
Of nature's works to me expung'd and ras'd,
And wisdom at one entrance quite shut out.
So much the rather thou, celestial Light,
Shine inward, and the mind through all her powers
Irradiate; there plant eyes, all mist from thence
Purge and disperse, that I may see and tell
Of things invisible to mortal sight.
Now had the Almighty Father from above,
From the pure empyrean where he sits

High thron'd above all hight, bent down his eye
His own works and their works at once to view:
About him all the Sanctities of Heaven
Stood thick as stars, and from his sight receiv'd
Beatitude past utterance; on his right
The radiant image of his glory sat,
His only son; on earth he first beheld
Our two first parents, yet the only two
Of mankind in the happy garden plac'd
Reaping immortal fruits of joy and love,
Uninterrupted joy, unrivall'd love,
In blissful solitude; he then survey'd
Hell and the gulf between, and Satan there
Coasting the wall of Heaven on this side Night
In the dun air sublime, and ready now
To stoop with wearied wings, and willing feet,
On the bare outside of this world, that seem'd
Firm land imbosom'd, without firmament,
Uncertain which, in ocean or in air.
Him God beholding from his prospect high,
Wherein past, present, future, he beholds,
Thus to his only Son foreseeing spake.
"Only begotten Son, seest thou what rage
Transports our Adversary? whom no bounds
Prescrib'd no bars of Hell, nor all the chains
Heap'd on him there, nor yet the main abyss
Wide interrupt, can hold; so bent he seems
On desperate revenge, that shall redound
Upon his own rebellious head. And now,
Through all restraint broke loose, he wings his way
Not far off Heaven, in the precincts of light,
Directly towards the new created world,
And man there plac'd, with purpose to assay
If him by force he can destroy, or, worse,
By some false guile pervert; and shall pervert;

For man will hearken to his glozing lies,
And easily transgress the sole command,
Sole pledge of his obedience: So will fall
He and his faithless progeny: Whose fault?
Whose but his own? ingrate, he had of me
All he could have; I made him just and right,
Sufficient to have stood, though free to fall.
Such I created all the ethereal Powers
And Spirits, both them who stood, and them who fail'd;
Freely they stood who stood, and fell who fell.
Not free, what proof could they have given sincere
Of true allegiance, constant faith or love,
Where only what they needs must do appear'd,
Not what they would? what praise could they receive?
What pleasure I from such obedience paid,
When will and reason (reason also is choice)
Useless and vain, of freedom both despoil'd,
Made passive both, had serv'd necessity,
Not me. They therefore, as to right belong'd,
So were created, nor can justly accuse
Their Maker, or their making, or their fate,
As if predestination over-rul'd
Their will dispos'd by absolute decree
Or high foreknowledge they themselves decreed
Their own revolt, not I; if I foreknew,
Foreknowledge had no influence on their fault,
Which had no less proved certain unforeknown.
So without least impulse or shadow of fate,
Or aught by me immutably foreseen,
They trespass, authors to themselves in all
Both what they judge, and what they choose; for so
I form'd them free: and free they must remain,
Till they enthrall themselves; I else must change
Their nature, and revoke the high decree
Unchangeable, eternal, which ordain'd

Their freedom: they themselves ordain'd their fall.
The first sort by their own suggestion fell,
Self-tempted, self-deprav'd: Man falls, deceiv'd
By the other first: Man therefore shall find grace,
The other none: In mercy and justice both,
Through Heaven and Earth, so shall my glory excel;
But Mercy, first and last, shall brightest shine."
Thus while God spake, ambrosial fragrance fill'd
All Heaven, and in the blessed Spirits elect
Sense of new joy ineffable diffus'd.
Beyond compare the Son of God was seen
Most glorious; in him all his Father shone
Substantially express'd; and in his face
Divine compassion visibly appear'd,
Love without end, and without measure grace,
Which uttering, thus he to his Father spake.
"O Father, gracious was that word which clos'd
Thy sovran command, that Man should find grace;
For which both Heaven and earth shall high extol
Thy praises, with the innumerable sound
Of hymns and sacred songs, wherewith thy throne
Encompass'd shall resound thee ever blest.
For should Man finally be lost, should Man,
Thy creature late so lov'd, thy youngest son,
Fall circumvented thus by fraud, though join'd
With his own folly? that be from thee far,
That far be from thee, Father, who art judge
Of all things made, and judgest only right.
Or shall the Adversary thus obtain
His end, and frustrate thine? shall he fulfill
His malice, and thy goodness bring to nought,
Or proud return, though to his heavier doom,
Yet with revenge accomplish'd, and to Hell
Draw after him the whole race of mankind,
By him corrupted? or wilt thou thyself

Abolish thy creation, and unmake
For him, what for thy glory thou hast made?
So should thy goodness and thy greatness both
Be question'd and blasphem'd without defence."
To whom the great Creator thus replied.
"O son, in whom my soul hath chief delight,
Son of my bosom, Son who art alone.
My word, my wisdom, and effectual might,
All hast thou spoken as my thoughts are, all
As my eternal purpose hath decreed;
Man shall not quite be lost, but sav'd who will;
Yet not of will in him, but grace in me
Freely vouchsaf'd; once more I will renew
His lapsed powers, though forfeit; and enthrall'd
By sin to foul exorbitant desires;
Upheld by me, yet once more he shall stand
On even ground against his mortal foe;
By me upheld, that he may know how frail
His fallen condition is, and to me owe
All his deliverance, and to none but me.
Some I have chosen of peculiar grace,
Elect above the rest; so is my will:
The rest shall hear me call, and oft be warn'd
Their sinful state, and to appease betimes
The incensed Deity, while offer'd grace
Invites; for I will clear their senses dark,
What may suffice, and soften stony hearts
To pray, repent, and bring obedience due.
To prayer, repentance, and obedience due,
Though but endeavour'd with sincere intent,
Mine ear shall not be slow, mine eye not shut.
And I will place within them as a guide,
My umpire Conscience; whom if they will hear,
Light after light, well us'd, they shall attain,
And to the end, persisting, safe arrive.

This my long sufferance, and my day of grace,
They who neglect and scorn, shall never taste;
But hard be harden'd, blind be blinded more,
That they may stumble on, and deeper fall;
And none but such from mercy I exclude.
But yet all is not done; Man disobeying,
Disloyal, breaks his fealty, and sins
Against the high supremacy of Heaven,
Affecting God-head, and, so losing all,
To expiate his treason hath nought left,
But to destruction sacred and devote,
He, with his whole posterity, must die,
Die he or justice must; unless for him
Some other able, and as willing, pay
The rigid satisfaction, death for death.
Say, heavenly Powers, where shall we find such love?
Which of you will be mortal, to redeem
Man's mortal crime, and just the unjust to save?
Dwells in all Heaven charity so dear?"
He ask'd, but all the heavenly quire stood mute,
And silence was in Heaven: on Man's behalf
Patron or intercessour none appear'd,
Much less that durst upon his own head draw
The deadly forfeiture, and ransom set.
And now without redemption all mankind
Must have been lost, adjudg'd to Death and Hell
By doom severe, had not the Son of God,
In whom the fulness dwells of love divine,
His dearest mediation thus renew'd.
"Father, thy word is past, Man shall find grace;
And shall grace not find means, that finds her way,
The speediest of thy winged messengers,
To visit all thy creatures, and to all
Comes unprevented, unimplor'd, unsought?
Happy for Man, so coming; he her aid

Can never seek, once dead in sins, and lost;
Atonement for himself, or offering meet,
Indebted and undone, hath none to bring;
Behold me then: me for him, life for life
I offer: on me let thine anger fall;
Account me Man; I for his sake will leave
Thy bosom, and this glory next to thee
Freely put off, and for him lastly die
Well pleased; on me let Death wreak all his rage.
Under his gloomy power I shall not long
Lie vanquished. Thou hast given me to possess
Life in myself for ever; by thee I live;
Though now to Death I yield, and am his due,
All that of me can die, yet, that debt paid,
Thou wilt not leave me in the loathsome grave
His prey, nor suffer my unspotted soul
For ever with corruption there to dwell;
But I shall rise victorious, and subdue
My vanquisher, spoiled of his vaunted spoil.
Death his death's wound shall then receive, and stoop
Inglorious, of his mortal sting disarmed;
I through the ample air in triumph high
Shall lead Hell captive maugre Hell, and show
The powers of darkness bound. Thou, at the sight
Pleased, out of Heaven shalt look down and smile,
While, by thee raised, I ruin all my foes;
Death last, and with his carcass glut the grave;
Then, with the multitude of my redeemed,
Shall enter Heaven, long absent, and return,
Father, to see thy face, wherein no cloud
Of anger shall remain, but peace assured
And reconcilement: wrath shall be no more
Thenceforth, but in thy presence joy entire."
His words here ended; but his meek aspect
Silent yet spake, and breathed immortal love

To mortal men, above which only shone
Filial obedience: as a sacrifice
Glad to be offered, he attends the will
Of his great Father. Admiration seized
All Heaven, what this might mean, and whither tend,
Wondering; but soon th' Almighty thus replied:
"O thou in Heaven and Earth the only peace
Found out for mankind under wrath, O thou
My sole complacence! Well thou know'st how dear
To me are all my works; nor Man the least,
Though last created, that for him I spare
Thee from my bosom and right hand, to save,
By losing thee a while, the whole race lost.
Thou, therefore, whom thou only canst redeem,
Their nature also to thy nature join;
And be thyself Man among men on Earth,
Made flesh, when time shall be, of virgin seed,
By wondrous birth; be thou in Adam's room
The head of all mankind, though Adam's son.
As in him perish all men, so in thee,
As from a second root, shall be restored
As many as are restored, without thee none.
His crime makes guilty all his sons; thy merit,
Imputed, shall absolve them who renounce
Their own both righteous and unrighteous deeds,
And live in thee transplanted, and from thee
Receive new life. So Man, as is most just,
Shall satisfy for Man, be judged and die,
And dying rise, and rising with him raise
His brethren, ransomed with his own dear life.
So heavenly love shall outdo hellish hate,
Giving to death, and dying to redeem,
So dearly to redeem what hellish hate
So easily destroyed, and still destroys
In those who, when they may, accept not grace.

Nor shalt thou, by descending to assume
Man's nature, lessen or degrade thine own.
Because thou hast, though throned in highest bliss
Equal to God, and equally enjoying
God-like fruition, quitted all, to save
A world from utter loss, and hast been found
By merit more than birthright Son of God,
Found worthiest to be so by being good,
Far more than great or high; because in thee
Love hath abounded more than glory abounds;
Therefore thy humiliation shall exalt
With thee thy manhood also to this throne:
Here shalt thou sit incarnate, here shalt reign
Both God and Man, Son both of God and Man,
Anointed universal King; all power
I give thee; reign for ever, and assume
Thy merits; under thee, as head supreme,
Thrones, Princedoms, Powers, Dominions, I reduce:
All knees to thee shall bow, of them that bide
In Heaven, or Earth, or under Earth in Hell.
When thou, attended gloriously from Heaven,
Shalt in the sky appear, and from thee send
The summoning Arch-Angels to proclaim
Thy dread tribunal; forthwith from all winds,
The living, and forthwith the cited dead
Of all past ages, to the general doom
Shall hasten; such a peal shall rouse their sleep.
Then, all thy saints assembled, thou shalt judge
Bad Men and Angels; they, arraigned, shall sink
Beneath thy sentence; Hell, her numbers full,
Thenceforth shall be for ever shut. Meanwhile
The world shall burn, and from her ashes spring
New Heaven and Earth, wherein the just shall dwell,
And, after all their tribulations long,
See golden days, fruitful of golden deeds,

With joy and peace triumphing, and fair truth.
Then thou thy regal scepter shalt lay by,
For regal scepter then no more shall need,
God shall be all in all. But, all ye Gods,
Adore him, who to compass all this dies;
Adore the Son, and honour him as me."
No sooner had the Almighty ceased, but all
The multitude of Angels, with a shout
Loud as from numbers without number, sweet
As from blest voices, uttering joy, Heaven rung
With jubilee, and loud Hosannas filled
The eternal regions: Lowly reverent
Towards either throne they bow, and to the ground
With solemn adoration down they cast
Their crowns inwove with amarant and gold;
Immortal amarant, a flower which once
In Paradise, fast by the tree of life,
Began to bloom; but soon for man's offence
To Heaven removed, where first it grew, there grows,
And flowers aloft shading the fount of life,
And where the river of bliss through midst of Heaven
Rolls o'er Elysian flowers her amber stream;
With these that never fade the Spirits elect
Bind their resplendent locks inwreathed with beams;
Now in loose garlands thick thrown off, the bright
Pavement, that like a sea of jasper shone,
Impurpled with celestial roses smiled.
Then, crowned again, their golden harps they took,
Harps ever tuned, that glittering by their side
Like quivers hung, and with preamble sweet
Of charming symphony they introduce
Their sacred song, and waken raptures high;
No voice exempt, no voice but well could join
Melodious part, such concord is in Heaven.
Thee, Father, first they sung Omnipotent,

Immutable, Immortal, Infinite,
Eternal King; the Author of all being,
Fountain of light, thyself invisible
Amidst the glorious brightness where thou sit'st
Throned inaccessible, but when thou shadest
The full blaze of thy beams, and, through a cloud
Drawn round about thee like a radiant shrine,
Dark with excessive bright thy skirts appear,
Yet dazzle Heaven, that brightest Seraphim
Approach not, but with both wings veil their eyes.
Thee next they sang of all creation first,
Begotten Son, Divine Similitude,
In whose conspicuous countenance, without cloud
Made visible, the Almighty Father shines,
Whom else no creature can behold; on thee
Impressed the effulgence of his glory abides,
Transfused on thee his ample Spirit rests.
He Heaven of Heavens and all the Powers therein
By thee created; and by thee threw down
The aspiring Dominations: Thou that day
Thy Father's dreadful thunder didst not spare,
Nor stop thy flaming chariot-wheels, that shook
Heaven's everlasting frame, while o'er the necks
Thou drovest of warring Angels disarrayed.
Back from pursuit thy Powers with loud acclaim
Thee only extolled, Son of thy Father's might,
To execute fierce vengeance on his foes,
Not so on Man: Him through their malice fallen,
Father of mercy and grace, thou didst not doom
So strictly, but much more to pity incline:
No sooner did thy dear and only Son
Perceive thee purposed not to doom frail Man
So strictly, but much more to pity inclined,
He to appease thy wrath, and end the strife
Of mercy and justice in thy face discerned,

Regardless of the bliss wherein he sat
Second to thee, offered himself to die
For Man's offence. O unexampled love,
Love nowhere to be found less than Divine!
Hail, Son of God, Saviour of Men! Thy name
Shall be the copious matter of my song
Henceforth, and never shall my heart thy praise
Forget, nor from thy Father's praise disjoin.
Thus they in Heaven, above the starry sphere,
Their happy hours in joy and hymning spent.
Meanwhile upon the firm opacous globe
Of this round world, whose first convex divides
The luminous inferior orbs, enclosed
From Chaos, and the inroad of Darkness old,
Satan alighted walks: A globe far off
It seemed, now seems a boundless continent
Dark, waste, and wild, under the frown of Night
Starless exposed, and ever-threatening storms
Of Chaos blustering round, inclement sky;
Save on that side which from the wall of Heaven,
Though distant far, some small reflection gains
Of glimmering air less vexed with tempest loud:
Here walked the Fiend at large in spacious field.
As when a vulture on Imaus bred,
Whose snowy ridge the roving Tartar bounds,
Dislodging from a region scarce of prey
To gorge the flesh of lambs or yeanling kids,
On hills where flocks are fed, flies toward the springs
Of Ganges or Hydaspes, Indian streams;
But in his way lights on the barren plains
Of Sericana, where Chineses drive
With sails and wind their cany wagons light:
So, on this windy sea of land, the Fiend
Walked up and down alone, bent on his prey;
Alone, for other creature in this place,

Living or lifeless, to be found was none;
None yet, but store hereafter from the earth
Up hither like aerial vapours flew
Of all things transitory and vain, when sin
With vanity had filled the works of men:
Both all things vain, and all who in vain things
Built their fond hopes of glory or lasting fame,
Or happiness in this or the other life;
All who have their reward on earth, the fruits
Of painful superstition and blind zeal,
Nought seeking but the praise of men, here find
Fit retribution, empty as their deeds;
All the unaccomplished works of Nature's hand,
Abortive, monstrous, or unkindly mixed,
Dissolved on earth, fleet hither, and in vain,
Till final dissolution, wander here;
Not in the neighbouring moon as some have dreamed;
Those argent fields more likely habitants,
Translated Saints, or middle Spirits hold
Betwixt the angelical and human kind.
Hither of ill-joined sons and daughters born
First from the ancient world those giants came
With many a vain exploit, though then renowned:
The builders next of Babel on the plain
Of Sennaar, and still with vain design,
New Babels, had they wherewithal, would build:
Others came single; he, who, to be deemed
A God, leaped fondly into Aetna flames,
Empedocles; and he, who, to enjoy
Plato's Elysium, leaped into the sea,
Cleombrotus; and many more too long,
Embryos, and idiots, eremites, and friars
White, black, and gray, with all their trumpery.
Here pilgrims roam, that strayed so far to seek
In Golgotha him dead, who lives in Heaven;

And they, who to be sure of Paradise,
Dying, put on the weeds of Dominick,
Or in Franciscan think to pass disguised;
They pass the planets seven, and pass the fixed,
And that crystalling sphere whose balance weighs
The trepidation talked, and that first moved;
And now Saint Peter at Heaven's wicket seems
To wait them with his keys, and now at foot
Of Heaven's ascent they lift their feet, when lo
A violent cross wind from either coast
Blows them transverse, ten thousand leagues awry
Into the devious air: Then might ye see
Cowls, hoods, and habits, with their wearers, tost
And fluttered into rags; then reliques, beads,
Indulgences, dispenses, pardons, bulls,
The sport of winds: All these, upwhirled aloft,
Fly o'er the backside of the world far off
Into a Limbo large and broad, since called
The Paradise of Fools, to few unknown
Long after; now unpeopled, and untrod.
All this dark globe the Fiend found as he passed,
And long he wandered, till at last a gleam
Of dawning light turned thither-ward in haste
His travelled steps: far distant he descries
Ascending by degrees magnificent
Up to the wall of Heaven a structure high;
At top whereof, but far more rich, appeared
The work as of a kingly palace-gate,
With frontispiece of diamond and gold
Embellished; thick with sparkling orient gems
The portal shone, inimitable on earth
By model, or by shading pencil, drawn.
These stairs were such as whereon Jacob saw
Angels ascending and descending, bands
Of guardians bright, when he from Esau fled

To Padan-Aram, in the field of Luz
Dreaming by night under the open sky
And waking cried, "This is the gate of Heaven."
Each stair mysteriously was meant, nor stood
There always, but drawn up to Heaven sometimes
Viewless; and underneath a bright sea flowed
Of jasper, or of liquid pearl, whereon
Who after came from earth, failing arrived
Wafted by Angels, or flew o'er the lake
Rapt in a chariot drawn by fiery steeds.
The stairs were then let down, whether to dare
The Fiend by easy ascent, or aggravate
His sad exclusion from the doors of bliss:
Direct against which opened from beneath,
Just o'er the blissful seat of Paradise,
A passage down to the Earth, a passage wide,
Wider by far than that of after-times
Over mount Sion, and, though that were large,
Over the Promised Land to God so dear;
By which, to visit oft those happy tribes,
On high behests his angels to and fro
Passed frequent, and his eye with choice regard
From Paneas, the fount of Jordan's flood,
To Beersaba, where the Holy Land
Borders on Egypt and the Arabian shore;
So wide the opening seemed, where bounds were set
To darkness, such as bound the ocean wave.
Satan from hence, now on the lower stair,
That scaled by steps of gold to Heaven-gate,
Looks down with wonder at the sudden view
Of all this world at once. As when a scout,
Through dark and desert ways with peril gone
All night; at last by break of cheerful dawn
Obtains the brow of some high-climbing hill,
Which to his eye discovers unaware

The goodly prospect of some foreign land
First seen, or some renowned metropolis
With glistering spires and pinnacles adorned,
Which now the rising sun gilds with his beams:
Such wonder seized, though after Heaven seen,
The Spirit malign, but much more envy seized,
At sight of all this world beheld so fair.
Round he surveys (and well might, where he stood
So high above the circling canopy
Of night's extended shade,) from eastern point
Of Libra to the fleecy star that bears
Andromeda far off Atlantic seas
Beyond the horizon; then from pole to pole
He views in breadth, and without longer pause
Down right into the world's first region throws
His flight precipitant, and winds with ease
Through the pure marble air his oblique way
Amongst innumerable stars, that shone
Stars distant, but nigh hand seemed other worlds;
Or other worlds they seemed, or happy isles,
Like those Hesperian gardens famed of old,
Fortunate fields, and groves, and flowery vales,
Thrice happy isles; but who dwelt happy there
He staid not to inquire: Above them all
The golden sun, in splendour likest Heaven,
Allured his eye; thither his course he bends
Through the calm firmament, (but up or down,
By center, or eccentric, hard to tell,
Or longitude,) where the great luminary
Aloof the vulgar constellations thick,
That from his lordly eye keep distance due,
Dispenses light from far; they, as they move
Their starry dance in numbers that compute
Days, months, and years, towards his all-cheering lamp
Turn swift their various motions, or are turned

By his magnetic beam, that gently warms
The universe, and to each inward part
With gentle penetration, though unseen,
Shoots invisible virtue even to the deep;
So wonderously was set his station bright.
There lands the Fiend, a spot like which perhaps
Astronomer in the sun's lucent orb
Through his glazed optic tube yet never saw.
The place he found beyond expression bright,
Compared with aught on earth, metal or stone;
Not all parts like, but all alike informed
With radiant light, as glowing iron with fire;
If metal, part seemed gold, part silver clear;
If stone, carbuncle most or chrysolite,
Ruby or topaz, to the twelve that shone
In Aaron's breast-plate, and a stone besides
Imagined rather oft than elsewhere seen,
That stone, or like to that which here below
Philosophers in vain so long have sought,
In vain, though by their powerful art they bind
Volatile Hermes, and call up unbound
In various shapes old Proteus from the sea,
Drained through a limbeck to his native form.
What wonder then if fields and regions here
Breathe forth Elixir pure, and rivers run
Potable gold, when with one virtuous touch
The arch-chemic sun, so far from us remote,
Produces, with terrestrial humour mixed,
Here in the dark so many precious things
Of colour glorious, and effect so rare?
Here matter new to gaze the Devil met
Undazzled; far and wide his eye commands;
For sight no obstacle found here, nor shade,
But all sun-shine, as when his beams at noon
Culminate from the equator, as they now

Shot upward still direct, whence no way round
Shadow from body opaque can fall; and the air,
Nowhere so clear, sharpened his visual ray
To objects distant far, whereby he soon
Saw within ken a glorious Angel stand,
The same whom John saw also in the sun:
His back was turned, but not his brightness hid;
Of beaming sunny rays a golden tiar
Circled his head, nor less his locks behind
Illustrious on his shoulders fledge with wings
Lay waving round; on some great charge employed
He seemed, or fixed in cogitation deep.
Glad was the Spirit impure, as now in hope
To find who might direct his wandering flight
To Paradise, the happy seat of Man,
His journey's end and our beginning woe.
But first he casts to change his proper shape,
Which else might work him danger or delay:
And now a stripling Cherub he appears,
Not of the prime, yet such as in his face
Youth smiled celestial, and to every limb
Suitable grace diffused, so well he feigned:
Under a coronet his flowing hair
In curls on either cheek played; wings he wore
Of many a coloured plume, sprinkled with gold;
His habit fit for speed succinct, and held
Before his decent steps a silver wand.
He drew not nigh unheard; the Angel bright,
Ere he drew nigh, his radiant visage turned,
Admonished by his ear, and straight was known
The Arch-Angel Uriel, one of the seven
Who in God's presence, nearest to his throne,
Stand ready at command, and are his eyes
That run through all the Heavens, or down to the Earth
Bear his swift errands over moist and dry,

O'er sea and land: him Satan thus accosts.
"Uriel, for thou of those seven Spirits that stand
In sight of God's high throne, gloriously bright,
The first art wont his great authentic will
Interpreter through highest Heaven to bring,
Where all his sons thy embassy attend;
And here art likeliest by supreme decree
Like honour to obtain, and as his eye
To visit oft this new creation round;
Unspeakable desire to see, and know
All these his wonderous works, but chiefly Man,
His chief delight and favour, him for whom
All these his works so wonderous he ordained,
Hath brought me from the quires of Cherubim
Alone thus wandering. Brightest Seraph, tell
In which of all these shining orbs hath Man
His fixed seat, or fixed seat hath none,
But all these shining orbs his choice to dwell;
That I may find him, and with secret gaze
Or open admiration him behold,
On whom the great Creator hath bestowed
Worlds, and on whom hath all these graces poured;
That both in him and all things, as is meet,
The universal Maker we may praise;
Who justly hath driven out his rebel foes
To deepest Hell, and, to repair that loss,
Created this new happy race of Men
To serve him better: Wise are all his ways."
So spake the false dissembler unperceived;
For neither Man nor Angel can discern
Hypocrisy, the only evil that walks
Invisible, except to God alone,
By his permissive will, through Heaven and Earth:
And oft, though wisdom wake, suspicion sleeps
At wisdom's gate, and to simplicity

Resigns her charge, while goodness thinks no ill
Where no ill seems: Which now for once beguiled
Uriel, though regent of the sun, and held
The sharpest-sighted Spirit of all in Heaven;
Who to the fraudulent impostor foul,
In his uprightness, answer thus returned.
"Fair Angel, thy desire, which tends to know
The works of God, thereby to glorify
The great Work-master, leads to no excess
That reaches blame, but rather merits praise
The more it seems excess, that led thee hither
From thy empyreal mansion thus alone,
To witness with thine eyes what some perhaps,
Contented with report, hear only in Heaven:
For wonderful indeed are all his works,
Pleasant to know, and worthiest to be all
Had in remembrance always with delight;
But what created mind can comprehend
Their number, or the wisdom infinite
That brought them forth, but hid their causes deep?
I saw when at his word the formless mass,
This world's material mould, came to a heap:
Confusion heard his voice, and wild uproar
Stood ruled, stood vast infinitude confined;
Till at his second bidding Darkness fled,
Light shone, and order from disorder sprung:
Swift to their several quarters hasted then
The cumbrous elements, earth, flood, air, fire;
And this ethereal quintessence of Heaven
Flew upward, spirited with various forms,
That rolled orbicular, and turned to stars
Numberless, as thou seest, and how they move;
Each had his place appointed, each his course;
The rest in circuit walls this universe.
Look downward on that globe, whose hither side

With light from hence, though but reflected, shines;
That place is Earth, the seat of Man; that light
His day, which else, as the other hemisphere,
Night would invade; but there the neighbouring moon
(So call that opposite fair star) her aid
Timely interposes, and her monthly round
Still ending, still renewing, through mid Heaven,
With borrowed light her countenance triform
Hence fills and empties to enlighten the Earth,
And in her pale dominion checks the night.
That spot, to which I point, is Paradise,
Adam's abode; those lofty shades, his bower.
Thy way thou canst not miss, me mine requires."
Thus said, he turned; and Satan, bowing low,
As to superior Spirits is wont in Heaven,
Where honour due and reverence none neglects,
Took leave, and toward the coast of earth beneath,
Down from the ecliptic, sped with hoped success,
Throws his steep flight in many an aery wheel;
Nor staid, till on Niphates' top he lights.

BOOK IV

O, for that warning voice, which he, who saw
The Apocalypse, heard cry in Heaven aloud,
Then when the Dragon, put to second rout,
Came furious down to be revenged on men,
"Woe to the inhabitants on earth!" that now,
While time was, our first parents had been warned
The coming of their secret foe, and 'scaped,
Haply so 'scaped his mortal snare: For now
Satan, now first inflamed with rage, came down,
The tempter ere the accuser of mankind,
To wreak on innocent frail Man his loss
Of that first battle, and his flight to Hell:
Yet, not rejoicing in his speed, though bold
Far off and fearless, nor with cause to boast,
Begins his dire attempt; which nigh the birth
Now rolling boils in his tumultuous breast,
And like a devilish engine back recoils
Upon himself; horror and doubt distract
His troubled thoughts, and from the bottom stir
The Hell within him; for within him Hell
He brings, and round about him, nor from Hell
One step, no more than from himself, can fly

By change of place: Now conscience wakes despair,
That slumbered; wakes the bitter memory
Of what he was, what is, and what must be
Worse; of worse deeds worse sufferings must ensue.
Sometimes towards Eden, which now in his view
Lay pleasant, his grieved look he fixes sad;
Sometimes towards Heaven, and the full-blazing sun,
Which now sat high in his meridian tower:
Then, much revolving, thus in sighs began.
"O thou, that, with surpassing glory crowned,
Lookest from thy sole dominion like the God
Of this new world; at whose sight all the stars
Hide their diminished heads; to thee I call,
But with no friendly voice, and add thy name,
Of Sun! to tell thee how I hate thy beams,
That bring to my remembrance from what state
I fell, how glorious once above thy sphere;
Till pride and worse ambition threw me down
Warring in Heaven against Heaven's matchless King:
Ah, wherefore! he deserved no such return
From me, whom he created what I was
In that bright eminence, and with his good
Upbraided none; nor was his service hard.
What could be less than to afford him praise,
The easiest recompense, and pay him thanks,
How due! yet all his good proved ill in me,
And wrought but malice; lifted up so high
I 'sdeined subjection, and thought one step higher
Would set me highest, and in a moment quit
The debt immense of endless gratitude,
So burdensome still paying, still to owe,
Forgetful what from him I still received,
And understood not that a grateful mind
By owing owes not, but still pays, at once
Indebted and discharged; what burden then

O, had his powerful destiny ordained
Me some inferior Angel, I had stood
Then happy; no unbounded hope had raised
Ambition! Yet why not some other Power
As great might have aspired, and me, though mean,
Drawn to his part; but other Powers as great
Fell not, but stand unshaken, from within
Or from without, to all temptations armed.
Hadst thou the same free will and power to stand?
Thou hadst: whom hast thou then or what to accuse,
But Heaven's free love dealt equally to all?
Be then his love accursed, since love or hate,
To me alike, it deals eternal woe.
Nay, cursed be thou; since against his thy will
Chose freely what it now so justly rues.
Me miserable! which way shall I fly
Infinite wrath, and infinite despair?
Which way I fly is Hell; myself am Hell;
And, in the lowest deep, a lower deep
Still threatening to devour me opens wide,
To which the Hell I suffer seems a Heaven.
O, then, at last relent: Is there no place
Left for repentance, none for pardon left?
None left but by submission; and that word
Disdain forbids me, and my dread of shame
Among the Spirits beneath, whom I seduced
With other promises and other vaunts
Than to submit, boasting I could subdue
The Omnipotent. Ay me! they little know
How dearly I abide that boast so vain,
Under what torments inwardly I groan,
While they adore me on the throne of Hell.
With diadem and scepter high advanced,
The lower still I fall, only supreme
In misery: Such joy ambition finds.

But say I could repent, and could obtain,
By act of grace, my former state; how soon
Would hight recall high thoughts, how soon unsay
What feigned submission swore? Ease would recant
Vows made in pain, as violent and void.
For never can true reconcilement grow,
Where wounds of deadly hate have pierced so deep:
Which would but lead me to a worse relapse
And heavier fall: so should I purchase dear
Short intermission bought with double smart.
This knows my Punisher; therefore as far
From granting he, as I from begging, peace;
All hope excluded thus, behold, instead
Of us outcast, exil'd, his new delight,
Mankind created, and for him this world.
So farewell, hope; and with hope farewell, fear,
Farewell, remorse! all good to me is lost;
Evil, be thou my good; by thee at least
Divided empire with Heaven's King I hold,
By thee, and more than half perhaps will reign;
As Man ere long, and this new world, shall know."
Thus while he spake, each passion dimmed his face
Thrice changed with pale, ire, envy, and despair;
Which marred his borrowed visage, and betrayed
Him counterfeit, if any eye beheld.
For heavenly minds from such distempers foul
Are ever clear. Whereof he soon aware,
Each perturbation smoothed with outward calm,
Artificer of fraud; and was the first
That practised falsehood under saintly show,
Deep malice to conceal, couched with revenge:
Yet not enough had practised to deceive
Uriel once warned; whose eye pursued him down
The way he went, and on the Assyrian mount
Saw him disfigured, more than could befall

Spirit of happy sort; his gestures fierce
He marked and mad demeanour, then alone,
As he supposed, all unobserved, unseen.
So on he fares, and to the border comes
Of Eden, where delicious Paradise,
Now nearer, crowns with her enclosure green,
As with a rural mound, the champaign head
Of a steep wilderness, whose hairy sides
With thicket overgrown, grotesque and wild,
Access denied; and overhead upgrew
Insuperable height of loftiest shade,
Cedar, and pine, and fir, and branching palm,
A sylvan scene, and, as the ranks ascend,
Shade above shade, a woody theatre
Of stateliest view. Yet higher than their tops
The verdurous wall of Paradise upsprung;
Which to our general sire gave prospect large
Into his nether empire neighbouring round.
And higher than that wall a circling row
Of goodliest trees, loaden with fairest fruit,
Blossoms and fruits at once of golden hue,
Appeared, with gay enamelled colours mixed:
On which the sun more glad impressed his beams
Than in fair evening cloud, or humid bow,
When God hath showered the earth; so lovely seemed
That landskip: And of pure now purer air
Meets his approach, and to the heart inspires
Vernal delight and joy, able to drive
All sadness but despair: Now gentle gales,
Fanning their odoriferous wings, dispense
Native perfumes, and whisper whence they stole
Those balmy spoils. As when to them who fail
Beyond the Cape of Hope, and now are past
Mozambic, off at sea north-east winds blow
Sabean odours from the spicy shore

Of Araby the blest; with such delay
Well pleased they slack their course, and many a league
Cheered with the grateful smell old Ocean smiles:
So entertained those odorous sweets the Fiend,
Who came their bane; though with them better pleased
Than Asmodeus with the fishy fume
That drove him, though enamoured, from the spouse
Of Tobit's son, and with a vengeance sent
From Media post to Egypt, there fast bound.
Now to the ascent of that steep savage hill
Satan had journeyed on, pensive and slow;
But further way found none, so thick entwined,
As one continued brake, the undergrowth
Of shrubs and tangling bushes had perplexed
All path of man or beast that passed that way.
One gate there only was, and that looked east
On the other side: which when the arch-felon saw,
Due entrance he disdained; and, in contempt,
At one flight bound high over-leaped all bound
Of hill or highest wall, and sheer within
Lights on his feet. As when a prowling wolf,
Whom hunger drives to seek new haunt for prey,
Watching where shepherds pen their flocks at eve
In hurdled cotes amid the field secure,
Leaps o'er the fence with ease into the fold:
Or as a thief, bent to unhoard the cash
Of some rich burgher, whose substantial doors,
Cross-barred and bolted fast, fear no assault,
In at the window climbs, or o'er the tiles:
So clomb this first grand thief into God's fold;
So since into his church lewd hirelings climb.
Thence up he flew, and on the tree of life,
The middle tree and highest there that grew,
Sat like a cormorant; yet not true life
Thereby regained, but sat devising death

To them who lived; nor on the virtue thought
Of that life-giving plant, but only used
For prospect, what well used had been the pledge
Of immortality. So little knows
Any, but God alone, to value right
The good before him, but perverts best things
To worst abuse, or to their meanest use.
Beneath him with new wonder now he views,
To all delight of human sense exposed,
In narrow room, Nature's whole wealth, yea more,
A Heaven on Earth: For blissful Paradise
Of God the garden was, by him in the east
Of Eden planted; Eden stretched her line
From Auran eastward to the royal towers
Of great Seleucia, built by Grecian kings,
Or where the sons of Eden long before
Dwelt in Telassar: In this pleasant soil
His far more pleasant garden God ordained;
Out of the fertile ground he caused to grow
All trees of noblest kind for sight, smell, taste;
And all amid them stood the tree of life,
High eminent, blooming ambrosial fruit
Of vegetable gold; and next to life,
Our death, the tree of knowledge, grew fast by,
Knowledge of good bought dear by knowing ill.
Southward through Eden went a river large,
Nor changed his course, but through the shaggy hill
Passed underneath engulfed; for God had thrown
That mountain as his garden-mould high raised
Upon the rapid current, which, through veins
Of porous earth with kindly thirst up-drawn,
Rose a fresh fountain, and with many a rill
Watered the garden; thence united fell
Down the steep glade, and met the nether flood,
Which from his darksome passage now appears,

And now, divided into four main streams,
Runs diverse, wandering many a famous realm
And country, whereof here needs no account;
But rather to tell how, if Art could tell,
How from that sapphire fount the crisped brooks,
Rolling on orient pearl and sands of gold,
With mazy error under pendant shades
Ran nectar, visiting each plant, and fed
Flowers worthy of Paradise, which not nice Art
In beds and curious knots, but Nature boon
Poured forth profuse on hill, and dale, and plain,
Both where the morning sun first warmly smote
The open field, and where the unpierced shade
Embrowned the noontide bowers: Thus was this place
A happy rural seat of various view;
Groves whose rich trees wept odorous gums and balm,
Others whose fruit, burnished with golden rind,
Hung amiable, Hesperian fables true,
If true, here only, and of delicious taste:
Betwixt them lawns, or level downs, and flocks
Grazing the tender herb, were interposed,
Or palmy hillock; or the flowery lap
Of some irriguous valley spread her store,
Flowers of all hue, and without thorn the rose:
Another side, umbrageous grots and caves
Of cool recess, o'er which the mantling vine
Lays forth her purple grape, and gently creeps
Luxuriant; meanwhile murmuring waters fall
Down the slope hills, dispersed, or in a lake,
That to the fringed bank with myrtle crowned
Her crystal mirror holds, unite their streams.
The birds their quire apply; airs, vernal airs,
Breathing the smell of field and grove, attune
The trembling leaves, while universal Pan,
Knit with the Graces and the Hours in dance,

Led on the eternal Spring. Not that fair field
Of Enna, where Proserpine gathering flowers,
Herself a fairer flower by gloomy Dis
Was gathered, which cost Ceres all that pain
To seek her through the world; nor that sweet grove
Of Daphne by Orontes, and the inspired
Castalian spring, might with this Paradise
Of Eden strive; nor that Nyseian isle
Girt with the river Triton, where old Cham,
Whom Gentiles Ammon call and Libyan Jove,
Hid Amalthea, and her florid son
Young Bacchus, from his stepdame Rhea's eye;
Nor where Abassin kings their issue guard,
Mount Amara, though this by some supposed
True Paradise under the Ethiop line
By Nilus' head, enclosed with shining rock,
A whole day's journey high, but wide remote
From this Assyrian garden, where the Fiend
Saw, undelighted, all delight, all kind
Of living creatures, new to sight, and strange
Two of far nobler shape, erect and tall,
Godlike erect, with native honour clad
In naked majesty seemed lords of all:
And worthy seemed; for in their looks divine
The image of their glorious Maker shone,
Truth, wisdom, sanctitude severe and pure,
(Severe, but in true filial freedom placed,)
Whence true authority in men; though both
Not equal, as their sex not equal seemed;
For contemplation he and valour formed;
For softness she and sweet attractive grace;
He for God only, she for God in him:
His fair large front and eye sublime declared
Absolute rule; and hyacinthine locks
Round from his parted forelock manly hung

Clustering, but not beneath his shoulders broad:
She, as a veil, down to the slender waist
Her unadorned golden tresses wore
Dishevelled, but in wanton ringlets waved
As the vine curls her tendrils, which implied
Subjection, but required with gentle sway,
And by her yielded, by him best received,
Yielded with coy submission, modest pride,
And sweet, reluctant, amorous delay.
Nor those mysterious parts were then concealed;
Then was not guilty shame, dishonest shame
Of nature's works, honour dishonourable,
Sin-bred, how have ye troubled all mankind
With shows instead, mere shows of seeming pure,
And banished from man's life his happiest life,
Simplicity and spotless innocence!
So passed they naked on, nor shunned the sight
Of God or Angel; for they thought no ill:
So hand in hand they passed, the loveliest pair,
That ever since in love's embraces met;
Adam the goodliest man of men since born
His sons, the fairest of her daughters Eve.
Under a tuft of shade that on a green
Stood whispering soft, by a fresh fountain side
They sat them down; and, after no more toil
Of their sweet gardening labour than sufficed
To recommend cool Zephyr, and made ease
More easy, wholesome thirst and appetite
More grateful, to their supper-fruits they fell,
Nectarine fruits which the compliant boughs
Yielded them, side-long as they sat recline
On the soft downy bank damasked with flowers:
The savoury pulp they chew, and in the rind,
Still as they thirsted, scoop the brimming stream;
Nor gentle purpose, nor endearing smiles

Wanted, nor youthful dalliance, as beseems
Fair couple, linked in happy nuptial league,
Alone as they. About them frisking played
All beasts of the earth, since wild, and of all chase
In wood or wilderness, forest or den;
Sporting the lion ramped, and in his paw
Dandled the kid; bears, tigers, ounces, pards,
Gambolled before them; the unwieldy elephant,
To make them mirth, used all his might, and wreathed
His lithe proboscis; close the serpent sly,
Insinuating, wove with Gordian twine
His braided train, and of his fatal guile
Gave proof unheeded; others on the grass
Couched, and now filled with pasture gazing sat,
Or bedward ruminating; for the sun,
Declined, was hasting now with prone career
To the ocean isles, and in the ascending scale
Of Heaven the stars that usher evening rose:
When Satan still in gaze, as first he stood,
Scarce thus at length failed speech recovered sad.
"O Hell! what do mine eyes with grief behold!
Into our room of bliss thus high advanced
Creatures of other mould, earth-born perhaps,
Not Spirits, yet to heavenly Spirits bright
Little inferior; whom my thoughts pursue
With wonder, and could love, so lively shines
In them divine resemblance, and such grace
The hand that formed them on their shape hath poured.
Ah! gentle pair, ye little think how nigh
Your change approaches, when all these delights
Will vanish, and deliver ye to woe;
More woe, the more your taste is now of joy;
Happy, but for so happy ill secured
Long to continue, and this high seat your Heaven
Ill fenced for Heaven to keep out such a foe

As now is entered; yet no purposed foe
To you, whom I could pity thus forlorn,
Though I unpitied: League with you I seek,
And mutual amity, so strait, so close,
That I with you must dwell, or you with me
Henceforth; my dwelling haply may not please,
Like this fair Paradise, your sense; yet such
Accept your Maker's work; he gave it me,
Which I as freely give: Hell shall unfold,
To entertain you two, her widest gates,
And send forth all her kings; there will be room,
Not like these narrow limits, to receive
Your numerous offspring; if no better place,
Thank him who puts me loth to this revenge
On you who wrong me not for him who wronged.
And should I at your harmless innocence
Melt, as I do, yet public reason just,
Honour and empire with revenge enlarged,
By conquering this new world, compels me now
To do what else, though damned, I should abhor."
So spake the Fiend, and with necessity,
The tyrant's plea, excused his devilish deeds.
Then from his lofty stand on that high tree
Down he alights among the sportful herd
Of those four-footed kinds, himself now one,
Now other, as their shape served best his end
Nearer to view his prey, and, unespied,
To mark what of their state he more might learn,
By word or action marked. About them round
A lion now he stalks with fiery glare;
Then as a tiger, who by chance hath spied
In some purlieu two gentle fawns at play,
Straight couches close, then, rising, changes oft
His couchant watch, as one who chose his ground,
Whence rushing, he might surest seize them both,

Gripped in each paw: when, Adam first of men
To first of women Eve thus moving speech,
Turned him, all ear to hear new utterance flow.
"Sole partner, and sole part, of all these joys,
Dearer thyself than all; needs must the Power
That made us, and for us this ample world,
Be infinitely good, and of his good
As liberal and free as infinite;
That raised us from the dust, and placed us here
In all this happiness, who at his hand
Have nothing merited, nor can perform
Aught whereof he hath need; he who requires
From us no other service than to keep
This one, this easy charge, of all the trees
In Paradise that bear delicious fruit
So various, not to taste that only tree
Of knowledge, planted by the tree of life;
So near grows death to life, whate'er death is,
Some dreadful thing no doubt; for well thou knowest
God hath pronounced it death to taste that tree,
The only sign of our obedience left,
Among so many signs of power and rule
Conferred upon us, and dominion given
Over all other creatures that possess
Earth, air, and sea. Then let us not think hard
One easy prohibition, who enjoy
Free leave so large to all things else, and choice
Unlimited of manifold delights:
But let us ever praise him, and extol
His bounty, following our delightful task,
To prune these growing plants, and tend these flowers,
Which were it toilsome, yet with thee were sweet."
To whom thus Eve replied. "O thou for whom
And from whom I was formed, flesh of thy flesh,
And without whom am to no end, my guide

And head! what thou hast said is just and right.
For we to him indeed all praises owe,
And daily thanks; I chiefly, who enjoy
So far the happier lot, enjoying thee
Pre-eminent by so much odds, while thou
Like consort to thyself canst no where find.
That day I oft remember, when from sleep
I first awaked, and found myself reposed
Under a shade on flowers, much wondering where
And what I was, whence thither brought, and how.
Not distant far from thence a murmuring sound
Of waters issued from a cave, and spread
Into a liquid plain, then stood unmoved
Pure as the expanse of Heaven; I thither went
With unexperienced thought, and laid me down
On the green bank, to look into the clear
Smooth lake, that to me seemed another sky.
As I bent down to look, just opposite
A shape within the watery gleam appeared,
Bending to look on me: I started back,
It started back; but pleased I soon returned,
Pleased it returned as soon with answering looks
Of sympathy and love: There I had fixed
Mine eyes till now, and pined with vain desire,
Had not a voice thus warned me; 'What thou seest,
What there thou seest, fair Creature, is thyself;
With thee it came and goes: but follow me,
And I will bring thee where no shadow stays
Thy coming, and thy soft embraces, he
Whose image thou art; him thou shalt enjoy
Inseparably thine, to him shalt bear
Multitudes like thyself, and thence be called
Mother of human race.' What could I do,
But follow straight, invisibly thus led?
Till I espied thee, fair indeed and tall,

Under a platane; yet methought less fair,
Less winning soft, less amiably mild,
Than that smooth watery image: Back I turned;
Thou following cryedst aloud, 'Return, fair Eve;
Whom flyest thou? whom thou flyest, of him thou art,
His flesh, his bone; to give thee being I lent
Out of my side to thee, nearest my heart,
Substantial life, to have thee by my side
Henceforth an individual solace dear;
Part of my soul I seek thee, and thee claim
My other half:' With that thy gentle hand
Seized mine: I yielded; and from that time see
How beauty is excelled by manly grace,
And wisdom, which alone is truly fair."
So spake our general mother, and with eyes
Of conjugal attraction unreproved,
And meek surrender, half-embracing leaned
On our first father; half her swelling breast
Naked met his, under the flowing gold
Of her loose tresses hid: he in delight
Both of her beauty, and submissive charms,
Smiled with superior love, as Jupiter
On Juno smiles, when he impregns the clouds
That shed Mayflowers; and pressed her matron lip
With kisses pure: Aside the Devil turned
For envy; yet with jealous leer malign
Eyed them askance, and to himself thus plained.
"Sight hateful, sight tormenting! thus these two,
Imparadised in one another's arms,
The happier Eden, shall enjoy their fill
Of bliss on bliss; while I to Hell am thrust,
Where neither joy nor love, but fierce desire,
Among our other torments not the least,
Still unfulfilled with pain of longing pines.
Yet let me not forget what I have gained

From their own mouths: All is not theirs, it seems;
One fatal tree there stands, of knowledge called,
Forbidden them to taste: Knowledge forbidden
Suspicious, reasonless. Why should their Lord
Envy them that? Can it be sin to know?
Can it be death? And do they only stand
By ignorance? Is that their happy state,
The proof of their obedience and their faith?
O fair foundation laid whereon to build
Their ruin! hence I will excite their minds
With more desire to know, and to reject
Envious commands, invented with design
To keep them low, whom knowledge might exalt
Equal with Gods: aspiring to be such,
They taste and die: What likelier can ensue
But first with narrow search I must walk round
This garden, and no corner leave unspied;
A chance but chance may lead where I may meet
Some wandering Spirit of Heaven by fountain side,
Or in thick shade retired, from him to draw
What further would be learned. Live while ye may,
Yet happy pair; enjoy, till I return,
Short pleasures, for long woes are to succeed!"
So saying, his proud step he scornful turned,
But with sly circumspection, and began
Through wood, through waste, o'er hill, o'er dale, his roam
Meanwhile in utmost longitude, where Heaven
With earth and ocean meets, the setting sun
Slowly descended, and with right aspect
Against the eastern gate of Paradise
Levelled his evening rays: It was a rock
Of alabaster, piled up to the clouds,
Conspicuous far, winding with one ascent
Accessible from earth, one entrance high;
The rest was craggy cliff, that overhung

Still as it rose, impossible to climb.
Betwixt these rocky pillars Gabriel sat,
Chief of the angelic guards, awaiting night;
About him exercised heroic games
The unarmed youth of Heaven, but nigh at hand
Celestial armoury, shields, helms, and spears,
Hung high with diamond flaming, and with gold.
Thither came Uriel, gliding through the even
On a sun-beam, swift as a shooting star
In autumn thwarts the night, when vapours fired
Impress the air, and shows the mariner
From what point of his compass to beware
Impetuous winds: He thus began in haste.
"Gabriel, to thee thy course by lot hath given
Charge and strict watch, that to this happy place
No evil thing approach or enter in.
This day at hight of noon came to my sphere
A Spirit, zealous, as he seemed, to know
More of the Almighty's works, and chiefly Man,
God's latest image: I described his way
Bent all on speed, and marked his aery gait;
But in the mount that lies from Eden north,
Where he first lighted, soon discerned his looks
Alien from Heaven, with passions foul obscured:
Mine eye pursued him still, but under shade
Lost sight of him: One of the banished crew,
I fear, hath ventured from the deep, to raise
New troubles; him thy care must be to find."
To whom the winged warrior thus returned.
"Uriel, no wonder if thy perfect sight,
Amid the sun's bright circle where thou sitst,
See far and wide: In at this gate none pass
The vigilance here placed, but such as come
Well known from Heaven; and since meridian hour
No creature thence: If Spirit of other sort,

So minded, have o'er-leaped these earthly bounds
On purpose, hard thou knowest it to exclude
Spiritual substance with corporeal bar.
But if within the circuit of these walks,
In whatsoever shape he lurk, of whom
Thou tellest, by morrow dawning I shall know."
So promised he; and Uriel to his charge
Returned on that bright beam, whose point now raised
Bore him slope downward to the sun now fallen
Beneath the Azores; whether the prime orb,
Incredible how swift, had thither rolled
Diurnal, or this less voluble earth,
By shorter flight to the east, had left him there
Arraying with reflected purple and gold
The clouds that on his western throne attend.
Now came still Evening on, and Twilight gray
Had in her sober livery all things clad;
Silence accompanied; for beast and bird,
They to their grassy couch, these to their nests
Were slunk, all but the wakeful nightingale;
She all night long her amorous descant sung;
Silence was pleased: Now glowed the firmament
With living sapphires: Hesperus, that led
The starry host, rode brightest, till the moon,
Rising in clouded majesty, at length
Apparent queen unveiled her peerless light,
And o'er the dark her silver mantle threw.
When Adam thus to Eve. "Fair Consort, the hour
Of night, and all things now retired to rest,
Mind us of like repose; since God hath set
Labour and rest, as day and night, to men
Successive; and the timely dew of sleep,
Now falling with soft slumbrous weight, inclines
Our eye-lids: Other creatures all day long
Rove idle, unemployed, and less need rest;

Man hath his daily work of body or mind
Appointed, which declares his dignity,
And the regard of Heaven on all his ways;
While other animals unactive range,
And of their doings God takes no account.
To-morrow, ere fresh morning streak the east
With first approach of light, we must be risen,
And at our pleasant labour, to reform
Yon flowery arbours, yonder alleys green,
Our walk at noon, with branches overgrown,
That mock our scant manuring, and require
More hands than ours to lop their wanton growth:
Those blossoms also, and those dropping gums,
That lie bestrown, unsightly and unsmooth,
Ask riddance, if we mean to tread with ease;
Meanwhile, as Nature wills, night bids us rest."
To whom thus Eve, with perfect beauty adorned
"My Author and Disposer, what thou bidst
Unargued I obey: So God ordains;
God is thy law, thou mine: To know no more
Is woman's happiest knowledge, and her praise.
With thee conversing I forget all time;
All seasons, and their change, all please alike.
Sweet is the breath of Morn, her rising sweet,
With charm of earliest birds: pleasant the sun,
When first on this delightful land he spreads
His orient beams, on herb, tree, fruit, and flower,
Glistering with dew; fragrant the fertile earth
After soft showers; and sweet the coming on
Of grateful Evening mild; then silent Night,
With this her solemn bird, and this fair moon,
And these the gems of Heaven, her starry train:
But neither breath of Morn, when she ascends
With charm of earliest birds; nor rising sun
On this delightful land; nor herb, fruit, flower,

Glistering with dew; nor fragrance after showers;
Nor grateful Evening mild; nor silent Night,
With this her solemn bird, nor walk by moon,
Or glittering star-light, without thee is sweet.
But wherefore all night long shine these? for whom
This glorious sight, when sleep hath shut all eyes?"
To whom our general ancestor replied.
"Daughter of God and Man, accomplished Eve,
These have their course to finish round the earth,
By morrow evening, and from land to land
In order, though to nations yet unborn,
Ministring light prepared, they set and rise;
Lest total Darkness should by night regain
Her old possession, and extinguish life
In Nature and all things; which these soft fires
Not only enlighten, but with kindly heat
Of various influence foment and warm,
Temper or nourish, or in part shed down
Their stellar virtue on all kinds that grow
On earth, made hereby apter to receive
Perfection from the sun's more potent ray.
These then, though unbeheld in deep of night,
Shine not in vain; nor think, though men were none,
That Heaven would want spectators, God want praise:
Millions of spiritual creatures walk the earth
Unseen, both when we wake, and when we sleep:
All these with ceaseless praise his works behold
Both day and night: How often from the steep
Of echoing hill or thicket have we heard
Celestial voices to the midnight air,
Sole, or responsive each to others note,
Singing their great Creator? oft in bands
While they keep watch, or nightly rounding walk,
With heavenly touch of instrumental sounds
In full harmonic number joined, their songs

Divide the night, and lift our thoughts to Heaven."
Thus talking, hand in hand alone they passed
On to their blissful bower: it was a place
Chosen by the sovran Planter, when he framed
All things to Man's delightful use; the roof
Of thickest covert was inwoven shade
Laurel and myrtle, and what higher grew
Of firm and fragrant leaf; on either side
Acanthus, and each odorous bushy shrub,
Fenced up the verdant wall; each beauteous flower,
Iris all hues, roses, and jessamin,
Reared high their flourished heads between, and wrought
Mosaic; underfoot the violet,
Crocus, and hyacinth, with rich inlay
Broidered the ground, more coloured than with stone
Of costliest emblem: Other creature here,
Bird, beast, insect, or worm, durst enter none,
Such was their awe of Man. In shadier bower
More sacred and sequestered, though but feigned,
Pan or Sylvanus never slept, nor Nymph
Nor Faunus haunted. Here, in close recess,
With flowers, garlands, and sweet-smelling herbs,
Espoused Eve decked first her nuptial bed;
And heavenly quires the hymenaean sung,
What day the genial Angel to our sire
Brought her in naked beauty more adorned,
More lovely, than Pandora, whom the Gods
Endowed with all their gifts, and O! too like
In sad event, when to the unwiser son
Of Japhet brought by Hermes, she ensnared
Mankind with her fair looks, to be avenged
On him who had stole Jove's authentic fire.
Thus, at their shady lodge arrived, both stood,
Both turned, and under open sky adored
The God that made both sky, air, earth, and heaven,

Which they beheld, the moon's resplendent globe,
And starry pole: "Thou also madest the night,
Maker Omnipotent, and thou the day,
Which we, in our appointed work employed,
Have finished, happy in our mutual help
And mutual love, the crown of all our bliss
Ordained by thee; and this delicious place
For us too large, where thy abundance wants
Partakers, and uncropt falls to the ground.
But thou hast promised from us two a race
To fill the earth, who shall with us extol
Thy goodness infinite, both when we wake,
And when we seek, as now, thy gift of sleep."
This said unanimous, and other rites
Observing none, but adoration pure
Which God likes best, into their inmost bower
Handed they went; and, eased the putting off
These troublesome disguises which we wear,
Straight side by side were laid; nor turned, I ween,
Adam from his fair spouse, nor Eve the rites
Mysterious of connubial love refused:
Whatever hypocrites austerely talk
Of purity, and place, and innocence,
Defaming as impure what God declares
Pure, and commands to some, leaves free to all.
Our Maker bids encrease; who bids abstain
But our Destroyer, foe to God and Man?
Hail, wedded Love, mysterious law, true source
Of human offspring, sole propriety
In Paradise of all things common else!
By thee adulterous Lust was driven from men
Among the bestial herds to range; by thee
Founded in reason, loyal, just, and pure,
Relations dear, and all the charities
Of father, son, and brother, first were known.

Far be it, that I should write thee sin or blame,
Or think thee unbefitting holiest place,
Perpetual fountain of domestick sweets,
Whose bed is undefiled and chaste pronounced,
Present, or past, as saints and patriarchs used.
Here Love his golden shafts employs, here lights
His constant lamp, and waves his purple wings,
Reigns here and revels; not in the bought smile
Of harlots, loveless, joyless, unendeared,
Casual fruition; nor in court-amours,
Mixed dance, or wanton mask, or midnight ball,
Or serenade, which the starved lover sings
To his proud fair, best quitted with disdain.
These, lulled by nightingales, embracing slept,
And on their naked limbs the flowery roof
Showered roses, which the morn repaired. Sleep on,
Blest pair; and O! yet happiest, if ye seek
No happier state, and know to know no more.
Now had night measured with her shadowy cone
Half way up hill this vast sublunar vault,
And from their ivory port the Cherubim,
Forth issuing at the accustomed hour, stood armed
To their night watches in warlike parade;
When Gabriel to his next in power thus spake.
"Uzziel, half these draw off, and coast the south
With strictest watch; these other wheel the north;
Our circuit meets full west." As flame they part,
Half wheeling to the shield, half to the spear.
From these, two strong and subtle Spirits he called
That near him stood, and gave them thus in charge.
"Ithuriel and Zephon, with winged speed
Search through this garden, leave unsearched no nook;
But chiefly where those two fair creatures lodge,
Now laid perhaps asleep, secure of harm.
This evening from the sun's decline arrived,

Who tells of some infernal Spirit seen
Hitherward bent (who could have thought?) escaped
The bars of Hell, on errand bad no doubt:
Such, where ye find, seize fast, and hither bring."
So saying, on he led his radiant files,
Dazzling the moon; these to the bower direct
In search of whom they sought: Him there they found
Squat like a toad, close at the ear of Eve,
Assaying by his devilish art to reach
The organs of her fancy, and with them forge
Illusions, as he list, phantasms and dreams;
Or if, inspiring venom, he might taint
The animal spirits, that from pure blood arise
Like gentle breaths from rivers pure, thence raise
At least distempered, discontented thoughts,
Vain hopes, vain aims, inordinate desires,
Blown up with high conceits ingendering pride.
Him thus intent Ithuriel with his spear
Touched lightly; for no falsehood can endure
Touch of celestial temper, but returns
Of force to its own likeness: Up he starts
Discovered and surprised. As when a spark
Lights on a heap of nitrous powder, laid
Fit for the tun some magazine to store
Against a rumoured war, the smutty grain,
With sudden blaze diffused, inflames the air;
So started up in his own shape the Fiend.
Back stept those two fair Angels, half amazed
So sudden to behold the grisly king;
Yet thus, unmoved with fear, accost him soon.
"Which of those rebel Spirits adjudged to Hell
Comest thou, escaped thy prison? and, transformed,
Why sat'st thou like an enemy in wait,
Here watching at the head of these that sleep?"
"Know ye not then" said Satan, filled with scorn,

"Know ye not me? ye knew me once no mate
For you, there sitting where ye durst not soar:
Not to know me argues yourselves unknown,
The lowest of your throng; or, if ye know,
Why ask ye, and superfluous begin
Your message, like to end as much in vain?"
To whom thus Zephon, answering scorn with scorn.
"Think not, revolted Spirit, thy shape the same,
Or undiminished brightness to be known,
As when thou stoodest in Heaven upright and pure;
That glory then, when thou no more wast good,
Departed from thee; and thou resemblest now
Thy sin and place of doom obscure and foul.
But come, for thou, be sure, shalt give account
To him who sent us, whose charge is to keep
This place inviolable, and these from harm."
So spake the Cherub; and his grave rebuke,
Severe in youthful beauty, added grace
Invincible: Abashed the Devil stood,
And felt how awful goodness is, and saw
Virtue in her shape how lovely; saw, and pined
His loss; but chiefly to find here observed
His lustre visibly impaired; yet seemed
Undaunted. "If I must contend," said he,
"Best with the best, the sender, not the sent,
Or all at once; more glory will be won,
Or less be lost." "Thy fear," said Zephon bold,
"Will save us trial what the least can do
Single against thee wicked, and thence weak."
The Fiend replied not, overcome with rage;
But, like a proud steed reined, went haughty on,
Champing his iron curb: To strive or fly
He held it vain; awe from above had quelled
His heart, not else dismayed. Now drew they nigh
The western point, where those half-rounding guards

Just met, and closing stood in squadron joined,
Awaiting next command. To whom their Chief,
Gabriel, from the front thus called aloud.
"O friends! I hear the tread of nimble feet
Hasting this way, and now by glimpse discern
Ithuriel and Zephon through the shade;
And with them comes a third of regal port,
But faded splendour wan; who by his gait
And fierce demeanour seems the Prince of Hell,
Not likely to part hence without contest;
Stand firm, for in his look defiance lours."
He scarce had ended, when those two approached,
And brief related whom they brought, where found,
How busied, in what form and posture couched.
To whom with stern regard thus Gabriel spake.
"Why hast thou, Satan, broke the bounds prescribed
To thy transgressions, and disturbed the charge
Of others, who approve not to transgress
By thy example, but have power and right
To question thy bold entrance on this place;
Employed, it seems, to violate sleep, and those
Whose dwelling God hath planted here in bliss!"
To whom thus Satan with contemptuous brow.
"Gabriel, thou hadst in Heaven the esteem of wise,
And such I held thee; but this question asked
Puts me in doubt. Lives there who loves his pain!
Who would not, finding way, break loose from Hell,
Though thither doomed! Thou wouldst thyself, no doubt
And boldly venture to whatever place
Farthest from pain, where thou mightst hope to change
Torment with ease, and soonest recompense
Dole with delight, which in this place I sought;
To thee no reason, who knowest only good,
But evil hast not tried: and wilt object
His will who bounds us! Let him surer bar

His iron gates, if he intends our stay
In that dark durance: Thus much what was asked.
The rest is true, they found me where they say;
But that implies not violence or harm."
Thus he in scorn. The warlike Angel moved,
Disdainfully half smiling, thus replied.
"O loss of one in Heaven to judge of wise
Since Satan fell, whom folly overthrew,
And now returns him from his prison 'scaped,
Gravely in doubt whether to hold them wise
Or not, who ask what boldness brought him hither
Unlicensed from his bounds in Hell prescribed;
So wise he judges it to fly from pain
However, and to 'scape his punishment!
So judge thou still, presumptuous! till the wrath,
Which thou incurrest by flying, meet thy flight
Sevenfold, and scourge that wisdom back to Hell,
Which taught thee yet no better, that no pain
Can equal anger infinite provoked.
But wherefore thou alone? wherefore with thee
Came not all hell broke loose? or thou than they
Less hardy to endure? Courageous Chief!
The first in flight from pain! hadst thou alleged
To thy deserted host this cause of flight,
Thou surely hadst not come sole fugitive."
To which the Fiend thus answered, frowning stern.
"Not that I less endure, or shrink from pain,
Insulting Angel! well thou knowest I stood
Thy fiercest, when in battle to thy aid
The blasting volleyed thunder made all speed,
And seconded thy else not dreaded spear.
But still thy words at random, as before,
Argue thy inexperience what behoves
From hard assays and ill successes past
A faithful leader, not to hazard all

Through ways of danger by himself untried:
I, therefore, I alone first undertook
To wing the desolate abyss, and spy
This new created world, whereof in Hell
Fame is not silent, here in hope to find
Better abode, and my afflicted Powers
To settle here on earth, or in mid air;
Though for possession put to try once more
What thou and thy gay legions dare against;
Whose easier business were to serve their Lord
High up in Heaven, with songs to hymn his throne,
And practised distances to cringe, not fight,"
To whom the warrior Angel soon replied.
"To say and straight unsay, pretending first
Wise to fly pain, professing next the spy,
Argues no leader but a liar traced,
Satan, and couldst thou faithful add? O name,
O sacred name of faithfulness profaned!
Faithful to whom? to thy rebellious crew?
Army of Fiends, fit body to fit head.
Was this your discipline and faith engaged,
Your military obedience, to dissolve
Allegiance to the acknowledged Power supreme?
And thou, sly hypocrite, who now wouldst seem
Patron of liberty, who more than thou
Once fawned, and cringed, and servilely adored
Heaven's awful Monarch? wherefore, but in hope
To dispossess him, and thyself to reign?
But mark what I arreed thee now, Avant;
Fly neither whence thou fledst! If from this hour
Within these hallowed limits thou appear,
Back to the infernal pit I drag thee chained,
And seal thee so, as henceforth not to scorn
The facile gates of Hell too slightly barred."
So threatened he; but Satan to no threats

Gave heed, but waxing more in rage replied.
"Then when I am thy captive talk of chains,
Proud limitary Cherub! but ere then
Far heavier load thyself expect to feel
From my prevailing arm, though Heaven's King
Ride on thy wings, and thou with thy compeers,
Us'd to the yoke, drawest his triumphant wheels
In progress through the road of Heaven star-paved."
While thus he spake, the angelic squadron bright
Turned fiery red, sharpening in mooned horns
Their phalanx, and began to hem him round
With ported spears, as thick as when a field
Of Ceres ripe for harvest waving bends
Her bearded grove of ears, which way the wind
Sways them; the careful plowman doubting stands,
Left on the threshing floor his hopeless sheaves
Prove chaff. On the other side, Satan, alarmed,
Collecting all his might, dilated stood,
Like Teneriff or Atlas, unremoved:
His stature reached the sky, and on his crest
Sat Horror plumed; nor wanted in his grasp
What seemed both spear and shield: Now dreadful deeds
Might have ensued, nor only Paradise
In this commotion, but the starry cope
Of Heaven perhaps, or all the elements
At least had gone to wrack, disturbed and torn
With violence of this conflict, had not soon
The Eternal, to prevent such horrid fray,
Hung forth in Heaven his golden scales, yet seen
Betwixt Astrea and the Scorpion sign,
Wherein all things created first he weighed,
The pendulous round earth with balanced air
In counterpoise, now ponders all events,
Battles and realms: In these he put two weights,
The sequel each of parting and of fight:

The latter quick up flew, and kicked the beam,
Which Gabriel spying, thus bespake the Fiend.
"Satan, I know thy strength, and thou knowest mine;
Neither our own, but given: What folly then
To boast what arms can do? since thine no more
Than Heaven permits, nor mine, though doubled now
To trample thee as mire: For proof look up,
And read thy lot in yon celestial sign;
Where thou art weighed, and shown how light, how weak,
If thou resist." The Fiend looked up, and knew
His mounted scale aloft: Nor more; but fled
Murmuring, and with him fled the shades of night.

BOOK V

Now Morn, her rosy steps in the eastern clime
Advancing, sowed the earth with orient pearl,
When Adam waked, so customed; for his sleep
Was aery-light, from pure digestion bred,
And temperate vapours bland, which the only sound
Of leaves and fuming rills, Aurora's fan,
Lightly dispersed, and the shrill matin song
Of birds on every bough; so much the more
His wonder was to find unwakened Eve
With tresses discomposed, and glowing cheek,
As through unquiet rest: He, on his side
Leaning half raised, with looks of cordial love
Hung over her enamoured, and beheld
Beauty, which, whether waking or asleep,
Shot forth peculiar graces; then with voice
Mild, as when Zephyrus on Flora breathes,
Her hand soft touching, whispered thus. Awake,
My fairest, my espoused, my latest found,
Heaven's last best gift, my ever new delight!
Awake: The morning shines, and the fresh field
Calls us; we lose the prime, to mark how spring
Our tender plants, how blows the citron grove,

What drops the myrrh, and what the balmy reed,
How nature paints her colours, how the bee
Sits on the bloom extracting liquid sweet.
Such whispering waked her, but with startled eye
On Adam, whom embracing, thus she spake.
"O sole in whom my thoughts find all repose,
My glory, my perfection! glad I see
Thy face, and morn returned; for I this night
(Such night till this I never passed) have dreamed,
If dreamed, not, as I oft am wont, of thee,
Works of day past, or morrow's next design,
But of offence and trouble, which my mind
Knew never till this irksome night: Methought,
Close at mine ear one called me forth to walk
With gentle voice; I thought it thine: It said,
'Why sleepest thou, Eve? now is the pleasant time,
The cool, the silent, save where silence yields
To the night-warbling bird, that now awake
Tunes sweetest his love-laboured song; now reigns
Full-orbed the moon, and with more pleasing light
Shadowy sets off the face of things; in vain,
If none regard; Heaven wakes with all his eyes,
Whom to behold but thee, Nature's desire?
In whose sight all things joy, with ravishment
Attracted by thy beauty still to gaze.'
I rose as at thy call, but found thee not;
To find thee I directed then my walk;
And on, methought, alone I passed through ways
That brought me on a sudden to the tree
Of interdicted knowledge: fair it seemed,
Much fairer to my fancy than by day:
And, as I wondering looked, beside it stood
One shaped and winged like one of those from Heaven
By us oft seen; his dewy locks distilled
Ambrosia; on that tree he also gazed;

And 'O fair plant,' said he, 'with fruit surcharged,
Deigns none to ease thy load, and taste thy sweet,
Nor God, nor Man? Is knowledge so despised?
Or envy, or what reserve forbids to taste?
Forbid who will, none shall from me withhold
Longer thy offered good; why else set here?'
This said, he paused not, but with venturous arm
He plucked, he tasted; me damp horror chilled
At such bold words vouched with a deed so bold:
But he thus, overjoyed; 'O fruit divine,
Sweet of thyself, but much more sweet thus cropt,
Forbidden here, it seems, as only fit
For Gods, yet able to make Gods of Men:
And why not Gods of Men; since good, the more
Communicated, more abundant grows,
The author not impaired, but honoured more?
Here, happy creature, fair angelic Eve!
Partake thou also; happy though thou art,
Happier thou mayest be, worthier canst not be:
Taste this, and be henceforth among the Gods
Thyself a Goddess, not to earth confined,
But sometimes in the air, as we, sometimes
Ascend to Heaven, by merit thine, and see
What life the Gods live there, and such live thou!'
So saying, he drew nigh, and to me held,
Even to my mouth of that same fruit held part
Which he had plucked; the pleasant savoury smell
So quickened appetite, that I, methought,
Could not but taste. Forthwith up to the clouds
With him I flew, and underneath beheld
The earth outstretched immense, a prospect wide
And various: Wondering at my flight and change
To this high exaltation; suddenly
My guide was gone, and I, methought, sunk down,
And fell asleep; but O, how glad I waked

To find this but a dream!" Thus Eve her night
Related, and thus Adam answered sad.
"Best image of myself, and dearer half,
The trouble of thy thoughts this night in sleep
Affects me equally; nor can I like
This uncouth dream, of evil sprung, I fear;
Yet evil whence? in thee can harbour none,
Created pure. But know that in the soul
Are many lesser faculties, that serve
Reason as chief; among these Fancy next
Her office holds; of all external things
Which the five watchful senses represent,
She forms imaginations, aery shapes,
Which Reason, joining or disjoining, frames
All what we affirm or what deny, and call
Our knowledge or opinion; then retires
Into her private cell, when nature rests.
Oft in her absence mimic Fancy wakes
To imitate her; but, misjoining shapes,
Wild work produces oft, and most in dreams;
Ill matching words and deeds long past or late.
Some such resemblances, methinks, I find
Of our last evening's talk, in this thy dream,
But with addition strange; yet be not sad.
Evil into the mind of God or Man
May come and go, so unreproved, and leave
No spot or blame behind: Which gives me hope
That what in sleep thou didst abhor to dream,
Waking thou never will consent to do.
Be not disheartened then, nor cloud those looks,
That wont to be more cheerful and serene,
Than when fair morning first smiles on the world;
And let us to our fresh employments rise
Among the groves, the fountains, and the flowers
That open now their choicest bosomed smells,

Reserved from night, and kept for thee in store."
So cheered he his fair spouse, and she was cheered;
But silently a gentle tear let fall
From either eye, and wiped them with her hair;
Two other precious drops that ready stood,
Each in their crystal sluice, he ere they fell
Kissed, as the gracious signs of sweet remorse
And pious awe, that feared to have offended.
So all was cleared, and to the field they haste.
But first, from under shady arborous roof
Soon as they forth were come to open sight
Of day-spring, and the sun, who, scarce up-risen,
With wheels yet hovering o'er the ocean-brim,
Shot parallel to the earth his dewy ray,
Discovering in wide landskip all the east
Of Paradise and Eden's happy plains,
Lowly they bowed adoring, and began
Their orisons, each morning duly paid
In various style; for neither various style
Nor holy rapture wanted they to praise
Their Maker, in fit strains pronounced, or sung
Unmeditated; such prompt eloquence
Flowed from their lips, in prose or numerous verse,
More tuneable than needed lute or harp
To add more sweetness; and they thus began.
"These are thy glorious works, Parent of good,
Almighty! Thine this universal frame,
Thus wonderous fair; Thyself how wonderous then!
Unspeakable, who sitst above these heavens
To us invisible, or dimly seen
In these thy lowest works; yet these declare
Thy goodness beyond thought, and power divine.
Speak, ye who best can tell, ye sons of light,
Angels; for ye behold him, and with songs
And choral symphonies, day without night,

Circle his throne rejoicing; ye in Heaven
On Earth join all ye Creatures to extol
Him first, him last, him midst, and without end.
Fairest of stars, last in the train of night,
If better thou belong not to the dawn,
Sure pledge of day, that crownest the smiling morn
With thy bright circlet, praise him in thy sphere,
While day arises, that sweet hour of prime.
Thou Sun, of this great world both eye and soul,
Acknowledge him thy greater; sound his praise
In thy eternal course, both when thou climbest,
And when high noon hast gained, and when thou fallest.
Moon, that now meetest the orient sun, now flyest,
With the fixed Stars, fixed in their orb that flies;
And ye five other wandering Fires, that move
In mystic dance not without song, resound
His praise, who out of darkness called up light.
Air, and ye Elements, the eldest birth
Of Nature's womb, that in quaternion run
Perpetual circle, multiform; and mix
And nourish all things; let your ceaseless change
Vary to our great Maker still new praise.
Ye Mists and Exhalations, that now rise
From hill or steaming lake, dusky or gray,
Till the sun paint your fleecy skirts with gold,
In honour to the world's great Author rise;
Whether to deck with clouds the uncoloured sky,
Or wet the thirsty earth with falling showers,
Rising or falling still advance his praise.
His praise, ye Winds, that from four quarters blow,
Breathe soft or loud; and, wave your tops, ye Pines,
With every plant, in sign of worship wave.
Fountains, and ye that warble, as ye flow,
Melodious murmurs, warbling tune his praise.
Join voices, all ye living Souls: Ye Birds,

That singing up to Heaven-gate ascend,
Bear on your wings and in your notes his praise.
Ye that in waters glide, and ye that walk
The earth, and stately tread, or lowly creep;
Witness if I be silent, morn or even,
To hill, or valley, fountain, or fresh shade,
Made vocal by my song, and taught his praise.
Hail, universal Lord, be bounteous still
To give us only good; and if the night
Have gathered aught of evil, or concealed,
Disperse it, as now light dispels the dark!"
So prayed they innocent, and to their thoughts
Firm peace recovered soon, and wonted calm.
On to their morning's rural work they haste,
Among sweet dews and flowers; where any row
Of fruit-trees over-woody reached too far
Their pampered boughs, and needed hands to check
Fruitless embraces: or they led the vine
To wed her elm; she, spoused, about him twines
Her marriageable arms, and with him brings
Her dower, the adopted clusters, to adorn
His barren leaves. Them thus employed beheld
With pity Heaven's high King, and to him called
Raphael, the sociable Spirit, that deigned
To travel with Tobias, and secured
His marriage with the seven-times-wedded maid.
"Raphael," said he, "thou hearest what stir on Earth
Satan, from Hell 'scaped through the darksome gulf,
Hath raised in Paradise; and how disturbed
This night the human pair; how he designs
In them at once to ruin all mankind.
Go therefore, half this day as friend with friend
Converse with Adam, in what bower or shade
Thou findest him from the heat of noon retired,
To respite his day-labour with repast,

Or with repose; and such discourse bring on,
As may advise him of his happy state,
Happiness in his power left free to will,
Left to his own free will, his will though free,
Yet mutable; whence warn him to beware
He swerve not, too secure: Tell him withal
His danger, and from whom; what enemy,
Late fallen himself from Heaven, is plotting now
The fall of others from like state of bliss;
By violence? no, for that shall be withstood;
But by deceit and lies: This let him know,
Lest, wilfully transgressing, he pretend
Surprisal, unadmonished, unforewarned."
So spake the Eternal Father, and fulfilled
All justice: Nor delayed the winged Saint
After his charge received; but from among
Thousand celestial Ardours, where he stood
Veiled with his gorgeous wings, up springing light,
Flew through the midst of Heaven; the angelic choirs,
On each hand parting, to his speed gave way
Through all the empyreal road; till, at the gate
Of Heaven arrived, the gate self-opened wide
On golden hinges turning, as by work
Divine the sovran Architect had framed.
From hence no cloud, or, to obstruct his sight,
Star interposed, however small he sees,
Not unconformed to other shining globes,
Earth, and the garden of God, with cedars crowned
Above all hills. As when by night the glass
Of Galileo, less assured, observes
Imagined lands and regions in the moon:
Or pilot, from amidst the Cyclades
Delos or Samos first appearing, kens
A cloudy spot. Down thither prone in flight
He speeds, and through the vast ethereal sky

Sails between worlds and worlds, with steady wing
Now on the polar winds, then with quick fan
Winnows the buxom air; till, within soar
Of towering eagles, to all the fowls he seems
A phoenix, gazed by all as that sole bird,
When, to enshrine his relics in the Sun's
Bright temple, to Egyptian Thebes he flies.
At once on the eastern cliff of Paradise
He lights, and to his proper shape returns
A Seraph winged: Six wings he wore, to shade
His lineaments divine; the pair that clad
Each shoulder broad, came mantling o'er his breast
With regal ornament; the middle pair
Girt like a starry zone his waist, and round
Skirted his loins and thighs with downy gold
And colours dipt in Heaven; the third his feet
Shadowed from either heel with feathered mail,
Sky-tinctured grain. Like Maia's son he stood,
And shook his plumes, that heavenly fragrance filled
The circuit wide. Straight knew him all the bands
Of Angels under watch; and to his state,
And to his message high, in honour rise;
For on some message high they guessed him bound.
Their glittering tents he passed, and now is come
Into the blissful field, through groves of myrrh,
And flowering odours, cassia, nard, and balm;
A wilderness of sweets; for Nature here
Wantoned as in her prime, and played at will
Her virgin fancies pouring forth more sweet,
Wild above rule or art, enormous bliss.
Him through the spicy forest onward come
Adam discerned, as in the door he sat
Of his cool bower, while now the mounted sun
Shot down direct his fervid rays to warm
Earth's inmost womb, more warmth than Adam needs:

And Eve within, due at her hour prepared
For dinner savoury fruits, of taste to please
True appetite, and not disrelish thirst
Of nectarous draughts between, from milky stream,
Berry or grape: To whom thus Adam called:
"Haste hither, Eve, and worth thy sight behold
Eastward among those trees, what glorious shape
Comes this way moving; seems another morn
Risen on mid-noon; some great behest from Heaven
To us perhaps he brings, and will vouchsafe
This day to be our guest. But go with speed,
And, what thy stores contain, bring forth, and pour
Abundance, fit to honour and receive
Our heavenly stranger: Well we may afford
Our givers their own gifts, and large bestow
From large bestowed, where Nature multiplies
Her fertile growth, and by disburthening grows
More fruitful, which instructs us not to spare.
To whom thus Eve. "Adam, earth's hallowed mould,
Of God inspired! small store will serve, where store,
All seasons, ripe for use hangs on the stalk;
Save what by frugal storing firmness gains
To nourish, and superfluous moist consumes:
But I will haste, and from each bough and brake,
Each plant and juciest gourd, will pluck such choice
To entertain our Angel-guest, as he
Beholding shall confess, that here on Earth
God hath dispensed his bounties as in Heaven."
So saying, with dispatchful looks in haste
She turns, on hospitable thoughts intent
What choice to choose for delicacy best,
What order, so contrived as not to mix
Tastes, not well joined, inelegant, but bring
Taste after taste upheld with kindliest change;
Bestirs her then, and from each tender stalk

Whatever Earth, all-bearing mother, yields
In India East or West, or middle shore
In Pontus or the Punick coast, or where
Alcinous reigned, fruit of all kinds, in coat
Rough, or smooth rind, or bearded husk, or shell,
She gathers, tribute large, and on the board
Heaps with unsparing hand; for drink the grape
She crushes, inoffensive must, and meaths
From many a berry, and from sweet kernels pressed
She tempers dulcet creams; nor these to hold
Wants her fit vessels pure; then strows the ground
With rose and odours from the shrub unfumed.
Meanwhile our primitive great sire, to meet
His God-like guest, walks forth, without more train
Accompanied than with his own complete
Perfections; in himself was all his state,
More solemn than the tedious pomp that waits
On princes, when their rich retinue long
Of horses led, and grooms besmeared with gold,
Dazzles the crowd, and sets them all agape.
Nearer his presence Adam, though not awed,
Yet with submiss approach and reverence meek,
As to a superior nature bowing low,
Thus said: "Native of Heaven, for other place
None can than Heaven such glorious shape contain;
Since, by descending from the thrones above,
Those happy places thou hast deigned a while
To want, and honour these, vouchsafe with us
Two only, who yet by sovran gift possess
This spacious ground, in yonder shady bower
To rest; and what the garden choicest bears
To sit and taste, till this meridian heat
Be over, and the sun more cool decline."
Whom thus the angelic Virtue answered mild:
"Adam, I therefore came; nor art thou such

Created, or such place hast here to dwell,
As may not oft invite, though Spirits of Heaven,
To visit thee; lead on then where thy bower
O'ershades; for these mid-hours, till evening rise,
I have at will." So to the sylvan lodge
They came, that like Pomona's arbour smiled,
With flowerets decked, and fragrant smells; but Eve,
Undecked save with herself, more lovely fair
Than Wood-Nymph, or the fairest Goddess feigned
Of three that in mount Ida naked strove,
Stood to entertain her guest from Heaven; no veil
She needed, virtue-proof; no thought infirm
Altered her cheek. On whom the Angel "Hail"
Bestowed, the holy salutation used
Long after to blest Mary, second Eve.
"Hail, Mother of Mankind, whose fruitful womb
Shall fill the world more numerous with thy sons,
Than with these various fruits the trees of God
Have heaped this table!" Raised of grassy turf
Their table was, and mossy seats had round,
And on her ample square from side to side
All autumn piled, though spring and autumn here
Danced hand in hand. A while discourse they hold;
No fear lest dinner cool; when thus began
Our author. "Heavenly stranger, please to taste
These bounties, which our Nourisher, from whom
All perfect good, unmeasured out, descends,
To us for food and for delight hath caused
The earth to yield; unsavoury food perhaps
To spiritual natures; only this I know,
That one celestial Father gives to all."
To whom the Angel. "Therefore what he gives
(Whose praise be ever sung) to Man in part
Spiritual, may of purest Spirits be found
No ingrateful food: And food alike those pure

Intelligential substances require,
As doth your rational; and both contain
Within them every lower faculty
Of sense, whereby they hear, see, smell, touch, taste,
Tasting concoct, digest, assimilate,
And corporeal to incorporeal turn.
For know, whatever was created, needs
To be sustained and fed: Of elements
The grosser feeds the purer, earth the sea,
Earth and the sea feed air, the air those fires
Ethereal, and as lowest first the moon;
Whence in her visage round those spots, unpurged
Vapours not yet into her substance turned.
Nor doth the moon no nourishment exhale
From her moist continent to higher orbs.
The sun that light imparts to all, receives
From all his alimental recompense
In humid exhalations, and at even
Sups with the ocean. Though in Heaven the trees
Of life ambrosial fruitage bear, and vines
Yield nectar; though from off the boughs each morn
We brush mellifluous dews, and find the ground
Covered with pearly grain: Yet God hath here
Varied his bounty so with new delights,
As may compare with Heaven; and to taste
Think not I shall be nice." So down they sat,
And to their viands fell; nor seemingly
The Angel, nor in mist, the common gloss
Of Theologians; but with keen dispatch
Of real hunger, and concoctive heat
To transubstantiate: What redounds, transpires
Through Spirits with ease; nor wonder; if by fire
Of sooty coal the empiric alchemist
Can turn, or holds it possible to turn,
Metals of drossiest ore to perfect gold,

As from the mine. Meanwhile at table Eve
Ministered naked, and their flowing cups
With pleasant liquours crowned: O innocence
Deserving Paradise! if ever, then,
Then had the sons of God excuse to have been
Enamoured at that sight; but in those hearts
Love unlibidinous reigned, nor jealousy
Was understood, the injured lover's hell.
Thus when with meats and drinks they had sufficed,
Not burdened nature, sudden mind arose
In Adam, not to let the occasion pass
Given him by this great conference to know
Of things above his world, and of their being
Who dwell in Heaven, whose excellence he saw
Transcend his own so far; whose radiant forms,
Divine effulgence, whose high power, so far
Exceeded human; and his wary speech
Thus to the empyreal minister he framed.
"Inhabitant with God, now know I well
Thy favour, in this honour done to Man;
Under whose lowly roof thou hast vouchsafed
To enter, and these earthly fruits to taste,
Food not of Angels, yet accepted so,
As that more willingly thou couldst not seem
At Heaven's high feasts to have fed: yet what compare?"
To whom the winged Hierarch replied.
"O Adam, One Almighty is, from whom
All things proceed, and up to him return,
If not depraved from good, created all
Such to perfection, one first matter all,
Endued with various forms, various degrees
Of substance, and, in things that live, of life;
But more refined, more spiritous, and pure,
As nearer to him placed, or nearer tending
Each in their several active spheres assigned,

Till body up to spirit work, in bounds
Proportioned to each kind. So from the root
Springs lighter the green stalk, from thence the leaves
More airy, last the bright consummate flower
Spirits odorous breathes: flowers and their fruit,
Man's nourishment, by gradual scale sublimed,
To vital spirits aspire, to animal,
To intellectual; give both life and sense,
Fancy and understanding; whence the soul
Reason receives, and reason is her being,
Discursive, or intuitive; discourse
Is oftest yours, the latter most is ours,
Differing but in degree, of kind the same.
Wonder not then, what God for you saw good
If I refuse not, but convert, as you
To proper substance. Time may come, when Men
With Angels may participate, and find
No inconvenient diet, nor too light fare;
And from these corporal nutriments perhaps
Your bodies may at last turn all to spirit,
Improved by tract of time, and, winged, ascend
Ethereal, as we; or may, at choice,
Here or in heavenly Paradises dwell;
If ye be found obedient, and retain
Unalterably firm his love entire,
Whose progeny you are. Meanwhile enjoy
Your fill what happiness this happy state
Can comprehend, incapable of more."
To whom the patriarch of mankind replied.
"O favourable Spirit, propitious guest,
Well hast thou taught the way that might direct
Our knowledge, and the scale of nature set
From center to circumference; whereon,
In contemplation of created things,
By steps we may ascend to God. But say,

What meant that caution joined, If ye be found
Obedient? Can we want obedience then
To him, or possibly his love desert,
Who formed us from the dust and placed us here
Full to the utmost measure of what bliss
Human desires can seek or apprehend?"
To whom the Angel: "Son of Heaven and Earth,
Attend! That thou art happy, owe to God;
That thou continuest such, owe to thyself,
That is, to thy obedience; therein stand.
This was that caution given thee; be advised.
God made thee perfect, not immutable;
And good he made thee, but to persevere
He left it in thy power; ordained thy will
By nature free, not over-ruled by fate
Inextricable, or strict necessity:
Our voluntary service he requires,
Not our necessitated; such with him
Finds no acceptance, nor can find; for how
Can hearts, not free, be tried whether they serve
Willing or no, who will but what they must
By destiny, and can no other choose?
Myself, and all the angelic host, that stand
In sight of God, enthroned, our happy state
Hold, as you yours, while our obedience holds;
On other surety none: Freely we serve,
Because we freely love, as in our will
To love or not; in this we stand or fall:
And some are fallen, to disobedience fallen,
And so from Heaven to deepest Hell; O fall
From what high state of bliss, into what woe!"
To whom our great progenitor: "Thy words
Attentive, and with more delighted ear,
Divine instructor, I have heard, than when
Cherubic songs by night from neighbouring hills

Aerial music send: Nor knew I not
To be both will and deed created free;
Yet that we never shall forget to love
Our Maker, and obey him whose command
Single is yet so just, my constant thoughts
Assured me, and still assure: Though what thou tellest
Hath passed in Heaven, some doubt within me move,
But more desire to hear, if thou consent,
The full relation, which must needs be strange,
Worthy of sacred silence to be heard;
And we have yet large day, for scarce the sun
Hath finished half his journey, and scarce begins
His other half in the great zone of Heaven."
Thus Adam made request; and Raphael,
After short pause assenting, thus began:
"High matter thou enjoinest me, O prime of men,
Sad task and hard: For how shall I relate
To human sense the invisible exploits
Of warring Spirits? how, without remorse,
The ruin of so many glorious once
And perfect while they stood? how last unfold
The secrets of another world, perhaps
Not lawful to reveal? yet for thy good
This is dispensed; and what surmounts the reach
Of human sense, I shall delineate so,
By likening spiritual to corporal forms,
As may express them best; though what if Earth
Be but a shadow of Heaven, and things therein
Each to other like, more than on earth is thought?
As yet this world was not, and Chaos wild
Reigned where these Heavens now roll, where Earth now
    rests
Upon her center poised; when on a day
(For time, though in eternity, applied
To motion, measures all things durable

By present, past, and future,) on such day
As Heaven's great year brings forth, the empyreal host
Of Angels by imperial summons called,
Innumerable before the Almighty's throne
Forthwith, from all the ends of Heaven, appeared
Under their Hierarchs in orders bright:
Ten thousand thousand ensigns high advanced,
Standards and gonfalons 'twixt van and rear
Stream in the air, and for distinction serve
Of hierarchies, of orders, and degrees;
Or in their glittering tissues bear imblazed
Holy memorials, acts of zeal and love
Recorded eminent. Thus when in orbs
Of circuit inexpressible they stood,
Orb within orb, the Father Infinite,
By whom in bliss imbosomed sat the Son,
Amidst as from a flaming mount, whose top
Brightness had made invisible, thus spake.
'Hear, all ye Angels, progeny of light,
Thrones, Dominations, Princedoms, Virtues, Powers;
Hear my decree, which unrevoked shall stand.
This day I have begot whom I declare
My only Son, and on this holy hill
Him have anointed, whom ye now behold
At my right hand; your head I him appoint;
And by myself have sworn, to him shall bow
All knees in Heaven, and shall confess him Lord:
Under his great vice-gerent reign abide
United, as one individual soul,
For ever happy: Him who disobeys,
Me disobeys, breaks union, and that day,
Cast out from God and blessed vision, falls
Into utter darkness, deep ingulfed, his place
Ordained without redemption, without end.'
So spake the Omnipotent, and with his words

All seemed well pleased; all seemed, but were not all.
That day, as other solemn days, they spent
In song and dance about the sacred hill;
Mystical dance, which yonder starry sphere
Of planets, and of fixed, in all her wheels
Resembles nearest, mazes intricate,
Eccentric, intervolved, yet regular
Then most, when most irregular they seem;
And in their motions harmony divine
So smooths her charming tones, that God's own ear
Listens delighted. Evening now approached,
(For we have also our evening and our morn,
We ours for change delectable, not need;)
Forthwith from dance to sweet repast they turn
Desirous; all in circles as they stood,
Tables are set, and on a sudden piled
With Angels food, and rubied nectar flows
In pearl, in diamond, and massy gold,
Fruit of delicious vines, the growth of Heaven.
On flowers reposed, and with fresh flowerets crowned,
They eat, they drink, and in communion sweet
Quaff immortality and joy, secure
Of surfeit, where full measure only bounds
Excess, before the all-bounteous King, who showered
With copious hand, rejoicing in their joy.
Now when ambrosial night with clouds exhaled
From that high mount of God, whence light and shade
Spring both, the face of brightest Heaven had changed
To grateful twilight, (for night comes not there
In darker veil) and roseate dews disposed
All but the unsleeping eyes of God to rest;
Wide over all the plain, and wider far
Than all this globous earth in plain outspread,
(Such are the courts of God) the angelic throng,
Dispersed in bands and files, their camp extend

By living streams among the trees of life,
Pavilions numberless, and sudden reared,
Celestial tabernacles, where they slept
Fanned with cool winds; save those, who, in their course,
Melodious hymns about the sovran throne
Alternate all night long: but not so waked
Satan; so call him now, his former name
Is heard no more in Heaven; he of the first,
If not the first Arch-Angel, great in power,
In favour and pre-eminence, yet fraught
With envy against the Son of God, that day
Honoured by his great Father, and proclaimed
Messiah King anointed, could not bear
Through pride that sight, and thought himself impaired.
Deep malice thence conceiving and disdain,
Soon as midnight brought on the dusky hour
Friendliest to sleep and silence, he resolved
With all his legions to dislodge, and leave
Unworshipt, unobeyed, the throne supreme,
Contemptuous; and his next subordinate
Awakening, thus to him in secret spake.
"'Sleepest thou, Companion dear? What sleep can close
Thy eye-lids? and rememberest what decree
Of yesterday, so late hath passed the lips
Of Heaven's Almighty. Thou to me thy thoughts
Wast wont, I mine to thee was wont to impart;
Both waking we were one; how then can now
Thy sleep dissent? New laws thou seest imposed;
New laws from him who reigns, new minds may raise
In us who serve, new counsels to debate
What doubtful may ensue: More in this place
To utter is not safe. Assemble thou
Of all those myriads which we lead the chief;
Tell them, that by command, ere yet dim night
Her shadowy cloud withdraws, I am to haste,

And all who under me their banners wave,
Homeward, with flying march, where we possess
The quarters of the north; there to prepare
Fit entertainment to receive our King,
The great Messiah, and his new commands,
Who speedily through all the hierarchies
Intends to pass triumphant, and give laws.'
So spake the false Arch-Angel, and infused
Bad influence into the unwary breast
Of his associate: He together calls,
Or several one by one, the regent Powers,
Under him Regent; tells, as he was taught,
That the Most High commanding, now ere night,
Now ere dim night had disincumbered Heaven,
The great hierarchal standard was to move;
Tells the suggested cause, and casts between
Ambiguous words and jealousies, to sound
Or taint integrity: But all obeyed
The wonted signal, and superior voice
Of their great Potentate; for great indeed
His name, and high was his degree in Heaven;
His countenance, as the morning-star that guides
The starry flock, allured them, and with lies
Drew after him the third part of Heaven's host.
Meanwhile the Eternal eye, whose sight discerns
Abstrusest thoughts, from forth his holy mount,
And from within the golden lamps that burn
Nightly before him, saw without their light
Rebellion rising; saw in whom, how spread
Among the sons of morn, what multitudes
Were banded to oppose his high decree;
And, smiling, to his only Son thus said.
'Son, thou in whom my glory I behold
In full resplendence, Heir of all my might,
Nearly it now concerns us to be sure

Of our Omnipotence, and with what arms
We mean to hold what anciently we claim
Of deity or empire: Such a foe
Is rising, who intends to erect his throne
Equal to ours, throughout the spacious north;
Nor so content, hath in his thought to try
In battle, what our power is, or our right.
Let us advise, and to this hazard draw
With speed what force is left, and all employ
In our defence; lest unawares we lose
This our high place, our sanctuary, our hill.'
To whom the Son with calm aspect and clear,
Lightning divine, ineffable, serene,
Made answer. 'Mighty Father, thou thy foes
Justly hast in derision, and, secure,
Laughest at their vain designs and tumults vain,
Matter to me of glory, whom their hate
Illustrates, when they see all regal power
Given me to quell their pride, and in event
Know whether I be dextrous to subdue
Thy rebels, or be found the worst in Heaven.'
So spake the Son; but Satan, with his Powers,
Far was advanced on winged speed; an host
Innumerable as the stars of night,
Or stars of morning, dew-drops, which the sun
Impearls on every leaf and every flower.
Regions they passed, the mighty regencies
Of Seraphim, and Potentates, and Thrones,
In their triple degrees; regions to which
All thy dominion, Adam, is no more
Than what this garden is to all the earth,
And all the sea, from one entire globose
Stretched into longitude; which having passed,
At length into the limits of the north
They came; and Satan to his royal seat

High on a hill, far blazing, as a mount
Raised on a mount, with pyramids and towers
From diamond quarries hewn, and rocks of gold;
The palace of great Lucifer, (so call
That structure in the dialect of men
Interpreted,) which not long after, he
Affecting all equality with God,
In imitation of that mount whereon
Messiah was declared in sight of Heaven,
The Mountain of the Congregation called;
For thither he assembled all his train,
Pretending so commanded to consult
About the great reception of their King,
Thither to come, and with calumnious art
Of counterfeited truth thus held their ears.
'Thrones, Dominations, Princedoms, Virtues, Powers;
If these magnifick titles yet remain
Not merely titular, since by decree
Another now hath to himself engrossed
All power, and us eclipsed under the name
Of King anointed, for whom all this haste
Of midnight-march, and hurried meeting here,
This only to consult how we may best,
With what may be devised of honours new,
Receive him coming to receive from us
Knee-tribute yet unpaid, prostration vile!
Too much to one! but double how endured,
To one, and to his image now proclaimed?
But what if better counsels might erect
Our minds, and teach us to cast off this yoke?
Will ye submit your necks, and choose to bend
The supple knee? Ye will not, if I trust
To know ye right, or if ye know yourselves
Natives and sons of Heaven possessed before
By none; and if not equal all, yet free,

Equally free; for orders and degrees
Jar not with liberty, but well consist.
Who can in reason then, or right, assume
Monarchy over such as live by right
His equals, if in power and splendour less,
In freedom equal? or can introduce
Law and edict on us, who without law
Err not? much less for this to be our Lord,
And look for adoration, to the abuse
Of those imperial titles, which assert
Our being ordained to govern, not to serve.'
Thus far his bold discourse without controul
Had audience; when among the Seraphim
Abdiel, than whom none with more zeal adored
The Deity, and divine commands obeyed,
Stood up, and in a flame of zeal severe
The current of his fury thus opposed.
'O argument blasphemous, false, and proud!
Words which no ear ever to hear in Heaven
Expected, least of all from thee, Ingrate,
In place thyself so high above thy peers.
Canst thou with impious obloquy condemn
The just decree of God, pronounced and sworn,
That to his only Son, by right endued
With regal scepter, every soul in Heaven
Shall bend the knee, and in that honour due
Confess him rightful King? unjust, thou sayest,
Flatly unjust, to bind with laws the free,
And equal over equals to let reign,
One over all with unsucceeded power.
Shalt thou give law to God? shalt thou dispute
With him the points of liberty, who made
Thee what thou art, and formed the Powers of Heaven
Such as he pleased, and circumscribed their being?
Yet, by experience taught, we know how good,

And of our good and of our dignity
How provident he is; how far from thought
To make us less, bent rather to exalt
Our happy state, under one head more near
United. But to grant it thee unjust,
That equal over equals monarch reign:
Thyself, though great and glorious, dost thou count,
Or all angelic nature joined in one,
Equal to him begotten Son? by whom,
As by his Word, the Mighty Father made
All things, even thee; and all the Spirits of Heaven
By him created in their bright degrees,
Crowned them with glory, and to their glory named
Thrones, Dominations, Princedoms, Virtues, Powers,
Essential Powers; nor by his reign obscured,
But more illustrious made; since he the head
One of our number thus reduced becomes;
His laws our laws; all honour to him done
Returns our own. Cease then this impious rage,
And tempt not these; but hasten to appease
The incensed Father, and the incensed Son,
While pardon may be found in time besought.'
So spake the fervent Angel; but his zeal
None seconded, as out of season judged,
Or singular and rash: Whereat rejoiced
The Apostate, and, more haughty, thus replied.
'That we were formed then sayest thou? and the work
Of secondary hands, by task transferred
From Father to his Son? strange point and new!
Doctrine which we would know whence learned: who saw
When this creation was? rememberest thou
Thy making, while the Maker gave thee being?
We know no time when we were not as now;
Know none before us, self-begot, self-raised
By our own quickening power, when fatal course

Had circled his full orb, the birth mature
Of this our native Heaven, ethereal sons.
Our puissance is our own; our own right hand
Shall teach us highest deeds, by proof to try
Who is our equal: Then thou shalt behold
Whether by supplication we intend
Address, and to begirt the almighty throne
Beseeching or besieging. This report,
These tidings carry to the anointed King;
And fly, ere evil intercept thy flight.'
He said; and, as the sound of waters deep,
Hoarse murmur echoed to his words applause
Through the infinite host; nor less for that
The flaming Seraph fearless, though alone
Encompassed round with foes, thus answered bold.
'O alienate from God, O Spirit accursed,
Forsaken of all good! I see thy fall
Determined, and thy hapless crew involved
In this perfidious fraud, contagion spread
Both of thy crime and punishment: Henceforth
No more be troubled how to quit the yoke
Of God's Messiah; those indulgent laws
Will not be now vouchsafed; other decrees
Against thee are gone forth without recall;
That golden scepter, which thou didst reject,
Is now an iron rod to bruise and break
Thy disobedience. Well thou didst advise;
Yet not for thy advice or threats I fly
These wicked tents devoted, lest the wrath
Impendent, raging into sudden flame,
Distinguish not: For soon expect to feel
His thunder on thy head, devouring fire.
Then who created thee lamenting learn,
When who can uncreate thee thou shalt know.'
So spake the Seraph Abdiel, faithful found

Among the faithless, faithful only he;
Among innumerable false, unmoved,
Unshaken, unseduced, unterrified,
His loyalty he kept, his love, his zeal;
Nor number, nor example, with him wrought
To swerve from truth, or change his constant mind,
Though single. From amidst them forth he passed,
Long way through hostile scorn, which he sustained
Superior, nor of violence feared aught;
And, with retorted scorn, his back he turned
On those proud towers to swift destruction doomed."

BOOK VI

All night the dreadless Angel, unpursued,
Through Heaven's wide champaign held his way; till Morn,
Waked by the circling Hours, with rosy hand
Unbarred the gates of light. There is a cave
Within the mount of God, fast by his throne,
Where light and darkness in perpetual round
Lodge and dislodge by turns, which makes through Heaven
Grateful vicissitude, like day and night;
Light issues forth, and at the other door
Obsequious darkness enters, till her hour
To veil the Heaven, though darkness there might well
Seem twilight here: And now went forth the Morn
Such as in highest Heaven arrayed in gold
Empyreal; from before her vanished Night,
Shot through with orient beams; when all the plain
Covered with thick embattled squadrons bright,
Chariots, and flaming arms, and fiery steeds,
Reflecting blaze on blaze, first met his view:
War he perceived, war in procinct; and found
Already known what he for news had thought
To have reported: Gladly then he mixed
Among those friendly Powers, who him received

With joy and acclamations loud, that one,
That of so many myriads fallen, yet one
Returned not lost. On to the sacred hill
They led him high applauded, and present
Before the seat supreme; from whence a voice,
From midst a golden cloud, thus mild was heard.
"'Servant of God. Well done; well hast thou fought
The better fight, who single hast maintained
Against revolted multitudes the cause
Of truth, in word mightier than they in arms;
And for the testimony of truth hast borne
Universal reproach, far worse to bear
Than violence; for this was all thy care
To stand approved in sight of God, though worlds
Judged thee perverse: The easier conquest now
Remains thee, aided by this host of friends,
Back on thy foes more glorious to return,
Than scorned thou didst depart; and to subdue
By force, who reason for their law refuse,
Right reason for their law, and for their King
Messiah, who by right of merit reigns.
Go, Michael, of celestial armies prince,
And thou, in military prowess next,
Gabriel, lead forth to battle these my sons
Invincible; lead forth my armed Saints,
By thousands and by millions, ranged for fight,
Equal in number to that Godless crew
Rebellious: Them with fire and hostile arms
Fearless assault; and, to the brow of Heaven
Pursuing, drive them out from God and bliss,
Into their place of punishment, the gulf
Of Tartarus, which ready opens wide
His fiery Chaos to receive their fall.'
So spake the Sovran Voice, and clouds began
To darken all the hill, and smoke to roll

In dusky wreaths, reluctant flames, the sign
Of wrath awaked; nor with less dread the loud
Ethereal trumpet from on high gan blow:
At which command the Powers militant,
That stood for Heaven, in mighty quadrate joined
Of union irresistible, moved on
In silence their bright legions, to the sound
Of instrumental harmony, that breathed
Heroic ardour to adventurous deeds
Under their God-like leaders, in the cause
Of God and his Messiah. On they move
Indissolubly firm; nor obvious hill,
Nor straitening vale, nor wood, nor stream, divides
Their perfect ranks; for high above the ground
Their march was, and the passive air upbore
Their nimble tread; as when the total kind
Of birds, in orderly array on wing,
Came summoned over Eden to receive
Their names of thee; so over many a tract
Of Heaven they marched, and many a province wide,
Tenfold the length of this terrene: At last,
Far in the horizon to the north appeared
From skirt to skirt a fiery region, stretched
In battailous aspect, and nearer view
Bristled with upright beams innumerable
Of rigid spears, and helmets thronged, and shields
Various, with boastful argument portrayed,
The banded Powers of Satan hasting on
With furious expedition; for they weened
That self-same day, by fight or by surprise,
To win the mount of God, and on his throne
To set the Envier of his state, the proud
Aspirer; but their thoughts proved fond and vain
In the mid way: Though strange to us it seemed
At first, that Angel should with Angel war,

And in fierce hosting meet, who wont to meet
So oft in festivals of joy and love
Unanimous, as sons of one great Sire,
Hymning the Eternal Father: But the shout
Of battle now began, and rushing sound
Of onset ended soon each milder thought.
High in the midst, exalted as a God,
The Apostate in his sun-bright chariot sat,
Idol of majesty divine, enclosed
With flaming Cherubim, and golden shields;
Then lighted from his gorgeous throne, for now
'Twixt host and host but narrow space was left,
A dreadful interval, and front to front
Presented stood in terrible array
Of hideous length: Before the cloudy van,
On the rough edge of battle ere it joined,
Satan, with vast and haughty strides advanced,
Came towering, armed in adamant and gold;
Abdiel that sight endured not, where he stood
Among the mightiest, bent on highest deeds,
And thus his own undaunted heart explores.
'O Heaven! that such resemblance of the Highest
Should yet remain, where faith and realty
Remain not: Wherefore should not strength and might
There fail where virtue fails, or weakest prove
Where boldest, though to fight unconquerable?
His puissance, trusting in the Almighty's aid,
I mean to try, whose reason I have tried
Unsound and false; nor is it aught but just,
That he, who in debate of truth hath won,
Should win in arms, in both disputes alike
Victor; though brutish that contest and foul,
When reason hath to deal with force, yet so
Most reason is that reason overcome.'
So pondering, and from his armed peers

Forth stepping opposite, half-way he met
His daring foe, at this prevention more
Incensed, and thus securely him defied.
'Proud, art thou met? thy hope was to have reached
The hight of thy aspiring unopposed,
The throne of God unguarded, and his side
Abandoned, at the terror of thy power
Or potent tongue: Fool! not to think how vain
Against the Omnipotent to rise in arms;
Who out of smallest things could, without end,
Have raised incessant armies to defeat
Thy folly; or with solitary hand
Reaching beyond all limit, at one blow,
Unaided, could have finished thee, and whelmed
Thy legions under darkness: But thou seest
All are not of thy train; there be, who faith
Prefer, and piety to God, though then
To thee not visible, when I alone
Seemed in thy world erroneous to dissent
From all: My sect thou seest; now learn too late
How few sometimes may know, when thousands err.'
Whom the grand foe, with scornful eye askance,
Thus answered. 'Ill for thee, but in wished hour
Of my revenge, first sought for, thou returnest
From flight, seditious Angel! to receive
Thy merited reward, the first assay
Of this right hand provoked, since first that tongue,
Inspired with contradiction, durst oppose
A third part of the Gods, in synod met
Their deities to assert; who, while they feel
Vigour divine within them, can allow
Omnipotence to none. But well thou comest
Before thy fellows, ambitious to win
From me some plume, that thy success may show
Destruction to the rest: This pause between,

(Unanswered lest thou boast) to let thee know,
At first I thought that Liberty and Heaven
To heavenly souls had been all one; but now
I see that most through sloth had rather serve,
Ministring Spirits, trained up in feast and song!
Such hast thou armed, the minstrelsy of Heaven,
Servility with freedom to contend,
As both their deeds compared this day shall prove.'
To whom in brief thus Abdiel stern replied.
'Apostate! still thou err'st, nor end wilt find
Of erring, from the path of truth remote:
Unjustly thou depravest it with the name
Of servitude, to serve whom God ordains,
Or Nature: God and Nature bid the same,
When he who rules is worthiest, and excels
Them whom he governs. This is servitude,
To serve the unwise, or him who hath rebelled
Against his worthier, as thine now serve thee,
Thyself not free, but to thyself enthralled;
Yet lewdly darest our ministring upbraid.
Reign thou in Hell, thy kingdom; let me serve
In Heaven God ever blest, and his divine
Behests obey, worthiest to be obeyed;
Yet chains in Hell, not realms, expect: Meanwhile
From me returned, as erst thou saidst, from flight,
This greeting on thy impious crest receive.'
So saying, a noble stroke he lifted high,
Which hung not, but so swift with tempest fell
On the proud crest of Satan, that no sight,
Nor motion of swift thought, less could his shield,
Such ruin intercept: Ten paces huge
He back recoiled; the tenth on bended knee
His massy spear upstaid; as if on earth
Winds under ground, or waters forcing way,
Sidelong had pushed a mountain from his seat,

Half sunk with all his pines. Amazement seized
The rebel Thrones, but greater rage, to see
Thus foiled their mightiest; ours joy filled, and shout,
Presage of victory, and fierce desire
Of battle: Whereat Michael bid sound
The Arch-Angel trumpet; through the vast of Heaven
It sounded, and the faithful armies rung
Hosanna to the Highest: Nor stood at gaze
The adverse legions, nor less hideous joined
The horrid shock. Now storming fury rose,
And clamour such as heard in Heaven till now
Was never; arms on armour clashing brayed
Horrible discord, and the madding wheels
Of brazen chariots raged; dire was the noise
Of conflict; over head the dismal hiss
Of fiery darts in flaming vollies flew,
And flying vaulted either host with fire.
So under fiery cope together rushed
Both battles main, with ruinous assault
And inextinguishable rage. All Heaven
Resounded; and had Earth been then, all Earth
Had to her center shook. What wonder? when
Millions of fierce encountering Angels fought
On either side, the least of whom could wield
These elements, and arm him with the force
Of all their regions: How much more of power
Army against army numberless to raise
Dreadful combustion warring, and disturb,
Though not destroy, their happy native seat;
Had not the Eternal King Omnipotent,
From his strong hold of Heaven, high over-ruled
And limited their might; though numbered such
As each divided legion might have seemed
A numerous host; in strength each armed hand
A legion; led in fight, yet leader seemed

Each warrior single as in chief, expert
When to advance, or stand, or turn the sway
Of battle, open when, and when to close
The ridges of grim war: No thought of flight,
None of retreat, no unbecoming deed
That argued fear; each on himself relied,
As only in his arm the moment lay
Of victory: Deeds of eternal fame
Were done, but infinite; for wide was spread
That war and various; sometimes on firm ground
A standing fight, then, soaring on main wing,
Tormented all the air; all air seemed then
Conflicting fire. Long time in even scale
The battle hung; till Satan, who that day
Prodigious power had shown, and met in arms
No equal, ranging through the dire attack
Of fighting Seraphim confused, at length
Saw where the sword of Michael smote, and felled
Squadrons at once; with huge two-handed sway
Brandished aloft, the horrid edge came down
Wide-wasting; such destruction to withstand
He hasted, and opposed the rocky orb
Of tenfold adamant, his ample shield,
A vast circumference. At his approach
The great Arch-Angel from his warlike toil
Surceased, and glad, as hoping here to end
Intestine war in Heaven, the arch-foe subdued
Or captive dragged in chains, with hostile frown
And visage all inflamed first thus began.
'Author of evil, unknown till thy revolt,
Unnamed in Heaven, now plenteous as thou seest
These acts of hateful strife, hateful to all,
Though heaviest by just measure on thyself,
And thy adherents: How hast thou disturbed
Heaven's blessed peace, and into nature brought

Misery, uncreated till the crime
Of thy rebellion! how hast thou instilled
Thy malice into thousands, once upright
And faithful, now proved false! But think not here
To trouble holy rest; Heaven casts thee out
From all her confines. Heaven, the seat of bliss,
Brooks not the works of violence and war.
Hence then, and evil go with thee along,
Thy offspring, to the place of evil, Hell;
Thou and thy wicked crew! there mingle broils,
Ere this avenging sword begin thy doom,
Or some more sudden vengeance, winged from God,
Precipitate thee with augmented pain.'
So spake the Prince of Angels; to whom thus
The Adversary. 'Nor think thou with wind
Of aery threats to awe whom yet with deeds
Thou canst not. Hast thou turned the least of these
To flight, or if to fall, but that they rise
Unvanquished, easier to transact with me
That thou shouldst hope, imperious, and with threats
To chase me hence? err not, that so shall end
The strife which thou callest evil, but we style
The strife of glory; which we mean to win,
Or turn this Heaven itself into the Hell
Thou fablest; here however to dwell free,
If not to reign: Meanwhile thy utmost force,
And join him named Almighty to thy aid,
I fly not, but have sought thee far and nigh.'
They ended parle, and both addressed for fight
Unspeakable; for who, though with the tongue
Of Angels, can relate, or to what things
Liken on earth conspicuous, that may lift
Human imagination to such hight
Of Godlike power? for likest Gods they seemed,
Stood they or moved, in stature, motion, arms,

Fit to decide the empire of great Heaven.
Now waved their fiery swords, and in the air
Made horrid circles; two broad suns their shields
Blazed opposite, while Expectation stood
In horror: From each hand with speed retired,
Where erst was thickest fight, the angelic throng,
And left large field, unsafe within the wind
Of such commotion; such as, to set forth
Great things by small, if, nature's concord broke,
Among the constellations war were sprung,
Two planets, rushing from aspect malign
Of fiercest opposition, in mid sky
Should combat, and their jarring spheres confound.
Together both with next to almighty arm
Up-lifted imminent, one stroke they aimed
That might determine, and not need repeat,
As not of power at once; nor odds appeared
In might or swift prevention: But the sword
Of Michael from the armoury of God
Was given him tempered so, that neither keen
Nor solid might resist that edge: it met
The sword of Satan, with steep force to smite
Descending, and in half cut sheer; nor staid,
But with swift wheel reverse, deep entering, shared
All his right side: Then Satan first knew pain,
And writhed him to and fro convolved; so sore
The griding sword with discontinuous wound
Passed through him: But the ethereal substance closed,
Not long divisible; and from the gash
A stream of necturous humour issuing flowed
Sanguine, such as celestial Spirits may bleed,
And all his armour stained, ere while so bright.
Forthwith on all sides to his aid was run
By Angels many and strong, who interposed
Defence, while others bore him on their shields

Back to his chariot, where it stood retired
From off the files of war: There they him laid
Gnashing for anguish, and despite, and shame,
To find himself not matchless, and his pride
Humbled by such rebuke, so far beneath
His confidence to equal God in power.
Yet soon he healed; for Spirits that live throughout
Vital in every part, not as frail man
In entrails, heart of head, liver or reins,
Cannot but by annihilating die;
Nor in their liquid texture mortal wound
Receive, no more than can the fluid air:
All heart they live, all head, all eye, all ear,
All intellect, all sense; and, as they please,
They limb themselves, and colour, shape, or size
Assume, as likes them best, condense or rare.
Meanwhile in other parts like deeds deserved
Memorial, where the might of Gabriel fought,
And with fierce ensigns pierced the deep array
Of Moloch, furious king; who him defied,
And at his chariot-wheels to drag him bound
Threatened, nor from the Holy One of Heaven
Refrained his tongue blasphemous; but anon
Down cloven to the waist, with shattered arms
And uncouth pain fled bellowing. On each wing
Uriel, and Raphael, his vaunting foe,
Though huge, and in a rock of diamond armed,
Vanquished Adramelech, and Asmadai,
Two potent Thrones, that to be less than Gods
Disdained, but meaner thoughts learned in their flight,
Mangled with ghastly wounds through plate and mail.
Nor stood unmindful Abdiel to annoy
The atheist crew, but with redoubled blow
Ariel, and Arioch, and the violence
Of Ramiel scorched and blasted, overthrew.

I might relate of thousands, and their names
Eternize here on earth; but those elect
Angels, contented with their fame in Heaven,
Seek not the praise of men: The other sort,
In might though wonderous and in acts of war,
Nor of renown less eager, yet by doom
Cancelled from Heaven and sacred memory,
Nameless in dark oblivion let them dwell.
For strength from truth divided, and from just,
Illaudable, nought merits but dispraise
And ignominy; yet to glory aspires
Vain-glorious, and through infamy seeks fame:
Therefore eternal silence be their doom.
And now, their mightiest quelled, the battle swerved,
With many an inroad gored; deformed rout
Entered, and foul disorder; all the ground
With shivered armour strown, and on a heap
Chariot and charioteer lay overturned,
And fiery-foaming steeds; what stood, recoiled
O'er-wearied, through the faint Satanic host
Defensive scarce, or with pale fear surprised,
Then first with fear surprised, and sense of pain,
Fled ignominious, to such evil brought
By sin of disobedience; till that hour
Not liable to fear, or flight, or pain.
Far otherwise the inviolable Saints,
In cubic phalanx firm, advanced entire,
Invulnerable, impenetrably armed;
Such high advantages their innocence
Gave them above their foes; not to have sinned,
Not to have disobeyed; in fight they stood
Unwearied, unobnoxious to be pained
By wound, though from their place by violence moved,
Now Night her course began, and, over Heaven
Inducing darkness, grateful truce imposed,

And silence on the odious din of war:
Under her cloudy covert both retired,
Victor and vanquished: On the foughten field
Michael and his Angels prevalent
Encamping, placed in guard their watches round,
Cherubic waving fires: On the other part,
Satan with his rebellious disappeared,
Far in the dark dislodged; and, void of rest,
His potentates to council called by night;
And in the midst thus undismayed began.
'O now in danger tried, now known in arms
Not to be overpowered, Companions dear,
Found worthy not of liberty alone,
Too mean pretence! but what we more affect,
Honour, dominion, glory, and renown;
Who have sustained one day in doubtful fight,
(And if one day, why not eternal days?)
What Heaven's Lord had powerfullest to send
Against us from about his throne, and judged
Sufficient to subdue us to his will,
But proves not so: Then fallible, it seems,
Of future we may deem him, though till now
Omniscient thought. True is, less firmly armed,
Some disadvantage we endured and pain,
Till now not known, but, known, as soon contemned;
Since now we find this our empyreal form
Incapable of mortal injury,
Imperishable, and, though pierced with wound,
Soon closing, and by native vigour healed.
Of evil then so small as easy think
The remedy; perhaps more valid arms,
Weapons more violent, when next we meet,
May serve to better us, and worse our foes,
Or equal what between us made the odds,
In nature none: If other hidden cause

Left them superior, while we can preserve
Unhurt our minds, and understanding sound,
Due search and consultation will disclose.'
He sat; and in the assembly next upstood
Nisroch, of Principalities the prime;
As one he stood escaped from cruel fight,
Sore toiled, his riven arms to havock hewn,
And cloudy in aspect thus answering spake.
'Deliverer from new Lords, leader to free
Enjoyment of our right as Gods; yet hard
For Gods, and too unequal work we find,
Against unequal arms to fight in pain,
Against unpained, impassive; from which evil
Ruin must needs ensue; for what avails
Valour or strength, though matchless, quelled with pain
Which all subdues, and makes remiss the hands
Of mightiest? Sense of pleasure we may well
Spare out of life perhaps, and not repine,
But live content, which is the calmest life:
But pain is perfect misery, the worst
Of evils, and, excessive, overturns
All patience. He, who therefore can invent
With what more forcible we may offend
Our yet unwounded enemies, or arm
Ourselves with like defence, to me deserves
No less than for deliverance what we owe.'
Whereto with look composed Satan replied.
'Not uninvented that, which thou aright
Believest so main to our success, I bring.
Which of us who beholds the bright surface
Of this ethereous mould whereon we stand,
This continent of spacious Heaven, adorned
With plant, fruit, flower ambrosial, gems, and gold;
Whose eye so superficially surveys
These things, as not to mind from whence they grow

Deep under ground, materials dark and crude,
Of spiritous and fiery spume, till touched
With Heaven's ray, and tempered, they shoot forth
So beauteous, opening to the ambient light?
These in their dark nativity the deep
Shall yield us, pregnant with infernal flame;
Which, into hollow engines, long and round,
Thick rammed, at the other bore with touch of fire
Dilated and infuriate, shall send forth
From far, with thundering noise, among our foes
Such implements of mischief, as shall dash
To pieces, and o'erwhelm whatever stands
Adverse, that they shall fear we have disarmed
The Thunderer of his only dreaded bolt.
Nor long shall be our labour; yet ere dawn,
Effect shall end our wish. Meanwhile revive;
Abandon fear; to strength and counsel joined
Think nothing hard, much less to be despaired.'
He ended, and his words their drooping cheer
Enlightened, and their languished hope revived.
The invention all admired, and each, how he
To be the inventor missed; so easy it seemed
Once found, which yet unfound most would have thought
Impossible: Yet, haply, of thy race
In future days, if malice should abound,
Some one intent on mischief, or inspired
With devilish machination, might devise
Like instrument to plague the sons of men
For sin, on war and mutual slaughter bent.
Forthwith from council to the work they flew;
None arguing stood; innumerable hands
Were ready; in a moment up they turned
Wide the celestial soil, and saw beneath
The originals of nature in their crude
Conception; sulphurous and nitrous foam

They found, they mingled, and, with subtle art,
Concocted and adusted they reduced
To blackest grain, and into store conveyed:
Part hidden veins digged up (nor hath this earth
Entrails unlike) of mineral and stone,
Whereof to found their engines and their balls
Of missive ruin; part incentive reed
Provide, pernicious with one touch to fire.
So all ere day-spring, under conscious night,
Secret they finished, and in order set,
With silent circumspection, unespied.
Now when fair morn orient in Heaven appeared,
Up rose the victor-Angels, and to arms
The matin trumpet sung: In arms they stood
Of golden panoply, refulgent host,
Soon banded; others from the dawning hills
Look round, and scouts each coast light-armed scour,
Each quarter to descry the distant foe,
Where lodged, or whither fled, or if for fight,
In motion or in halt: Him soon they met
Under spread ensigns moving nigh, in slow
But firm battalion; back with speediest sail
Zophiel, of Cherubim the swiftest wing,
Came flying, and in mid air aloud thus cried.
'Arm, Warriors, arm for fight; the foe at hand,
Whom fled we thought, will save us long pursuit
This day; fear not his flight; so thick a cloud
He comes, and settled in his face I see
Sad resolution, and secure: Let each
His adamantine coat gird well, and each
Fit well his helm, gripe fast his orbed shield,
Borne even or high; for this day will pour down,
If I conjecture aught, no drizzling shower,
But rattling storm of arrows barbed with fire.'
So warned he them, aware themselves, and soon

In order, quit of all impediment;
Instant without disturb they took alarm,
And onward moved embattled: When behold!
Not distant far with heavy pace the foe
Approaching gross and huge, in hollow cube
Training his devilish enginery, impaled
On every side with shadowing squadrons deep,
To hide the fraud. At interview both stood
Awhile; but suddenly at head appeared
Satan, and thus was heard commanding loud.
'Vanguard, to right and left the front unfold;
That all may see who hate us, how we seek
Peace and composure, and with open breast
Stand ready to receive them, if they like
Our overture; and turn not back perverse:
But that I doubt; however witness, Heaven!
Heaven, witness thou anon! while we discharge
Freely our part: ye, who appointed stand
Do as you have in charge, and briefly touch
What we propound, and loud that all may hear!'
So scoffing in ambiguous words, he scarce
Had ended; when to right and left the front
Divided, and to either flank retired:
Which to our eyes discovered, new and strange,
A triple mounted row of pillars laid
On wheels (for like to pillars most they seemed,
Or hollowed bodies made of oak or fir,
With branches lopt, in wood or mountain felled,)
Brass, iron, stony mould, had not their mouths
With hideous orifice gaped on us wide,
Portending hollow truce: At each behind
A Seraph stood, and in his hand a reed
Stood waving tipt with fire; while we, suspense,
Collected stood within our thoughts amused,
Not long; for sudden all at once their reeds

Put forth, and to a narrow vent applied
With nicest touch. Immediate in a flame,
But soon obscured with smoke, all Heaven appeared,
From those deep-throated engines belched, whose roar
Embowelled with outrageous noise the air,
And all her entrails tore, disgorging foul
Their devilish glut, chained thunderbolts and hail
Of iron globes; which, on the victor host
Levelled, with such impetuous fury smote,
That, whom they hit, none on their feet might stand,
Though standing else as rocks, but down they fell
By thousands, Angel on Arch-Angel rolled;
The sooner for their arms; unarmed, they might
Have easily, as Spirits, evaded swift
By quick contraction or remove; but now
Foul dissipation followed, and forced rout;
Nor served it to relax their serried files.
What should they do? if on they rushed, repulse
Repeated, and indecent overthrow
Doubled, would render them yet more despised,
And to their foes a laughter; for in view
Stood ranked of Seraphim another row,
In posture to displode their second tire
Of thunder: Back defeated to return
They worse abhorred. Satan beheld their plight,
And to his mates thus in derision called.
'O Friends! why come not on these victors proud
Ere while they fierce were coming; and when we,
To entertain them fair with open front
And breast, (what could we more?) propounded terms
Of composition, straight they changed their minds,
Flew off, and into strange vagaries fell,
As they would dance; yet for a dance they seemed
Somewhat extravagant and wild; perhaps
For joy of offered peace: But I suppose,

If our proposals once again were heard,
We should compel them to a quick result.'
To whom thus Belial, in like gamesome mood.
Leader! the terms we sent were terms of weight,
Of hard contents, and full of force urged home;
Such as we might perceive amused them all,
And stumbled many: Who receives them right,
Had need from head to foot well understand;
Not understood, this gift they have besides,
They show us when our foes walk not upright.
So they among themselves in pleasant vein
Stood scoffing, hightened in their thoughts beyond
All doubt of victory: Eternal Might
To match with their inventions they presumed
So easy, and of his thunder made a scorn,
And all his host derided, while they stood
Awhile in trouble: But they stood not long;
Rage prompted them at length, and found them arms
Against such hellish mischief fit to oppose.
Forthwith (behold the excellence, the power,
Which God hath in his mighty Angels placed!)
Their arms away they threw, and to the hills
(For Earth hath this variety from Heaven
Of pleasure situate in hill and dale,)
Light as the lightning glimpse they ran, they flew;
From their foundations loosening to and fro,
They plucked the seated hills, with all their load,
Rocks, waters, woods, and by the shaggy tops
Up-lifting bore them in their hands: Amaze,
Be sure, and terror, seized the rebel host,
When coming towards them so dread they saw
The bottom of the mountains upward turned;
Till on those cursed engines' triple-row
They saw them whelmed, and all their confidence
Under the weight of mountains buried deep;

Themselves invaded next, and on their heads
Main promontories flung, which in the air
Came shadowing, and oppressed whole legions armed;
Their armour helped their harm, crushed in and bruised
Into their substance pent, which wrought them pain
Implacable, and many a dolorous groan;
Long struggling underneath, ere they could wind
Out of such prison, though Spirits of purest light,
Purest at first, now gross by sinning grown.
The rest, in imitation, to like arms
Betook them, and the neighbouring hills uptore:
So hills amid the air encountered hills,
Hurled to and fro with jaculation dire;
That under ground they fought in dismal shade;
Infernal noise! war seemed a civil game
To this uproar; horrid confusion heaped
Upon confusion rose: And now all Heaven
Had gone to wrack, with ruin overspread;
Had not the Almighty Father, where he sits
Shrined in his sanctuary of Heaven secure,
Consulting on the sum of things, foreseen
This tumult, and permitted all, advised:
That his great purpose he might so fulfil,
To honour his anointed Son avenged
Upon his enemies, and to declare
All power on him transferred: Whence to his Son,
The Assessour of his throne, he thus began.
'Effulgence of my glory, Son beloved,
Son, in whose face invisible is beheld
Visibly, what by Deity I am;
And in whose hand what by decree I do,
Second Omnipotence! two days are past,
Two days, as we compute the days of Heaven,
Since Michael and his Powers went forth to tame
These disobedient: Sore hath been their fight,

As likeliest was, when two such foes met armed;
For to themselves I left them; and thou knowest,
Equal in their creation they were formed,
Save what sin hath impaired; which yet hath wrought
Insensibly, for I suspend their doom;
Whence in perpetual fight they needs must last
Endless, and no solution will be found:
War wearied hath performed what war can do,
And to disordered rage let loose the reins
With mountains, as with weapons, armed; which makes
Wild work in Heaven, and dangerous to the main.
Two days are therefore past, the third is thine;
For thee I have ordained it; and thus far
Have suffered, that the glory may be thine
Of ending this great war, since none but Thou
Can end it. Into thee such virtue and grace
Immense I have transfused, that all may know
In Heaven and Hell thy power above compare;
And, this perverse commotion governed thus,
To manifest thee worthiest to be Heir
Of all things; to be Heir, and to be King
By sacred unction, thy deserved right.
Go then, Thou Mightiest, in thy Father's might;
Ascend my chariot, guide the rapid wheels
That shake Heaven's basis, bring forth all my war,
My bow and thunder, my almighty arms
Gird on, and sword upon thy puissant thigh;
Pursue these sons of darkness, drive them out
From all Heaven's bounds into the utter deep:
There let them learn, as likes them, to despise
God, and Messiah his anointed King.'
He said, and on his Son with rays direct
Shone full; he all his Father full expressed
Ineffably into his face received;
And thus the Filial Godhead answering spake.

'O Father, O Supreme of heavenly Thrones,
First, Highest, Holiest, Best; thou always seek'st
To glorify thy Son, I always thee,
As is most just: This I my glory account,
My exaltation, and my whole delight,
That thou, in me well pleased, declarest thy will
Fulfilled, which to fulfil is all my bliss.
Scepter and power, thy giving, I assume,
And gladlier shall resign, when in the end
Thou shalt be all in all, and I in thee
For ever; and in me all whom thou lovest:
But whom thou hatest, I hate, and can put on
Thy terrors, as I put thy mildness on,
Image of thee in all things; and shall soon,
Armed with thy might, rid Heaven of these rebelled;
To their prepared ill mansion driven down,
To chains of darkness, and the undying worm;
That from thy just obedience could revolt,
Whom to obey is happiness entire.
Then shall thy Saints unmixed, and from the impure
Far separate, circling thy holy mount,
Unfeigned Hallelujahs to thee sing,
Hymns of high praise, and I among them Chief.'
So said, he, o'er his scepter bowing, rose
From the right hand of Glory where he sat;
And the third sacred morn began to shine,
Dawning through Heaven. Forth rushed with whirlwind
    sound
The chariot of Paternal Deity,
Flashing thick flames, wheel within wheel undrawn,
Itself instinct with Spirit, but convoyed
By four Cherubic shapes; four faces each
Had wonderous; as with stars, their bodies all
And wings were set with eyes; with eyes the wheels
Of beryl, and careering fires between;

Over their heads a crystal firmament,
Whereon a sapphire throne, inlaid with pure
Amber, and colours of the showery arch.
He, in celestial panoply all armed
Of radiant Urim, work divinely wrought,
Ascended; at his right hand Victory
Sat eagle-winged; beside him hung his bow
And quiver with three-bolted thunder stored;
And from about him fierce effusion rolled
Of smoke, and bickering flame, and sparkles dire:
Attended with ten thousand thousand Saints,
He onward came; far off his coming shone;
And twenty thousand (I their number heard)
Chariots of God, half on each hand, were seen;
He on the wings of Cherub rode sublime
On the crystalline sky, in sapphire throned,
Illustrious far and wide; but by his own
First seen: Them unexpected joy surprised,
When the great ensign of Messiah blazed
Aloft by Angels borne, his sign in Heaven;
Under whose conduct Michael soon reduced
His army, circumfused on either wing,
Under their Head embodied all in one.
Before him Power Divine his way prepared;
At his command the uprooted hills retired
Each to his place; they heard his voice, and went
Obsequious; Heaven his wonted face renewed,
And with fresh flowerets hill and valley smiled.
This saw his hapless foes, but stood obdured,
And to rebellious fight rallied their Powers,
Insensate, hope conceiving from despair.
In heavenly Spirits could such perverseness dwell?
But to convince the proud what signs avail,
Or wonders move the obdurate to relent?
They, hardened more by what might most reclaim,

Grieving to see his glory, at the sight
Took envy; and, aspiring to his hight,
Stood re-embattled fierce, by force or fraud
Weening to prosper, and at length prevail
Against God and Messiah, or to fall
In universal ruin last; and now
To final battle drew, disdaining flight,
Or faint retreat; when the great Son of God
To all his host on either hand thus spake.
'Stand still in bright array, ye Saints; here stand,
Ye Angels armed; this day from battle rest:
Faithful hath been your warfare, and of God
Accepted, fearless in his righteous cause;
And as ye have received, so have ye done,
Invincibly: But of this cursed crew
The punishment to other hand belongs;
Vengeance is his, or whose he sole appoints:
Number to this day's work is not ordained,
Nor multitude; stand only, and behold
God's indignation on these godless poured
By me; not you, but me, they have despised,
Yet envied; against me is all their rage,
Because the Father, to whom in Heaven s'preme
Kingdom, and power, and glory appertains,
Hath honoured me, according to his will.
Therefore to me their doom he hath assigned;
That they may have their wish, to try with me
In battle which the stronger proves; they all,
Or I alone against them; since by strength
They measure all, of other excellence
Not emulous, nor care who them excels;
Nor other strife with them do I vouchsafe.'
So spake the Son, and into terror changed
His countenance too severe to be beheld,
And full of wrath bent on his enemies.

At once the Four spread out their starry wings
With dreadful shade contiguous, and the orbs
Of his fierce chariot rolled, as with the sound
Of torrent floods, or of a numerous host.
He on his impious foes right onward drove,
Gloomy as night; under his burning wheels
The steadfast empyrean shook throughout,
All but the throne itself of God. Full soon
Among them he arrived; in his right hand
Grasping ten thousand thunders, which he sent
Before him, such as in their souls infixed
Plagues: They, astonished, all resistance lost,
All courage; down their idle weapons dropt:
O'er shields, and helms, and helmed heads he rode
Of Thrones and mighty Seraphim prostrate,
That wished the mountains now might be again
Thrown on them, as a shelter from his ire.
Nor less on either side tempestuous fell
His arrows, from the fourfold-visaged Four
Distinct with eyes, and from the living wheels
Distinct alike with multitude of eyes;
One Spirit in them ruled; and every eye
Glared lightning, and shot forth pernicious fire
Among the accursed, that withered all their strength,
And of their wonted vigour left them drained,
Exhausted, spiritless, afflicted, fallen.
Yet half his strength he put not forth, but checked
His thunder in mid volley; for he meant
Not to destroy, but root them out of Heaven:
The overthrown he raised, and as a herd
Of goats or timorous flock together thronged
Drove them before him thunder-struck, pursued
With terrors, and with furies, to the bounds
And crystal wall of Heaven; which, opening wide,
Rolled inward, and a spacious gap disclosed

Into the wasteful deep: The monstrous sight
Struck them with horror backward, but far worse
Urged them behind: Headlong themselves they threw
Down from the verge of Heaven; eternal wrath
Burnt after them to the bottomless pit.
Hell heard the unsufferable noise, Hell saw
Heaven ruining from Heaven, and would have fled
Affrighted; but strict Fate had cast too deep
Her dark foundations, and too fast had bound.
Nine days they fell: Confounded Chaos roared,
And felt tenfold confusion in their fall
Through his wild anarchy, so huge a rout
Incumbered him with ruin: Hell at last
Yawning received them whole, and on them closed;
Hell, their fit habitation, fraught with fire
Unquenchable, the house of woe and pain.
Disburdened Heaven rejoiced, and soon repaired
Her mural breach, returning whence it rolled.
Sole victor, from the expulsion of his foes,
Messiah his triumphal chariot turned:
To meet him all his Saints, who silent stood
Eye-witnesses of his almighty acts,
With jubilee advanced; and, as they went,
Shaded with branching palm, each Order bright,
Sung triumph, and him sung victorious King,
Son, Heir, and Lord, to him dominion given,
Worthiest to reign: He, celebrated, rode
Triumphant through mid Heaven, into the courts
And temple of his Mighty Father throned
On high; who into glory him received,
Where now he sits at the right hand of bliss.
Thus, measuring things in Heaven by things on Earth,
At thy request, and that thou mayest beware
By what is past, to thee I have revealed
What might have else to human race been hid;

The discord which befell, and war in Heaven
Among the angelic Powers, and the deep fall
Of those too high aspiring, who rebelled
With Satan; he who envies now thy state,
Who now is plotting how he may seduce
Thee also from obedience, that, with him
Bereaved of happiness, thou mayest partake
His punishment, eternal misery;
Which would be all his solace and revenge,
As a despite done against the Most High,
Thee once to gain companion of his woe.
But listen not to his temptations, warn
Thy weaker; let it profit thee to have heard,
By terrible example, the reward
Of disobedience; firm they might have stood,
Yet fell; remember, and fear to transgress."

BOOK VII

Descend from Heaven, Urania, by that name
If rightly thou art called, whose voice divine
Following, above the Olympian hill I soar,
Above the flight of Pegasean wing!
The meaning, not the name, I call: for thou
Nor of the Muses nine, nor on the top
Of old Olympus dwellest; but, heavenly-born,
Before the hills appeared, or fountain flowed,
Thou with eternal Wisdom didst converse,
Wisdom thy sister, and with her didst play
In presence of the Almighty Father, pleased
With thy celestial song. Up led by thee
Into the Heaven of Heavens I have presumed,
An earthly guest, and drawn empyreal air,
Thy tempering: with like safety guided down
Return me to my native element:
Lest from this flying steed unreined, (as once
Bellerophon, though from a lower clime,)
Dismounted, on the Aleian field I fall,
Erroneous there to wander, and forlorn.
Half yet remains unsung, but narrower bound
Within the visible diurnal sphere;

Standing on earth, not rapt above the pole,
More safe I sing with mortal voice, unchanged
To hoarse or mute, though fallen on evil days,
On evil days though fallen, and evil tongues;
In darkness, and with dangers compassed round,
And solitude; yet not alone, while thou
Visitest my slumbers nightly, or when morn
Purples the east: still govern thou my song,
Urania, and fit audience find, though few.
But drive far off the barbarous dissonance
Of Bacchus and his revellers, the race
Of that wild rout that tore the Thracian bard
In Rhodope, where woods and rocks had ears
To rapture, till the savage clamour drowned
Both harp and voice; nor could the Muse defend
Her son. So fail not thou, who thee implores:
For thou art heavenly, she an empty dream.
Say, Goddess, what ensued when Raphael,
The affable Arch-Angel, had forewarned
Adam, by dire example, to beware
Apostasy, by what befell in Heaven
To those apostates; lest the like befall
In Paradise to Adam or his race,
Charged not to touch the interdicted tree,
If they transgress, and slight that sole command,
So easily obeyed amid the choice
Of all tastes else to please their appetite,
Though wandering. He, with his consorted Eve,
The story heard attentive, and was filled
With admiration and deep muse, to hear
Of things so high and strange; things, to their thought
So unimaginable, as hate in Heaven,
And war so near the peace of God in bliss,
With such confusion: but the evil, soon
Driven back, redounded as a flood on those

From whom it sprung; impossible to mix
With blessedness. Whence Adam soon repealed
The doubts that in his heart arose: and now
Led on, yet sinless, with desire to know
What nearer might concern him, how this world
Of Heaven and Earth conspicuous first began;
When, and whereof created; for what cause;
What within Eden, or without, was done
Before his memory; as one whose drouth
Yet scarce allayed still eyes the current stream,
Whose liquid murmur heard new thirst excites,
Proceeded thus to ask his heavenly guest.
"Great things, and full of wonder in our ears,
Far differing from this world, thou hast revealed,
Divine interpreter! by favour sent
Down from the empyrean, to forewarn
Us timely of what might else have been our loss,
Unknown, which human knowledge could not reach;
For which to the infinitely Good we owe
Immortal thanks, and his admonishment
Receive, with solemn purpose to observe
Immutably his sovran will, the end
Of what we are. But since thou hast vouchsafed
Gently, for our instruction, to impart
Things above earthly thought, which yet concerned
Our knowing, as to highest wisdom seemed,
Deign to descend now lower, and relate
What may no less perhaps avail us known,
How first began this Heaven which we behold
Distant so high, with moving fires adorned
Innumerable; and this which yields or fills
All space, the ambient air wide interfused
Embracing round this floried Earth; what cause
Moved the Creator, in his holy rest
Through all eternity, so late to build

In Chaos; and the work begun, how soon
Absolved; if unforbid thou mayest unfold
What we, not to explore the secrets ask
Of his eternal empire, but the more
To magnify his works, the more we know.
And the great light of day yet wants to run
Much of his race though steep; suspense in Heaven,
Held by thy voice, thy potent voice, he hears,
And longer will delay to hear thee tell
His generation, and the rising birth
Of Nature from the unapparent Deep:
Or if the star of evening and the moon
Haste to thy audience, Night with her will bring,
Silence; and Sleep, listening to thee, will watch;
Or we can bid his absence, till thy song
End, and dismiss thee ere the morning shine."
Thus Adam his illustrious guest besought:
And thus the Godlike Angel answered mild.
"This also thy request, with caution asked,
Obtain; though to recount almighty works
What words or tongue of Seraph can suffice,
Or heart of man suffice to comprehend?
Yet what thou canst attain, which best may serve
To glorify the Maker, and infer
Thee also happier, shall not be withheld
Thy hearing; such commission from above
I have received, to answer thy desire
Of knowledge within bounds; beyond, abstain
To ask; nor let thine own inventions hope
Things not revealed, which the invisible King,
Only Omniscient, hath suppressed in night;
To none communicable in Earth or Heaven:
Enough is left besides to search and know.
But knowledge is as food, and needs no less
Her temperance over appetite, to know

In measure what the mind may well contain;
Oppresses else with surfeit, and soon turns
Wisdom to folly, as nourishment to wind.
Know then, that, after Lucifer from Heaven
(So call him, brighter once amidst the host
Of Angels, than that star the stars among,)
Fell with his flaming legions through the deep
Into his place, and the great Son returned
Victorious with his Saints, the Omnipotent
Eternal Father from his throne beheld
Their multitude, and to his Son thus spake.
'At least our envious Foe hath failed, who thought
All like himself rebellious, by whose aid
This inaccessible high strength, the seat
Of Deity supreme, us dispossessed,
He trusted to have seized, and into fraud
Drew many, whom their place knows here no more:
Yet far the greater part have kept, I see,
Their station; Heaven, yet populous, retains
Number sufficient to possess her realms
Though wide, and this high temple to frequent
With ministeries due, and solemn rites:
But, lest his heart exalt him in the harm
Already done, to have dispeopled Heaven,
My damage fondly deemed, I can repair
That detriment, if such it be to lose
Self-lost; and in a moment will create
Another world, out of one man a race
Of men innumerable, there to dwell,
Not here; till, by degrees of merit raised,
They open to themselves at length the way
Up hither, under long obedience tried;
And Earth be changed to Heaven, and Heaven to Earth,
One kingdom, joy and union without end.
Meanwhile inhabit lax, ye Powers of Heaven;

And thou my Word, begotten Son, by thee
This I perform; speak thou, and be it done!
My overshadowing Spirit and Might with thee
I send along; ride forth, and bid the Deep
Within appointed bounds be Heaven and Earth;
Boundless the Deep, because I Am who fill
Infinitude, nor vacuous the space.
Though I, uncircumscribed myself, retire,
And put not forth my goodness, which is free
To act or not, Necessity and Chance
Approach not me, and what I will is Fate.'
So spake the Almighty, and to what he spake
His Word, the Filial Godhead, gave effect.
Immediate are the acts of God, more swift
Than time or motion, but to human ears
Cannot without process of speech be told,
So told as earthly notion can receive.
Great triumph and rejoicing was in Heaven,
When such was heard declared the Almighty's will;
'Glory' they sung to the Most High, 'good will
To future men, and in their dwellings peace;
Glory to Him, whose just avenging ire
Had driven out the ungodly from his sight
And the habitations of the just; to Him
Glory and praise, whose wisdom had ordained
Good out of evil to create; instead
Of Spirits malign, a better race to bring
Into their vacant room, and thence diffuse
His good to worlds and ages infinite.'
So sang the Hierarchies: Meanwhile the Son
On his great expedition now appeared,
Girt with Omnipotence, with radiance crowned
Of Majesty Divine; sapience and love
Immense, and all his Father in him shone.
About his chariot numberless were poured

Cherub, and Seraph, Potentates, and Thrones,
And Virtues, winged Spirits, and chariots winged
From the armoury of God; where stand of old
Myriads, between two brazen mountains lodged
Against a solemn day, harnessed at hand,
Celestial equipage; and now came forth
Spontaneous, for within them Spirit lived,
Attendant on their Lord: Heaven opened wide
Her ever-during gates, harmonious sound
On golden hinges moving, to let forth
The King of Glory, in his powerful Word
And Spirit, coming to create new worlds.
On heavenly ground they stood; and from the shore
They viewed the vast immeasurable abyss
Outrageous as a sea, dark, wasteful, wild,
Up from the bottom turned by furious winds
And surging waves, as mountains, to assault
Heaven's hight, and with the center mix the pole.
'Silence, ye troubled Waves, and thou Deep, peace,'
Said then the Omnifick Word; 'your discord end!'
Nor staid; but, on the wings of Cherubim
Uplifted, in paternal glory rode
Far into Chaos, and the world unborn;
For Chaos heard his voice: Him all his train
Followed in bright procession, to behold
Creation, and the wonders of his might.
Then staid the fervid wheels, and in his hand
He took the golden compasses, prepared
In God's eternal store, to circumscribe
This universe, and all created things:
One foot he centered, and the other turned
Round through the vast profundity obscure;
And said, Thus far extend, thus far thy bounds,
This be thy just circumference, O World!
Thus God the Heaven created, thus the Earth,

Matter unformed and void: Darkness profound
Covered the abyss: but on the watery calm
His brooding wings the Spirit of God outspread,
And vital virtue infused, and vital warmth
Throughout the fluid mass; but downward purged
The black tartareous cold infernal dregs,
Adverse to life: then founded, then conglobed
Like things to like; the rest to several place
Disparted, and between spun out the air;
And Earth self-balanced on her center hung.
'Let there be light,' said God; and forthwith Light
Ethereal, first of things, quintessence pure,
Sprung from the deep; and from her native east
To journey through the aery gloom began,
Sphered in a radiant cloud, for yet the sun
Was not; she in a cloudy tabernacle
Sojourned the while. God saw the light was good;
And light from darkness by the hemisphere
Divided: light the Day, and darkness Night,
He named. Thus was the first day even and morn:
Nor past uncelebrated, nor unsung
By the celestial quires, when orient light
Exhaling first from darkness they beheld;
Birth-day of Heaven and Earth; with joy and shout
The hollow universal orb they filled,
And touched their golden harps, and hymning praised
God and his works; Creator him they sung,
Both when first evening was, and when first morn.
Again, God said, Let there be firmament
Amid the waters, and let it divide
The waters from the waters; and God made
The firmament, expanse of liquid, pure,
Transparent, elemental air, diffused
In circuit to the uttermost convex
Of this great round; partition firm and sure,

The waters underneath from those above
Dividing: for as earth, so he the world
Built on circumfluous waters calm, in wide
Crystalline ocean, and the loud misrule
Of Chaos far removed; lest fierce extremes
Contiguous might distemper the whole frame:
And Heaven he named the Firmament: So even
And morning chorus sung the second day.
The Earth was formed, but in the womb as yet
Of waters, embryon immature involved,
Appeared not: over all the face of Earth
Main ocean flowed, not idle; but, with warm
Prolific humour softening all her globe,
Fermented the great mother to conceive,
Satiate with genial moisture; when God said,
'Be gathered now ye waters under Heaven
Into one place, and let dry land appear.'
Immediately the mountains huge appear
Emergent, and their broad bare backs upheave
Into the clouds; their tops ascend the sky:
So high as heaved the tumid hills, so low
Down sunk a hollow bottom broad and deep,
Capacious bed of waters: Thither they
Hasted with glad precipitance, uprolled,
As drops on dust conglobing from the dry:
Part rise in crystal wall, or ridge direct,
For haste; such flight the great command impressed
On the swift floods: As armies at the call
Of trumpet (for of armies thou hast heard)
Troop to their standard; so the watery throng,
Wave rolling after wave, where way they found,
If steep, with torrent rapture, if through plain,
Soft-ebbing; nor withstood them rock or hill;
But they, or under ground, or circuit wide
With serpent error wandering, found their way,

And on the washy ooze deep channels wore;
Easy, ere God had bid the ground be dry,
All but within those banks, where rivers now
Stream, and perpetual draw their humid train.
The dry land, Earth; and the great receptacle
Of congregated waters, he called Seas:
And saw that it was good; and said, 'Let the Earth
Put forth the verdant grass, herb yielding seed,
And fruit-tree yielding fruit after her kind,
Whose seed is in herself upon the Earth.'
He scarce had said, when the bare Earth, till then
Desart and bare, unsightly, unadorned,
Brought forth the tender grass, whose verdure clad
Her universal face with pleasant green;
Then herbs of every leaf, that sudden flowered
Opening their various colours, and made gay
Her bosom, smelling sweet: and, these scarce blown,
Forth flourished thick the clustering vine, forth crept
The swelling gourd, up stood the corny reed
Embattled in her field, and the humble shrub,
And bush with frizzled hair implicit: Last
Rose, as in dance, the stately trees, and spread
Their branches hung with copious fruit, or gemmed
Their blossoms: With high woods the hills were crowned;
With tufts the valleys, and each fountain side;
With borders long the rivers: that Earth now
Seemed like to Heaven, a seat where Gods might dwell,
Or wander with delight, and love to haunt
Her sacred shades: though God had yet not rained
Upon the Earth, and man to till the ground
None was; but from the Earth a dewy mist
Went up, and watered all the ground, and each
Plant of the field; which, ere it was in the Earth,
God made, and every herb, before it grew
On the green stem: God saw that it was good:

So even and morn recorded the third day.
Again the Almighty spake, 'Let there be lights
High in the expanse of Heaven, to divide
The day from night; and let them be for signs,
For seasons, and for days, and circling years;
And let them be for lights, as I ordain
Their office in the firmament of Heaven,
To give light on the Earth'; and it was so.
And God made two great lights, great for their use
To Man, the greater to have rule by day,
The less by night, altern; and made the stars,
And set them in the firmament of Heaven
To illuminate the Earth, and rule the day
In their vicissitude, and rule the night,
And light from darkness to divide. God saw,
Surveying his great work, that it was good:
For of celestial bodies first the sun
A mighty sphere he framed, unlightsome first,
Though of ethereal mould: then formed the moon
Globose, and every magnitude of stars,
And sowed with stars the Heaven, thick as a field:
Of light by far the greater part he took,
Transplanted from her cloudy shrine, and placed
In the sun's orb, made porous to receive
And drink the liquid light; firm to retain
Her gathered beams, great palace now of light.
Hither, as to their fountain, other stars
Repairing, in their golden urns draw light,
And hence the morning-planet gilds her horns;
By tincture or reflection they augment
Their small peculiar, though from human sight
So far remote, with diminution seen,
First in his east the glorious lamp was seen,
Regent of day, and all the horizon round
Invested with bright rays, jocund to run

His longitude through Heaven's high road; the gray
Dawn, and the Pleiades, before him danced,
Shedding sweet influence: Less bright the moon,
But opposite in levelled west was set,
His mirror, with full face borrowing her light
From him; for other light she needed none
In that aspect, and still that distance keeps
Till night; then in the east her turn she shines,
Revolved on Heaven's great axle, and her reign
With thousand lesser lights dividual holds,
With thousand thousand stars, that then appeared
Spangling the hemisphere: Then first adorned
With their bright luminaries that set and rose,
Glad evening and glad morn crowned the fourth day.
And God said, 'Let the waters generate
Reptile with spawn abundant, living soul:
And let fowl fly above the Earth, with wings
Displayed on the open firmament of Heaven.'
And God created the great whales, and each
Soul living, each that crept, which plenteously
The waters generated by their kinds;
And every bird of wing after his kind;
And saw that it was good, and blessed them, saying.
'Be fruitful, multiply, and in the seas,
And lakes, and running streams, the waters fill;
And let the fowl be multiplied, on the Earth.'
Forthwith the sounds and seas, each creek and bay,
With fry innumerable swarm, and shoals
Of fish that with their fins, and shining scales,
Glide under the green wave, in sculls that oft
Bank the mid sea: part single, or with mate,
Graze the sea-weed their pasture, and through groves
Of coral stray; or, sporting with quick glance,
Show to the sun their waved coats dropt with gold;
Or, in their pearly shells at ease, attend

Moist nutriment; or under rocks their food
In jointed armour watch: on smooth the seal
And bended dolphins play: part huge of bulk
Wallowing unwieldy, enormous in their gait,
Tempest the ocean: there leviathan,
Hugest of living creatures, on the deep
Stretched like a promontory sleeps or swims,
And seems a moving land; and at his gills
Draws in, and at his trunk spouts out, a sea.
Meanwhile the tepid caves, and fens, and shores,
Their brood as numerous hatch, from the egg that soon
Bursting with kindly rupture forth disclosed
Their callow young; but feathered soon and fledge
They summed their pens; and, soaring the air sublime,
With clang despised the ground, under a cloud
In prospect; there the eagle and the stork
On cliffs and cedar tops their eyries build:
Part loosely wing the region, part more wise
In common, ranged in figure, wedge their way,
Intelligent of seasons, and set forth
Their aery caravan, high over seas
Flying, and over lands, with mutual wing
Easing their flight; so steers the prudent crane
Her annual voyage, borne on winds; the air
Floats as they pass, fanned with unnumbered plumes:
From branch to branch the smaller birds with song
Solaced the woods, and spread their painted wings
Till even; nor then the solemn nightingale
Ceased warbling, but all night tun'd her soft lays:
Others, on silver lakes and rivers, bathed
Their downy breast; the swan with arched neck,
Between her white wings mantling proudly, rows
Her state with oary feet; yet oft they quit
The dank, and, rising on stiff pennons, tower
The mid aereal sky: Others on ground

Walked firm; the crested cock whose clarion sounds
The silent hours, and the other whose gay train
Adorns him, coloured with the florid hue
Of rainbows and starry eyes. The waters thus
With fish replenished, and the air with fowl,
Evening and morn solemnized the fifth day.
The sixth, and of creation last, arose
With evening harps and matin; when God said,
'Let the Earth bring forth soul living in her kind,
Cattle, and creeping things, and beast of the Earth,
Each in their kind.' The Earth obeyed, and straight
Opening her fertile womb teemed at a birth
Innumerous living creatures, perfect forms,
Limbed and full grown: Out of the ground up rose,
As from his lair, the wild beast where he wons
In forest wild, in thicket, brake, or den;
Among the trees in pairs they rose, they walked:
The cattle in the fields and meadows green:
Those rare and solitary, these in flocks
Pasturing at once, and in broad herds upsprung.
The grassy clods now calved; now half appeared
The tawny lion, pawing to get free
His hinder parts, then springs as broke from bonds,
And rampant shakes his brinded mane; the ounce,
The libbard, and the tiger, as the mole
Rising, the crumbled earth above them threw
In hillocks: The swift stag from under ground
Bore up his branching head: Scarce from his mould
Behemoth biggest born of earth upheaved
His vastness: Fleeced the flocks and bleating rose,
As plants: Ambiguous between sea and land
The river-horse, and scaly crocodile.
At once came forth whatever creeps the ground,
Insect or worm: those waved their limber fans
For wings, and smallest lineaments exact

In all the liveries decked of summer's pride
With spots of gold and purple, azure and green:
These, as a line, their long dimension drew,
Streaking the ground with sinuous trace; not all
Minims of nature; some of serpent-kind,
Wonderous in length and corpulence, involved
Their snaky folds, and added wings. First crept
The parsimonious emmet, provident
Of future; in small room large heart enclosed;
Pattern of just equality perhaps
Hereafter, joined in her popular tribes
Of commonalty: Swarming next appeared
The female bee, that feeds her husband drone
Deliciously, and builds her waxen cells
With honey stored: The rest are numberless,
And thou their natures knowest, and gavest them names,
Needless to thee repeated; nor unknown
The serpent, subtlest beast of all the field,
Of huge extent sometimes, with brazen eyes
And hairy mane terrific, though to thee
Not noxious, but obedient at thy call.
Now Heaven in all her glory shone, and rolled
Her motions, as the great first Mover's hand
First wheeled their course: Earth in her rich attire
Consummate lovely smiled; air, water, earth,
By fowl, fish, beast, was flown, was swum, was walked,
Frequent; and of the sixth day yet remained:
There wanted yet the master-work, the end
Of all yet done; a creature, who, not prone
And brute as other creatures, but endued
With sanctity of reason, might erect
His stature, and upright with front serene
Govern the rest, self-knowing; and from thence
Magnanimous to correspond with Heaven,
But grateful to acknowledge whence his good

Descends, thither with heart, and voice, and eyes
Directed in devotion, to adore
And worship God Supreme, who made him chief
Of all his works: therefore the Omnipotent
Eternal Father (for where is not he
Present?) thus to his Son audibly spake.
'Let us make now Man in our image, Man
In our similitude, and let them rule
Over the fish and fowl of sea and air,
Beast of the field, and over all the Earth,
And every creeping thing that creeps the ground.'
This said, he formed thee, Adam, thee, O Man,
Dust of the ground, and in thy nostrils breathed
The breath of life; in his own image he
Created thee, in the image of God
Express; and thou becamest a living soul.
Male he created thee; but thy consort
Female, for race; then blessed mankind, and said,
'Be fruitful, multiply, and fill the Earth;
Subdue it, and throughout dominion hold
Over fish of the sea, and fowl of the air,
And every living thing that moves on the Earth.'
Wherever thus created, for no place
Is yet distinct by name, thence, as thou knowest,
He brought thee into this delicious grove,
This garden, planted with the trees of God,
Delectable both to behold and taste;
And freely all their pleasant fruit for food
Gave thee; all sorts are here that all the Earth yields,
Variety without end; but of the tree,
Which, tasted, works knowledge of good and evil,
Thou mayest not; in the day thou eatest, thou diest;
Death is the penalty imposed; beware,
And govern well thy appetite; lest Sin
Surprise thee, and her black attendant Death.

Here finished he, and all that he had made
Viewed, and behold all was entirely good;
So even and morn accomplished the sixth day:
Yet not till the Creator from his work
Desisting, though unwearied, up returned,
Up to the Heaven of Heavens, his high abode;
Thence to behold this new created world,
The addition of his empire, how it showed
In prospect from his throne, how good, how fair,
Answering his great idea. Up he rode
Followed with acclamation, and the sound
Symphonious of ten thousand harps, that tuned
Angelic harmonies: The earth, the air
Resounded, (thou rememberest, for thou heardst,)
The heavens and all the constellations rung,
The planets in their station listening stood,
While the bright pomp ascended jubilant.
'Open, ye everlasting gates!' they sung,
'Open, ye Heavens! your living doors; let in
The great Creator from his work returned
Magnificent, his six days work, a World;
Open, and henceforth oft; for God will deign
To visit oft the dwellings of just men,
Delighted; and with frequent intercourse
Thither will send his winged messengers
On errands of supernal grace.' So sung
The glorious train ascending: He through Heaven,
That opened wide her blazing portals, led
To God's eternal house direct the way;
A broad and ample road, whose dust is gold
And pavement stars, as stars to thee appear,
Seen in the galaxy, that milky way,
Which nightly, as a circling zone, thou seest
Powdered with stars. And now on Earth the seventh
Evening arose in Eden, for the sun

Was set, and twilight from the east came on,
Forerunning night; when at the holy mount
Of Heaven's high-seated top, the imperial throne
Of Godhead, fixed for ever firm and sure,
The Filial Power arrived, and sat him down
With his great Father; for he also went
Invisible, yet staid, (such privilege
Hath Omnipresence) and the work ordained,
Author and End of all things; and, from work
Now resting, blessed and hallowed the seventh day,
As resting on that day from all his work,
But not in silence holy kept: the harp
Had work and rested not; the solemn pipe,
And dulcimer, all organs of sweet stop,
All sounds on fret by string or golden wire,
Tempered soft tunings, intermixed with voice
Choral or unison: of incense clouds,
Fuming from golden censers, hid the mount.
Creation and the six days acts they sung:
'Great are thy works, Jehovah! infinite
Thy power! what thought can measure thee, or tongue
Relate thee! Greater now in thy return
Than from the giant Angels: Thee that day
Thy thunders magnified; but to create
Is greater than created to destroy.
Who can impair thee, Mighty King, or bound
Thy empire! Easily the proud attempt
Of Spirits apostate, and their counsels vain,
Thou hast repelled; while impiously they thought
Thee to diminish, and from thee withdraw
The number of thy worshippers. Who seeks
To lessen thee, against his purpose serves
To manifest the more thy might: his evil
Thou usest, and from thence createst more good.
Witness this new-made world, another Heaven

From Heaven-gate not far, founded in view
On the clear hyaline, the glassy sea;
Of amplitude almost immense, with stars
Numerous, and every star perhaps a world
Of destined habitation; but thou knowest
Their seasons: among these the seat of Men,
Earth, with her nether ocean circumfused,
Their pleasant dwelling-place. Thrice happy Men,
And sons of Men, whom God hath thus advanced!
Created in his image, there to dwell
And worship him; and in reward to rule
Over his works, on earth, in sea, or air,
And multiply a race of worshippers
Holy and just: Thrice happy, if they know
Their happiness, and persevere upright!'
So sung they, and the empyrean rung
With halleluiahs: Thus was sabbath kept.
And thy request think now fulfilled, that asked
How first this world and face of things began,
And what before thy memory was done
From the beginning; that posterity,
Informed by thee, might know: If else thou seekest
Aught, not surpassing human measure, say."

BOOK VIII

The Angel ended, and in Adam's ear
So charming left his voice, that he a while
Thought him still speaking, still stood fixed to hear;
Then, as new waked, thus gratefully replied.
"What thanks sufficient, or what recompence
Equal, have I to render thee, divine
Historian, who thus largely hast allayed
The thirst I had of knowledge, and vouchsafed
This friendly condescension to relate
Things, else by me unsearchable; now heard
With wonder, but delight, and, as is due,
With glory attributed to the high
Creator! Something yet of doubt remains,
Which only thy solution can resolve.
When I behold this goodly frame, this world,
Of Heaven and Earth consisting; and compute
Their magnitudes; this Earth, a spot, a grain,
An atom, with the firmament compared
And all her numbered stars, that seem to roll
Spaces incomprehensible, (for such
Their distance argues, and their swift return
Diurnal,) merely to officiate light
Round this opacous Earth, this punctual spot,

One day and night; in all her vast survey
Useless besides; reasoning I oft admire,
How Nature wise and frugal could commit
Such disproportions, with superfluous hand
So many nobler bodies to create,
Greater so manifold, to this one use,
For aught appears, and on their orbs impose
Such restless revolution day by day
Repeated; while the sedentary Earth,
That better might with far less compass move,
Served by more noble than herself, attains
Her end without least motion, and receives,
As tribute, such a sumless journey brought
Of incorporeal speed, her warmth and light;
Speed, to describe whose swiftness number fails."
So spake our sire, and by his countenance seemed
Entering on studious thoughts abstruse; which Eve
Perceiving, where she sat retired in sight,
With lowliness majestick from her seat,
And grace that won who saw to wish her stay,
Rose, and went forth among her fruits and flowers,
To visit how they prospered, bud and bloom,
Her nursery; they at her coming sprung,
And, touched by her fair tendance, gladlier grew.
Yet went she not, as not with such discourse
Delighted, or not capable her ear
Of what was high: such pleasure she reserved,
Adam relating, she sole auditress;
Her husband the relater she preferred
Before the Angel, and of him to ask
Chose rather; he, she knew, would intermix
Grateful digressions, and solve high dispute
With conjugal caresses: from his lip
Not words alone pleased her. O! when meet now
Such pairs, in love and mutual honour joined?

With Goddess-like demeanour forth she went,
Not unattended; for on her, as Queen,
A pomp of winning Graces waited still,
And from about her shot darts of desire
Into all eyes, to wish her still in sight.
And Raphael now, to Adam's doubt proposed,
Benevolent and facile thus replied.
"To ask or search, I blame thee not; for Heaven
Is as the book of God before thee set,
Wherein to read his wonderous works, and learn
His seasons, hours, or days, or months, or years:
This to attain, whether Heaven move or Earth,
Imports not, if thou reckon right; the rest
From Man or Angel the great Architect
Did wisely to conceal, and not divulge
His secrets to be scanned by them who ought
Rather admire; or, if they list to try
Conjecture, he his fabric of the Heavens
Hath left to their disputes, perhaps to move
His laughter at their quaint opinions wide
Hereafter; when they come to model Heaven
And calculate the stars, how they will wield
The mighty frame; how build, unbuild, contrive
To save appearances; how gird the sphere
With centric and eccentric scribbled o'er,
Cycle and epicycle, orb in orb:
Already by thy reasoning this I guess,
Who art to lead thy offspring, and supposest
That bodies bright and greater should not serve
The less not bright, nor Heaven such journeys run,
Earth sitting still, when she alone receives
The benefit: Consider first, that great
Or bright infers not excellence: the Earth
Though, in comparison of Heaven, so small,
Nor glistering, may of solid good contain

More plenty than the sun that barren shines;
Whose virtue on itself works no effect,
But in the fruitful Earth; there first received,
His beams, unactive else, their vigour find.
Yet not to Earth are those bright luminaries
Officious; but to thee, Earth's habitant.
And for the Heaven's wide circuit, let it speak
The Maker's high magnificence, who built
So spacious, and his line stretched out so far,
That Man may know he dwells not in his own;
An edifice too large for him to fill,
Lodged in a small partition; and the rest
Ordained for uses to his Lord best known.
The swiftness of those circles attribute,
Though numberless, to his Omnipotence,
That to corporeal substances could add
Speed almost spiritual: Me thou thinkest not slow,
Who since the morning-hour set out from Heaven
Where God resides, and ere mid-day arrived
In Eden; distance inexpressible
By numbers that have name. But this I urge,
Admitting motion in the Heavens, to show
Invalid that which thee to doubt it moved;
Not that I so affirm, though so it seem
To thee who hast thy dwelling here on Earth.
God, to remove his ways from human sense,
Placed Heaven from Earth so far, that earthly sight,
If it presume, might err in things too high,
And no advantage gain. What if the sun
Be center to the world; and other stars,
By his attractive virtue and their own
Incited, dance about him various rounds?
Their wandering course now high, now low, then hid,
Progressive, retrograde, or standing still,
In six thou seest; and what if seventh to these

The planet earth, so steadfast though she seem,
Insensibly three different motions move?
Which else to several spheres thou must ascribe,
Moved contrary with thwart obliquities;
Or save the sun his labour, and that swift
Nocturnal and diurnal rhomb supposed,
Invisible else above all stars, the wheel
Of day and night; which needs not thy belief,
If earth, industrious of herself, fetch day
Travelling east, and with her part averse
From the sun's beam meet night, her other part
Still luminous by his ray. What if that light,
Sent from her through the wide transpicuous air,
To the terrestrial moon be as a star,
Enlightening her by day, as she by night
This earth? reciprocal, if land be there,
Fields and inhabitants: Her spots thou seest
As clouds, and clouds may rain, and rain produce
Fruits in her softened soil for some to eat
Allotted there; and other suns perhaps,
With their attendant moons, thou wilt descry,
Communicating male and female light;
Which two great sexes animate the world,
Stored in each orb perhaps with some that live.
For such vast room in Nature unpossessed
By living soul, desart and desolate,
Only to shine, yet scarce to contribute
Each orb a glimpse of light, conveyed so far
Down to this habitable, which returns
Light back to them, is obvious to dispute.
But whether thus these things, or whether not;
But whether the sun, predominant in Heaven,
Rise on the earth; or earth rise on the sun;
He from the east his flaming road begin;
Or she from west her silent course advance,

With inoffensive pace that spinning sleeps
On her soft axle, while she paces even,
And bears thee soft with the smooth hair along;
Solicit not thy thoughts with matters hid;
Leave them to God above; him serve, and fear!
Of other creatures, as him pleases best,
Wherever placed, let him dispose; joy thou
In what he gives to thee, this Paradise
And thy fair Eve; Heaven is for thee too high
To know what passes there; be lowly wise:
Think only what concerns thee, and thy being;
Dream not of other worlds, what creatures there
Live, in what state, condition, or degree;
Contented that thus far hath been revealed
Not of Earth only, but of highest Heaven."
To whom thus Adam, cleared of doubt, replied.
"How fully hast thou satisfied me, pure
Intelligence of Heaven, Angel serene!
And, freed from intricacies, taught to live
The easiest way; nor with perplexing thoughts
To interrupt the sweet of life, from which
God hath bid dwell far off all anxious cares,
And not molest us; unless we ourselves
Seek them with wandering thoughts, and notions vain.
But apt the mind or fancy is to rove
Unchecked, and of her roving is no end;
Till warned, or by experience taught, she learn,
That, not to know at large of things remote
From use, obscure and subtle; but, to know
That which before us lies in daily life,
Is the prime wisdom: What is more, is fume,
Or emptiness, or fond impertinence:
And renders us, in things that most concern,
Unpractised, unprepared, and still to seek.
Therefore from this high pitch let us descend

A lower flight, and speak of things at hand
Useful; whence, haply, mention may arise
Of something not unseasonable to ask,
By sufferance, and thy wonted favour, deigned.
Thee I have heard relating what was done
Ere my remembrance: now, hear me relate
My story, which perhaps thou hast not heard;
And day is not yet spent; till then thou seest
How subtly to detain thee I devise;
Inviting thee to hear while I relate;
Fond! were it not in hope of thy reply:
For, while I sit with thee, I seem in Heaven;
And sweeter thy discourse is to my ear
Than fruits of palm-tree pleasantest to thirst
And hunger both, from labour, at the hour
Of sweet repast; they satiate, and soon fill,
Though pleasant; but thy words, with grace divine
Imbued, bring to their sweetness no satiety."
To whom thus Raphael answered heavenly meek.
"Nor are thy lips ungraceful, Sire of men,
Nor tongue ineloquent; for God on thee
Abundantly his gifts hath also poured
Inward and outward both, his image fair:
Speaking, or mute, all comeliness and grace
Attends thee; and each word, each motion, forms;
Nor less think we in Heaven of thee on Earth
Than of our fellow-servant, and inquire
Gladly into the ways of God with Man:
For God, we see, hath honoured thee, and set
On Man his equal love: Say therefore on;
For I that day was absent, as befell,
Bound on a voyage uncouth and obscure,
Far on excursion toward the gates of Hell;
Squared in full legion (such command we had)
To see that none thence issued forth a spy,

Or enemy, while God was in his work;
Lest he, incensed at such eruption bold,
Destruction with creation might have mixed.
Not that they durst without his leave attempt;
But us he sends upon his high behests
For state, as Sovran King; and to inure
Our prompt obedience. Fast we found, fast shut,
The dismal gates, and barricadoed strong;
But long ere our approaching heard within
Noise, other than the sound of dance or song,
Torment, and loud lament, and furious rage.
Glad we returned up to the coasts of light
Ere sabbath-evening: so we had in charge.
But thy relation now; for I attend,
Pleased with thy words no less than thou with mine."
So spake the Godlike Power, and thus our Sire.
"For Man to tell how human life began
Is hard; for who himself beginning knew
Desire with thee still longer to converse
Induced me. As new waked from soundest sleep,
Soft on the flowery herb I found me laid,
In balmy sweat; which with his beams the sun
Soon dried, and on the reeking moisture fed.
Straight toward Heaven my wondering eyes I turned,
And gazed a while the ample sky; till, raised
By quick instinctive motion, up I sprung,
As thitherward endeavouring, and upright
Stood on my feet: about me round I saw
Hill, dale, and shady woods, and sunny plains,
And liquid lapse of murmuring streams; by these,
Creatures that lived and moved, and walked, or flew;
Birds on the branches warbling; all things smiled;
With fragrance and with joy my heart o'erflowed.
Myself I then perused, and limb by limb
Surveyed, and sometimes went, and sometimes ran

With supple joints, as lively vigour led:
But who I was, or where, or from what cause,
Knew not; to speak I tried, and forthwith spake;
My tongue obeyed, and readily could name
Whate'er I saw. 'Thou Sun,' said I, 'fair light,
And thou enlightened Earth, so fresh and gay,
Ye Hills, and Dales, ye Rivers, Woods, and Plains,
And ye that live and move, fair Creatures, tell,
Tell, if ye saw, how I came thus, how here?—
Not of myself;—by some great Maker then,
In goodness and in power pre-eminent:
Tell me, how may I know him, how adore,
From whom I have that thus I move and live,
And feel that I am happier than I know.'
While thus I called, and strayed I knew not whither,
From where I first drew air, and first beheld
This happy light; when, answer none returned,
On a green shady bank, profuse of flowers,
Pensive I sat me down: There gentle sleep
First found me, and with soft oppression seized
My droused sense, untroubled, though I thought
I then was passing to my former state
Insensible, and forthwith to dissolve:
When suddenly stood at my head a dream,
Whose inward apparition gently moved
My fancy to believe I yet had being,
And lived: One came, methought, of shape divine,
And said, 'Thy mansion wants thee, Adam; rise,
First Man, of men innumerable ordained
First Father! called by thee, I come thy guide
To the garden of bliss, thy seat prepared.'
So saying, by the hand he took me raised,
And over fields and waters, as in air
Smooth-sliding without step, last led me up
A woody mountain; whose high top was plain,

A circuit wide, enclosed, with goodliest trees
Planted, with walks, and bowers; that what I saw
Of Earth before scarce pleasant seemed. Each tree,
Loaden with fairest fruit that hung to the eye
Tempting, stirred in me sudden appetite
To pluck and eat; whereat I waked, and found
Before mine eyes all real, as the dream
Had lively shadowed: Here had new begun
My wandering, had not he, who was my guide
Up hither, from among the trees appeared,
Presence Divine. Rejoicing, but with awe,
In adoration at his feet I fell
Submiss: He reared me, and 'Whom thou soughtest I am,'
Said mildly, 'Author of all this thou seest
Above, or round about thee, or beneath.
This Paradise I give thee, count it thine
To till and keep, and of the fruit to eat:
Of every tree that in the garden grows
Eat freely with glad heart; fear here no dearth:
But of the tree whose operation brings
Knowledge of good and ill, which I have set
The pledge of thy obedience and thy faith,
Amid the garden by the tree of life,
Remember what I warn thee, shun to taste,
And shun the bitter consequence: for know,
The day thou eatest thereof, my sole command
Transgressed, inevitably thou shalt die,
From that day mortal; and this happy state
Shalt lose, expelled from hence into a world
Of woe and sorrow.' Sternly he pronounced
The rigid interdiction, which resounds
Yet dreadful in mine ear, though in my choice
Not to incur; but soon his clear aspect
Returned, and gracious purpose thus renewed.
'Not only these fair bounds, but all the Earth

To thee and to thy race I give; as lords
Possess it, and all things that therein live,
Or live in sea, or air; beast, fish, and fowl.
In sign whereof, each bird and beast behold
After their kinds; I bring them to receive
From thee their names, and pay thee fealty
With low subjection; understand the same
Of fish within their watery residence,
Not hither summoned, since they cannot change
Their element, to draw the thinner air.'
As thus he spake, each bird and beast behold
Approaching two and two; these cowering low
With blandishment; each bird stooped on his wing.
I named them, as they passed, and understood
Their nature, with such knowledge God endued
My sudden apprehension: But in these
I found not what methought I wanted still;
And to the heavenly Vision thus presumed.
'O, by what name, for thou above all these,
Above mankind, or aught than mankind higher,
Surpassest far my naming; how may I
Adore thee, Author of this universe,
And all this good to man? for whose well being
So amply, and with hands so liberal,
Thou hast provided all things: But with me
I see not who partakes. In solitude
What happiness, who can enjoy alone,
Or, all enjoying, what contentment find?'
Thus I presumptuous; and the Vision bright,
As with a smile more brightened, thus replied.
'What callest thou solitude? Is not the Earth
With various living creatures, and the air
Replenished, and all these at thy command
To come and play before thee? Knowest thou not
Their language and their ways? They also know,

And reason not contemptibly: With these
Find pastime, and bear rule; thy realm is large.'
So spake the Universal Lord, and seemed
So ordering: I, with leave of speech implored,
And humble deprecation, thus replied.
'Let not my words offend thee, Heavenly Power;
My Maker, be propitious while I speak.
Hast thou not made me here thy substitute,
And these inferior far beneath me set?
Among unequals what society
Can sort, what harmony, or true delight?
Which must be mutual, in proportion due
Given and received; but, in disparity
The one intense, the other still remiss,
Cannot well suit with either, but soon prove
Tedious alike: Of fellowship I speak
Such as I seek, fit to participate
All rational delight: wherein the brute
Cannot be human consort: They rejoice
Each with their kind, lion with lioness;
So fitly them in pairs thou hast combined:
Much less can bird with beast, or fish with fowl
So well converse, nor with the ox the ape;
Worse then can man with beast, and least of all.'
Whereto the Almighty answered, not displeased.
'A nice and subtle happiness, I see,
Thou to thyself proposest, in the choice
Of thy associates, Adam! and wilt taste
No pleasure, though in pleasure, solitary.
What thinkest thou then of me, and this my state?
Seem I to thee sufficiently possessed
Of happiness, or not? who am alone
From all eternity; for none I know
Second to me or like, equal much less.
How have I then with whom to hold converse,

Save with the creatures which I made, and those
To me inferior, infinite descents
Beneath what other creatures are to thee?'
He ceased; I lowly answered. 'To attain
The hight and depth of thy eternal ways
All human thoughts come short, Supreme of things!
Thou in thyself art perfect, and in thee
Is no deficience found: Not so is Man,
But in degree; the cause of his desire
By conversation with his like to help
Or solace his defects. No need that thou
Shouldst propagate, already Infinite;
And through all numbers absolute, though One:
But Man by number is to manifest
His single imperfection, and beget
Like of his like, his image multiplied,
In unity defective; which requires
Collateral love, and dearest amity.
Thou in thy secrecy although alone,
Best with thyself accompanied, seekest not
Social communication; yet, so pleased,
Canst raise thy creature to what hight thou wilt
Of union or communion, deified:
I, by conversing, cannot these erect
From prone; nor in their ways complacence find.'
Thus I emboldened spake, and freedom used
Permissive, and acceptance found; which gained
This answer from the gracious Voice Divine.
'Thus far to try thee, Adam, I was pleased;
And find thee knowing, not of beasts alone,
Which thou hast rightly named, but of thyself;
Expressing well the spirit within thee free,
My image, not imparted to the brute;
Whose fellowship therefore unmeet for thee
Good reason was thou freely shouldst dislike;

And be so minded still: I, ere thou spakest,
Knew it not good for Man to be alone;
And no such company as then thou sawest
Intended thee; for trial only brought,
To see how thou couldest judge of fit and meet:
What next I bring shall please thee, be assured,
Thy likeness, thy fit help, thy other self,
Thy wish exactly to thy heart's desire.'
He ended, or I heard no more; for now
My earthly by his heavenly overpowered,
Which it had long stood under, strained to the hight
In that celestial colloquy sublime,
As with an object that excels the sense
Dazzled and spent, sunk down; and sought repair
Of sleep, which instantly fell on me, called
By Nature as in aid, and closed mine eyes.
Mine eyes he closed, but open left the cell
Of fancy, my internal sight; by which,
Abstract as in a trance, methought I saw,
Though sleeping, where I lay, and saw the shape
Still glorious before whom awake I stood:
Who stooping opened my left side, and took
From thence a rib, with cordial spirits warm,
And life-blood streaming fresh; wide was the wound,
But suddenly with flesh filled up and healed:
The rib he formed and fashioned with his hands;
Under his forming hands a creature grew,
Man-like, but different sex; so lovely fair,
That what seemed fair in all the world, seemed now
Mean, or in her summed up, in her contained
And in her looks; which from that time infused
Sweetness into my heart, unfelt before,
And into all things from her air inspired
The spirit of love and amorous delight.
She disappeared, and left me dark; I waked

To find her, or for ever to deplore
Her loss, and other pleasures all abjure:
When out of hope, behold her, not far off,
Such as I saw her in my dream, adorned
With what all Earth or Heaven could bestow
To make her amiable: On she came,
Led by her heavenly Maker, though unseen,
And guided by his voice; nor uninformed
Of nuptial sanctity, and marriage rites:
Grace was in all her steps, Heaven in her eye,
In every gesture dignity and love.
I, overjoyed, could not forbear aloud.
'This turn hath made amends; thou hast fulfilled
Thy words, Creator bounteous and benign,
Giver of all things fair! but fairest this
Of all thy gifts! nor enviest. I now see
Bone of my bone, flesh of my flesh, myself
Before me: Woman is her name; of Man
Extracted: for this cause he shall forego
Father and mother, and to his wife adhere;
And they shall be one flesh, one heart, one soul.'
She heard me thus; and though divinely brought,
Yet innocence, and virgin modesty,
Her virtue, and the conscience of her worth,
That would be wooed, and not unsought be won,
Not obvious, not obtrusive, but, retired,
The more desirable; or, to say all,
Nature herself, though pure of sinful thought,
Wrought in her so, that, seeing me, she turned:
I followed her; she what was honour knew,
And with obsequious majesty approved
My pleaded reason. To the nuptial bower
I led her blushing like the morn: All Heaven,
And happy constellations, on that hour
Shed their selectest influence; the Earth

Gave sign of gratulation, and each hill;
Joyous the birds; fresh gales and gentle airs
Whispered it to the woods, and from their wings
Flung rose, flung odours from the spicy shrub,
Disporting, till the amorous bird of night
Sung spousal, and bid haste the evening-star
On his hill top, to light the bridal lamp.
Thus have I told thee all my state, and brought
My story to the sum of earthly bliss,
Which I enjoy; and must confess to find
In all things else delight indeed, but such
As, used or not, works in the mind no change,
Nor vehement desire; these delicacies
I mean of taste, sight, smell, herbs, fruits, and flowers,
Walks, and the melody of birds: but here
Far otherwise, transported I behold,
Transported touch; here passion first I felt,
Commotion strange! in all enjoyments else
Superior and unmoved; here only weak
Against the charm of Beauty's powerful glance.
Or Nature failed in me, and left some part
Not proof enough such object to sustain;
Or, from my side subducting, took perhaps
More than enough; at least on her bestowed
Too much of ornament, in outward show
Elaborate, of inward less exact.
For well I understand in the prime end
Of Nature her the inferior, in the mind
And inward faculties, which most excel;
In outward also her resembling less
His image who made both, and less expressing
The character of that dominion given
O'er other creatures: Yet when I approach
Her loveliness, so absolute she seems
And in herself complete, so well to know

Her own, that what she wills to do or say,
Seems wisest, virtuousest, discreetest, best:
All higher knowledge in her presence falls
Degraded; Wisdom in discourse with her
Loses discountenanced, and like Folly shows;
Authority and Reason on her wait,
As one intended first, not after made
Occasionally; and, to consummate all,
Greatness of mind and Nobleness their seat
Build in her loveliest, and create an awe
About her, as a guard angelic placed.
To whom the Angel with contracted brow.
Accuse not Nature, she hath done her part;
Do thou but thine; and be not diffident
Of Wisdom; she deserts thee not, if thou
Dismiss not her, when most thou needest her nigh,
By attributing overmuch to things
Less excellent, as thou thyself perceivest.
For, what admirest thou, what transports thee so,
An outside? fair, no doubt, and worthy well
Thy cherishing, thy honouring, and thy love;
Not thy subjection: Weigh with her thyself;
Then value: Oft-times nothing profits more
Than self-esteem, grounded on just and right
Well managed; of that skill the more thou knowest,
The more she will acknowledge thee her head,
And to realities yield all her shows:
Made so adorn for thy delight the more,
So awful, that with honour thou mayest love
Thy mate, who sees when thou art seen least wise.
But if the sense of touch, whereby mankind
Is propagated, seem such dear delight
Beyond all other; think the same vouchsafed
To cattle and each beast; which would not be
To them made common and divulged, if aught

Therein enjoyed were worthy to subdue
The soul of man, or passion in him move.
What higher in her society thou findest
Attractive, human, rational, love still;
In loving thou dost well, in passion not,
Wherein true love consists not: Love refines
The thoughts, and heart enlarges; hath his seat
In reason, and is judicious; is the scale
By which to heavenly love thou mayest ascend,
Not sunk in carnal pleasure; for which cause,
Among the beasts no mate for thee was found."
To whom thus, half abashed, Adam replied.
"Neither her outside formed so fair, nor aught
In procreation common to all kinds,
(Though higher of the genial bed by far,
And with mysterious reverence I deem,)
So much delights me, as those graceful acts,
Those thousand decencies, that daily flow
From all her words and actions mixed with love
And sweet compliance, which declare unfeigned
Union of mind, or in us both one soul;
Harmony to behold in wedded pair
More grateful than harmonious sound to the ear.
Yet these subject not; I to thee disclose
What inward thence I feel, not therefore foiled,
Who meet with various objects, from the sense
Variously representing; yet, still free,
Approve the best, and follow what I approve.
To love, thou blamest me not; for Love, thou sayest,
Leads up to Heaven, is both the way and guide;
Bear with me then, if lawful what I ask:
Love not the heavenly Spirits, and how their love
Express they? by looks only? or do they mix
Irradiance, virtual or immediate touch?"
To whom the Angel, with a smile that glowed

Celestial rosy red, Love's proper hue,
Answered. "Let it suffice thee that thou knowest
Us happy, and without love no happiness.
Whatever pure thou in the body enjoyest,
(And pure thou wert created) we enjoy
In eminence; and obstacle find none
Of membrane, joint, or limb, exclusive bars;
Easier than air with air, if Spirits embrace,
Total they mix, union of pure with pure
Desiring, nor restrained conveyance need,
As flesh to mix with flesh, or soul with soul.
But I can now no more; the parting sun
Beyond the Earth's green Cape and verdant Isles
Hesperian sets, my signal to depart.
Be strong, live happy, and love! But, first of all,
Him, whom to love is to obey, and keep
His great command; take heed lest passion sway
Thy judgement to do aught, which else free will
Would not admit: thine, and of all thy sons,
The weal or woe in thee is placed; beware!
I in thy persevering shall rejoice,
And all the Blest: Stand fast; to stand or fall
Free in thine own arbitrement it lies.
Perfect within, no outward aid require;
And all temptation to transgress repel."
So saying, he arose; whom Adam thus
Followed with benediction. "Since to part,
Go, heavenly guest, ethereal Messenger,
Sent from whose sovran goodness I adore!
Gentle to me and affable hath been
Thy condescension, and shall be honoured ever
With grateful memory: Thou to mankind
Be good and friendly still, and oft return!"
So parted they; the Angel up to Heaven
From the thick shade, and Adam to his bower.

BOOK IX

No more of talk where God or Angel guest
With Man, as with his friend, familiar us'd,
To sit indulgent, and with him partake
Rural repast; permitting him the while
Venial discourse unblam'd. I now must change
Those notes to tragic; foul distrust, and breach
Disloyal on the part of Man, revolt,
And disobedience: on the part of Heaven
Now alienated, distance and distaste,
Anger and just rebuke, and judgement given,
That brought into this world a world of woe,
Sin and her shadow Death, and Misery
Death's harbinger: Sad task! yet argument
Not less but more heroic than the wrath
Of stern Achilles on his foe pursued
Thrice fugitive about Troy wall; or rage
Of Turnus for Lavinia disespous'd;
Or Neptune's ire, or Juno's, that so long
Perplexed the Greek, and Cytherea's son:
If answerable style I can obtain
Of my celestial patroness, who deigns
Her nightly visitation unimplor'd,

And dictates to me slumbering; or inspires
Easy my unpremeditated verse:
Since first this subject for heroic song
Pleas'd me long choosing, and beginning late;
Not sedulous by nature to indite
Wars, hitherto the only argument
Heroic deem'd chief mastery to dissect
With long and tedious havock fabled knights
In battles feign'd; the better fortitude
Of patience and heroic martyrdom
Unsung; or to describe races and games,
Or tilting furniture, imblazon'd shields,
Impresses quaint, caparisons and steeds,
Bases and tinsel trappings, gorgeous knights
At joust and tournament; then marshall'd feast
Serv'd up in hall with sewers and seneshals;
The skill of artifice or office mean,
Not that which justly gives heroic name
To person, or to poem. Me, of these
Nor skill'd nor studious, higher argument
Remains; sufficient of itself to raise
That name, unless an age too late, or cold
Climate, or years, damp my intended wing
Depress'd; and much they may, if all be mine,
Not hers, who brings it nightly to my ear.
The sun was sunk, and after him the star
Of Hesperus, whose office is to bring
Twilight upon the earth, short arbiter
'Twixt day and night, and now from end to end
Night's hemisphere had veil'd the horizon round:
When satan, who late fled before the threats
Of Gabriel out of Eden, now improv'd
In meditated fraud and malice, bent
On Man's destruction, maugre what might hap
Of heavier on himself, fearless returned

By night he fled, and at midnight returned
From compassing the earth; cautious of day,
Since Uriel, regent of the sun, descried
His entrance, and forewarned the Cherubim
That kept their watch; thence full of anguish driven,
The space of seven continued nights he rode
With darkness; thrice the equinoctial line
He circled; four times crossed the car of night
From pole to pole, traversing each colure;
On the eighth returned; and, on the coast averse
From entrance or Cherubic watch, by stealth
Found unsuspected way. There was a place,
Now not, though sin, not time, first wrought the change,
Where Tigris, at the foot of Paradise,
Into a gulf shot under ground, till part
Rose up a fountain by the tree of life:
In with the river sunk, and with it rose
Satan, involved in rising mist; then sought
Where to lie hid; sea he had searched, and land,
From Eden over Pontus and the pool
Maeotis, up beyond the river Ob;
Downward as far antarctic; and in length,
West from Orontes to the ocean barred
At Darien; thence to the land where flows
Ganges and Indus: Thus the orb he roamed
With narrow search; and with inspection deep
Considered every creature, which of all
Most opportune might serve his wiles; and found
The Serpent subtlest beast of all the field.
Him after long debate, irresolute
Of thoughts revolved, his final sentence chose
Fit vessel, fittest imp of fraud, in whom
To enter, and his dark suggestions hide
From sharpest sight: for, in the wily snake
Whatever sleights, none would suspicious mark,

As from his wit and native subtlety
Proceeding; which, in other beasts observed,
Doubt might beget of diabolic power
Active within, beyond the sense of brute.
Thus he resolved, but first from inward grief
His bursting passion into plaints thus poured.
More justly, seat worthier of Gods, as built
With second thoughts, reforming what was old!
"O Earth, how like to Heaven, if not preferred
For what God, after better, worse would build?
Terrestrial Heaven, danced round by other Heavens
That shine, yet bear their bright officious lamps,
Light above light, for thee alone, as seems,
In thee concentring all their precious beams
Of sacred influence! As God in Heaven
Is center, yet extends to all; so thou,
Centring, receivest from all those orbs: in thee,
Not in themselves, all their known virtue appears
Productive in herb, plant, and nobler birth
Of creatures animate with gradual life
Of growth, sense, reason, all summed up in Man.
With what delight could I have walked thee round,
If I could joy in aught, sweet interchange
Of hill, and valley, rivers, woods, and plains,
Now land, now sea and shores with forest crowned,
Rocks, dens, and caves! But I in none of these
Find place or refuge; and the more I see
Pleasures about me, so much more I feel
Torment within me, as from the hateful siege
Of contraries: all good to me becomes
Bane, and in Heaven much worse would be my state.
But neither here seek I, no nor in Heaven
To dwell, unless by mastering Heaven's Supreme;
Nor hope to be myself less miserable
By what I seek, but others to make such

As I, though thereby worse to me redound:
For only in destroying I find ease
To my relentless thoughts; and, him destroyed,
Or won to what may work his utter loss,
For whom all this was made, all this will soon
Follow, as to him linked in weal or woe;
In woe then; that destruction wide may range:
To me shall be the glory sole among
The infernal Powers, in one day to have marred
What he, Almighty styled, six nights and days
Continued making; and who knows how long
Before had been contriving? though perhaps
Not longer than since I, in one night, freed
From servitude inglorious well nigh half
The angelic name, and thinner left the throng
Of his adorers: He, to be avenged,
And to repair his numbers thus impaired,
Whether such virtue spent of old now failed
More Angels to create, if they at least
Are his created, or, to spite us more,
Determined to advance into our room
A creature formed of earth, and him endow,
Exalted from so base original,
With heavenly spoils, our spoils: What he decreed,
He effected; Man he made, and for him built
Magnificent this world, and earth his seat,
Him lord pronounced; and, O indignity!
Subjected to his service angel-wings,
And flaming ministers to watch and tend
Their earthly charge: Of these the vigilance
I dread; and, to elude, thus wrapt in mist
Of midnight vapour glide obscure, and pry
In every bush and brake, where hap may find
The serpent sleeping; in whose mazy folds
To hide me, and the dark intent I bring.

O foul descent! that I, who erst contended
With Gods to sit the highest, am now constrained
Into a beast; and, mixed with bestial slime,
This essence to incarnate and imbrute,
That to the hight of Deity aspired!
But what will not ambition and revenge
Descend to? Who aspires, must down as low
As high he soared; obnoxious, first or last,
To basest things. Revenge, at first though sweet,
Bitter ere long, back on itself recoils:
Let it; I reck not, so it light well aimed,
Since higher I fall short, on him who next
Provokes my envy, this new favourite
Of Heaven, this man of clay, son of despite,
Whom, us the more to spite, his Maker raised
From dust: Spite then with spite is best repaid."
So saying, through each thicket dank or dry,
Like a black mist low-creeping, he held on
His midnight-search, where soonest he might find
The serpent; him fast-sleeping soon he found
In labyrinth of many a round self-rolled,
His head the midst, well stored with subtile wiles:
Not yet in horrid shade or dismal den,
Nor nocent yet; but, on the grassy herb,
Fearless unfeared he slept: in at his mouth
The Devil entered; and his brutal sense,
In heart or head, possessing, soon inspired
With act intelligential; but his sleep
Disturbed not, waiting close the approach of morn.
Now, when as sacred light began to dawn
In Eden on the humid flowers, that breathed
Their morning incense, when all things, that breathe,
From the Earth's great altar send up silent praise
To the Creator, and his nostrils fill
With grateful smell, forth came the human pair,

And joined their vocal worship to the quire
Of creatures wanting voice; that done, partake
The season prime for sweetest scents and airs:
Then commune, how that day they best may ply
Their growing work: for much their work out-grew
The hands' dispatch of two gardening so wide,
And Eve first to her husband thus began.
"Adam, well may we labour still to dress
This garden, still to tend plant, herb, and flower,
Our pleasant task enjoined; but, till more hands
Aid us, the work under our labour grows,
Luxurious by restraint; what we by day
Lop overgrown, or prune, or prop, or bind,
One night or two with wanton growth derides
Tending to wild. Thou therefore now advise,
Or bear what to my mind first thoughts present:
Let us divide our labours; thou, where choice
Leads thee, or where most needs, whether to wind
The woodbine round this arbour, or direct
The clasping ivy where to climb; while I,
In yonder spring of roses intermixed
With myrtle, find what to redress till noon:
For, while so near each other thus all day
Our task we choose, what wonder if so near
Looks intervene and smiles, or object new
Casual discourse draw on; which intermits
Our day's work, brought to little, though begun
Early, and the hour of supper comes unearned?"
To whom mild answer Adam thus returned.
"Sole Eve, associate sole, to me beyond
Compare above all living creatures dear!
Well hast thou motioned, well thy thoughts employed,
How we might best fulfil the work which here
God hath assigned us; nor of me shalt pass
Unpraised: for nothing lovelier can be found

In woman, than to study household good,
And good works in her husband to promote.
Yet not so strictly hath our Lord imposed
Labour, as to debar us when we need
Refreshment, whether food, or talk between,
Food of the mind, or this sweet intercourse
Of looks and smiles; for smiles from reason flow,
To brute denied, and are of love the food;
Love, not the lowest end of human life.
For not to irksome toil, but to delight,
He made us, and delight to reason joined.
These paths and bowers doubt not but our joint hands
Will keep from wilderness with ease, as wide
As we need walk, till younger hands ere long
Assist us; But, if much converse perhaps
Thee satiate, to short absence I could yield:
For solitude sometimes is best society,
And short retirement urges sweet return.
But other doubt possesses me, lest harm
Befall thee severed from me; for thou knowest
What hath been warned us, what malicious foe
Envying our happiness, and of his own
Despairing, seeks to work us woe and shame
By sly assault; and somewhere nigh at hand
Watches, no doubt, with greedy hope to find
His wish and best advantage, us asunder;
Hopeless to circumvent us joined, where each
To other speedy aid might lend at need:
Whether his first design be to withdraw
Our fealty from God, or to disturb
Conjugal love, than which perhaps no bliss
Enjoyed by us excites his envy more;
Or this, or worse, leave not the faithful side
That gave thee being, still shades thee, and protects.
The wife, where danger or dishonour lurks,

Safest and seemliest by her husband stays,
Who guards her, or with her the worst endures."
To whom the virgin majesty of Eve,
As one who loves, and some unkindness meets,
With sweet austere composure thus replied.
"Offspring of Heaven and Earth, and all Earth's Lord!
That such an enemy we have, who seeks
Our ruin, both by thee informed I learn,
And from the parting Angel over-heard,
As in a shady nook I stood behind,
Just then returned at shut of evening flowers.
But, that thou shouldst my firmness therefore doubt
To God or thee, because we have a foe
May tempt it, I expected not to hear.
His violence thou fearest not, being such
As we, not capable of death or pain,
Can either not receive, or can repel.
His fraud is then thy fear; which plain infers
Thy equal fear, that my firm faith and love
Can by his fraud be shaken or seduced;
Thoughts, which how found they harbour in thy breast,
Adam, mis-thought of her to thee so dear?"
To whom with healing words Adam replied.
"Daughter of God and Man, immortal Eve!
For such thou art; from sin and blame entire:
Not diffident of thee do I dissuade
Thy absence from my sight, but to avoid
The attempt itself, intended by our foe.
For he who tempts, though in vain, at least asperses
The tempted with dishonour foul; supposed
Not incorruptible of faith, not proof
Against temptation: Thou thyself with scorn
And anger wouldst resent the offered wrong,
Though ineffectual found: misdeem not then,
If such affront I labour to avert

From thee alone, which on us both at once
The enemy, though bold, will hardly dare;
Or daring, first on me the assault shall light.
Nor thou his malice and false guile contemn;
Subtle he needs must be, who could seduce
Angels; nor think superfluous other's aid.
I, from the influence of thy looks, receive
Access in every virtue; in thy sight
More wise, more watchful, stronger, if need were
Of outward strength; while shame, thou looking on,
Shame to be overcome or over-reached,
Would utmost vigour raise, and raised unite.
Why shouldst not thou like sense within thee feel
When I am present, and thy trial choose
With me, best witness of thy virtue tried?"
So spake domestick Adam in his care
And matrimonial love; but Eve, who thought
Less attributed to her faith sincere,
Thus her reply with accent sweet renewed.
"If this be our condition, thus to dwell
In narrow circuit straitened by a foe,
Subtle or violent, we not endued
Single with like defence, wherever met;
How are we happy, still in fear of harm?
But harm precedes not sin: only our foe,
Tempting, affronts us with his foul esteem
Of our integrity: his foul esteem
Sticks no dishonour on our front, but turns
Foul on himself; then wherefore shunned or feared
By us? who rather double honour gain
From his surmise proved false; find peace within,
Favour from Heaven, our witness, from the event.
And what is faith, love, virtue, unassayed
Alone, without exteriour help sustained?
Let us not then suspect our happy state

Left so imperfect by the Maker wise,
As not secure to single or combined.
Frail is our happiness, if this be so,
And Eden were no Eden, thus exposed."
To whom thus Adam fervently replied.
"O Woman, best are all things as the will
Of God ordained them: His creating hand
Nothing imperfect or deficient left
Of all that he created, much less Man,
Or aught that might his happy state secure,
Secure from outward force; within himself
The danger lies, yet lies within his power:
Against his will he can receive no harm.
But God left free the will; for what obeys
Reason, is free; and Reason he made right,
But bid her well be ware, and still erect;
Lest, by some fair-appearing good surprised,
She dictate false; and mis-inform the will
To do what God expressly hath forbid.
Not then mistrust, but tender love, enjoins,
That I should mind thee oft; and mind thou me.
Firm we subsist, yet possible to swerve;
Since Reason not impossibly may meet
Some specious object by the foe suborned,
And fall into deception unaware,
Not keeping strictest watch, as she was warned.
Seek not temptation then, which to avoid
Were better, and most likely if from me
Thou sever not: Trial will come unsought.
Wouldst thou approve thy constancy, approve
First thy obedience; the other who can know,
Not seeing thee attempted, who attest?
But, if thou think, trial unsought may find
Us both securer than thus warned thou seemest,
Go; for thy stay, not free, absents thee more;

Go in thy native innocence, rely
On what thou hast of virtue; summon all!
For God towards thee hath done his part, do thine."
So spake the patriarch of mankind; but Eve
Persisted; yet submiss, though last, replied.
"With thy permission then, and thus forewarned
Chiefly by what thy own last reasoning words
Touched only; that our trial, when least sought,
May find us both perhaps far less prepared,
The willinger I go, nor much expect
A foe so proud will first the weaker seek;
So bent, the more shall shame him his repulse."
Thus saying, from her husband's hand her hand
Soft she withdrew; and, like a Wood-Nymph light,
Oread or Dryad, or of Delia's train,
Betook her to the groves; but Delia's self
In gait surpassed, and Goddess-like deport,
Though not as she with bow and quiver armed,
But with such gardening tools as Art yet rude,
Guiltless of fire, had formed, or Angels brought.
To Pales, or Pomona, thus adorned,
Likest she seemed, Pomona when she fled
Vertumnus, or to Ceres in her prime,
Yet virgin of Proserpina from Jove.
Her long with ardent look his eye pursued
Delighted, but desiring more her stay.
Oft he to her his charge of quick return
Repeated; she to him as oft engaged
To be returned by noon amid the bower,
And all things in best order to invite
Noontide repast, or afternoon's repose.
O much deceived, much failing, hapless Eve,
Of thy presumed return! event perverse!
Thou never from that hour in Paradise
Foundst either sweet repast, or sound repose;

Such ambush, hid among sweet flowers and shades,
Waited with hellish rancour imminent
To intercept thy way, or send thee back
Despoiled of innocence, of faith, of bliss!
For now, and since first break of dawn, the Fiend,
Mere serpent in appearance, forth was come;
And on his quest, where likeliest he might find
The only two of mankind, but in them
The whole included race, his purposed prey.
In bower and field he sought, where any tuft
Of grove or garden-plot more pleasant lay,
Their tendance, or plantation for delight;
By fountain or by shady rivulet
He sought them both, but wished his hap might find
Eve separate; he wished, but not with hope
Of what so seldom chanced; when to his wish,
Beyond his hope, Eve separate he spies,
Veiled in a cloud of fragrance, where she stood,
Half spied, so thick the roses blushing round
About her glowed, oft stooping to support
Each flower of slender stalk, whose head, though gay
Carnation, purple, azure, or specked with gold,
Hung drooping unsustained; them she upstays
Gently with myrtle band, mindless the while
Herself, though fairest unsupported flower,
From her best prop so far, and storm so nigh.
Nearer he drew, and many a walk traversed
Of stateliest covert, cedar, pine, or palm;
Then voluble and bold, now hid, now seen,
Among thick-woven arborets, and flowers
Embordered on each bank, the hand of Eve:
Spot more delicious than those gardens feigned
Or of revived Adonis, or renowned
Alcinous, host of old Laertes' son;
Or that, not mystick, where the sapient king

Held dalliance with his fair Egyptian spouse.
Much he the place admired, the person more.
As one who long in populous city pent,
Where houses thick and sewers annoy the air,
Forth issuing on a summer's morn, to breathe
Among the pleasant villages and farms
Adjoined, from each thing met conceives delight;
The smell of grain, or tedded grass, or kine,
Or dairy, each rural sight, each rural sound;
If chance, with nymph-like step, fair virgin pass,
What pleasing seemed, for her now pleases more;
She most, and in her look sums all delight:
Such pleasure took the Serpent to behold
This flowery plat, the sweet recess of Eve
Thus early, thus alone: Her heavenly form
Angelic, but more soft, and feminine,
Her graceful innocence, her every air
Of gesture, or least action, overawed
His malice, and with rapine sweet bereaved
His fierceness of the fierce intent it brought:
That space the Evil-one abstracted stood
From his own evil, and for the time remained
Stupidly good; of enmity disarmed,
Of guile, of hate, of envy, of revenge:
But the hot Hell that always in him burns,
Though in mid Heaven, soon ended his delight,
And tortures him now more, the more he sees
Of pleasure, not for him ordained: then soon
Fierce hate he recollects, and all his thoughts
Of mischief, gratulating, thus excites.
"Thoughts, whither have ye led me! with what sweet
Compulsion thus transported, to forget
What hither brought us! hate, not love; nor hope
Of Paradise for Hell, hope here to taste
Of pleasure; but all pleasure to destroy,

Save what is in destroying; other joy
To me is lost. Then, let me not let pass
Occasion which now smiles; behold alone
The woman, opportune to all attempts,
Her husband, for I view far round, not nigh,
Whose higher intellectual more I shun,
And strength, of courage haughty, and of limb
Heroic built, though of terrestrial mould;
Foe not informidable! exempt from wound,
I not; so much hath Hell debased, and pain
Enfeebled me, to what I was in Heaven.
She fair, divinely fair, fit love for Gods!
Not terrible, though terrour be in love
And beauty, not approached by stronger hate,
Hate stronger, under show of love well feigned;
The way which to her ruin now I tend."
So spake the enemy of mankind, enclosed
In serpent, inmate bad! and toward Eve
Addressed his way: not with indented wave,
Prone on the ground, as since; but on his rear,
Circular base of rising folds, that towered
Fold above fold, a surging maze! his head
Crested aloft, and carbuncle his eyes;
With burnished neck of verdant gold, erect
Amidst his circling spires, that on the grass
Floated redundant: pleasing was his shape
And lovely; never since of serpent-kind
Lovelier, not those that in Illyria changed,
Hermione and Cadmus, or the god
In Epidaurus; nor to which transformed
Ammonian Jove, or Capitoline, was seen;
He with Olympias; this with her who bore
Scipio, the hight of Rome. With tract oblique
At first, as one who sought access, but feared
To interrupt, side-long he works his way.

As when a ship, by skilful steersmen wrought
Nigh river's mouth or foreland, where the wind
Veers oft, as oft so steers, and shifts her sail:
So varied he, and of his tortuous train
Curled many a wanton wreath in sight of Eve,
To lure her eye; she, busied, heard the sound
Of rusling leaves, but minded not, as used
To such disport before her through the field,
From every beast; more duteous at her call,
Than at Circean call the herd disguised.
He, bolder now, uncalled before her stood,
But as in gaze admiring: oft he bowed
His turret crest, and sleek enamelled neck,
Fawning; and licked the ground whereon she trod.
His gentle dumb expression turned at length
The eye of Eve to mark his play; he, glad
Of her attention gained, with serpent-tongue
Organick, or impulse of vocal air,
His fraudulent temptation thus began.
"Wonder not, sovran Mistress, if perhaps
Thou canst, who art sole wonder! much less arm
Thy looks, the Heaven of mildness, with disdain,
Displeased that I approach thee thus, and gaze
Insatiate; I thus single; nor have feared
Thy awful brow, more awful thus retired.
Fairest resemblance of thy Maker fair,
Thee all things living gaze on, all things thine
By gift, and thy celestial beauty adore
With ravishment beheld! there best beheld,
Where universally admired; but here
In this enclosure wild, these beasts among,
Beholders rude, and shallow to discern
Half what in thee is fair, one man except,
Who sees thee? and what is one? who should be seen
A Goddess among Gods, adored and served

By Angels numberless, thy daily train."
So glozed the Tempter, and his proem tuned:
Into the heart of Eve his words made way,
Though at the voice much marvelling; at length,
Not unamazed, she thus in answer spake.
"What may this mean? language of man pronounced
By tongue of brute, and human sense expressed?
The first, at least, of these I thought denied
To beasts; whom God, on their creation-day,
Created mute to all articulate sound:
The latter I demur; for in their looks
Much reason, and in their actions, oft appears.
Thee, Serpent, subtlest beast of all the field
I knew, but not with human voice endued;
Redouble then this miracle, and say,
How camest thou speakable of mute, and how
To me so friendly grown above the rest
Of brutal kind, that daily are in sight?
Say, for such wonder claims attention due."
To whom the guileful Tempter thus replied.
"Empress of this fair world, resplendent Eve!
Easy to me it is to tell thee all
What thou commandest; and right thou shouldst be
    obeyed:
I was at first as other beasts that graze
The trodden herb, of abject thoughts and low,
As was my food; nor aught but food discerned
Or sex, and apprehended nothing high:
Till, on a day roving the field, I chanced
A goodly tree far distant to behold
Loaden with fruit of fairest colours mixed,
Ruddy and gold: I nearer drew to gaze;
When from the boughs a savoury odour blown,
Grateful to appetite, more pleased my sense
Than smell of sweetest fennel, or the teats

Of ewe or goat dropping with milk at even,
Unsucked of lamb or kid, that tend their play.
To satisfy the sharp desire I had
Of tasting those fair apples, I resolved
Not to defer; hunger and thirst at once,
Powerful persuaders, quickened at the scent
Of that alluring fruit, urged me so keen.
About the mossy trunk I wound me soon;
For, high from ground, the branches would require
Thy utmost reach or Adam's: Round the tree
All other beasts that saw, with like desire
Longing and envying stood, but could not reach.
Amid the tree now got, where plenty hung
Tempting so nigh, to pluck and eat my fill
I spared not; for, such pleasure till that hour,
At feed or fountain, never had I found.
Sated at length, ere long I might perceive
Strange alteration in me, to degree
Of reason in my inward powers; and speech
Wanted not long; though to this shape retained.
Thenceforth to speculations high or deep
I turned my thoughts, and with capacious mind
Considered all things visible in Heaven,
Or Earth, or Middle; all things fair and good:
But all that fair and good in thy divine
Semblance, and in thy beauty's heavenly ray,
United I beheld; no fair to thine
Equivalent or second! which compelled
Me thus, though importune perhaps, to come
And gaze, and worship thee of right declared
Sovran of creatures, universal Dame!"
So talked the spirited sly Snake; and Eve,
Yet more amazed, unwary thus replied.
"Serpent, thy overpraising leaves in doubt
The virtue of that fruit, in thee first proved:

But say, where grows the tree? from hence how far?
For many are the trees of God that grow
In Paradise, and various, yet unknown
To us; in such abundance lies our choice,
As leaves a greater store of fruit untouched,
Still hanging incorruptible, till men
Grow up to their provision, and more hands
Help to disburden Nature of her birth."
To whom the wily Adder, blithe and glad.
"Empress, the way is ready, and not long;
Beyond a row of myrtles, on a flat,
Fast by a fountain, one small thicket past
Of blowing myrrh and balm: if thou accept
My conduct, I can bring thee thither soon."
"Lead then," said Eve. He, leading, swiftly rolled
In tangles, and made intricate seem straight,
To mischief swift. Hope elevates, and joy
Brightens his crest; as when a wandering fire,
Compact of unctuous vapour, which the night
Condenses, and the cold environs round,
Kindled through agitation to a flame,
Which oft, they say, some evil Spirit attends,
Hovering and blazing with delusive light,
Misleads the amazed night-wanderer from his way
To bogs and mires, and oft through pond or pool;
There swallowed up and lost, from succour far.
So glistered the dire Snake, and into fraud
Led Eve, our credulous mother, to the tree
Of prohibition, root of all our woe;
Which when she saw, thus to her guide she spake.
"Serpent, we might have spared our coming hither,
Fruitless to me, though fruit be here to excess,
The credit of whose virtue rest with thee;
Wonderous indeed, if cause of such effects.
But of this tree we may not taste nor touch;

God so commanded, and left that command
Sole daughter of his voice; the rest, we live
Law to ourselves; our reason is our law."
To whom the Tempter guilefully replied.
"Indeed! hath God then said that of the fruit
Of all these garden-trees ye shall not eat,
Yet Lords declared of all in earth or air?"
To whom thus Eve, yet sinless: "Of the fruit
Of each tree in the garden we may eat;
But of the fruit of this fair tree amidst
The garden, God hath said, 'Ye shall not eat
Thereof, nor shall ye touch it, lest ye die.'"
She scarce had said, though brief, when now more bold
The Tempter, but with show of zeal and love
To Man, and indignation at his wrong,
New part puts on; and, as to passion moved,
Fluctuates disturbed, yet comely and in act
Raised, as of some great matter to begin.
As when of old some orator renowned,
In Athens or free Rome, where eloquence
Flourished, since mute! to some great cause addressed,
Stood in himself collected; while each part,
Motion, each act, won audience ere the tongue;
Sometimes in hight began, as no delay
Of preface brooking, through his zeal of right:
So standing, moving, or to hight up grown,
The Tempter, all impassioned, thus began.
"O sacred, wise, and wisdom-giving Plant,
Mother of science! now I feel thy power
Within me clear; not only to discern
Things in their causes, but to trace the ways
Of highest agents, deemed however wise.
Queen of this universe! do not believe
Those rigid threats of death: ye shall not die:
How should you? by the fruit? it gives you life

To knowledge; by the threatener? look on me,
Me, who have touched and tasted; yet both live,
And life more perfect have attained than Fate
Meant me, by venturing higher than my lot.
Shall that be shut to Man, which to the Beast
Is open? or will God incense his ire
For such a petty trespass? and not praise
Rather your dauntless virtue, whom the pain
Of death denounced, whatever thing death be,
Deterred not from achieving what might lead
To happier life, knowledge of good and evil;
Of good, how just? of evil, if what is evil
Be real, why not known, since easier shunned?
God therefore cannot hurt ye, and be just;
Not just, not God; not feared then, nor obeyed:
Your fear itself of death removes the fear.
Why then was this forbid? Why, but to awe;
Why, but to keep ye low and ignorant,
His worshippers? He knows that in the day
Ye eat thereof, your eyes that seem so clear,
Yet are but dim, shall perfectly be then
Opened and cleared, and ye shall be as Gods,
Knowing both good and evil, as they know.
That ye shall be as Gods, since I as Man,
Internal Man, is but proportion meet;
I, of brute, human; ye, of human, Gods.
So ye shall die perhaps, by putting off
Human, to put on Gods; death to be wished,
Though threatened, which no worse than this can bring.
And what are Gods, that Man may not become
As they, participating God-like food?
The Gods are first, and that advantage use
On our belief, that all from them proceeds:
I question it; for this fair earth I see,
Warmed by the sun, producing every kind;

Them, nothing: if they all things, who enclosed
Knowledge of good and evil in this tree,
That whoso eats thereof, forthwith attains
Wisdom without their leave? and wherein lies
The offence, that Man should thus attain to know?
What can your knowledge hurt him, or this tree
Impart against his will, if all be his?
Or is it envy? and can envy dwell
In heavenly breasts? These, these, and many more
Causes import your need of this fair fruit.
Goddess humane, reach then, and freely taste!"
He ended; and his words, replete with guile,
Into her heart too easy entrance won:
Fixed on the fruit she gazed, which to behold
Might tempt alone; and in her ears the sound
Yet rung of his persuasive words, impregned
With reason, to her seeming, and with truth:
Meanwhile the hour of noon drew on, and waked
An eager appetite, raised by the smell
So savoury of that fruit, which with desire,
Inclinable now grown to touch or taste,
Solicited her longing eye; yet first
Pausing a while, thus to herself she mused.
"Great are thy virtues, doubtless, best of fruits,
Though kept from man, and worthy to be admired;
Whose taste, too long forborn, at first assay
Gave elocution to the mute, and taught
The tongue not made for speech to speak thy praise:
Thy praise he also, who forbids thy use,
Conceals not from us, naming thee the tree
Of knowledge, knowledge both of good and evil;
Forbids us then to taste! but his forbidding
Commends thee more, while it infers the good
By thee communicated, and our want:
For good unknown sure is not had; or, had

And yet unknown, is as not had at all.
In plain then, what forbids he but to know,
Forbids us good, forbids us to be wise?
Such prohibitions bind not. But, if death
Bind us with after-bands, what profits then
Our inward freedom? In the day we eat
Of this fair fruit, our doom is, we shall die!
How dies the Serpent? he hath eaten and lives,
And knows, and speaks, and reasons, and discerns,
Irrational till then. For us alone
Was death invented? or to us denied
This intellectual food, for beasts reserved?
For beasts it seems: yet that one beast which first
Hath tasted envies not, but brings with joy
The good befallen him, author unsuspect,
Friendly to man, far from deceit or guile.
What fear I then? rather, what know to fear
Under this ignorance of good and evil,
Of God or death, of law or penalty?
Here grows the cure of all, this fruit divine,
Fair to the eye, inviting to the taste,
Of virtue to make wise: What hinders then
To reach, and feed at once both body and mind?"
So saying, her rash hand in evil hour
Forth reaching to the fruit, she plucked, she eat!
Earth felt the wound; and Nature from her seat,
Sighing through all her works, gave signs of woe,
That all was lost. Back to the thicket slunk
The guilty Serpent; and well might; for Eve,
Intent now wholly on her taste, nought else
Regarded; such delight till then, as seemed,
In fruit she never tasted, whether true
Or fancied so, through expectation high
Of knowledge; not was Godhead from her thought.
Greedily she ingorged without restraint,

And knew not eating death: Satiate at length,
And hightened as with wine, jocund and boon,
Thus to herself she pleasingly began.
"O sovran, virtuous, precious of all trees
In Paradise! of operation blest
To sapience, hitherto obscured, infamed.
And thy fair fruit let hang, as to no end
Created; but henceforth my early care,
Not without song, each morning, and due praise,
Shall tend thee, and the fertile burden ease
Of thy full branches offered free to all;
Till, dieted by thee, I grow mature
In knowledge, as the Gods, who all things know;
Though others envy what they cannot give:
For, had the gift been theirs, it had not here
Thus grown. Experience, next, to thee I owe,
Best guide; not following thee, I had remained
In ignorance; thou openest wisdom's way,
And givest access, though secret she retire.
And I perhaps am secret: Heaven is high,
High, and remote to see from thence distinct
Each thing on Earth; and other care perhaps
May have diverted from continual watch
Our great Forbidder, safe with all his spies
About him. But to Adam in what sort
Shall I appear? shall I to him make known
As yet my change, and give him to partake
Full happiness with me, or rather not,
But keeps the odds of knowledge in my power
Without copartner? so to add what wants
In female sex, the more to draw his love,
And render me more equal; and perhaps,
A thing not undesirable, sometime
Superior; for, inferior, who is free
This may be well: But what if God have seen,

And death ensue? then I shall be no more!
And Adam, wedded to another Eve,
Shall live with her enjoying, I extinct;
A death to think! Confirmed then I resolve,
Adam shall share with me in bliss or woe:
So dear I love him, that with him all deaths
I could endure, without him live no life."
So saying, from the tree her step she turned;
But first low reverence done, as to the Power
That dwelt within, whose presence had infused
Into the plant sciential sap, derived
From nectar, drink of Gods. Adam the while,
Waiting desirous her return, had wove
Of choicest flowers a garland, to adorn
Her tresses, and her rural labours crown;
As reapers oft are wont their harvest-queen.
Great joy he promised to his thoughts, and new
Solace in her return, so long delayed:
Yet oft his heart, divine of something ill,
Misgave him; he the faltering measure felt;
And forth to meet her went, the way she took
That morn when first they parted: by the tree
Of knowledge he must pass; there he her met,
Scarce from the tree returning; in her hand
A bough of fairest fruit, that downy smiled,
New gathered, and ambrosial smell diffused.
To him she hasted; in her face excuse
Came prologue, and apology too prompt;
Which, with bland words at will, she thus addressed.
"Hast thou not wondered, Adam, at my stay?
Thee I have missed, and thought it long, deprived
Thy presence; agony of love till now
Not felt, nor shall be twice; for never more
Mean I to try, what rash untried I sought,
The pain of absence from thy sight. But strange

Hath been the cause, and wonderful to hear:
This tree is not, as we are told, a tree
Of danger tasted, nor to evil unknown
Opening the way, but of divine effect
To open eyes, and make them Gods who taste;
And hath been tasted such: The serpent wise,
Or not restrained as we, or not obeying,
Hath eaten of the fruit; and is become,
Not dead, as we are threatened, but thenceforth
Endued with human voice and human sense,
Reasoning to admiration; and with me
Persuasively hath so prevailed, that I
Have also tasted, and have also found
The effects to correspond; opener mine eyes,
Dim erst, dilated spirits, ampler heart,
And growing up to Godhead; which for thee
Chiefly I sought, without thee can despise.
For bliss, as thou hast part, to me is bliss;
Tedious, unshared with thee, and odious soon.
Thou therefore also taste, that equal lot
May join us, equal joy, as equal love;
Lest, thou not tasting, different degree
Disjoin us, and I then too late renounce
Deity for thee, when Fate will not permit."
Thus Eve with countenance blithe her story told;
But in her cheek distemper flushing glowed.
On the other side Adam, soon as he heard
The fatal trespass done by Eve, amazed,
Astonied stood and blank, while horror chill
Ran through his veins, and all his joints relaxed;
From his slack hand the garland wreathed for Eve
Down dropt, and all the faded roses shed:
Speechless he stood and pale, till thus at length
First to himself he inward silence broke.
"O fairest of Creation, last and best

Of all God's works, Creature in whom excelled
Whatever can to sight or thought be formed,
Holy, divine, good, amiable, or sweet!
How art thou lost! how on a sudden lost,
Defaced, deflowered, and now to death devote!
Rather, how hast thou yielded to transgress
The strict forbiddance, how to violate
The sacred fruit forbidden! Some cursed fraud
Of enemy hath beguiled thee, yet unknown,
And me with thee hath ruined; for with thee
Certain my resolution is to die:
How can I live without thee! how forego
Thy sweet converse, and love so dearly joined,
To live again in these wild woods forlorn!
Should God create another Eve, and I
Another rib afford, yet loss of thee
Would never from my heart: no, no! I feel
The link of Nature draw me: flesh of flesh,
Bone of my bone thou art, and from thy state
Mine never shall be parted, bliss or woe."
So having said, as one from sad dismay
Recomforted, and after thoughts disturbed
Submitting to what seemed remediless,
Thus in calm mood his words to Eve he turned.
"Bold deed thou hast presumed, adventurous Eve,
And peril great provoked, who thus hast dared,
Had it been only coveting to eye
That sacred fruit, sacred to abstinence,
Much more to taste it under ban to touch.
But past who can recall, or done undo?
Not God Omnipotent, nor Fate; yet so
Perhaps thou shalt not die, perhaps the fact
Is not so heinous now, foretasted fruit,
Profaned first by the serpent, by him first
Made common, and unhallowed, ere our taste;

Nor yet on him found deadly; yet he lives;
Lives, as thou saidst, and gains to live, as Man,
Higher degree of life; inducement strong
To us, as likely tasting to attain
Proportional ascent; which cannot be
But to be Gods, or Angels, demi-Gods.
Nor can I think that God, Creator wise,
Though threatening, will in earnest so destroy
Us his prime creatures, dignified so high,
Set over all his works; which in our fall,
For us created, needs with us must fail,
Dependant made; so God shall uncreate,
Be frustrate, do, undo, and labour lose;
Not well conceived of God, who, though his power
Creation could repeat, yet would be loth
Us to abolish, lest the Adversary
Triumph, and say; 'Fickle their state whom God
Most favours; who can please him long? Me first
He ruined, now Mankind; whom will he next?'
Matter of scorn, not to be given the Foe.
However I with thee have fixed my lot,
Certain to undergo like doom: If death
Consort with thee, death is to me as life;
So forcible within my heart I feel
The bond of Nature draw me to my own;
My own in thee, for what thou art is mine;
Our state cannot be severed; we are one,
One flesh; to lose thee were to lose myself."
So Adam; and thus Eve to him replied.
"O glorious trial of exceeding love,
Illustrious evidence, example high!
Engaging me to emulate; but, short
Of thy perfection, how shall I attain,
Adam, from whose dear side I boast me sprung,
And gladly of our union hear thee speak,

One heart, one soul in both; whereof good proof
This day affords, declaring thee resolved,
Rather than death, or aught than death more dread,
Shall separate us, linked in love so dear,
To undergo with me one guilt, one crime,
If any be, of tasting this fair fruit;
Whose virtue for of good still good proceeds,
Direct, or by occasion, hath presented
This happy trial of thy love, which else
So eminently never had been known?
Were it I thought death menaced would ensue
This my attempt, I would sustain alone
The worst, and not persuade thee, rather die
Deserted, than oblige thee with a fact
Pernicious to thy peace; chiefly assured
Remarkably so late of thy so true,
So faithful, love unequalled: but I feel
Far otherwise the event; not death, but life
Augmented, opened eyes, new hopes, new joys,
Taste so divine, that what of sweet before
Hath touched my sense, flat seems to this, and harsh.
On my experience, Adam, freely taste,
And fear of death deliver to the winds."
So saying, she embraced him, and for joy
Tenderly wept; much won, that he his love
Had so ennobled, as of choice to incur
Divine displeasure for her sake, or death.
In recompence (for such compliance bad
Such recompence best merits) from the bough
She gave him of that fair enticing fruit
With liberal hand: he scrupled not to eat,
Against his better knowledge; not deceived,
But fondly overcome with female charm.
Earth trembled from her entrails, as again
In pangs; and Nature gave a second groan;

Sky loured; and, muttering thunder, some sad drops
Wept at completing of the mortal sin
Original: while Adam took no thought,
Eating his fill; nor Eve to iterate
Her former trespass feared, the more to sooth
Him with her loved society; that now,
As with new wine intoxicated both,
They swim in mirth, and fancy that they feel
Divinity within them breeding wings,
Wherewith to scorn the earth: But that false fruit
Far other operation first displayed,
Carnal desire inflaming; he on Eve
Began to cast lascivious eyes; she him
As wantonly repaid; in lust they burn:
Till Adam thus 'gan Eve to dalliance move.
"Eve, now I see thou art exact of taste,
And elegant, of sapience no small part;
Since to each meaning savour we apply,
And palate call judicious; I the praise
Yield thee, so well this day thou hast purveyed.
Much pleasure we have lost, while we abstained
From this delightful fruit, nor known till now
True relish, tasting; if such pleasure be
In things to us forbidden, it might be wished,
For this one tree had been forbidden ten.
But come, so well refreshed, now let us play,
As meet is, after such delicious fare;
For never did thy beauty, since the day
I saw thee first and wedded thee, adorned
With all perfections, so inflame my sense
With ardour to enjoy thee, fairer now
Than ever; bounty of this virtuous tree!"
So said he, and forbore not glance or toy
Of amorous intent; well understood
Of Eve, whose eye darted contagious fire.

Her hand he seized; and to a shady bank,
Thick over-head with verdant roof embowered,
He led her nothing loth; flowers were the couch,
Pansies, and violets, and asphodel,
And hyacinth; Earth's freshest softest lap.
There they their fill of love and love's disport
Took largely, of their mutual guilt the seal,
The solace of their sin; till dewy sleep
Oppressed them, wearied with their amorous play,
Soon as the force of that fallacious fruit,
That with exhilarating vapour bland
About their spirits had played, and inmost powers
Made err, was now exhaled; and grosser sleep,
Bred of unkindly fumes, with conscious dreams
Encumbered, now had left them; up they rose
As from unrest; and, each the other viewing,
Soon found their eyes how opened, and their minds
How darkened; innocence, that as a veil
Had shadowed them from knowing ill, was gone;
Just confidence, and native righteousness,
And honour, from about them, naked left
To guilty Shame; he covered, but his robe
Uncovered more. So rose the Danite strong,
Herculean Samson, from the harlot-lap
Of Philistean Dalilah, and waked
Shorn of his strength. They destitute and bare
Of all their virtue: Silent, and in face
Confounded, long they sat, as strucken mute:
Till Adam, though not less than Eve abashed,
At length gave utterance to these words constrained.
"O Eve, in evil hour thou didst give ear
To that false worm, of whomsoever taught
To counterfeit Man's voice; true in our fall,
False in our promised rising; since our eyes
Opened we find indeed, and find we know

Both good and evil; good lost, and evil got;
Bad fruit of knowledge, if this be to know;
Which leaves us naked thus, of honour void,
Of innocence, of faith, of purity,
Our wonted ornaments now soiled and stained,
And in our faces evident the signs
Of foul concupiscence; whence evil store;
Even shame, the last of evils; of the first
Be sure then. How shall I behold the face
Henceforth of God or Angel, erst with joy
And rapture so oft beheld? Those heavenly shapes
Will dazzle now this earthly with their blaze
Insufferably bright. O! might I here
In solitude live savage; in some glade
Obscured, where highest woods, impenetrable
To star or sun-light, spread their umbrage broad
And brown as evening: Cover me, ye Pines!
Ye Cedars, with innumerable boughs
Hide me, where I may never see them more!—
But let us now, as in bad plight, devise
What best may for the present serve to hide
The parts of each from other, that seem most
To shame obnoxious, and unseemliest seen;
Some tree, whose broad smooth leaves together sewed,
And girded on our loins, may cover round
Those middle parts; that this new comer, Shame,
There sit not, and reproach us as unclean."
So counselled he, and both together went
Into the thickest wood; there soon they chose
The fig-tree; not that kind for fruit renowned,
But such as at this day, to Indians known,
In Malabar or Decan spreads her arms
Branching so broad and long, that in the ground
The bended twigs take root, and daughters grow
About the mother tree, a pillared shade

High over-arched, and echoing walks between:
There oft the Indian herdsman, shunning heat,
Shelters in cool, and tends his pasturing herds
At loop-holes cut through thickest shade: Those leaves
They gathered, broad as Amazonian targe;
And, with what skill they had, together sewed,
To gird their waist; vain covering, if to hide
Their guilt and dreaded shame! O, how unlike
To that first naked glory! Such of late
Columbus found the American, so girt
With feathered cincture; naked else, and wild
Among the trees on isles and woody shores.
Thus fenced, and, as they thought, their shame in part
Covered, but not at rest or ease of mind,
They sat them down to weep; nor only tears
Rained at their eyes, but high winds worse within
Began to rise, high passions, anger, hate,
Mistrust, suspicion, discord; and shook sore
Their inward state of mind, calm region once
And full of peace, now tost and turbulent:
For Understanding ruled not, and the Will
Heard not her lore; both in subjection now
To sensual Appetite, who from beneath
Usurping over sovran Reason claimed
Superior sway: From thus distempered breast,
Adam, estranged in look and altered style,
Speech intermitted thus to Eve renewed.
"Would thou hadst hearkened to my words, and staid
With me, as I besought thee, when that strange
Desire of wandering, this unhappy morn,
I know not whence possessed thee; we had then
Remained still happy; not, as now, despoiled
Of all our good; shamed, naked, miserable!
Let none henceforth seek needless cause to approve
The faith they owe; when earnestly they seek

Such proof, conclude, they then begin to fail."
To whom, soon moved with touch of blame, thus Eve.
"What words have passed thy lips, Adam severe!
Imputest thou that to my default, or will
Of wandering, as thou callest it, which who knows
But might as ill have happened thou being by,
Or to thyself perhaps? Hadst thou been there,
Or here the attempt, thou couldst not have discerned
Fraud in the Serpent, speaking as he spake;
No ground of enmity between us known,
Why he should mean me ill, or seek to harm.
Was I to have never parted from thy side?
As good have grown there still a lifeless rib.
Being as I am, why didst not thou, the head,
Command me absolutely not to go,
Going into such danger, as thou saidst?
Too facile then, thou didst not much gainsay;
Nay, didst permit, approve, and fair dismiss.
Hadst thou been firm and fixed in thy dissent,
Neither had I transgressed, nor thou with me."
To whom, then first incensed, Adam replied.
"Is this the love, is this the recompence
Of mine to thee, ingrateful Eve! expressed
Immutable, when thou wert lost, not I;
Who might have lived, and joyed immortal bliss,
Yet willingly chose rather death with thee?
And am I now upbraided as the cause
Of thy transgressing? Not enough severe,
It seems, in thy restraint: What could I more
I warned thee, I admonished thee, foretold
The danger, and the lurking enemy
That lay in wait; beyond this, had been force;
And force upon free will hath here no place.
But confidence then bore thee on; secure
Either to meet no danger, or to find

Matter of glorious trial; and perhaps
I also erred, in overmuch admiring
What seemed in thee so perfect, that I thought
No evil durst attempt thee; but I rue
The error now, which is become my crime,
And thou the accuser. Thus it shall befall
Him, who, to worth in women overtrusting,
Lets her will rule: restraint she will not brook;
And, left to herself, if evil thence ensue,
She first his weak indulgence will accuse."
Thus they in mutual accusation spent
The fruitless hours, but neither self-condemning;
And of their vain contest appeared no end.

BOOK X

Meanwhile the heinous and despiteful act
Of Satan, done in Paradise; and how
He, in the serpent, had perverted Eve,
Her husband she, to taste the fatal fruit,
Was known in Heaven; for what can 'scape the eye
Of God all-seeing, or deceive his heart
Omniscient? who, in all things wise and just,
Hindered not Satan to attempt the mind
Of Man, with strength entire and free will armed,
Complete to have discovered and repulsed
Whatever wiles of foe or seeming friend.
For still they knew, and ought to have still remembered,
The high injunction, not to taste that fruit,
Whoever tempted; which they not obeying,
(Incurred what could they less?) the penalty;
And, manifold in sin, deserved to fall.
Up into Heaven from Paradise in haste
The angelic guards ascended, mute, and sad,
For Man; for of his state by this they knew,
Much wondering how the subtle Fiend had stolen
Entrance unseen. Soon as the unwelcome news
From Earth arrived at Heaven-gate, displeased

All were who heard; dim sadness did not spare
That time celestial visages, yet, mixed
With pity, violated not their bliss.
About the new-arrived, in multitudes
The ethereal people ran, to hear and know
How all befell: They towards the throne supreme,
Accountable, made haste, to make appear,
With righteous plea, their utmost vigilance
And easily approved; when the Most High
Eternal Father, from his secret cloud,
Amidst in thunder uttered thus his voice.
"Assembled Angels, and ye Powers returned
From unsuccessful charge; be not dismayed,
Nor troubled at these tidings from the earth,
Which your sincerest care could not prevent;
Foretold so lately what would come to pass,
When first this tempter crossed the gulf from Hell.
I told ye then he should prevail, and speed
On his bad errand; Man should be seduced,
And flattered out of all, believing lies
Against his Maker; no decree of mine
Concurring to necessitate his fall,
Or touch with lightest moment of impulse
His free will, to her own inclining left
In even scale. But fallen he is; and now
What rests, but that the mortal sentence pass
On his transgression, death denounced that day?
Which he presumes already vain and void,
Because not yet inflicted, as he feared,
By some immediate stroke; but soon shall find
Forbearance no acquittance, ere day end.
Justice shall not return as bounty scorned.
But whom send I to judge them? whom but thee,
Vicegerent Son? To thee I have transferred
All judgement, whether in Heaven, or Earth, or Hell.

Easy it may be seen that I intend
Mercy colleague with justice, sending thee
Man's friend, his Mediator, his designed
Both ransom and Redeemer voluntary,
And destined Man himself to judge Man fallen."
So spake the Father; and, unfolding bright
Toward the right hand his glory, on the Son
Blazed forth unclouded Deity: He full
Resplendent all his Father manifest
Expressed, and thus divinely answered mild.
"Father Eternal, thine is to decree;
Mine, both in Heaven and Earth, to do thy will
Supreme; that thou in me, thy Son beloved,
Mayest ever rest well pleased. I go to judge
On earth these thy transgressors; but thou knowest,
Whoever judged, the worst on me must light,
When time shall be; for so I undertook
Before thee; and, not repenting, this obtain
Of right, that I may mitigate their doom
On me derived; yet I shall temper so
Justice with mercy, as may illustrate most
Them fully satisfied, and thee appease.
Attendance none shall need, nor train, where none
Are to behold the judgement, but the judged,
Those two; the third best absent is condemned,
Convict by flight, and rebel to all law:
Conviction to the serpent none belongs."
Thus saying, from his radiant seat he rose
Of high collateral glory: Him Thrones, and Powers,
Princedoms, and Dominations ministrant,
Accompanied to Heaven-gate; from whence
Eden, and all the coast, in prospect lay.
Down he descended straight; the speed of Gods
Time counts not, though with swiftest minutes winged.
Now was the sun in western cadence low

From noon, and gentle airs, due at their hour,
To fan the earth now waked, and usher in
The evening cool; when he, from wrath more cool,
Came the mild Judge, and Intercessor both,
To sentence Man: The voice of God they heard
Now walking in the garden, by soft winds
Brought to their ears, while day declined; they heard,
And from his presence hid themselves among
The thickest trees, both man and wife; till God,
Approaching, thus to Adam called aloud.
"Where art thou, Adam, wont with joy to meet
My coming seen far off? I miss thee here,
Not pleased, thus entertained with solitude,
Where obvious duty ere while appeared unsought:
Or come I less conspicuous, or what change
Absents thee, or what chance detains? Come forth!"
He came; and with him Eve, more loth, though first
To offend; discountenanced both, and discomposed;
Love was not in their looks, either to God,
Or to each other; but apparent guilt,
And shame, and perturbation, and despair,
Anger, and obstinacy, and hate, and guile.
Whence Adam, faltering long, thus answered brief.
"I heard thee in the garden, and of thy voice
Afraid, being naked, hid myself." To whom
The gracious Judge without revile replied.
"My voice thou oft hast heard, and hast not feared,
But still rejoiced; how is it now become
So dreadful to thee? That thou art naked, who
Hath told thee? Hast thou eaten of the tree,
Whereof I gave thee charge thou shouldst not eat?"
To whom thus Adam sore beset replied.
"O Heaven! in evil strait this day I stand
Before my Judge; either to undergo
Myself the total crime, or to accuse

My other self, the partner of my life;
Whose failing, while her faith to me remains,
I should conceal, and not expose to blame
By my complaint: but strict necessity
Subdues me, and calamitous constraint;
Lest on my head both sin and punishment,
However insupportable, be all
Devolved; though should I hold my peace, yet thou
Wouldst easily detect what I conceal.
This Woman, whom thou madest to be my help,
And gavest me as thy perfect gift, so good,
So fit, so acceptable, so divine,
That from her hand I could suspect no ill,
And what she did, whatever in itself,
Her doing seemed to justify the deed;
She gave me of the tree, and I did eat."
To whom the Sovran Presence thus replied.
"Was she thy God, that her thou didst obey
Before his voice? or was she made thy guide,
Superior, or but equal, that to her
Thou didst resign thy manhood, and the place
Wherein God set thee above her made of thee,
And for thee, whose perfection far excelled
Hers in all real dignity? Adorned
She was indeed, and lovely, to attract
Thy love, not thy subjection; and her gifts
Were such, as under government well seemed;
Unseemly to bear rule; which was thy part
And person, hadst thou known thyself aright."
So having said, he thus to Eve in few.
"Say, Woman, what is this which thou hast done?"
To whom sad Eve, with shame nigh overwhelmed,
Confessing soon, yet not before her Judge
Bold or loquacious, thus abashed replied.
"The Serpent me beguiled, and I did eat."

Which when the Lord God heard, without delay
To judgement he proceeded on the accused
Serpent, though brute; unable to transfer
The guilt on him, who made him instrument
Of mischief, and polluted from the end
Of his creation; justly then accursed,
As vitiated in nature: More to know
Concerned not Man, (since he no further knew)
Nor altered his offence; yet God at last
To Satan first in sin his doom applied,
Though in mysterious terms, judged as then best:
And on the Serpent thus his curse let fall.
"Because thou hast done this, thou art accursed
Above all cattle, each beast of the field;
Upon thy belly groveling thou shalt go,
And dust shalt eat all the days of thy life.
Between thee and the woman I will put
Enmity, and between thine and her seed;
Her seed shall bruise thy head, thou bruise his heel."
So spake this oracle, then verified
When Jesus, Son of Mary, second Eve,
Saw Satan fall, like lightning, down from Heaven,
Prince of the air; then, rising from his grave
Spoiled Principalities and Powers, triumphed
In open show; and, with ascension bright,
Captivity led captive through the air,
The realm itself of Satan, long usurped;
Whom he shall tread at last under our feet;
Even he, who now foretold his fatal bruise;
And to the Woman thus his sentence turned.
"Thy sorrow I will greatly multiply
By thy conception; children thou shalt bring
In sorrow forth; and to thy husband's will
Thine shall submit; he over thee shall rule."
On Adam last thus judgement he pronounced.

"Because thou hast hearkened to the voice of thy wife,
And eaten of the tree, concerning which
I charged thee, saying, Thou shalt not eat thereof:
Cursed is the ground for thy sake; thou in sorrow
Shalt eat thereof, all the days of thy life;
Thorns also and thistles it shall bring thee forth
Unbid; and thou shalt eat the herb of the field;
In the sweat of thy face shalt thou eat bread,
Till thou return unto the ground; for thou
Out of the ground wast taken, know thy birth,
For dust thou art, and shalt to dust return."
So judged he Man, both Judge and Saviour sent;
And the instant stroke of death, denounced that day,
Removed far off; then, pitying how they stood
Before him naked to the air, that now
Must suffer change, disdained not to begin
Thenceforth the form of servant to assume;
As when he washed his servants feet; so now,
As father of his family, he clad
Their nakedness with skins of beasts, or slain,
Or as the snake with youthful coat repaid;
And thought not much to clothe his enemies;
Nor he their outward only with the skins
Of beasts, but inward nakedness, much more.
Opprobrious, with his robe of righteousness,
Arraying, covered from his Father's sight.
To him with swift ascent he up returned,
Into his blissful bosom reassumed
In glory, as of old; to him appeased
All, though all-knowing, what had passed with Man
Recounted, mixing intercession sweet.
Meanwhile, ere thus was sinned and judged on Earth,
Within the gates of Hell sat Sin and Death,
In counterview within the gates, that now
Stood open wide, belching outrageous flame

Far into Chaos, since the Fiend passed through,
Sin opening; who thus now to Death began.
"O Son, why sit we here each other viewing
Idly, while Satan, our great author, thrives
In other worlds, and happier seat provides
For us, his offspring dear? It cannot be
But that success attends him; if mishap,
Ere this he had returned, with fury driven
By his avengers; since no place like this
Can fit his punishment, or their revenge.
Methinks I feel new strength within me rise,
Wings growing, and dominion given me large
Beyond this deep; whatever draws me on,
Or sympathy, or some connatural force,
Powerful at greatest distance to unite,
With secret amity, things of like kind,
By secretest conveyance. Thou, my shade
Inseparable, must with me along;
For Death from Sin no power can separate.
But, lest the difficulty of passing back
Stay his return perhaps over this gulf
Impassable, impervious; let us try
Adventurous work, yet to thy power and mine
Not unagreeable, to found a path
Over this main from Hell to that new world,
Where Satan now prevails; a monument
Of merit high to all the infernal host,
Easing their passage hence, for intercourse,
Or transmigration, as their lot shall lead.
Nor can I miss the way, so strongly drawn
By this new-felt attraction and instinct."
Whom thus the meager Shadow answered soon.
"Go, whither Fate, and inclination strong,
Leads thee; I shall not lag behind, nor err
The way, thou leading; such a scent I draw

Of carnage, prey innumerable, and taste
The savour of death from all things there that live:
Nor shall I to the work thou enterprisest
Be wanting, but afford thee equal aid."
So saying, with delight he snuffed the smell
Of mortal change on earth. As when a flock
Of ravenous fowl, though many a league remote,
Against the day of battle, to a field,
Where armies lie encamped, come flying, lured
With scent of living carcasses designed
For death, the following day, in bloody fight:
So scented the grim Feature, and upturned
His nostril wide into the murky air;
Sagacious of his quarry from so far.
Then both from out Hell-gates, into the waste
Wide anarchy of Chaos, damp and dark,
Flew diverse; and with power (their power was great)
Hovering upon the waters, what they met
Solid or slimy, as in raging sea
Tost up and down, together crouded drove,
From each side shoaling towards the mouth of Hell;
As when two polar winds, blowing adverse
Upon the Cronian sea, together drive
Mountains of ice, that stop the imagined way
Beyond Petsora eastward, to the rich
Cathaian coast. The aggregated soil
Death with his mace petrific, cold and dry,
As with a trident, smote; and fixed as firm
As Delos, floating once; the rest his look
Bound with Gorgonian rigour not to move;
And with Asphaltic slime, broad as the gate,
Deep to the roots of Hell the gathered beach
They fastened, and the mole immense wrought on
Over the foaming deep high-arched, a bridge
Of length prodigious, joining to the wall

Immoveable of this now fenceless world,
Forfeit to Death; from hence a passage broad,
Smooth, easy, inoffensive, down to Hell.
So, if great things to small may be compared,
Xerxes, the liberty of Greece to yoke,
From Susa, his Memnonian palace high,
Came to the sea: and, over Hellespont
Bridging his way, Europe with Asia joined,
And scourged with many a stroke the indignant waves.
Now had they brought the work by wonderous art
Pontifical, a ridge of pendant rock,
Over the vexed abyss, following the track
Of Satan to the self-same place where he
First lighted from his wing, and landed safe
From out of Chaos, to the outside bare
Of this round world: With pins of adamant
And chains they made all fast, too fast they made
And durable! And now in little space
The confines met of empyrean Heaven,
And of this World; and, on the left hand, Hell
With long reach interposed; three several ways
In sight, to each of these three places led.
And now their way to Earth they had descried,
To Paradise first tending; when, behold!
Satan, in likeness of an Angel bright,
Betwixt the Centaur and the Scorpion steering
His zenith, while the sun in Aries rose:
Disguised he came; but those his children dear
Their parent soon discerned, though in disguise.
He, after Eve seduced, unminded slunk
Into the wood fast by; and, changing shape,
To observe the sequel, saw his guileful act
By Eve, though all unweeting, seconded
Upon her husband; saw their shame that sought
Vain covertures; but when he saw descend

The Son of God to judge them, terrified
He fled; not hoping to escape, but shun
The present; fearing, guilty, what his wrath
Might suddenly inflict; that past, returned
By night, and listening where the hapless pair
Sat in their sad discourse, and various plaint,
Thence gathered his own doom; which understood
Not instant, but of future time, with joy
And tidings fraught, to Hell he now returned;
And at the brink of Chaos, near the foot
Of this new wonderous pontifice, unhoped
Met, who to meet him came, his offspring dear.
Great joy was at their meeting, and at sight
Of that stupendous bridge his joy increased.
Long he admiring stood, till Sin, his fair
Enchanting daughter, thus the silence broke.
"O Parent, these are thy magnific deeds,
Thy trophies! which thou viewest as not thine own;
Thou art their author, and prime architect:
For I no sooner in my heart divined,
My heart, which by a secret harmony
Still moves with thine, joined in connexion sweet,
That thou on earth hadst prospered, which thy looks
Now also evidence, but straight I felt,
Though distant from thee worlds between, yet felt,
That I must after thee, with this thy son;
Such fatal consequence unites us three!
Hell could no longer hold us in our bounds,
Nor this unvoyageable gulf obscure
Detain from following thy illustrious track.
Thou hast achieved our liberty, confined
Within Hell-gates till now; thou us impowered
To fortify thus far, and overlay,
With this portentous bridge, the dark abyss.
Thine now is all this world; thy virtue hath won

What thy hands builded not; thy wisdom gained
With odds what war hath lost, and fully avenged
Our foil in Heaven; here thou shalt monarch reign,
There didst not; there let him still victor sway,
As battle hath adjudged; from this new world
Retiring, by his own doom alienated;
And henceforth monarchy with thee divide
Of all things, parted by the empyreal bounds,
His quadrature, from thy orbicular world;
Or try thee now more dangerous to his throne."
Whom thus the Prince of darkness answered glad.
"Fair Daughter, and thou Son and Grandchild both;
High proof ye now have given to be the race
Of Satan (for I glory in the name,
Antagonist of Heaven's Almighty King,)
Amply have merited of me, of all
The infernal empire, that so near Heaven's door
Triumphal with triumphal act have met,
Mine, with this glorious work; and made one realm,
Hell and this world, one realm, one continent
Of easy thorough-fare. Therefore, while I
Descend through darkness, on your road with ease,
To my associate Powers, them to acquaint
With these successes, and with them rejoice;
You two this way, among these numerous orbs,
All yours, right down to Paradise descend;
There dwell, and reign in bliss; thence on the earth
Dominion exercise and in the air,
Chiefly on Man, sole lord of all declared;
Him first make sure your thrall, and lastly kill.
My substitutes I send ye, and create
Plenipotent on earth, of matchless might
Issuing from me: on your joint vigour now
My hold of this new kingdom all depends,
Through Sin to Death exposed by my exploit.

If your joint power prevail, the affairs of Hell
No detriment need fear; go, and be strong!"
So saying he dismissed them; they with speed
Their course through thickest constellations held,
Spreading their bane; the blasted stars looked wan,
And planets, planet-struck, real eclipse
Then suffered. The other way Satan went down
The causey to Hell-gate: On either side
Disparted Chaos overbuilt exclaimed,
And with rebounding surge the bars assailed,
That scorned his indignation: Through the gate,
Wide open and unguarded, Satan passed,
And all about found desolate; for those,
Appointed to sit there, had left their charge,
Flown to the upper world; the rest were all
Far to the inland retired, about the walls
Of Pandemonium; city and proud seat
Of Lucifer, so by allusion called
Of that bright star to Satan paragoned;
There kept their watch the legions, while the Grand
In council sat, solicitous what chance
Might intercept their emperor sent; so he
Departing gave command, and they observed.
As when the Tartar from his Russian foe,
By Astracan, over the snowy plains,
Retires; or Bactrin Sophi, from the horns
Of Turkish crescent, leaves all waste beyond
The realm of Aladule, in his retreat
To Tauris or Casbeen: So these, the late
Heaven-banished host, left desart utmost Hell
Many a dark league, reduced in careful watch
Round their metropolis; and now expecting
Each hour their great adventurer, from the search
Of foreign worlds: He through the midst unmarked,
In show plebeian Angel militant

Of lowest order, passed; and from the door
Of that Plutonian hall, invisible
Ascended his high throne; which, under state
Of richest texture spread, at the upper end
Was placed in regal lustre. Down a while
He sat, and round about him saw unseen:
At last, as from a cloud, his fulgent head
And shape star-bright appeared, or brighter, clad
With what permissive glory since his fall
Was left him, or false glitter: All amazed
At that so sudden blaze the Stygian throng
Bent their aspect, and whom they wished beheld,
Their mighty Chief returned: loud was the acclaim:
Forth rushed in haste the great consulting peers,
Raised from their dark Divan, and with like joy
Congratulant approached him; who with hand
Silence, and with these words attention, won.
"Thrones, Dominations, Princedoms, Virtues, Powers;
For in possession such, not only of right,
I call ye, and declare ye now; returned
Successful beyond hope, to lead ye forth
Triumphant out of this infernal pit
Abominable, accursed, the house of woe,
And dungeon of our tyrant: Now possess,
As Lords, a spacious world, to our native Heaven
Little inferior, by my adventure hard
With peril great achieved. Long were to tell
What I have done; what suffered; with what pain
Voyaged th' unreal, vast, unbounded deep
Of horrible confusion; over which
By Sin and Death a broad way now is paved,
To expedite your glorious march; but I
Toiled out my uncouth passage, forced to ride
The untractable abyss, plunged in the womb
Of unoriginal Night and Chaos wild;

That, jealous of their secrets, fiercely opposed
My journey strange, with clamorous uproar
Protesting Fate supreme; thence how I found
The new created world, which fame in Heaven
Long had foretold, a fabric wonderful
Of absolute perfection! therein Man
Placed in a Paradise, by our exile
Made happy: Him by fraud I have seduced
From his Creator; and, the more to increase
Your wonder, with an apple; he, thereat
Offended, worth your laughter! hath given up
Both his beloved Man, and all his world,
To Sin and Death a prey, and so to us,
Without our hazard, labour, or alarm;
To range in, and to dwell, and over Man
To rule, as over all he should have ruled.
True is, me also he hath judged, or rather
Me not, but the brute serpent in whose shape
Man I deceived: that which to me belongs,
Is enmity which he will put between
Me and mankind; I am to bruise his heel;
His seed, when is not set, shall bruise my head:
A world who would not purchase with a bruise,
Or much more grievous pain?—Ye have the account
Of my performance: What remains, ye Gods,
But up, and enter now into full bliss?"
So having said, a while he stood, expecting
Their universal shout, and high applause,
To fill his ear; when, contrary, he hears
On all sides, from innumerable tongues,
A dismal universal hiss, the sound
Of public scorn; he wondered, but not long
Had leisure, wondering at himself now more,
His visage drawn he felt to sharp and spare;
His arms clung to his ribs; his legs entwining

Each other, till supplanted down he fell
A monstrous serpent on his belly prone,
Reluctant, but in vain; a greater power
Now ruled him, punished in the shape he sinned,
According to his doom: he would have spoke,
But hiss for hiss returned with forked tongue
To forked tongue; for now were all transformed
Alike, to serpents all, as accessories
To his bold riot: Dreadful was the din
Of hissing through the hall, thick swarming now
With complicated monsters head and tail,
Scorpion, and Asp, and Amphisbaena dire,
Cerastes horned, Hydrus, and Elops drear,
And Dipsas; (not so thick swarmed once the soil
Bedropt with blood of Gorgon, or the isle
Ophiusa,) but still greatest he the midst,
Now Dragon grown, larger than whom the sun
Engendered in the Pythian vale or slime,
Huge Python, and his power no less he seemed
Above the rest still to retain; they all
Him followed, issuing forth to the open field,
Where all yet left of that revolted rout,
Heaven-fallen, in station stood or just array;
Sublime with expectation when to see
In triumph issuing forth their glorious Chief;
They saw, but other sight instead! a crowd
Of ugly serpents; horror on them fell,
And horrid sympathy; for, what they saw,
They felt themselves, now changing; down their arms,
Down fell both spear and shield; down they as fast;
And the dire hiss renewed, and the dire form
Catched, by contagion; like in punishment,
As in their crime. Thus was the applause they meant,
Turned to exploding hiss, triumph to shame
Cast on themselves from their own mouths. There stood

A grove hard by, sprung up with this their change,
His will who reigns above, to aggravate
Their penance, laden with fair fruit, like that
Which grew in Paradise, the bait of Eve
Used by the Tempter: on that prospect strange
Their earnest eyes they fixed, imagining
For one forbidden tree a multitude
Now risen, to work them further woe or shame;
Yet, parched with scalding thirst and hunger fierce,
Though to delude them sent, could not abstain;
But on they rolled in heaps, and, up the trees
Climbing, sat thicker than the snaky locks
That curled Megaera: greedily they plucked
The fruitage fair to sight, like that which grew
Near that bituminous lake where Sodom flamed;
This more delusive, not the touch, but taste
Deceived; they, fondly thinking to allay
Their appetite with gust, instead of fruit
Chewed bitter ashes, which the offended taste
With spattering noise rejected: oft they assayed,
Hunger and thirst constraining; drugged as oft,
With hatefullest disrelish writhed their jaws,
With soot and cinders filled; so oft they fell
Into the same illusion, not as Man
Whom they triumphed once lapsed. Thus were they
    plagued
And worn with famine, long and ceaseless hiss,
Till their lost shape, permitted, they resumed;
Yearly enjoined, some say, to undergo,
This annual humbling certain numbered days,
To dash their pride, and joy, for Man seduced.
However, some tradition they dispersed
Among the Heathen, of their purchase got,
And fabled how the Serpent, whom they called
Ophion, with Eurynome, the wide—

Encroaching Eve perhaps, had first the rule
Of high Olympus; thence by Saturn driven
And Ops, ere yet Dictaean Jove was born.
Meanwhile in Paradise the hellish pair
Too soon arrived; Sin, there in power before,
Once actual; now in body, and to dwell
Habitual habitant; behind her Death,
Close following pace for pace, not mounted yet
On his pale horse: to whom Sin thus began.
"Second of Satan sprung, all-conquering Death!
What thinkest thou of our empire now, though earned
With travel difficult, not better far
Than still at Hell's dark threshold to have sat watch,
Unnamed, undreaded, and thyself half starved?"
Whom thus the Sin-born monster answered soon.
"To me, who with eternal famine pine,
Alike is Hell, or Paradise, or Heaven;
There best, where most with ravine I may meet;
Which here, though plenteous, all too little seems
To stuff this maw, this vast unhide-bound corpse."
To whom the incestuous mother thus replied.
"Thou therefore on these herbs, and fruits, and flowers,
Feed first; on each beast next, and fish, and fowl;
No homely morsels! and, whatever thing
The sithe of Time mows down, devour unspared;
Till I, in Man residing, through the race,
His thoughts, his looks, words, actions, all infect;
And season him thy last and sweetest prey."
This said, they both betook them several ways,
Both to destroy, or unimmortal make
All kinds, and for destruction to mature
Sooner or later; which the Almighty seeing,
From his transcendent seat the Saints among,
To those bright Orders uttered thus his voice.
"See, with what heat these dogs of Hell advance

To waste and havoc yonder world, which I
So fair and good created; and had still
Kept in that state, had not the folly of Man
Let in these wasteful furies, who impute
Folly to me; so doth the Prince of Hell
And his adherents, that with so much ease
I suffer them to enter and possess
A place so heavenly; and, conniving, seem
To gratify my scornful enemies,
That laugh, as if, transported with some fit
Of passion, I to them had quitted all,
At random yielded up to their misrule;
And know not that I called, and drew them thither,
My Hell-hounds, to lick up the draff and filth
Which Man's polluting sin with taint hath shed
On what was pure; til, crammed and gorged, nigh burst
With sucked and glutted offal, at one sling
Of thy victorious arm, well-pleasing Son,
Both Sin, and Death, and yawning Grave, at last,
Through Chaos hurled, obstruct the mouth of Hell
For ever, and seal up his ravenous jaws.
Then Heaven and Earth renewed shall be made pure
To sanctity, that shall receive no stain:
Till then, the curse pronounced on both precedes."
He ended, and the heavenly audience loud
Sung Halleluiah, as the sound of seas,
Through multitude that sung: "Just are thy ways,
Righteous are thy decrees on all thy works;
Who can extenuate thee? Next, to the Son,
Destined Restorer of mankind, by whom
New Heaven and Earth shall to the ages rise,
Or down from Heaven descend." Such was their song;
While the Creator, calling forth by name
His mighty Angels, gave them several charge,
As sorted best with present things. The sun

Had first his precept so to move, so shine,
As might affect the earth with cold and heat
Scarce tolerable; and from the north to call
Decrepit winter; from the south to bring
Solstitial summer's heat. To the blanc moon
Her office they prescribed; to the other five
Their planetary motions, and aspects,
In sextile, square, and trine, and opposite,
Of noxious efficacy, and when to join
In synod unbenign; and taught the fixed
Their influence malignant when to shower,
Which of them rising with the sun, or falling,
Should prove tempestuous: To the winds they set
Their corners, when with bluster to confound
Sea, air, and shore; the thunder when to roll
With terrour through the dark aereal hall.
Some say, he bid his Angels turn askanse
The poles of earth, twice ten degrees and more,
From the sun's axle; they with labour pushed
Oblique the centrick globe: Some say, the sun
Was bid turn reins from the equinoctial road
Like distant breadth to Taurus with the seven
Atlantic Sisters, and the Spartan Twins,
Up to the Tropic Crab: thence down amain
By Leo, and the Virgin, and the Scales,
As deep as Capricorn; to bring in change
Of seasons to each clime; else had the spring
Perpetual smiled on earth with vernant flowers,
Equal in days and nights, except to those
Beyond the polar circles; to them day
Had unbenighted shone, while the low sun,
To recompense his distance, in their sight
Had rounded still the horizon, and not known
Or east or west; which had forbid the snow
From cold Estotiland, and south as far

Beneath Magellan. At that tasted fruit
The sun, as from Thyestean banquet, turned
His course intended; else, how had the world
Inhabited, though sinless, more than now,
Avoided pinching cold and scorching heat?
These changes in the Heavens, though slow, produced
Like change on sea and land; sideral blast,
Vapour, and mist, and exhalation hot,
Corrupt and pestilent: Now from the north
Of Norumbega, and the Samoed shore,
Bursting their brazen dungeon, armed with ice,
And snow, and hail, and stormy gust and flaw,
Boreas, and Caecias, and Argestes loud,
And Thrascias, rend the woods, and seas upturn;
With adverse blast upturns them from the south
Notus, and Afer black with thunderous clouds
From Serraliona; thwart of these, as fierce,
Forth rush the Levant and the Ponent winds,
Eurus and Zephyr, with their lateral noise,
Sirocco and Libecchio. Thus began
Outrage from lifeless things; but Discord first,
Daughter of Sin, among the irrational
Death introduced, through fierce antipathy:
Beast now with beast 'gan war, and fowl with fowl,
And fish with fish; to graze the herb all leaving,
Devoured each other; nor stood much in awe
Of Man, but fled him; or, with countenance grim,
Glared on him passing. These were from without
The growing miseries, which Adam saw
Already in part, though hid in gloomiest shade,
To sorrow abandoned, but worse felt within;
And, in a troubled sea of passion tost,
Thus to disburden sought with sad complaint.
"O miserable of happy! Is this the end
Of this new glorious world, and me so late

The glory of that glory, who now become
Accursed, of blessed? hide me from the face
Of God, whom to behold was then my hight
Of happiness!—Yet well, if here would end
The misery; I deserved it, and would bear
My own deservings; but this will not serve:
All that I eat or drink, or shall beget,
Is propagated curse. O voice, once heard
Delightfully, Encrease and multiply;
Now death to hear! for what can I encrease,
Or multiply, but curses on my head?
Who of all ages to succeed, but, feeling
The evil on him brought by me, will curse
My head? Ill fare our ancestor impure,
For this we may thank Adam! but his thanks
Shall be the execration: so, besides
Mine own that bide upon me, all from me
Shall with a fierce reflux on me rebound;
On me, as on their natural center, light
Heavy, though in their place. O fleeting joys
Of Paradise, dear bought with lasting woes!
Did I request thee, Maker, from my clay
To mould me Man? did I solicit thee
From darkness to promote me, or here place
In this delicious garden? As my will
Concurred not to my being, it were but right
And equal to reduce me to my dust;
Desirous to resign and render back
All I received; unable to perform
Thy terms too hard, by which I was to hold
The good I sought not. To the loss of that,
Sufficient penalty, why hast thou added
The sense of endless woes? Inexplicable
Thy justice seems; yet to say truth, too late
I thus contest; then should have been refused

Those terms whatever, when they were proposed:
Thou didst accept them; wilt thou enjoy the good,
Then cavil the conditions? And, though God
Made thee without thy leave, what if thy son
Prove disobedient, and reproved, retort,
'Wherefore didst thou beget me? I sought it not!'
Wouldst thou admit for his contempt of thee
That proud excuse? yet him not thy election,
But natural necessity begot.
God made thee of choice his own, and of his own
To serve him; thy reward was of his grace;
Thy punishment then, justly is at his will.
Be it so, for I submit; his doom is fair,
That dust I am, and shall to dust return.
O welcome hour whenever! Why delays
His hand to execute what his decree
Fixed on this day? Why do I overlive,
Why am I mocked with death, and lengthened out
To deathless pain? How gladly would I meet
Mortality my sentence, and be earth
Insensible! How glad would lay me down
As in my mother's lap! There I should rest,
And sleep secure; his dreadful voice no more
Would thunder in my ears; no fear of worse
To me, and to my offspring, would torment me
With cruel expectation. Yet one doubt
Pursues me still, lest all I cannot die;
Lest that pure breath of life, the spirit of Man
Which God inspired, cannot together perish
With this corporeal clod; then, in the grave,
Or in some other dismal place, who knows
But I shall die a living death? O thought
Horrid, if true! Yet why? It was but breath
Of life that sinned; what dies but what had life
And sin? The body properly had neither,

All of me then shall die: let this appease
The doubt, since human reach no further knows.
For though the Lord of all be infinite,
Is his wrath also? Be it, Man is not so,
But mortal doomed. How can he exercise
Wrath without end on Man, whom death must end?
Can he make deathless death? That were to make
Strange contradiction, which to God himself
Impossible is held; as argument
Of weakness, not of power. Will he draw out,
For anger's sake, finite to infinite,
In punished Man, to satisfy his rigour,
Satisfied never? That were to extend
His sentence beyond dust and Nature's law;
By which all causes else, according still
To the reception of their matter, act;
Not to the extent of their own sphere. But say
That death be not one stroke, as I supposed,
Bereaving sense, but endless misery
From this day onward; which I feel begun
Both in me, and without me; and so last
To perpetuity;—Ay me! that fear
Comes thundering back with dreadful revolution
On my defenceless head; both Death and I
Am found eternal, and incorporate both;
Nor I on my part single; in me all
Posterity stands cursed: Fair patrimony
That I must leave ye, Sons! O, were I able
To waste it all myself, and leave ye none!
So disinherited, how would you bless
Me, now your curse! Ah, why should all mankind,
For one man's fault, thus guiltless be condemned,
It guiltless? But from me what can proceed,
But all corrupt; both mind and will depraved
Not to do only, but to will the same

With me? How can they then acquitted stand
In sight of God? Him, after all disputes,
Forced I absolve: all my evasions vain,
And reasonings, though through mazes, lead me still
But to my own conviction: first and last
On me, me only, as the source and spring
Of all corruption, all the blame lights due;
So might the wrath! Fond wish! couldst thou support
That burden, heavier than the earth to bear,
Than all the world much heavier, though divided
With that bad Woman? Thus, what thou desirest,
And what thou fearest, alike destroys all hope
Of refuge, and concludes thee miserable
Beyond all past example and future;
To Satan only like both crime and doom.
O Conscience! into what abyss of fears
And horrors hast thou driven me; out of which
I find no way, from deep to deeper plunged!"
Thus Adam to himself lamented loud,
Through the still night; not now, as ere Man fell,
Wholesome, and cool, and mild, but with black air
Accompanied; with damps, and dreadful gloom;
Which to his evil conscience represented
All things with double terrour: On the ground
Outstretched he lay, on the cold ground; and oft
Cursed his creation; Death as oft accused
Of tardy execution, since denounced
The day of his offence. "Why comes not Death,"
Said he, "with one thrice-acceptable stroke
To end me? Shall Truth fail to keep her word,
Justice Divine not hasten to be just?
But Death comes not at call; Justice Divine
Mends not her slowest pace for prayers or cries,
O woods, O fountains, hillocks, dales, and bowers!
With other echo late I taught your shades

To answer, and resound far other song."
Whom thus afflicted when sad Eve beheld,
Desolate where she sat, approaching nigh,
Soft words to his fierce passion she assayed:
But her with stern regard he thus repelled.
"Out of my sight, thou Serpent! That name best
Befits thee with him leagued, thyself as false
And hateful; nothing wants, but that thy shape,
Like his, and colour serpentine, may show
Thy inward fraud; to warn all creatures from thee
Henceforth; lest that too heavenly form, pretended
To hellish falsehood, snare them! But for thee
I had persisted happy; had not thy pride
And wandering vanity, when least was safe,
Rejected my forewarning, and disdained
Not to be trusted; longing to be seen,
Though by the Devil himself; him overweening
To over-reach; but, with the serpent meeting,
Fooled and beguiled; by him thou, I by thee
To trust thee from my side; imagined wise,
Constant, mature, proof against all assaults;
And understood not all was but a show,
Rather than solid virtue; all but a rib
Crooked by nature, bent, as now appears,
More to the part sinister, from me drawn;
Well if thrown out, as supernumerary
To my just number found. O! why did God,
Creator wise, that peopled highest Heaven
With Spirits masculine, create at last
This novelty on earth, this fair defect
Of nature, and not fill the world at once
With Men, as Angels, without feminine;
Or find some other way to generate
Mankind? This mischief had not been befallen,
And more that shall befall; innumerable

Disturbances on earth through female snares,
And strait conjunction with this sex: for either
He never shall find out fit mate, but such
As some misfortune brings him, or mistake;
Or whom he wishes most shall seldom gain
Through her perverseness, but shall see her gained
By a far worse; or, if she love, withheld
By parents; or his happiest choice too late
Shall meet, already linked and wedlock-bound
To a fell adversary, his hate or shame:
Which infinite calamity shall cause
To human life, and household peace confound."
He added not, and from her turned; but Eve,
Not so repulsed, with tears that ceased not flowing
And tresses all disordered, at his feet
Fell humble; and, embracing them, besought
His peace, and thus proceeded in her plaint.
"Forsake me not thus, Adam! witness Heaven
What love sincere, and reverence in my heart
I bear thee, and unweeting have offended,
Unhappily deceived! Thy suppliant
I beg, and clasp thy knees; bereave me not,
Whereon I live, thy gentle looks, thy aid,
Thy counsel, in this uttermost distress,
My only strength and stay: Forlorn of thee,
Whither shall I betake me, where subsist?
While yet we live, scarce one short hour perhaps,
Between us two let there be peace; both joining,
As joined in injuries, one enmity
Against a foe by doom express assigned us,
That cruel Serpent: On me exercise not
Thy hatred for this misery befallen;
On me already lost, me than thyself
More miserable! Both have sinned; but thou
Against God only; I against God and thee;

And to the place of judgement will return,
There with my cries importune Heaven; that all
The sentence, from thy head removed, may light
On me, sole cause to thee of all this woe;
Me, me only, just object of his ire!"
She ended weeping; and her lowly plight,
Immoveable, till peace obtained from fault
Acknowledged and deplored, in Adam wrought
Commiseration: Soon his heart relented
Towards her, his life so late, and sole delight,
Now at his feet submissive in distress;
Creature so fair his reconcilement seeking,
His counsel, whom she had displeased, his aid:
As one disarmed, his anger all he lost,
And thus with peaceful words upraised her soon.
"Unwary, and too desirous, as before,
So now of what thou knowest not, who desirest
The punishment all on thyself; alas!
Bear thine own first, ill able to sustain
His full wrath, whose thou feelest as yet least part,
And my displeasure bearest so ill. If prayers
Could alter high decrees, I to that place
Would speed before thee, and be louder heard,
That on my head all might be visited;
Thy frailty and infirmer sex forgiven,
To me committed, and by me exposed.
But rise; let us no more contend, nor blame
Each other, blamed enough elsewhere; but strive
In offices of love, how we may lighten
Each other's burden, in our share of woe;
Since this day's death denounced, if aught I see,
Will prove no sudden, but a slow-paced evil;
A long day's dying, to augment our pain;
And to our seed (O hapless seed!) derived."
To whom thus Eve, recovering heart, replied.

"Adam, by sad experiment I know
How little weight my words with thee can find,
Found so erroneous; thence by just event
Found so unfortunate: Nevertheless,
Restored by thee, vile as I am, to place
Of new acceptance, hopeful to regain
Thy love, the sole contentment of my heart
Living or dying, from thee I will not hide
What thoughts in my unquiet breast are risen,
Tending to some relief of our extremes,
Or end; though sharp and sad, yet tolerable,
As in our evils, and of easier choice.
If care of our descent perplex us most,
Which must be born to certain woe, devoured
By Death at last; and miserable it is
To be to others cause of misery,
Our own begotten, and of our loins to bring
Into this cursed world a woeful race,
That after wretched life must be at last
Food for so foul a monster; in thy power
It lies, yet ere conception to prevent
The race unblest, to being yet unbegot.
Childless thou art, childless remain: so Death
Shall be deceived his glut, and with us two
Be forced to satisfy his ravenous maw.
But if thou judge it hard and difficult,
Conversing, looking, loving, to abstain
From love's due rights, nuptial embraces sweet;
And with desire to languish without hope,
Before the present object languishing
With like desire; which would be misery
And torment less than none of what we dread;
Then, both ourselves and seed at once to free
From what we fear for both, let us make short,
Let us seek Death; or, he not found, supply

With our own hands his office on ourselves:
Why stand we longer shivering under fears,
That show no end but death, and have the power,
Of many ways to die the shortest choosing,
Destruction with destruction to destroy?"
She ended here, or vehement despair
Broke off the rest: so much of death her thoughts
Had entertained, as dyed her cheeks with pale.
But Adam, with such counsel nothing swayed,
To better hopes his more attentive mind
Labouring had raised; and thus to Eve replied.
"Eve, thy contempt of life and pleasure seems
To argue in thee something more sublime
And excellent, than what thy mind contemns;
But self-destruction therefore sought, refutes
That excellence thought in thee; and implies,
Not thy contempt, but anguish and regret
For loss of life and pleasure overloved.
Or if thou covet death, as utmost end
Of misery, so thinking to evade
The penalty pronounced; doubt not but God
Hath wiselier armed his vengeful ire, than so
To be forestalled; much more I fear lest death,
So snatched, will not exempt us from the pain
We are by doom to pay; rather, such acts
Of contumacy will provoke the Highest
To make death in us live: Then let us seek
Some safer resolution, which methinks
I have in view, calling to mind with heed
Part of our sentence, that thy seed shall bruise
The Serpent's head; piteous amends! unless
Be meant, whom I conjecture, our grand foe,
Satan; who, in the serpent, hath contrived
Against us this deceit: To crush his head
Would be revenge indeed! which will be lost

By death brought on ourselves, or childless days
Resolved, as thou proposest; so our foe
Shall 'scape his punishment ordained, and we
Instead shall double ours upon our heads.
No more be mentioned then of violence
Against ourselves; and wilful barrenness,
That cuts us off from hope; and savours only
Rancour and pride, impatience and despite,
Reluctance against God and his just yoke
Laid on our necks. Remember with what mild
And gracious temper he both heard, and judged,
Without wrath or reviling; we expected
Immediate dissolution, which we thought
Was meant by death that day; when lo! to thee
Pains only in child-bearing were foretold,
And bringing forth; soon recompensed with joy,
Fruit of thy womb: On me the curse aslope
Glanced on the ground; with labour I must earn
My bread; what harm? Idleness had been worse;
My labour will sustain me; and, lest cold
Or heat should injure us, his timely care
Hath, unbesought, provided; and his hands
Clothed us unworthy, pitying while he judged;
How much more, if we pray him, will his ear
Be open, and his heart to pity incline,
And teach us further by what means to shun
The inclement seasons, rain, ice, hail, and snow!
Which now the sky, with various face, begins
To show us in this mountain; while the winds
Blow moist and keen, shattering the graceful locks
Of these fair spreading trees; which bids us seek
Some better shroud, some better warmth to cherish
Our limbs benumbed, ere this diurnal star
Leave cold the night, how we his gathered beams
Reflected may with matter sere foment;

Or, by collision of two bodies, grind
The air attrite to fire; as late the clouds
Justling, or pushed with winds, rude in their shock,
Tine the slant lightning; whose thwart flame, driven down
Kindles the gummy bark of fir or pine;
And sends a comfortable heat from far,
Which might supply the sun: Such fire to use,
And what may else be remedy or cure
To evils which our own misdeeds have wrought,
He will instruct us praying, and of grace
Beseeching him; so as we need not fear
To pass commodiously this life, sustained
By him with many comforts, till we end
In dust, our final rest and native home.
What better can we do, than, to the place
Repairing where he judged us, prostrate fall
Before him reverent; and there confess
Humbly our faults, and pardon beg; with tears
Watering the ground, and with our sighs the air
Frequenting, sent from hearts contrite, in sign
Of sorrow unfeigned, and humiliation meek.
Undoubtedly he will relent, and turn
From his displeasure; in whose look serene,
When angry most he seemed and most severe,
What else but favour, grace, and mercy, shone?"
So spake our father penitent; nor Eve
Felt less remorse: they, forthwith to the place
Repairing where he judged them, prostrate fell
Before him reverent; and both confessed
Humbly their faults, and pardon begged; with tears
Watering the ground, and with their sighs the air
Frequenting, sent from hearts contrite, in sign
Of sorrow unfeigned, and humiliation meek.

BOOK XI

Thus they, in lowliest plight, repentant stood
Praying; for from the mercy-seat above
Prevenient grace descending had removed
The stony from their hearts, and made new flesh
Regenerate grow instead; that sighs now breathed
Unutterable; which the Spirit of prayer
Inspired, and winged for Heaven with speedier flight
Than loudest oratory: Yet their port
Not of mean suitors; nor important less
Seemed their petition, than when the ancient pair
In fables old, less ancient yet than these,
Deucalion and chaste Pyrrha, to restore
The race of mankind drowned, before the shrine
Of Themis stood devout. To Heaven their prayers
Flew up, nor missed the way, by envious winds
Blown vagabond or frustrate: in they passed
Dimensionless through heavenly doors; then clad
With incense, where the golden altar fumed,
By their great intercessor, came in sight
Before the Father's throne: them the glad Son
Presenting, thus to intercede began.
"See Father, what first-fruits on earth are sprung

From thy implanted grace in Man; these sighs
And prayers, which in this golden censer mixed
With incense, I thy priest before thee bring;
Fruits of more pleasing savour, from thy seed
Sown with contrition in his heart, than those
Which, his own hand manuring, all the trees
Of Paradise could have produced, ere fallen
From innocence. Now therefore, bend thine ear
To supplication; hear his sighs, though mute;
Unskilful with what words to pray, let me
Interpret for him; me, his advocate
And propitiation; all his works on me,
Good, or not good, ingraft; my merit those
Shall perfect, and for these my death shall pay.
Accept me; and, in me, from these receive
The smell of peace toward mankind: let him live
Before thee reconciled, at least his days
Numbered, though sad; till death, his doom, (which I
To mitigate thus plead, not to reverse,)
To better life shall yield him: where with me
All my redeemed may dwell in joy and bliss;
Made one with me, as I with thee am one."
To whom the Father, without cloud, serene.
"All thy request for Man, accepted Son,
Obtain; all thy request was my decree:
But, longer in that Paradise to dwell,
The law I gave to Nature him forbids:
Those pure immortal elements, that know,
No gross, no unharmonious mixture foul,
Eject him, tainted now; and purge him off,
As a distemper, gross, to air as gross,
And mortal food; as may dispose him best
For dissolution wrought by sin, that first
Distempered all things, and of incorrupt
Corrupted. I, at first, with two fair gifts

Created him endowed; with happiness,
And immortality: that fondly lost,
This other served but to eternize woe;
Till I provided death: so death becomes
His final remedy; and, after life,
Tried in sharp tribulation, and refined
By faith and faithful works, to second life,
Waked in the renovation of the just,
Resigns him up with Heaven and Earth renewed.
But let us call to synod all the Blest,
Through Heaven's wide bounds: from them I will not hide
My judgements; how with mankind I proceed,
As how with peccant Angels late they saw,
And in their state, though firm, stood more confirmed."
He ended, and the Son gave signal high
To the bright minister that watched; he blew
His trumpet, heard in Oreb since perhaps
When God descended, and perhaps once more
To sound at general doom. The angelic blast
Filled all the regions: from their blisful bowers
Of amarantine shade, fountain or spring,
By the waters of life, where'er they sat
In fellowships of joy, the sons of light
Hasted, resorting to the summons high;
And took their seats; till from his throne supreme
The Almighty thus pronounced his sovran will.
"O Sons, like one of us Man is become
To know both good and evil, since his taste
Of that defended fruit; but let him boast
His knowledge of good lost, and evil got;
Happier! had it sufficed him to have known
Good by itself, and evil not at all.
He sorrows now, repents, and prays contrite,
My motions in him; longer than they move,
His heart I know, how variable and vain,

Self-left. Lest therefore his now bolder hand
Reach also of the tree of life, and eat,
And live for ever, dream at least to live
For ever, to remove him I decree,
And send him from the garden forth to till
The ground whence he was taken, fitter soil.
Michael, this my behest have thou in charge;
Take to thee from among the Cherubim
Thy choice of flaming warriors, lest the Fiend,
Or in behalf of Man, or to invade
Vacant possession, some new trouble raise:
Haste thee, and from the Paradise of God
Without remorse drive out the sinful pair;
From hallowed ground the unholy; and denounce
To them, and to their progeny, from thence
Perpetual banishment. Yet, lest they faint
At the sad sentence rigorously urged,
(For I behold them softened, and with tears
Bewailing their excess,) all terrour hide.
If patiently thy bidding they obey,
Dismiss them not disconsolate; reveal
To Adam what shall come in future days,
As I shall thee enlighten; intermix
My covenant in the Woman's seed renewed;
So send them forth, though sorrowing, yet in peace:
And on the east side of the garden place,
Where entrance up from Eden easiest climbs,
Cherubic watch; and of a sword the flame
Wide-waving; all approach far off to fright,
And guard all passage to the tree of life:
Lest Paradise a receptacle prove
To Spirits foul, and all my trees their prey;
With whose stolen fruit Man once more to delude."
He ceased; and the arch-angelic Power prepared
For swift descent; with him the cohort bright

Of watchful Cherubim: four faces each
Had, like a double Janus; all their shape
Spangled with eyes more numerous than those
Of Argus, and more wakeful than to drouse,
Charmed with Arcadian pipe, the pastoral reed
Of Hermes, or his opiate rod. Meanwhile,
To re-salute the world with sacred light,
Leucothea waked; and with fresh dews imbalmed
The earth; when Adam and first matron Eve
Had ended now their orisons, and found
Strength added from above; new hope to spring
Out of despair; joy, but with fear yet linked;
Which thus to Eve his welcome words renewed.
"Eve, easily my faith admit, that all
The good which we enjoy from Heaven descends;
But, that from us aught should ascend to Heaven
So prevalent as to concern the mind
Of God high-blest, or to incline his will,
Hard to belief may seem; yet this will prayer
Or one short sigh of human breath, upborne
Even to the seat of God. For since I sought
By prayer the offended Deity to appease;
Kneeled, and before him humbled all my heart;
Methought I saw him placable and mild,
Bending his ear; persuasion in me grew
That I was heard with favour; peace returned
Home to my breast, and to my memory
His promise, that thy seed shall bruise our foe;
Which, then not minded in dismay, yet now
Assures me that the bitterness of death
Is past, and we shall live. Whence hail to thee,
Eve rightly called, mother of all mankind,
Mother of all things living, since by thee
Man is to live; and all things live for Man."
To whom thus Eve with sad demeanour meek.

"Ill-worthy I such title should belong
To me transgressour; who, for thee ordained
A help, became thy snare; to me reproach
Rather belongs, distrust, and all dispraise:
But infinite in pardon was my Judge,
That I, who first brought death on all, am graced
The source of life; next favourable thou,
Who highly thus to entitle me vouchsaf'st,
Far other name deserving. But the field
To labour calls us, now with sweat imposed,
Though after sleepless night; for see! the morn,
All unconcerned with our unrest, begins
Her rosy progress smiling: let us forth;
I never from thy side henceforth to stray,
Where'er our day's work lies, though now enjoined
Laborious, till day droop; while here we dwell,
What can be toilsome in these pleasant walks?
Here let us live, though in fallen state, content."
So spake, so wished much humbled Eve; but Fate
Subscribed not: Nature first gave signs, impressed
On bird, beast, air; air suddenly eclipsed,
After short blush of morn; nigh in her sight
The bird of Jove, stooped from his aery tour,
Two birds of gayest plume before him drove;
Down from a hill the beast that reigns in woods,
First hunter then, pursued a gentle brace,
Goodliest of all the forest, hart and hind;
Direct to the eastern gate was bent their flight.
Adam observed, and with his eye the chase
Pursuing, not unmoved, to Eve thus spake.
"O Eve, some further change awaits us nigh,
Which Heaven, by these mute signs in Nature, shows
Forerunners of his purpose; or to warn
Us, haply too secure, of our discharge
From penalty, because from death released

Some days: how long, and what till then our life,
Who knows? or more than this, that we are dust,
And thither must return, and be no more?
Why else this double object in our sight
Of flight pursued in the air, and o'er the ground,
One way the self-same hour? why in the east
Darkness ere day's mid-course, and morning-light
More orient in yon western cloud, that draws
O'er the blue firmament a radiant white,
And slow descends with something heavenly fraught?"
He erred not; for by this the heavenly bands
Down from a sky of jasper lighted now
In Paradise, and on a hill made halt;
A glorious apparition, had not doubt
And carnal fear that day dimmed Adam's eye.
Not that more glorious, when the Angels met
Jacob in Mahanaim, where he saw
The field pavilioned with his guardians bright;
Nor that, which on the flaming mount appeared
In Dothan, covered with a camp of fire,
Against the Syrian king, who to surprise
One man, assassin-like, had levied war,
War unproclaimed. The princely Hierarch
In their bright stand there left his Powers, to seise
Possession of the garden; he alone,
To find where Adam sheltered, took his way,
Not unperceived of Adam; who to Eve,
While the great visitant approached, thus spake.
"Eve, now expect great tidings, which perhaps
Of us will soon determine, or impose
New laws to be observed; for I descry,
From yonder blazing cloud that veils the hill,
One of the heavenly host; and, by his gait,
None of the meanest; some great Potentate
Or of the Thrones above; such majesty

Invests him coming! yet not terrible,
That I should fear; nor sociably mild,
As Raphael, that I should much confide;
But solemn and sublime; whom not to offend,
With reverence I must meet, and thou retire."
He ended: and the Arch-Angel soon drew nigh,
Not in his shape celestial, but as man
Clad to meet man; over his lucid arms
A military vest of purple flowed,
Livelier than Meliboean, or the grain
Of Sarra, worn by kings and heroes old
In time of truce; Iris had dipt the woof;
His starry helm unbuckled showed him prime
In manhood where youth ended; by his side,
As in a glistering zodiac, hung the sword,
Satan's dire dread; and in his hand the spear.
Adam bowed low; he, kingly, from his state
Inclined not, but his coming thus declared.
"Adam, Heaven's high behest no preface needs:
Sufficient that thy prayers are heard; and Death,
Then due by sentence when thou didst transgress,
Defeated of his seisure many days
Given thee of grace; wherein thou mayest repent,
And one bad act with many deeds well done
Mayest cover: Well may then thy Lord, appeased,
Redeem thee quite from Death's rapacious claim;
But longer in this Paradise to dwell
Permits not: to remove thee I am come,
And send thee from the garden forth to till
The ground whence thou wast taken, fitter soil."
He added not; for Adam at the news
Heart-struck with chilling gripe of sorrow stood,
That all his senses bound; Eve, who unseen
Yet all had heard, with audible lament
Discovered soon the place of her retire.

"O unexpected stroke, worse than of Death!
Must I thus leave thee Paradise? thus leave
Thee, native soil! these happy walks and shades,
Fit haunt of Gods? where I had hope to spend,
Quiet though sad, the respite of that day
That must be mortal to us both. O flowers,
That never will in other climate grow,
My early visitation, and my last
At even, which I bred up with tender hand
From the first opening bud, and gave ye names,
Who now shall rear ye to the sun, or rank
Your tribes, and water from the ambrosial fount?
Thee lastly, nuptial bower! by me adorned
With what to sight or smell was sweet! from thee
How shall I part, and whither wander down
Into a lower world; to this obscure
And wild, how shall we breathe in other air
Less pure, accustomed to immortal fruits?"
Whom thus the Angel interrupted mild.
"Lament not, Eve, but patiently resign
What justly thou hast lost, nor set thy heart,
Thus over-fond, on that which is not thine:
Thy going is not lonely; with thee goes
Thy husband; whom to follow thou art bound;
Where he abides, think there thy native soil."
Adam, by this from the cold sudden damp
Recovering, and his scattered spirits returned,
To Michael thus his humble words addressed.
"Celestial, whether among the Thrones, or named
Of them the highest; for such of shape may seem
Prince above princes! gently hast thou told
Thy message, which might else in telling wound,
And in performing end us; what besides
Of sorrow, and dejection, and despair,
Our frailty can sustain, thy tidings bring,

Departure from this happy place, our sweet
Recess, and only consolation left
Familiar to our eyes! all places else
Inhospitable appear, and desolate;
Nor knowing us, nor known: And, if by prayer
Incessant I could hope to change the will
Of Him who all things can, I would not cease
To weary him with my assiduous cries:
But prayer against his absolute decree
No more avails than breath against the wind,
Blown stifling back on him that breathes it forth:
Therefore to his great bidding I submit.
This most afflicts me, that, departing hence,
As from his face I shall be hid, deprived
His blessed countenance: Here I could frequent
With worship place by place where he vouchsafed
Presence Divine; and to my sons relate,
'On this mount he appeared; under this tree
Stood visible; among these pines his voice
I heard; here with him at this fountain talked:'
So many grateful altars I would rear
Of grassy turf, and pile up every stone
Of lustre from the brook, in memory,
Or monument to ages; and theron
Offer sweet-smelling gums, and fruits, and flowers:
In yonder nether world where shall I seek
His bright appearances, or foot-step trace?
For though I fled him angry, yet recalled
To life prolonged and promised race, I now
Gladly behold though but his utmost skirts
Of glory; and far off his steps adore."
To whom thus Michael with regard benign.
"Adam, thou knowest Heaven his, and all the Earth;
Not this rock only; his Omnipresence fills
Land, sea, and air, and every kind that lives,

Fomented by his virtual power and warmed:
All the earth he gave thee to possess and rule,
No despicable gift; surmise not then
His presence to these narrow bounds confined
Of Paradise, or Eden: this had been
Perhaps thy capital seat, from whence had spread
All generations; and had hither come
From all the ends of the earth, to celebrate
And reverence thee, their great progenitor.
But this pre-eminence thou hast lost, brought down
To dwell on even ground now with thy sons:
Yet doubt not but in valley, and in plain,
God is, as here; and will be found alike
Present; and of his presence many a sign
Still following thee, still compassing thee round
With goodness and paternal love, his face
Express, and of his steps the track divine.
Which that thou mayest believe, and be confirmed
Ere thou from hence depart; know, I am sent
To show thee what shall come in future days
To thee, and to thy offspring: good with bad
Expect to hear; supernal grace contending
With sinfulness of men; thereby to learn
True patience, and to temper joy with fear
And pious sorrow; equally inured
By moderation either state to bear,
Prosperous or adverse: so shalt thou lead
Safest thy life, and best prepared endure
Thy mortal passage when it comes. Ascend
This hill; let Eve (for I have drenched her eyes)
Here sleep below; while thou to foresight wakest;
As once thou sleptst, while she to life was formed."
To whom thus Adam gratefully replied.
"Ascend, I follow thee, safe Guide, the path
Thou leadest me; and to the hand of Heaven submit,

However chastening; to the evil turn
My obvious breast; arming to overcome
By suffering, and earn rest from labour won,
If so I may attain." So both ascend
In the visions of God. It was a hill,
Of Paradise the highest; from whose top
The hemisphere of earth, in clearest ken,
Stretched out to the amplest reach of prospect lay.
Not higher that hill, nor wider looking round,
Whereon, for different cause, the Tempter set
Our second Adam, in the wilderness;
To show him all Earth's kingdoms, and their glory.
His eye might there command wherever stood
City of old or modern fame, the seat
Of mightiest empire, from the destined walls
Of Cambalu, seat of Cathaian Can,
And Samarchand by Oxus, Temir's throne,
To Paquin of Sinaean kings; and thence
To Agra and Lahor of great Mogul,
Down to the golden Chersonese; or where
The Persian in Ecbatan sat, or since
In Hispahan; or where the Russian Ksar
In Mosco; or the Sultan in Bizance,
Turchestan-born; nor could his eye not ken
The empire of Negus to his utmost port
Ercoco, and the less maritim kings
Mombaza, and Quiloa, and Melind,
And Sofala, thought Ophir, to the realm
Of Congo, and Angola farthest south;
Or thence from Niger flood to Atlas mount
The kingdoms of Almansor, Fez and Sus,
Morocco, and Algiers, and Tremisen;
On Europe thence, and where Rome was to sway
The world: in spirit perhaps he also saw
Rich Mexico, the seat of Montezume,

And Cusco in Peru, the richer seat
Of Atabalipa; and yet unspoiled
Guiana, whose great city Geryon's sons
Call El Dorado. But to nobler sights
Michael from Adam's eyes the film removed,
Which that false fruit that promised clearer sight
Had bred; then purged with euphrasy and rue
The visual nerve, for he had much to see;
And from the well of life three drops instilled.
So deep the power of these ingredients pierced,
Even to the inmost seat of mental sight,
That Adam, now enforced to close his eyes,
Sunk down, and all his spirits became entranced;
But him the gentle Angel by the hand
Soon raised, and his attention thus recalled.
"Adam, now ope thine eyes; and first behold
The effects, which thy original crime hath wrought
In some to spring from thee; who never touched
The excepted tree; nor with the snake conspired;
Nor sinned thy sin; yet from that sin derive
Corruption, to bring forth more violent deeds."
His eyes he opened, and beheld a field,
Part arable and tilth, whereon were sheaves
New reaped; the other part sheep-walks and folds;
I' the midst an altar as the land-mark stood,
Rustic, of grassy sord; thither anon
A sweaty reaper from his tillage brought
First fruits, the green ear, and the yellow sheaf,
Unculled, as came to hand; a shepherd next,
More meek, came with the firstlings of his flock,
Choicest and best; then, sacrificing, laid
The inwards and their fat, with incense strowed,
On the cleft wood, and all due rights performed:
His offering soon propitious fire from Heaven
Consumed with nimble glance, and grateful steam;

The other's not, for his was not sincere;
Whereat he inly raged, and, as they talked,
Smote him into the midriff with a stone
That beat out life; he fell; and, deadly pale,
Groaned out his soul with gushing blood effused.
Much at that sight was Adam in his heart
Dismayed, and thus in haste to the Angel cried.
"O Teacher, some great mischief hath befallen
To that meek man, who well had sacrificed;
Is piety thus and pure devotion paid?"
To whom Michael thus, he also moved, replied.
"These two are brethren, Adam, and to come
Out of thy loins; the unjust the just hath slain,
For envy that his brother's offering found
From Heaven acceptance; but the bloody fact
Will be avenged; and the other's faith, approved,
Lose no reward; though here thou see him die,
Rolling in dust and gore." To which our sire.
"Alas! both for the deed, and for the cause!
But have I now seen Death? Is this the way
I must return to native dust? O sight
Of terrour, foul and ugly to behold,
Horrid to think, how horrible to feel!"
To whom thus Michael. "Death thou hast seen
In his first shape on Man; but many shapes
Of Death, and many are the ways that lead
To his grim cave, all dismal; yet to sense
More terrible at the entrance, than within.
Some, as thou sawest, by violent stroke shall die;
By fire, flood, famine, by intemperance more
In meats and drinks, which on the earth shall bring
Diseases dire, of which a monstrous crew
Before thee shall appear; that thou mayest know
What misery the inabstinence of Eve
Shall bring on Men." Immediately a place

Before his eyes appeared, sad, noisome, dark;
A lazar-house it seemed; wherein were laid
Numbers of all diseased; all maladies
Of ghastly spasm, or racking torture, qualms
Of heart-sick agony, all feverous kinds,
Convulsions, epilepsies, fierce catarrhs,
Intestine stone and ulcer, colic-pangs,
Demoniac phrenzy, moaping melancholy,
And moon-struck madness, pining atrophy,
Marasmus, and wide-wasting pestilence,
Dropsies, and asthmas, and joint-racking rheums.
Dire was the tossing, deep the groans; Despair
Tended the sick busiest from couch to couch;
And over them triumphant Death his dart
Shook, but delayed to strike, though oft invoked
With vows, as their chief good, and final hope.
Sight so deform what heart of rock could long
Dry-eyed behold? Adam could not, but wept,
Though not of woman born; compassion quelled
His best of man, and gave him up to tears
A space, till firmer thoughts restrained excess;
And, scarce recovering words, his plaint renewed.
"O miserable mankind, to what fall
Degraded, to what wretched state reserved!
Better end here unborn. Why is life given
To be thus wrested from us? rather, why
Obtruded on us thus? who, if we knew
What we receive, would either no accept
Life offered, or soon beg to lay it down;
Glad to be so dismissed in peace. Can thus
The image of God in Man, created once
So goodly and erect, though faulty since,
To such unsightly sufferings be debased
Under inhuman pains? Why should not Man,
Retaining still divine similitude

In part, from such deformities be free,
And, for his Maker's image sake, exempt?"
"Their Maker's image," answered Michael, "then
Forsook them, when themselves they vilified
To serve ungoverned Appetite; and took
His image whom they served, a brutish vice,
Inductive mainly to the sin of Eve.
Therefore so abject is their punishment,
Disfiguring not God's likeness, but their own;
Or if his likeness, by themselves defaced;
While they pervert pure Nature's healthful rules
To loathsome sickness; worthily, since they
God's image did not reverence in themselves."
"I yield it just," said Adam, "and submit.
But is there yet no other way, besides
These painful passages, how we may come
To death, and mix with our connatural dust?"
"There is," said Michael, "if thou well observe
The rule of Not too much; by temperance taught,
In what thou eatest and drinkest; seeking from thence
Due nourishment, not gluttonous delight,
Till many years over thy head return:
So mayest thou live; till, like ripe fruit, thou drop
Into thy mother's lap; or be with ease
Gathered, nor harshly plucked; for death mature:
This is Old Age; but then, thou must outlive
Thy youth, thy strength, thy beauty; which will change
To withered, weak, and gray; thy senses then,
Obtuse, all taste of pleasure must forego,
To what thou hast; and, for the air of youth,
Hopeful and cheerful, in thy blood will reign
A melancholy damp of cold and dry
To weigh thy spirits down, and last consume
The balm of life." To whom our ancestor.
"Henceforth I fly not death, nor would prolong

Life much; bent rather, how I may be quit,
Fairest and easiest, of this cumbrous charge;
Which I must keep till my appointed day
Of rendering up, and patiently attend
My dissolution." Michael replied.
"Nor love thy life, nor hate; but what thou livest
Live well; how long, or short, permit to Heaven:
And now prepare thee for another sight."
He looked, and saw a spacious plain, whereon
Were tents of various hue; by some, were herds
Of cattle grazing; others, whence the sound
Of instruments, that made melodious chime,
Was heard, of harp and organ; and, who moved
Their stops and chords, was seen; his volant touch,
Instinct through all proportions, low and high,
Fled and pursued transverse the resonant fugue.
In other part stood one who, at the forge
Labouring, two massy clods of iron and brass
Had melted, (whether found where casual fire
Had wasted woods on mountain or in vale,
Down to the veins of earth; thence gliding hot
To some cave's mouth; or whether washed by stream
From underground;) the liquid ore he drained
Into fit moulds prepared; from which he formed
First his own tools; then, what might else be wrought
Fusil or graven in metal. After these,
But on the hither side, a different sort
From the high neighbouring hills, which was their seat,
Down to the plain descended; by their guise
Just men they seemed, and all their study bent
To worship God aright, and know his works
Not hid; nor those things last, which might preserve
Freedom and peace to Men; they on the plain
Long had not walked, when from the tents, behold!
A bevy of fair women, richly gay

In gems and wanton dress; to the harp they sung
Soft amorous ditties, and in dance came on:
The men, though grave, eyed them; and let their eyes
Rove without rein; till, in the amorous net
Fast caught, they liked; and each his liking chose;
And now of love they treat, till the evening-star,
Love's harbinger, appeared; then, all in heat
They light the nuptial torch, and bid invoke
Hymen, then first to marriage rites invoked:
With feast and music all the tents resound.
Such happy interview, and fair event
Of love and youth not lost, songs, garlands, flowers,
And charming symphonies, attached the heart
Of Adam, soon inclined to admit delight,
The bent of nature; which he thus expressed.
"True opener of mine eyes, prime Angel blest;
Much better seems this vision, and more hope
Of peaceful days portends, than those two past;
Those were of hate and death, or pain much worse;
Here Nature seems fulfilled in all her ends."
To whom thus Michael. "Judge not what is best
By pleasure, though to nature seeming meet;
Created, as thou art, to nobler end
Holy and pure, conformity divine.
Those tents thou sawest so pleasant, were the tents
Of wickedness, wherein shall dwell his race
Who slew his brother; studious they appear
Of arts that polish life, inventors rare;
Unmindful of their Maker, though his Spirit
Taught them; but they his gifts acknowledged none.
Yet they a beauteous offspring shall beget;
For that fair female troop thou sawest, that seemed
Of Goddesses, so blithe, so smooth, so gay,
Yet empty of all good wherein consists
Woman's domestic honour and chief praise;

Bred only and completed to the taste
Of lustful appetence, to sing, to dance,
To dress, and troll the tongue, and roll the eye:
To these that sober race of men, whose lives
Religious titled them the sons of God,
Shall yield up all their virtue, all their fame
Ignobly, to the trains and to the smiles
Of these fair atheists; and now swim in joy,
Erelong to swim at large; and laugh, for which
The world erelong a world of tears must weep."
To whom thus Adam, of short joy bereft.
"O pity and shame, that they, who to live well
Entered so fair, should turn aside to tread
Paths indirect, or in the mid way faint!
But still I see the tenour of Man's woe
Holds on the same, from Woman to begin."
"From Man's effeminate slackness it begins,"
Said the Angel, "who should better hold his place
By wisdom, and superior gifts received.
But now prepare thee for another scene."
He looked, and saw wide territory spread
Before him, towns, and rural works between;
Cities of men with lofty gates and towers,
Concourse in arms, fierce faces threatening war,
Giants of mighty bone and bold emprise;
Part wield their arms, part curb the foaming steed,
Single or in array of battle ranged
Both horse and foot, nor idly mustering stood;
One way a band select from forage drives
A herd of beeves, fair oxen and fair kine,
From a fat meadow ground; or fleecy flock,
Ewes and their bleating lambs over the plain,
Their booty; scarce with life the shepherds fly,
But call in aid, which makes a bloody fray;
With cruel tournament the squadrons join;

Where cattle pastured late, now scattered lies
With carcasses and arms the ensanguined field,
Deserted: Others to a city strong
Lay siege, encamped; by battery, scale, and mine,
Assaulting; others from the wall defend
With dart and javelin, stones, and sulphurous fire;
On each hand slaughter, and gigantic deeds.
In other part the sceptered heralds call
To council, in the city-gates; anon
Gray-headed men and grave, with warriors mixed,
Assemble, and harangues are heard; but soon,
In factious opposition; till at last,
Of middle age one rising, eminent
In wise deport, spake much of right and wrong,
Of justice, or religion, truth, and peace,
And judgement from above: him old and young
Exploded, and had seized with violent hands,
Had not a cloud descending snatched him thence
Unseen amid the throng: so violence
Proceeded, and oppression, and sword-law,
Through all the plain, and refuge none was found.
Adam was all in tears, and to his guide
Lamenting turned full sad; "O! what are these,
Death's ministers, not men? who thus deal death
Inhumanly to men, and multiply
Ten thousandfold the sin of him who slew
His brother: for of whom such massacre
Make they, but of their brethren; men of men
But who was that just man, whom had not Heaven
Rescued, had in his righteousness been lost?"
To whom thus Michael. "These are the product
Of those ill-mated marriages thou sawest;
Where good with bad were matched, who of themselves
Abhor to join; and, by imprudence mixed,
Produce prodigious births of body or mind.

Such were these giants, men of high renown;
For in those days might only shall be admired,
And valour and heroic virtue called;
To overcome in battle, and subdue
Nations, and bring home spoils with infinite
Man-slaughter, shall be held the highest pitch
Of human glory; and for glory done
Of triumph, to be styled great conquerours
Patrons of mankind, Gods, and sons of Gods;
Destroyers rightlier called, and plagues of men.
Thus fame shall be achieved, renown on earth;
And what most merits fame, in silence hid.
But he, the seventh from thee, whom thou beheldst
The only righteous in a world preverse,
And therefore hated, therefore so beset
With foes, for daring single to be just,
And utter odious truth, that God would come
To judge them with his Saints; him the Most High
Rapt in a balmy cloud with winged steeds
Did, as thou sawest, receive, to walk with God
High in salvation and the climes of bliss,
Exempt from death; to show thee what reward
Awaits the good; the rest what punishment;
Which now direct thine eyes and soon behold."
He looked, and saw the face of things quite changed;
The brazen throat of war had ceased to roar;
All now was turned to jollity and game,
To luxury and riot, feast and dance;
Marrying or prostituting, as befell,
Rape or adultery, where passing fair
Allured them; thence from cups to civil broils.
At length a reverend sire among them came,
And of their doings great dislike declared,
And testified against their ways; he oft
Frequented their assemblies, whereso met,

Triumphs or festivals; and to them preached
Conversion and repentance, as to souls
In prison, under judgements imminent:
But all in vain: which when he saw, he ceased
Contending, and removed his tents far off;
Then, from the mountain hewing timber tall,
Began to build a vessel of huge bulk;
Measured by cubit, length, and breadth, and hight;
Smeared round with pitch; and in the side a door
Contrived; and of provisions laid in large,
For man and beast: when lo, a wonder strange!
Of every beast, and bird, and insect small,
Came sevens, and pairs; and entered in as taught
Their order: last the sire and his three sons,
With their four wives; and God made fast the door.
Meanwhile the south-wind rose, and, with black wings
Wide-hovering, all the clouds together drove
From under Heaven; the hills to their supply
Vapour, and exhalation dusk and moist,
Sent up amain; and now the thickened sky
Like a dark ceiling stood; down rushed the rain
Impetuous; and continued, till the earth
No more was seen: the floating vessel swum
Uplifted, and secure with beaked prow
Rode tilting o'er the waves; all dwellings else
Flood overwhelmed, and them with all their pomp
Deep under water rolled; sea covered sea,
Sea without shore; and in their palaces,
Where luxury late reigned, sea-monsters whelped
And stabled; of mankind, so numerous late,
All left, in one small bottom swum imbarked.
How didst thou grieve then, Adam, to behold
The end of all thy offspring, end so sad,
Depopulation! Thee another flood,
Of tears and sorrow a flood, thee also drowned,

And sunk thee as thy sons; till, gently reared
By the Angel, on thy feet thou stoodest at last,
Though comfortless; as when a father mourns
His children, all in view destroyed at once;
And scarce to the Angel utter'dst thus thy plaint.
"O visions ill foreseen! Better had I
Lived ignorant of future! so had borne
My part of evil only, each day's lot
Enough to bear; those now, that were dispensed
The burden of many ages, on me light
At once, by my foreknowledge gaining birth
Abortive, to torment me ere their being,
With thought that they must be. Let no man seek
Henceforth to be foretold, what shall befall
Him or his children; evil he may be sure,
Which neither his foreknowing can prevent;
And he the future evil shall no less
In apprehension than in substance feel,
Grievous to bear: but that care now is past,
Man is not whom to warn: those few escaped
Famine and anguish will at last consume,
Wandering that watery desart: I had hope,
When violence was ceased, and war on earth,
All would have then gone well; peace would have crowned
With length of happy days the race of Man;
But I was far deceived; for now I see
Peace to corrupt no less than war to waste.
How comes it thus? unfold, celestial Guide,
And whether here the race of Man will end."
To whom thus Michael. "Those, whom last thou sawest
In triumph and luxurious wealth, are they
First seen in acts of prowess eminent
And great exploits, but of true virtue void;
Who, having spilt much blood, and done much wast
Subduing nations, and achieved thereby

Fame in the world, high titles, and rich prey;
Shall change their course to pleasure, ease, and sloth,
Surfeit, and lust; till wantonness and pride
Raise out of friendship hostile deeds in peace.
The conquered also, and enslaved by war,
Shall, with their freedom lost, all virtue lose
And fear of God; from whom their piety feigned
In sharp contest of battle found no aid
Against invaders; therefore, cooled in zeal,
Thenceforth shall practice how to live secure,
Worldly or dissolute, on what their lords
Shall leave them to enjoy; for the earth shall bear
More than enough, that temperance may be tried:
So all shall turn degenerate, all depraved;
Justice and temperance, truth and faith, forgot;
One man except, the only son of light
In a dark age, against example good,
Against allurement, custom, and a world
Offended: fearless of reproach and scorn,
Or violence, he of their wicked ways
Shall them admonish; and before them set
The paths of righteousness, how much more safe
And full of peace; denouncing wrath to come
On their impenitence; and shall return
Of them derided, but of God observed
The one just man alive; by his command
Shall build a wonderous ark, as thou beheldst,
To save himself, and houshold, from amidst
A world devote to universal wrack.
No sooner he, with them of man and beast
Select for life, shall in the ark be lodged,
And sheltered round; but all the cataracts
Of Heaven set open on the Earth shall pour
Rain, day and night; all fountains of the deep,
Broke up, shall heave the ocean to usurp

Beyond all bounds; till inundation rise
Above the highest hills: Then shall this mount
Of Paradise by might of waves be moved
Out of his place, pushed by the horned flood,
With all his verdure spoiled, and trees adrift,
Down the great river to the opening gulf,
And there take root an island salt and bare,
The haunt of seals, and orcs, and sea-mews' clang:
To teach thee that God attributes to place
No sanctity, if none be thither brought
By men who there frequent, or therein dwell.
And now, what further shall ensue, behold."
He looked, and saw the ark hull on the flood,
Which now abated; for the clouds were fled,
Driven by a keen north-wind, that, blowing dry,
Wrinkled the face of deluge, as decayed;
And the clear sun on his wide watery glass
Gazed hot, and of the fresh wave largely drew,
As after thirst; which made their flowing shrink
From standing lake to tripping ebb, that stole
With soft foot towards the deep; who now had stopt
His sluices, as the Heaven his windows shut.
The ark no more now floats, but seems on ground,
Fast on the top of some high mountain fixed.
And now the tops of hills, as rocks, appear;
With clamour thence the rapid currents drive,
Towards the retreating sea, their furious tide.
Forthwith from out the ark a raven flies,
And after him, the surer messenger,
A dove sent forth once and again to spy
Green tree or ground, whereon his foot may light:
The second time returning, in his bill
An olive-leaf he brings, pacifick sign:
Anon dry ground appears, and from his ark
The ancient sire descends, with all his train;

Then with uplifted hands, and eyes devout,
Grateful to Heaven, over his head beholds
A dewy cloud, and in the cloud a bow
Conspicuous with three lifted colours gay,
Betokening peace from God, and covenant new.
Whereat the heart of Adam, erst so sad,
Greatly rejoiced; and thus his joy broke forth.
"O thou, who future things canst represent
As present, heavenly Instructor! I revive
At this last sight; assured that Man shall live,
With all the creatures, and their seed preserve.
Far less I now lament for one whole world
Of wicked sons destroyed, than I rejoice
For one man found so perfect, and so just,
That God vouchsafes to raise another world
From him, and all his anger to forget.
But say, what mean those coloured streaks in Heaven
Distended, as the brow of God appeased?
Or serve they, as a flowery verge, to bind
The fluid skirts of that same watery cloud,
Lest it again dissolve, and shower the earth?"
To whom the Arch-Angel. "Dextrously thou aimest;
So willingly doth God remit his ire,
Though late repenting him of Man depraved;
Grieved at his heart, when looking down he saw
The whole earth filled with violence, and all flesh
Corrupting each their way; yet, those removed,
Such grace shall one just man find in his sight,
That he relents, not to blot out mankind;
And makes a covenant never to destroy
The earth again by flood; nor let the sea
Surpass his bounds; nor rain to drown the world,
With man therein or beast; but, when he brings
Over the earth a cloud, will therein set
His triple-coloured bow, whereon to look,

And call to mind his covenant: Day and night,
Seed-time and harvest, heat and hoary frost,
Shall hold their course; till fire purge all things new,
Both Heaven and Earth, wherein the just shall dwell."

BOOK XII

As one who in his journey bates at noon,
Though bent on speed; so here the Arch-Angel paused
Betwixt the world destroyed and world restored,
If Adam aught perhaps might interpose;
Then, with transition sweet, new speech resumes.
"Thus thou hast seen one world begin, and end;
And Man, as from a second stock, proceed.
Much thou hast yet to see; but I perceive
Thy mortal sight to fail; objects divine
Must needs impair and weary human sense:
Henceforth what is to come I will relate;
Thou therefore give due audience, and attend.
This second source of Men, while yet but few,
And while the dread of judgement past remains
Fresh in their minds, fearing the Deity,
With some regard to what is just and right
Shall lead their lives, and multiply apace;
Labouring the soil, and reaping plenteous crop,
Corn, wine, and oil; and, from the herd or flock,
Oft sacrificing bullock, lamb, or kid,
With large wine-offerings poured, and sacred feast,
Shall spend their days in joy unblamed; and dwell

Long time in peace, by families and tribes,
Under paternal rule: till one shall rise
Of proud ambitious heart; who, not content
With fair equality, fraternal state,
Will arrogate dominion undeserved
Over his brethren, and quite dispossess
Concord and law of nature from the earth;
Hunting (and men not beasts shall be his game)
With war, and hostile snare, such as refuse
Subjection to his empire tyrannous:
A mighty hunter thence he shall be styled
Before the Lord; as in despite of Heaven,
Or from Heaven, claiming second sovranty;
And from rebellion shall derive his name,
Though of rebellion others he accuse.
He with a crew, whom like ambition joins
With him or under him to tyrannize,
Marching from Eden towards the west, shall find
The plain, wherein a black bituminous gurge
Boils out from under ground, the mouth of Hell:
Of brick, and of that stuff, they cast to build
A city and tower, whose top may reach to Heaven;
And get themselves a name; lest, far dispersed
In foreign lands, their memory be lost;
Regardless whether good or evil fame.
But God, who oft descends to visit men
Unseen, and through their habitations walks
To mark their doings, them beholding soon,
Comes down to see their city, ere the tower
Obstruct Heaven-towers, and in derision sets
Upon their tongues a various spirit, to rase
Quite out their native language; and, instead,
To sow a jangling noise of words unknown:
Forthwith a hideous gabble rises loud,
Among the builders; each to other calls

Not understood; till hoarse, and all in rage,
As mocked they storm: great laughter was in Heaven,
And looking down, to see the hubbub strange,
And hear the din: Thus was the building left
Ridiculous, and the work Confusion named."
Whereto thus Adam, fatherly displeased.
"O execrable son! so to aspire
Above his brethren; to himself assuming
Authority usurped, from God not given:
He gave us only over beast, fish, fowl,
Dominion absolute; that right we hold
By his donation; but man over men
He made not lord; such title to himself
Reserving, human left from human free.
But this usurper his encroachment proud
Stays not on Man; to God his tower intends
Siege and defiance: Wretched man! what food
Will he convey up thither, to sustain
Himself and his rash army; where thin air
Above the clouds will pine his entrails gross,
And famish him of breath, if not of bread?"
To whom thus Michael. "Justly thou abhorrest
That son, who on the quiet state of men
Such trouble brought, affecting to subdue
Rational liberty; yet know withal,
Since thy original lapse, true liberty
Is lost, which always with right reason dwells
Twinned, and from her hath no dividual being:
Reason in man obscured, or not obeyed,
Immediately inordinate desires,
And upstart passions, catch the government
From reason; and to servitude reduce
Man, till then free. Therefore, since he permits
Within himself unworthy powers to reign
Over free reason, God, in judgement just,

Subjects him from without to violent lords;
Who oft as undeservedly enthrall
His outward freedom: Tyranny must be;
Though to the tyrant thereby no excuse.
Yet sometimes nations will decline so low
From virtue, which is reason, that no wrong,
But justice, and some fatal curse annexed,
Deprives them of their outward liberty;
Their inward lost: Witness the irreverent son
Of him who built the ark; who, for the shame
Done to his father, heard this heavy curse,
Servant of servants, on his vicious race.
Thus will this latter, as the former world,
Still tend from bad to worse; till God at last,
Wearied with their iniquities, withdraw
His presence from among them, and avert
His holy eyes; resolving from thenceforth
To leave them to their own polluted ways;
And one peculiar nation to select
From all the rest, of whom to be invoked,
A nation from one faithful man to spring:
Him on this side Euphrates yet residing,
Bred up in idol-worship: O, that men
(Canst thou believe?) should be so stupid grown,
While yet the patriarch lived, who 'scaped the flood,
As to forsake the living God, and fall
To worship their own work in wood and stone
For Gods! Yet him God the Most High vouchsafes
To call by vision, from his father's house,
His kindred, and false Gods, into a land
Which he will show him; and from him will raise
A mighty nation; and upon him shower
His benediction so, that in his seed
All nations shall be blest: he straight obeys;
Not knowing to what land, yet firm believes:

I see him, but thou canst not, with what faith
He leaves his Gods, his friends, and native soil,
Ur of Chaldaea, passing now the ford
To Haran; after him a cumbrous train
Of herds and flocks, and numerous servitude;
Not wandering poor, but trusting all his wealth
With God, who called him, in a land unknown.
Canaan he now attains; I see his tents
Pitched about Sechem, and the neighbouring plain
Of Moreh; there by promise he receives
Gift to his progeny of all that land,
From Hameth northward to the Desert south;
(Things by their names I call, though yet unnamed;)
From Hermon east to the great western Sea;
Mount Hermon, yonder sea; each place behold
In prospect, as I point them; on the shore
Mount Carmel; here, the double-founted stream,
Jordan, true limit eastward; but his sons
Shall dwell to Senir, that long ridge of hills.
This ponder, that all nations of the earth
Shall in his seed be blessed: By that seed
Is meant thy great Deliverer, who shall bruise
The Serpent's head; whereof to thee anon
Plainlier shall be revealed. This patriarch blest,
Whom faithful Abraham due time shall call,
A son, and of his son a grand-child, leaves;
Like him in faith, in wisdom, and renown:
The grandchild, with twelve sons increased, departs
From Canaan to a land hereafter called
Egypt, divided by the river Nile
See where it flows, disgorging at seven mouths
Into the sea. To sojourn in that land
He comes, invited by a younger son
In time of dearth, a son whose worthy deeds
Raise him to be the second in that realm

Of Pharaoh. There he dies, and leaves his race
Growing into a nation, and now grown
Suspected to a sequent king, who seeks
To stop their overgrowth, as inmate guests
Too numerous; whence of guests he makes them slaves
Inhospitably, and kills their infant males:
Till by two brethren (these two brethren call
Moses and Aaron) sent from God to claim
His people from enthralment, they return,
With glory and spoil, back to their promised land.
But first, the lawless tyrant, who denies
To know their God, or message to regard,
Must be compelled by signs and judgements dire;
To blood unshed the rivers must be turned;
Frogs, lice, and flies, must all his palace fill
With loathed intrusion, and fill all the land;
His cattle must of rot and murren die;
Botches and blains must all his flesh emboss,
And all his people; thunder mixed with hail,
Hail mixed with fire, must rend the Egyptians sky,
And wheel on the earth, devouring where it rolls;
What it devours not, herb, or fruit, or grain,
A darksome cloud of locusts swarming down
Must eat, and on the ground leave nothing green;
Darkness must overshadow all his bounds,
Palpable darkness, and blot out three days;
Last, with one midnight stroke, all the first-born
Of Egypt must lie dead. Thus with ten wounds
The river-dragon tamed at length submits
To let his sojourners depart, and oft
Humbles his stubborn heart; but still, as ice
More hardened after thaw; till, in his rage
Pursuing whom he late dismissed, the sea
Swallows him with his host; but them lets pass,
As on dry land, between two crystal walls;

Awed by the rod of Moses so to stand
Divided, till his rescued gain their shore:
Such wondrous power God to his saint will lend,
Though present in his Angel; who shall go
Before them in a cloud, and pillar of fire;
By day a cloud, by night a pillar of fire;
To guide them in their journey, and remove
Behind them, while the obdurate king pursues:
All night he will pursue; but his approach
Darkness defends between till morning watch;
Then through the fiery pillar, and the cloud,
God looking forth will trouble all his host,
And craze their chariot-wheels: when by command
Moses once more his potent rod extends
Over the sea; the sea his rod obeys;
On their embattled ranks the waves return,
And overwhelm their war: The race elect
Safe toward Canaan from the shore advance
Through the wild Desart, not the readiest way;
Lest, entering on the Canaanite alarmed,
War terrify them inexpert, and fear
Return them back to Egypt, choosing rather
Inglorious life with servitude; for life
To noble and ignoble is more sweet
Untrained in arms, where rashness leads not on.
This also shall they gain by their delay
In the wide wilderness; there they shall found
Their government, and their great senate choose
Through the twelve tribes, to rule by laws ordained:
God from the mount of Sinai, whose gray top
Shall tremble, he descending, will himself
In thunder, lightning, and loud trumpets' sound,
Ordain them laws; part, such as appertain
To civil justice; part, religious rites
Of sacrifice; informing them, by types

And shadows, of that destined Seed to bruise
The Serpent, by what means he shall achieve
Mankind's deliverance. But the voice of God
To mortal ear is dreadful: They beseech
That Moses might report to them his will,
And terrour cease; he grants what they besought,
Instructed that to God is no access
Without Mediator, whose high office now
Moses in figure bears; to introduce
One greater, of whose day he shall foretell,
And all the Prophets in their age the times
Of great Messiah shall sing. Thus, laws and rites
Established, such delight hath God in Men
Obedient to his will, that he vouchsafes
Among them to set up his tabernacle;
The Holy One with mortal Men to dwell:
By his prescript a sanctuary is framed
Of cedar, overlaid with gold; therein
An ark, and in the ark his testimony,
The records of his covenant; over these
A mercy-seat of gold, between the wings
Of two bright Cherubim; before him burn
Seven lamps as in a zodiack representing
The heavenly fires; over the tent a cloud
Shall rest by day, a fiery gleam by night;
Save when they journey, and at length they come,
Conducted by his Angel, to the land
Promised to Abraham and his seed: The rest
Were long to tell; how many battles fought
How many kings destroyed; and kingdoms won;
Or how the sun shall in mid Heaven stand still
A day entire, and night's due course adjourn,
Man's voice commanding, 'Sun, in Gibeon stand,
And thou moon in the vale of Aialon,
Till Israel overcome!' so call the third

From Abraham, son of Isaac; and from him
His whole descent, who thus shall Canaan win."
Here Adam interposed. "O sent from Heaven,
Enlightener of my darkness, gracious things
Thou hast revealed; those chiefly, which concern
Just Abraham and his seed: now first I find
Mine eyes true-opening, and my heart much eased;
Erewhile perplexed with thoughts, what would become
Of me and all mankind: But now I see
His day, in whom all nations shall be blest;
Favour unmerited by me, who sought
Forbidden knowledge by forbidden means.
This yet I apprehend not, why to those
Among whom God will deign to dwell on earth
So many and so various laws are given;
So many laws argue so many sins
Among them; how can God with such reside?"
To whom thus Michael. "Doubt not but that sin
Will reign among them, as of thee begot;
And therefore was law given them, to evince
Their natural pravity, by stirring up
Sin against law to fight: that when they see
Law can discover sin, but not remove,
Save by those shadowy expiations weak,
The blood of bulls and goats, they may conclude
Some blood more precious must be paid for Man;
Just for unjust; that, in such righteousness
To them by faith imputed, they may find
Justification towards God, and peace
Of conscience; which the law by ceremonies
Cannot appease; nor Man the mortal part
Perform; and, not performing, cannot live.
So law appears imperfect; and but given
With purpose to resign them, in full time,
Up to a better covenant; disciplined

From shadowy types to truth; from flesh to spirit;
From imposition of strict laws to free
Acceptance of large grace; from servile fear
To filial; works of law to works of faith.
And therefore shall not Moses, though of God
Highly beloved, being but the minister
Of law, his people into Canaan lead;
But Joshua, whom the Gentiles Jesus call,
His name and office bearing, who shall quell
The adversary-Serpent, and bring back
Through the world's wilderness long-wandered Man
Safe to eternal Paradise of rest.
Meanwhile they, in their earthly Canaan placed,
Long time shall dwell and prosper, but when sins
National interrupt their public peace,
Provoking God to raise them enemies;
From whom as oft he saves them penitent
By Judges first, then under Kings; of whom
The second, both for piety renowned
And puissant deeds, a promise shall receive
Irrevocable, that his regal throne
For ever shall endure; the like shall sing
All Prophecy, that of the royal stock
Of David (so I name this king) shall rise
A Son, the Woman's seed to thee foretold,
Foretold to Abraham, as in whom shall trust
All nations; and to kings foretold, of kings
The last; for of his reign shall be no end.
But first, a long succession must ensue;
And his next son, for wealth and wisdom famed,
The clouded ark of God, till then in tents
Wandering, shall in a glorious temple enshrine.
Such follow him, as shall be registered
Part good, part bad; of bad the longer scroll;
Whose foul idolatries, and other faults

Heaped to the popular sum, will so incense
God, as to leave them, and expose their land,
Their city, his temple, and his holy ark,
With all his sacred things, a scorn and prey
To that proud city, whose high walls thou sawest
Left in confusion; Babylon thence called.
There in captivity he lets them dwell
The space of seventy years; then brings them back,
Remembering mercy, and his covenant sworn
To David, stablished as the days of Heaven.
Returned from Babylon by leave of kings
Their lords, whom God disposed, the house of God
They first re-edify; and for a while
In mean estate live moderate; till, grown
In wealth and multitude, factious they grow;
But first among the priests dissention springs,
Men who attend the altar, and should most
Endeavour peace: their strife pollution brings
Upon the temple itself: at last they seize
The scepter, and regard not David's sons;
Then lose it to a stranger, that the true
Anointed King Messiah might be born
Barred of his right; yet at his birth a star,
Unseen before in Heaven, proclaims him come;
And guides the eastern sages, who inquire
His place, to offer incense, myrrh, and gold:
His place of birth a solemn Angel tells
To simple shepherds, keeping watch by night;
They gladly thither haste, and by a quire
Of squadroned Angels hear his carol sung.
A virgin is his mother, but his sire
The power of the Most High: He shall ascend
The throne hereditary, and bound his reign
With Earth's wide bounds, his glory with the Heavens."
He ceased, discerning Adam with such joy

Surcharged, as had like grief been dewed in tears,
Without the vent of words; which these he breathed.
"O prophet of glad tidings, finisher
Of utmost hope! now clear I understand
What oft my steadiest thoughts have searched in vain;
Why our great Expectation should be called
The seed of Woman: Virgin Mother, hail,
High in the love of Heaven; yet from my loins
Thou shalt proceed, and from thy womb the Son
Of God Most High: so God with Man unites!
Needs must the Serpent now his capital bruise
Expect with mortal pain: Say where and when
Their fight, what stroke shall bruise the victor's heel."
To whom thus Michael. "Dream not of their fight,
As of a duel, or the local wounds
Of head or heel: Not therefore joins the Son
Manhood to Godhead, with more strength to foil
Thy enemy; nor so is overcome
Satan, whose fall from Heaven, a deadlier bruise,
Disabled, not to give thee thy death's wound:
Which he, who comes thy Saviour, shall recure,
Not by destroying Satan, but his works
In thee, and in thy seed: Nor can this be,
But by fulfilling that which thou didst want,
Obedience to the law of God, imposed
On penalty of death, and suffering death;
The penalty to thy transgression due,
And due to theirs which out of thine will grow:
So only can high Justice rest appaid.
The law of God exact he shall fulfil
Both by obedience and by love, though love
Alone fulfil the law; thy punishment
He shall endure, by coming in the flesh
To a reproachful life, and cursed death;
Proclaiming life to all who shall believe

In his redemption; and that his obedience,
Imputed, becomes theirs by faith; his merits
To save them, not their own, though legal, works.
For this he shall live hated, be blasphemed,
Seized on by force, judged, and to death condemned
A shameful and accursed, nailed to the cross
By his own nation; slain for bringing life:
But to the cross he nails thy enemies,
The law that is against thee, and the sins
Of all mankind, with him there crucified,
Never to hurt them more who rightly trust
In this his satisfaction; so he dies,
But soon revives; Death over him no power
Shall long usurp; ere the third dawning light
Return, the stars of morn shall see him rise
Out of his grave, fresh as the dawning light,
Thy ransom paid, which Man from death redeems,
His death for Man, as many as offered life
Neglect not, and the benefit embrace
By faith not void of works: This God-like act
Annuls thy doom, the death thou shouldest have died,
In sin for ever lost from life; this act
Shall bruise the head of Satan, crush his strength,
Defeating Sin and Death, his two main arms;
And fix far deeper in his head their stings
Than temporal death shall bruise the victor's heel,
Or theirs whom he redeems; a death, like sleep,
A gentle wafting to immortal life.
Nor after resurrection shall he stay
Longer on earth, than certain times to appear
To his disciples, men who in his life
Still followed him; to them shall leave in charge
To teach all nations what of him they learned
And his salvation; them who shall believe
Baptizing in the profluent stream, the sign

Of washing them from guilt of sin to life
Pure, and in mind prepared, if so befall,
For death, like that which the Redeemer died.
All nations they shall teach; for, from that day,
Not only to the sons of Abraham's loins
Salvation shall be preached, but to the sons
Of Abraham's faith wherever through the world;
So in his seed all nations shall be blest.
Then to the Heaven of Heavens he shall ascend
With victory, triumphing through the air
Over his foes and thine; there shall surprise
The Serpent, prince of air, and drag in chains
Through all his realm, and there confounded leave;
Then enter into glory, and resume
His seat at God's right hand, exalted high
Above all names in Heaven; and thence shall come,
When this world's dissolution shall be ripe,
With glory and power to judge both quick and dead;
To judge the unfaithful dead, but to reward
His faithful, and receive them into bliss,
Whether in Heaven or Earth; for then the Earth
Shall all be Paradise, far happier place
Than this of Eden, and far happier days."
So spake the Arch-Angel Michael; then paused,
As at the world's great period; and our sire,
Replete with joy and wonder, thus replied.
"O Goodness infinite, Goodness immense!
That all this good of evil shall produce,
And evil turn to good; more wonderful
Than that which by creation first brought forth
Light out of darkness! Full of doubt I stand,
Whether I should repent me now of sin
By me done, and occasioned; or rejoice
Much more, that much more good thereof shall spring;
To God more glory, more good-will to Men

From God, and over wrath grace shall abound.
But say, if our Deliverer up to Heaven
Must re-ascend, what will betide the few
His faithful, left among the unfaithful herd,
The enemies of truth? Who then shall guide
His people, who defend? Will they not deal
Worse with his followers than with him they dealt?"
"Be sure they will," said the Angel; "but from Heaven
He to his own a Comforter will send,
The promise of the Father, who shall dwell
His Spirit within them; and the law of faith,
Working through love, upon their hearts shall write,
To guide them in all truth; and also arm
With spiritual armour, able to resist
Satan's assaults, and quench his fiery darts;
What man can do against them, not afraid,
Though to the death; against such cruelties
With inward consolations recompensed,
And oft supported so as shall amaze
Their proudest persecutors: For the Spirit,
Poured first on his Apostles, whom he sends
To evangelize the nations, then on all
Baptized, shall them with wonderous gifts endue
To speak all tongues, and do all miracles,
As did their Lord before them. Thus they win
Great numbers of each nation to receive
With joy the tidings brought from Heaven: At length
Their ministry performed, and race well run,
Their doctrine and their story written left,
They die; but in their room, as they forewarn,
Wolves shall succeed for teachers, grievous wolves,
Who all the sacred mysteries of Heaven
To their own vile advantages shall turn
Of lucre and ambition; and the truth
With superstitions and traditions taint,

Left only in those written records pure,
Though not but by the Spirit understood.
Then shall they seek to avail themselves of names,
Places, and titles, and with these to join
Secular power; though feigning still to act
By spiritual, to themselves appropriating
The Spirit of God, promised alike and given
To all believers; and, from that pretence,
Spiritual laws by carnal power shall force
On every conscience; laws which none shall find
Left them inrolled, or what the Spirit within
Shall on the heart engrave. What will they then
But force the Spirit of Grace itself, and bind
His consort Liberty? what, but unbuild
His living temples, built by faith to stand,
Their own faith, not another's? for, on earth,
Who against faith and conscience can be heard
Infallible? yet many will presume:
Whence heavy persecution shall arise
On all, who in the worship persevere
Of spirit and truth; the rest, far greater part,
Will deem in outward rites and specious forms
Religion satisfied; Truth shall retire
Bestuck with slanderous darts, and works of faith
Rarely be found: So shall the world go on,
To good malignant, to bad men benign;
Under her own weight groaning; till the day
Appear of respiration to the just,
And vengeance to the wicked, at return
Of him so lately promised to thy aid,
The Woman's Seed; obscurely then foretold,
Now ampler known thy Saviour and thy Lord;
Last, in the clouds, from Heaven to be revealed
In glory of the Father, to dissolve
Satan with his perverted world; then raise

From the conflagrant mass, purged and refined,
New Heavens, new Earth, ages of endless date,
Founded in righteousness, and peace, and love;
To bring forth fruits, joy and eternal bliss."
He ended; and thus Adam last replied.
"How soon hath thy prediction, Seer blest,
Measured this transient world, the race of time,
Till time stand fixed! Beyond is all abyss,
Eternity, whose end no eye can reach.
Greatly-instructed I shall hence depart;
Greatly in peace of thought; and have my fill
Of knowledge, what this vessel can contain;
Beyond which was my folly to aspire.
Henceforth I learn, that to obey is best,
And love with fear the only God; to walk
As in his presence; ever to observe
His providence; and on him sole depend,
Merciful over all his works, with good
Still overcoming evil, and by small
Accomplishing great things, by things deemed weak
Subverting worldly strong, and worldly wise
By simply meek: that suffering for truth's sake
Is fortitude to highest victory,
And, to the faithful, death the gate of life;
Taught this by his example, whom I now
Acknowledge my Redeemer ever blest."
To whom thus also the Angel last replied.
"This having learned, thou hast attained the sum
Of wisdom; hope no higher, though all the stars
Thou knewest by name, and all the ethereal powers,
All secrets of the deep, all Nature's works,
Or works of God in Heaven, air, earth, or sea,
And all the riches of this world enjoyedst,
And all the rule, one empire; only add
Deeds to thy knowledge answerable; add faith,

Add virtue, patience, temperance; add love,
By name to come called charity, the soul
Of all the rest: then wilt thou not be loth
To leave this Paradise, but shalt possess
A Paradise within thee, happier far.—
Let us descend now therefore from this top
Of speculation; for the hour precise
Exacts our parting hence; and see the guards,
By me encamped on yonder hill, expect
Their motion; at whose front a flaming sword,
In signal of remove, waves fiercely round:
We may no longer stay: go, waken Eve;
Her also I with gentle dreams have calmed
Portending good, and all her spirits composed
To meek submission: thou, at season fit,
Let her with thee partake what thou hast heard;
Chiefly what may concern her faith to know,
The great deliverance by her seed to come
(For by the Woman's seed) on all mankind:
That ye may live, which will be many days,
Both in one faith unanimous, though sad,
With cause, for evils past; yet much more cheered
With meditation on the happy end."
He ended, and they both descend the hill;
Descended, Adam to the bower, where Eve
Lay sleeping, ran before; but found her waked;
And thus with words not sad she him received.
"Whence thou returnest, and whither wentest, I know;
For God is also in sleep; and dreams advise,
Which he hath sent propitious, some great good
Presaging, since with sorrow and heart's distress
Wearied I fell asleep: But now lead on;
In me is no delay; with thee to go,
Is to stay here; without thee here to stay,
Is to go hence unwilling; thou to me

Art all things under Heaven, all places thou,
Who for my wilful crime art banished hence.
This further consolation yet secure
I carry hence; though all by me is lost,
Such favour I unworthy am vouchsafed,
By me the Promised Seed shall all restore."
So spake our mother Eve; and Adam heard
Well pleased, but answered not: For now, too nigh
The Arch-Angel stood; and, from the other hill
To their fixed station, all in bright array
The Cherubim descended; on the ground
Gliding meteorous, as evening-mist
Risen from a river o'er the marish glides,
And gathers ground fast at the labourer's heel
Homeward returning. High in front advanced,
The brandished sword of God before them blazed,
Fierce as a comet; which with torrid heat,
And vapour as the Libyan air adust,
Began to parch that temperate clime; whereat
In either hand the hastening Angel caught
Our lingering parents, and to the eastern gate
Led them direct, and down the cliff as fast
To the subjected plain; then disappeared.
They, looking back, all the eastern side beheld
Of Paradise, so late their happy seat,
Waved over by that flaming brand; the gate
With dreadful faces thronged, and fiery arms:
Some natural tears they dropt, but wiped them soon;
The world was all before them, where to choose
Their place of rest, and Providence their guide:
They, hand in hand, with wandering steps and slow,
Through Eden took their solitary way.

PARADISE
REGAINED

THE FIRST BOOK

I, WHO erewhile the happy Garden sung
By one man's disobedience lost, now sing
Recovered Paradise to all mankind,
By one man's firm obedience fully tried
Through all temptation, and the Tempter foiled
In all his wiles, defeated and repulsed,
And Eden raised in the waste Wilderness.
Thou Spirit, who led'st this glorious Eremite
Into the desert, his victorious field
Against the spiritual foe, and brought'st him thence
By proof the undoubted Son of God, inspire,
As thou art wont, my prompted song, else mute,
And bear through hight or depth of Nature's bounds,
With prosperous wing full summed, to tell of deeds
Above heroic, though in secret done,
And unrecorded left through many an age:
Worthy to have not remained so long unsung.
Now had the great Proclaimer, with a voice
More awful than the sound of trumpet, cried
Repentance, and Heaven's kingdom nigh at hand
To all baptized. To his great baptism flocked
With awe the regions round, and with them came

From Nazareth the son of Joseph deemed
To the flood Jordan—came as then obscure,
Unmarked, unknown. But him the Baptist soon
Descried, divinely warned, and witness bore
As to his worthier, and would have resigned
To him his heavenly office. Nor was long
His witness unconfirmed: on him baptized
Heaven opened, and in likeness of a Dove
The Spirit descended, while the Father's voice
From Heaven pronounced him his beloved Son.
That heard the Adversary, who, roving still
About the world, at that assembly famed
Would not be last, and, with the voice divine
Nigh thunder-struck, the exalted man to whom
Such high attest was given a while surveyed
With wonder; then, with envy fraught and rage,
Flies to his place, nor rests, but in mid air
To council summons all his mighty Peers,
Within thick clouds and dark tenfold involved,
A gloomy consistory; and them amidst,
With looks aghast and sad, he thus bespake:—
"O ancient Powers of Air and this wide World
(For much more willingly I mention Air,
This our old conquest, than remember Hell,
Our hated habitation), well ye know
How many ages, as the years of men,
This Universe we have possessed, and ruled
In manner at our will the affairs of Earth,
Since Adam and his facile consort Eve
Lost Paradise, deceived by me, though since
With dread attending when that fatal wound
Shall be inflicted by the seed of Eve
Upon my head. Long the decrees of Heaven
Delay, for longest time to Him is short;
And now, too soon for us, the circling hours

This dreaded time have compassed, wherein we
Must bide the stroke of that long-threatened wound
(At least, if so we can, and by the head
Broken be not intended all our power
To be infringed, our freedom and our being
In this fair empire won of Earth and Air)—
For this ill news I bring: The Woman's Seed,
Destined to this, is late of woman born.
His birth to our just fear gave no small cause;
But his growth now to youth's full flower, displaying
All virtue, grace and wisdom to achieve
Things highest, greatest, multiplies my fear.
Before him a great Prophet, to proclaim
His coming, is sent harbinger, who all
Invites, and in the consecrated stream
Pretends to wash off sin, and fit them so
Purified to receive him pure, or rather
To do him honour as their King. All come,
And he himself among them was baptized—
Not thence to be more pure, but to receive
The testimony of Heaven, that who he is
Thenceforth the nations may not doubt. I saw
The Prophet do him reverence; on him, rising
Out of the water, Heaven above the clouds
Unfold her crystal doors; thence on his head
A perfet Dove descend (whate'er it meant);
And out of Heaven the sovraign voice I heard,
'This is my Son beloved,—in him am pleased.'
His mother, than, is mortal, but his Sire
He who obtains the monarchy of Heaven;
And what will He not do to advance his Son?
His first-begot we know, and sore have felt,
When his fierce thunder drove us to the Deep;
Who this is we must learn, for Man he seems
In all his lineaments, though in his face

The glimpses of his Father's glory shine.
Ye see our danger on the utmost edge
Of hazard, which admits no long debate,
But must with something sudden be opposed
(Not force, but well-couched fraud, well-woven snares),
Ere in the head of nations he appear,
Their king, their leader, and supreme on Earth.
I, when no other durst, sole undertook
The dismal expedition to find out
And ruin Adam, and the exploit performed
Successfully: a calmer voyage now
Will waft me; and the way found prosperous once
Induces best to hope of like success."
He ended, and his words impression left
Of much amazement to the infernal crew,
Distracted and surprised with deep dismay
At these sad tidings. But no time was then
For long indulgence to their fears or grief:
Unanimous they all commit the care
And management of this man enterprise
To him, their great Dictator, whose attempt
At first against mankind so well had thrived
In Adam's overthrow, and led their march
From Hell's deep-vaulted den to dwell in light,
Regents, and potentates, and kings, yea gods,
Of many a pleasant realm and province wide.
So to the coast of Jordan he directs
His easy steps, girded with snaky wiles,
Where he might likeliest find this new-declared,
This man of men, attested Son of God,
Temptation and all guile on him to try—
So to subvert whom he suspected raised
To end his reign on Earth so long enjoyed:
But, contrary, unweeting he fulfilled
The purposed counsel, pre-ordained and fixed,

Of the Most High, who, in full frequence bright
Of Angels, thus to Gabriel smiling spake:—
"Gabriel, this day, by proof, thou shalt behold,
Thou and all Angels conversant on Earth
With Man or men's affairs, how I begin
To verify that solemn message late,
On which I sent thee to the Virgin pure
In Galilee, that she should bear a son,
Great in renown, and called the Son of God.
Then told'st her, doubting how these things could be
To her a virgin, that on her should come
The Holy Ghost, and the power of the Highest
O'ershadow her. This Man, born and now upgrown,
To shew him worthy of his birth divine
And high prediction, henceforth I expose
To Satan; let him tempt, and now assay
His utmost subtlety, because he boasts
And vaunts of his great cunning to the throng
Of his Apostasy. He might have learnt
Less overweening, since he failed in Job,
Whose constant perseverance overcame
Whate'er his cruel malice could invent.
He now shall know I can produce a man,
Of female seed, far abler to resist
All his solicitations, and at length
All his vast force, and drive him back to Hell—
Winning by conquest what the first man lost
By fallacy surprised. But first I mean
To exercise him in the Wilderness;
There he shall first lay down the rudiments
Of his great warfare, ere I send him forth
To conquer Sin and Death, the two grand foes.
By humiliation and strong sufferance
His weakness shall o'ercome Satanic strength,
And all the world, and mass of sinful flesh;

That all the Angels and aethereal Powers—
They now, and men hereafter—may discern
From what consummate virtue I have chose
This perfet man, by merit called my Son,
To earn salvation for the sons of men."
So spake the Eternal Father, and all Heaven
Admiring stood a space; then into hymns
Burst forth, and in celestial measures moved,
Circling the throne and singing, while the hand
Sung with the voice, and this the argument:—
"Victory and triumph to the Son of God,
Now entering his great duel, not of arms,
But to vanquish by wisdom hellish wiles!
The Father knows the Son; therefore secure
Ventures his filial virtue, though untried,
Against whate'er may tempt, whate'er seduce,
Allure, or terrify, or undermine.
Be frustrate, all ye stratagems of Hell,
And, devilish machinations, come to nought!"
So they in Heaven their odes and vigils tuned.
Meanwhile the Son of God, who yet some days
Lodged in Bethabara, where John baptized,
Musing and much revolving in his breast
How best the mighty work he might begin
Of Saviour to mankind, and which way first
Publish his godlike office now mature,
One day forth walked alone, the Spirit leading
And his deep thoughts, the better to converse
With solitude, till, far from track of men,
Thought following thought, and step by step led on,
He entered now the bordering Desert wild,
And, with dark shades and rocks environed round,
His holy meditations thus pursued:—
"O what a multitude of thoughts at once
Awakened in me swarm, while I consider

What from within I feel myself, and hear
What from without comes often to my ears,
Ill sorting with my present state compared!
When I was yet a child, no childish play
To me was pleasing; all my mind was set
Serious to learn and know, and thence to do,
What might be public good; myself I thought
Born to that end, born to promote all truth,
All righteous things. Therefore, above my years,
The Law of God I read, and found it sweet;
Made it my whole delight, and in it grew
To such perfection that, ere yet my age
Had measured twice six years, at our great Feast
I went into the Temple, there to hear
The teachers of our Law, and to propose
What might improve my knowledge or their own,
And was admired by all. Yet this not all
To which my spirit aspired. Victorious deeds
Flamed in my heart, heroic acts—one while
To rescue Israel from the Roman yoke;
Then to subdue and quell, o'er all the earth,
Brute violence and proud tyrannic power,
Till truth were freed, and equity restored:
Yet held it more humane, more heavenly, first
By winning words to conquer willing hearts,
And make persuasion do the work of fear;
At least to try, and teach the erring soul,
Not wilfully misdoing, but unware
Misled; the stubborn only to subdue.
These growing thoughts my mother soon perceiving,
By words at times cast forth, inly rejoiced,
And said to me apart, 'High are thy thoughts,
O Son! but nourish them, and let them soar
To what hight sacred virtue and true worth
Can raise them, though above example high;

By matchless deeds express thy matchless Sire.
For know, thou art no son of mortal man;
Though men esteem thee low of parentage,
Thy Father is the Eternal King who rules
All Heaven and Earth, Angels and sons of men.
A messenger from God foretold thy birth
Conceived in me a virgin; he foretold
Thou shouldst be great, and sit on David's throne,
And of thy kingdom there should be no end.
At thy nativity a glorious quire
Of Angels, in the fields of Bethlehem, sung
To shepherds, watching at their folds by night,
And told them the Messiah now was born,
Where they might see him; and to thee they came,
Directed to the manger where thou lay'st;
For in the inn was left no better room.
A Star, not seen before, in heaven appearing,
Guided the Wise Men thither from the East,
To honour thee with incense, myrrh, and gold;
By whose bright course led on they found the place,
Affirming it thy star, new-graven in heaven,
By which they knew thee King of Israel born.
Just Simeon and prophetic Anna, warned
By vision, found thee in the Temple, and spake,
Before the altar and the vested priest,
Like things of thee to all that present stood.'
This having heart, straight I again revolved
The Law and Prophets, searching what was writ
Concerning the Messiah, to our scribes
Known partly, and soon found of whom they spake
I am—this chiefly, that my way must lie
Through many a hard assay, even to the death,
Ere I the promised kingdom can attain,
Or work redemption for mankind, whose sins'
Full weight must be transferred upon my head.

Yet, neither thus disheartened or dismayed,
The time prefixed I waited; when behold
The Baptist (of whose birth I oft had heard,
Not knew by sight) now come, who was to come
Before Messiah, and his way prepare!
I, as all others, to his baptism came,
Which I believed was from above; but he
Straight knew me, and with loudest voice proclaimed
Me him (for it was shewn him so from Heaven)—
Me him whose harbinger he was; and first
Refused on me his baptism to confer,
As much his greater, and was hardly won.
But, as I rose out of the laving stream,
Heaven opened her eternal doors, from whence
The Spirit descended on me like a Dove;
And last, the sum of all, my Father's voice,
Audibly heard from Heaven, pronounced me his,
Me his beloved Son, in whom alone
He was well pleased: by which I knew the time
Now full, that I no more should live obscure,
But openly begin, as best becomes
The authority which I derived from Heaven.
And now by some strong motion I am led
Into this wilderness; to what intent
I learn not yet. Perhaps I need not know;
For what concerns my knowledge God reveals."
So spake our Morning Star, then in his rise,
And, looking round, on every side beheld
A pathless desert, dusk with horrid shades.
The way he came, not having marked return,
Was difficult, by human steps untrod;
And he still on was led, but with such thoughts
Accompanied of things past and to come
Lodged in his breast as well might recommend
Such solitude before choicest society.

Full forty days he passed—whether on hill
Sometimes, anon in shady vale, each night
Under the covert of some ancient oak
Or cedar to defend him from the dew,
Or harboured in one cave, is not revealed;
Nor tasted human food, nor hunger felt,
Till those days ended; hungered then at last
Among wild beasts. They at his sight grew mild,
Nor sleeping him nor waking harmed; his walk
The fiery serpent fled and noxious worm;
The lion and fierce tiger glared aloof.
But now an aged man in rural weeds,
Following, as seemed, the quest of some stray eye,
Or withered sticks to gather, which might serve
Against a winter's day, when winds blow keen,
To warm him wet returned from field at eve,
He saw approach; who first with curious eye
Perused him, then with words thus uttered spake:—
"Sir, what ill chance hath brought thee to this place,
So far from path or road of men, who pass
In troop or caravan? for single none
Durst ever, who returned, and dropt not here
His carcass, pined with hunger and with droughth.
I ask the rather, and the more admire,
For that to me thou seem'st the man whom late
Our new baptizing Prophet at the ford
Of Jordan honoured so, and called thee Son
Of God. I saw and heard, for we sometimes
Who dwell this wild, constrained by want, come forth
To town or village nigh (nighest is far),
Where aught we hear, and curious are to hear,
What happens new; fame also finds us out."
To whom the Son of God: "Who brought me hither
Will bring me hence; no other guide I seek."
"By miracle he may," replied the swain;

"What other way I see not; for we here
Live on tough roots and stubs, to thirst inured
More than the camel, and to drink go far—
Men to much misery and hardship born.
But, if thou be the Son of God, command
That out of these hard stones be made thee bread;
So shalt thou save thyself, and us relieve
With food, whereof we wretched seldom taste."
He ended, and the Son of God replied:—
"Think'st thou such force in bread? Is it not written
(For I discern thee other than thou seem'st),
Man lives not by bread only, but each word
Proceeding from the mouth of God, who fed
Our fathers here with manna? In the Mount
Moses was forty days, nor eat nor drank;
And forty days Eliah without food
Wandered this barren waste; the same I now.
Why dost thou, then, suggest to me distrust
Knowing who I am, as I know who thou art?"
Whom thus answered the Arch-Fiend, now undisguised:—
"'Tis true, I am that Spirit unfortunate
Who, leagued with millions more in rash revolt,
Kept not my happy station, but was driven
With them from bliss to the bottomless Deep—
Yet to that hideous place not so confined
By rigour unconniving but that oft,
Leaving my dolorous prison, I enjoy
Large liberty to round this globe of Earth,
Or range in the Air; nor from the Heaven of Heavens
Hath he excluded my resort sometimes.
I came, among the Sons of God, when he
Gave up into my hands Uzzean Job,
To prove him, and illustrate his high worth;
And, when to all his Angels he proposed
To draw the proud king Ahab into fraud,

That he might fall in Ramoth, they demurring,
I undertook that office, and the tongues
Of all his flattering prophets glibbed with lies
To his destruction, as I had in charge:
For what he bids I do. Though I have lost
Much lustre of my native brightness, lost
To be beloved of God, I have not lost
To love, at least contemplate and admire,
What I see excellent in good, or fair,
Or virtuous; I should so have lost all sense.
What can be then less in me than desire
To see thee and approach thee, whom I know
Declared the Son of God, to hear attent
Thy wisdom, and behold thy godlike deeds?
Men generally think me much a foe
To all mankind. Why should I? they to me
Never did wrong or violence. By them
I lost not what I lost; rather by them
I gained what I have gained, and with them dwell
Copartner in these regions of the World,
If not disposer—lend them oft my aid,
Oft my advice by presages and signs,
And answers, oracles, portents, and dreams,
Whereby they may direct their future life.
Envy, they say, excites me, thus to gain
Companions of my misery and woe!
At first it may be; but, long since with woe
Nearer acquainted, now I feel by proof
That fellowship in pain divides not smart,
Nor lightens aught each man's peculiar load;
Small consolation, then, were Man adjoined.
This wounds me most (what can it less?) that Man,
Man fallen, shall be restored, I never more."
To whom our Saviour sternly thus replied:—
"Deservedly thou griev'st, composed of lies

From the beginning, and in lies wilt end,
Who boast'st release from Hell, and leave to come
Into the Heaven of Heavens. Thou com'st, indeed,
As a poor miserable captive thrall
Comes to the place where he before had sat
Among the prime in splendour, now deposed,
Ejected, emptied, gazed, unpitied, shunned,
A spectacle of ruin, or of scorn,
To all the host of Heaven. The happy place
Imparts to thee no happiness, no joy—
Rather inflames thy torment, representing
Lost bliss, to thee no more communicable;
So never more in Hell than when in Heaven.
But thou art serviceable to Heaven's King!
Wilt thou impute to obedience what thy fear
Extorts, or pleasure to do ill excites?
What but thy malice moved thee to misdeem
Of righteous Job, then cruelly to afflict him
With all inflictions? but his patience won.
The other service was thy chosen task,
To be a liar in four hundred mouths;
For lying is thy sustenance, thy food.
Yet thou pretend'st to truth! all oracles
By thee are given, and what confessed more true
Among the nations? That hath been thy craft,
By mixing somewhat true to vent more lies.
But what have been thy answers? what but dark,
Ambiguous, and with double sense deluding,
Which they who asked have seldom understood,
And, not well understood, as good not known?
Who ever, by consulting at thy shrine,
Returned the wiser, or the more instruct
To fly or follow what concerned him most,
And run not sooner to his fatal snare?
For God hath justly given the nations up

To thy delusions; justly, since they fell
Idolatrous. But, when his purpose is
Among them to declare his providence,
To thee not known, whence hast thou then thy truth,
But from him, or his Angels president
In every province, who, themselves disdaining
To approach thy temples, give thee in command
What, to the smallest tittle, thou shalt say
To thy adorers? Thou, with trembling fear,
Or like a fawning parasite, obey'st;
Then to thyself ascrib'st the truth foretold.
But this thy glory shall be soon retrenched;
No more shalt thou by oracling abuse
The Gentiles; henceforth oracles are ceased,
And thou no more with pomp and sacrifice
Shalt be enquired at Delphos or elsewhere—
At least in vain, for they shall find thee mute.
God hath now sent his living Oracle
Into the world to teach his final will,
And sends his Spirit of Truth henceforth to dwell
In pious hearts, an inward oracle
To all truth requisite for men to know."
So spake our Saviour; but the subtle Fiend,
Though inly stung with anger and disdain,
Dissembled, and this answer smooth returned:—
"Sharply thou hast insisted on rebuke,
And urged me hard with doings which not will,
But misery, hath wrested from me. Where
Easily canst thou find one miserable,
And not inforced oft-times to part from truth,
If it may stand him more in stead to lie,
Say and unsay, feign, flatter, or abjure?
But thou art placed above me; thou art Lord;
From thee I can, and must, submiss, endure
Cheek or reproof, and glad to scape so quit.

Hard are the ways of truth, and rough to walk,
Smooth on the tongue discoursed, pleasing to the ear,
And tunable as sylvan pipe or song;
What wonder, then, if I delight to hear
Her dictates from thy mouth? most men admire
Virtue who follow not her lore. Permit me
To hear thee when I come (since no man comes),
And talk at least, though I despair to attain.
Thy Father, who is holy, wise, and pure,
Suffers the hypocrite or atheous priest
To tread his sacred courts, and minister
About his altar, handling holy things,
Praying or vowing, and voutsafed his voice
To Balaam reprobate, a prophet yet
Inspired: disdain not such access to me."
To whom our Saviour, with unaltered brow:—
"Thy coming hither, though I know thy scope,
I bid not, or forbid. Do as thou find'st
Permission from above; thou canst not more."
He added not; and Satan, bowling low
His gray dissimulation, disappeared,
Into thin air diffused: for now began
Night with her sullen wing to double-shade
The desert; fowls in their clay nests were couched;
And now wild beasts came forth the woods to roam.

THE SECOND BOOK

MEANWHILE the new-baptized, who yet remained
At Jordan with the Baptist, and had seen
Him whom they heard so late expressly called
Jesus Messiah, Son of God, declared,
And on that high authority had believed,
And with him talked, and with him lodged—I mean
Andrew and Simon, famous after known,
With others, though in Holy Writ not named—
Now missing him, their joy so lately found,
So lately found and so abruptly gone,
Began to doubt, and doubted many days,
And, as the days increased, increased their doubt.
Sometimes they thought he might be only shewn,
And for a time caught up to God, as once
Moses was in the Mount and missing long,
And the great Thisbite, who on fiery wheels
Rode up to Heaven, yet once again to come.
Therefore, as those young prophets then with care
Sought lost Eliah, so in each place these
Nigh to Bethabara—in Jericho
The city of palms, AEnon, and Salem old,
Machaerus, and each town or city walled

On this side the broad lake Genezaret,
Or in Peraea—but returned in vain.
Then on the bank of Jordan, by a creek,
Where winds with reeds and osiers whispering play,
Plain fishermen (no greater men them call),
Close in a cottage low together got,
Their unexpected loss and plaints outbreathed:—
"Alas, from what high hope to what relapse
Unlooked for are we fallen! Our eyes beheld
Messiah certainly now come, so long
Expected of our fathers; we have heard
His words, his wisdom full of grace and truth.
'Now, now, for sure, deliverance is at hand;
The kingdom shall to Israel be restored:'
Thus we rejoiced, but soon our joy is turned
Into perplexity and new amaze.
For whither is he gone? what accident
Hath rapt him from us? will he now retire
After appearance, and again prolong
Our expectation? God of Israel,
Send thy Messiah forth; the time is come.
Behold the kings of the earth, how they oppress
Thy Chosen, to what hight their power unjust
They have exalted, and behind them cast
All fear of Thee; arise, and vindicate
Thy glory; free thy people from their yoke!
But let us wait; thus far He hath performed—
Sent his Anointed, and to us revealed him
By his great Prophet pointed at and shown
In public, and with him we have conversed.
Let us be glad of this, and all our fears
Lay on his providence; He will not fail,
Nor will withdraw him now, nor will recall—
Mock us with his blest sight, then snatch him hence:
Soon we shall see our hope, our joy, return."

Thus they out of their plaints new hope resume
To find whom at the first they found unsought.
But to his mother Mary, when she saw
Others returned from baptism, not her Son,
Nor left at Jordan tidings of him none,
Within her breast though calm, her breast though pure,
Motherly cares and fears got head, and raised
Some troubled thoughts, which she in sighs thus clad:—
"Oh, what avails me now that honour high,
To have conceived of God, or that salute,
'Hail, highly favoured, among women blest!'
While I to sorrows am no less advanced,
And fears as eminent above the lot
Of other women, by the birth I bore:
In such a season born, when scarce a shed
Could be obtained to shelter him or me
From the bleak air? A stable was our warmth,
A manger his; yet soon enforced to fly
Thence into Egypt, till the murderous king
Were dead, who sought his life, and, missing, filled
With infant blood the streets of Bethlehem.
From Egypt home returned, in Nazareth
Hath been our dwelling many years; his life
Private, unactive, calm, contemplative,
Little suspicious to any king. But now,
Full grown to man, acknowledged, as I hear,
By John the Baptist, and in public shewn,
Son owned from Heaven by his Father's voice,
I looked for some great change. To honour? no;
But trouble, as old Simeon plain foretold,
That to the fall and rising he should be
Of many in Israel, and to a sign
Spoken against—that through my very soul
A sword shall pierce. This is my favoured lot,
My exaltation to afflictions high!

Afflicted I may be, it seems, and blest!
I will not argue that, nor will repine.
But where delays he now? Some great intent
Conceals him. When twelve years he scarce had seen,
I lost him, but so found as well I saw
He could not lose himself, but went about
His Father's business. What he meant I mused—
Since understand; much more his absence now
Thus long to some great purpose he obscures.
But I to wait with patience am inured;
My heart hath been a storehouse long of things
And sayings laid up, pretending strange events."
Thus Mary, pondering oft, and oft to mind
Recalling what remarkably had passed
Since first her Salutation heard, with thoughts
Meekly composed awaited the fulfilling:
The while her Son, tracing the desert wild,
Sole, but with holiest meditations fed,
Into himself descended, and at once
All his great work to come before him set—
How to begin, how to accomplish best
His end of being on Earth, and mission high.
For Satan, with sly preface to return,
Had left him vacant, and with speed was gone
Up to the middle region of thick air,
Where all his Potentates in council sate.
There, without sign of boast, or sign of joy,
Solicitous and blank, he thus began:—
"Princes, Heaven's ancient Sons, AEthereal Thrones—
Daemonian Spirits now, from the element
Each of his reign allotted, rightlier called
Powers of Fire, Air, Water, and Earth beneath
(So may we hold our place and these mild seats
Without new trouble!)—such an enemy
Is risen to invade us, who no less

Threatens than our expulsion down to Hell.
I, as I undertook, and with the vote
Consenting in full frequence was impowered,
Have found him, viewed him, tasted him; but find
Far other labour to be undergone
Than when I dealt with Adam, first of men,
Though Adam by his wife's allurement fell,
However to this Man inferior far—
If he be Man by mother's side, at least
With more than human gifts from Heaven adorned,
Perfections absolute, graces divine,
And amplitude of mind to greatest deeds.
Therefore I am returned, lest confidence
Of my success with Eve in Paradise
Deceive ye to persuasion over-sure
Of like succeeding here. I summon all
Rather to be in readiness with hand
Or counsel to assist, lest I, who erst
Thought none my equal, now be overmatched."
So spake the old Serpent, doubting, and from all
With clamour was assured their utmost aid
At his command; when from amidst them rose
Belial, the dissolutest Spirit that fell,
The sensualest, and, after Asmodai,
The fleshliest Incubus, and thus advised:—
"Set women in his eye and in his walk,
Among daughters of men the fairest found.
Many are in each region passing fair
As the noon sky, more like to goddesses
Than mortal creatures, graceful and discreet,
Expert in amorous arts, enchanting tongues
Persuasive, virgin majesty with mild
And sweet allayed, yet terrible to approach,
Skilled to retire, and in retiring draw
Hearts after them tangled in amorous nets.

Such object hath the power to soften and tame
Severest temper, smooth the rugged'st brow,
Enerve, and with voluptuous hope dissolve,
Draw out with credulous desire, and lead
At will the manliest, resolutest breast,
As the magnetic hardest iron draws.
Women, when nothing else, beguiled the heart
Of wisest Solomon, and made him build,
And made him bow, to the gods of his wives."
To whom quick answer Satan thus returned:—
"Belial, in much uneven scale thou weigh'st
All others by thyself. Because of old
Thou thyself doat'st on womankind, admiring
Their shape, their colour, and attractive grace,
None are, thou think'st, but taken with such toys.
Before the Flood, thou, with thy lusty crew,
False titled Sons of God, roaming the Earth,
Cast wanton eyes on the daughters of men,
And coupled with them, and begot a race.
Have we not seen, or by relation heard,
In courts and regal chambers how thou lurk'st,
In wood or grove, by mossy fountain-side,
In valley or green meadow, to waylay
Some beauty rare, Calisto, Clymene,
Daphne, or Semele, Antiopa,
Or Amymone, Syrinx, many more
Too long—then lay'st thy scapes on names adored,
Apollo, Neptune, Jupiter, or Pan,
Satyr, or Faun, or Silvan? But these haunts
Delight not all. Among the sons of men
How many have with a smile made small account
Of beauty and her lures, easily scorned
All her assaults, on worthier things intent!
Remember that Pellean conqueror,
A youth, how all the beauties of the East

He slightly viewed, and slightly overpassed;
How he surnamed of Africa dismissed,
In his prime youth, the fair Iberian maid.
For Solomon, he lived at ease, and, full
Of honour, wealth, high fare, aimed not beyond
Higher design than to enjoy his state;
Thence to the bait of women lay exposed.
But he whom we attempt is wiser far
Than Solomon, of more exalted mind,
Made and set wholly on the accomplishment
Of greatest things. What woman will you find,
Though of this age the wonder and the fame,
On whom his leisure will voutsafe an eye
Of fond desire? Or should she, confident,
As sitting queen adored on Beauty's throne,
Descend with all her winning charms begirt
To enamour, as the zone of Venus once
Wrought that effect on Jove (so fables tell),
How would one look from his majestic brow,
Seated as on the top of Virtue's hill,
Discountenance her despised, and put to rout
All her array, her female pride deject,
Or turn to reverent awe! For Beauty stands
In the admiration only of weak minds
Led captive; cease to admire, and all her plumes
Fall flat, and shrink into a trivial toy,
At every sudden slighting quite abashed.
Therefore with manlier objects we must try
His constancy—with such as have more shew
Of worth, of honour, glory, and popular praise
(Rocks whereon greatest men have oftest wrecked);
Or that which only seems to satisfy
Lawful desires of nature, not beyond.
And now I know he hungers, where no food
Is to be found, in the wide Wilderness:

The rest commit to me; I shall let pass
No advantage, and his strength as oft assay."
He ceased, and heard their grant in loud acclaim;
Then forthwith to him takes a chosen band
Of Spirits likest to himself in guile,
To be at hand and at his beck appear,
If cause were to unfold some active scene
Of various persons, each to know his part;
Then to the desert takes with these his flight,
Where still, from shade to shade, the Son of God,
After forty days' fasting, had remained,
Now hungering first, and to himself thus said:—
"Where will this end? Four times ten days I have passed
Wandering this woody maze, and human food
Nor tasted, nor had appetite. That fast
To virtue I impute not, or count part
Of what I suffer here. If nature need not,
Or God support nature without repast,
Though needing, what praise is it to endure?
But now I feel I hunger; which declares
Nature hath need of what she asks. Yet God
Can satisfy that need some other way,
Though hunger still remain. So it remain
Without this body's wasting, I content me,
And from the sting of famine fear no harm;
Nor mind it, fed with better thoughts, that feed
Me hungering more to do my Father's will."
It was the hour of night, when thus the Son
Communed in silent walk, then laid him down
Under the hospitable covert nigh
Of trees thick interwoven. There he slept,
And dreamed, as appetite is wont to dream,
Of meats and drinks, nature's refreshment sweet.
Him thought he by the brook of Cherith stood,
And saw the ravens with their horny beaks

Food to Elijah bringing even and morn—
Though ravenous, taught to abstain from what they
    brought;
He saw the Prophet also, how he fled
Into the desert, and how there he slept
Under a juniper—then how, awaked,
He found his supper on the coals prepared,
And by the Angel was bid rise and eat,
And eat the second time after repose,
The strength whereof sufficed him forty days:
Sometimes that with Elijah he partook,
Or as a guest with Daniel at his pulse.
Thus wore out night; and now the harald Lark
Left his ground-nest, high towering to descry
The Morn's approach, and greet her with his song.
As lightly from his grassy couch up rose
Our Saviour, and found all was but a dream;
Fasting he went to sleep, and fasting waked.
Up to a hill anon his steps he reared,
From whose high top to ken the prospect round,
If cottage were in view, sheep-cote, or herd;
But cottage, herd, or sheep-cote, none he saw—
Only in a bottom saw a pleasant grove,
With chaunt of tuneful birds resounding loud.
Thither he bent his way, determined there
To rest at noon, and entered soon the shade
High-roofed, and walks beneath, and alleys brown,
That opened in the midst a woody scene;
Nature's own work it seemed (Nature taught Art),
And, to a superstitious eye, the haunt
Of wood-gods and wood-nymphs. He viewed it round;
When suddenly a man before him stood,
Not rustic as before, but seemlier clad,
As one in city or court or palace bred,
And with fair speech these words to him addressed:—

"With granted leave officious I return,
But much more wonder that the Son of God
In this wild solitude so long should bide,
Of all things destitute, and, well I know,
Not without hunger. Others of some note,
As story tells, have trod this wilderness:
The fugitive Bond-woman, with her son,
Outcast Nebaioth, yet found here relief
By a providing Angel; all the race
Of Israel here had famished, had not God
Rained from heaven manna; and that Prophet bold,
Native of Thebez, wandering here, was fed
Twice by a voice inviting him to eat.
Of thee those forty days none hath regard,
Forty and more deserted here indeed."
To whom thus Jesus: "What conclud'st thou hence?
They all had need; I, as thou seest, have none."
"How hast thou hunger then?" Satan replied.
"Tell me, if food were now before thee set,
Wouldst thou not eat?" "Thereafter as I like
the giver," answered Jesus. "Why should that
Cause thy refusal?" said the subtle Fiend.
"Hast thou not right to all created things?
Owe not all creatures, by just right, to thee
Duty and service, nor to stay till bid,
But tender all their power? Nor mention I
Meats by the law unclean, or offered first
To idols—those young Daniel could refuse;
Nor proffered by an enemy—though who
Would scruple that, with want oppressed? Behold,
Nature ashamed, or, better to express,
Troubled, that thou shouldst hunger, hath purveyed
From all the elements her choicest store,
To treat thee as beseems, and as her Lord
With honour. Only deign to sit and eat."

He spake no dream; for, as his words had end,
Our Saviour, lifting up his eyes, beheld,
In ample space under the broadest shade,
A table richly spread in regal mode,
With dishes piled and meats of noblest sort
And savour—beasts of chase, or fowl of game,
In pastry built, or from the spit, or boiled,
Grisamber-steamed; all fish, from sea or shore,
Freshet or purling brook, of shell or fin,
And exquisitest name, for which was drained
Pontus, and Lucrine bay, and Afric coast.
Alas! how simple, to these cates compared,
Was that crude Apple that diverted Eve!
And at a stately sideboard, by the wine,
That fragrant smell diffused, in order stood
Tall stripling youths rich-clad, of fairer hue
Than Ganymed or Hylas; distant more,
Under the trees now tripped, now solemn stood,
Nymphs of Diana's train, and Naiades
With fruits and flowers from Amalthea's horn,
And ladies of the Hesperides, that seemed
Fairer than feigned of old, or fabled since
Of faery damsels met in forest wide
By knights of Logres, or of Lyones,
Lancelot, or Pelleas, or Pellenore.
And all the while harmonious airs were heard
Of chiming strings or charming pipes; and winds
Of gentlest gale Arabian odours fanned
From their soft wings, and Flora's earliest smells.
Such was the splendour; and the Tempter now
His invitation earnestly renewed:—
"What doubts the Son of God to sit and eat?
These are not fruits forbidden; no interdict
Defends the touching of these viands pure;
Their taste no knowledge works, at least of evil,

But life preserves, destroys life's enemy,
Hunger, with sweet restorative delight.
All these are Spirits of air, and woods, and springs,
Thy gentle ministers, who come to pay
Thee homage, and acknowledge thee their Lord.
What doubt'st thou, Son of God? Sit down and eat."
To whom thus Jesus temperately replied:—
"Said'st thou not that to all things I had right?
And who withholds my power that right to use?
Shall I receive by gift what of my own,
When and where likes me best, I can command?
I can at will, doubt not, as soon as thou,
Command a table in this wilderness,
And call swift flights of Angels ministrant,
Arrayed in glory, on my cup to attend:
Why shouldst thou, then, obtrude this diligence
In vain, where no acceptance it can find?
And with my hunger what hast thou to do?
Thy pompous delicacies I contemn,
And count thy specious gifts no gifts, but guiles."
To whom thus answered Satan, malcontent:—
"That I have also power to give thou seest;
If of that power I bring thee voluntary
What I might have bestowed on whom I pleased,
And rather opportunely in this place
Chose to impart to thy apparent need,
Why shouldst thou not accept it? But I see
What I can do or offer is suspect.
Of these things others quickly will dispose,
Whose pains have earned the far-fet spoil." With that
Both table and provision vanished quite,
With sound of harpies' wings and talons heard;
Only the importune Tempter still remained,
And with these words his temptation pursued:—
"By hunger, that each other creature tames,

Thou art not to be harmed, therefore not moved;
Thy temperance, invincible besides,
For no allurement yields to appetite;
And all thy heart is set on high designs,
High actions. But wherewith to be achieved?
Great acts require great means of enterprise;
Thou art unknown, unfriended, low of birth,
A carpenter thy father known, thyself
Bred up in poverty and straits at home,
Lost in a desert here and hunger-bit.
Which way, or from what hope, dost thou aspire
To greatness? whence authority deriv'st?
What followers, what retinue canst thou gain,
Or at thy heels the dizzy multitude,
Longer than thou canst feed them on thy cost?
Money brings honour, friends, conquest, and realms.
What raised Antipater the Edomite,
And his son Herod placed on Juda's throne,
Thy throne, but gold, that got him puissant friends?
Therefore, if at great things thou wouldst arrive,
Get riches first, get wealth, and treasure heap—
Not difficult, if thou hearken to me.
Riches are mine, fortune is in my hand;
They whom I favour thrive in wealth amain,
While virtue, valour, wisdom, sit in want."
To whom thus Jesus patiently replied:—
"Yet wealth without these three is impotent
To gain dominion, or to keep it gained—
Witness those ancient empires of the earth,
In hight of all their flowing wealth dissolved;
But men endued with these have oft attained,
In lowest poverty, to highest deeds—
Gideon, and Jephtha, and the shepherd lad
Whose offspring on the throne of Juda sate
So many ages, and shall yet regain

That seat, and reign in Israel without end.
Among the Heathen (for throughout the world
To me is not unknown what hath been done
Worthy of memorial) canst thou not remember
Quintius, Fabricius, Curius, Regulus?
For I esteem those names of men so poor,
Who could do mighty things, and could contemn
Riches, though offered from the hand of kings.
And what in me seems wanting but that I
May also in this poverty as soon
Accomplish what they did, perhaps and more?
Extol not riches, then, the toil of fools,
The wise man's cumbrance, if not snare; more apt
To slacken virtue and abate her edge
Than prompt her to do aught may merit praise.
What if with like aversion I reject
Riches and realms! Yet not for that a crown,
Golden in shew, is but a wreath of thorns,
Brings dangers, troubles, cares, and sleepless nights,
To him who wears the regal diadem,
When on his shoulders each man's burden lies;
For therein stands the office of a king,
His honour, virtue, merit, and chief praise,
That for the public all this weight he bears.
Yet he who reigns within himself, and rules
Passions, desires, and fears, is more a king—
Which every wise and virtuous man attains;
And who attains not, ill aspires to rule
Cities of men, or headstrong multitudes,
Subject himself to anarchy within,
Or lawless passions in him, which he serves.
But to guide nations in the way of truth
By saving doctrine, and from error lead
To know, and, knowing, worship God aright,
Is yet more kingly. This attracts the soul,

Governs the inner man, the nobler part;
That other o'er the body only reigns,
And oft by force—which to a generous mind
So reigning can be no sincere delight.
Besides, to give a kingdom hath been thought
Greater and nobler done, and to lay down
Far more magnanimous, than to assume.
Riches are needless, then, both for themselves,
And for thy reason why they should be sought—
To gain a sceptre, oftest better missed."

THE THIRD BOOK

SO spake the Son of God; and Satan stood
A while as mute, confounded what to say,
What to reply, confuted and convinced
Of his weak arguing and fallacious drift;
At length, collecting all his serpent wiles,
With soothing words renewed, him thus accosts:—
"I see thou know'st what is of use to know,
What best to say canst say, to do canst do;
Thy actions to thy words accord; thy words
To thy large heart give utterance due; thy heart
Contains of good, wise, just, the perfet shape.
Should kings and nations from thy mouth consult,
Thy counsel would be as the oracle
Urim and Thummim, those oraculous gems
On Aaron's breast, or tongue of Seers old
Infallible; or, wert thou sought to deeds
That might require the array of war, thy skill
Of conduct would be such that all the world
Could not sustain thy prowess, or subsist
In battle, though against thy few in arms.
These godlike virtues wherefore dost thou hide?
Affecting private life, or more obscure
In savage wilderness, wherefore deprive

All Earth her wonder at thy acts, thyself
The fame and glory—glory, the reward
That sole excites to high attempts the flame
Of most erected spirits, most tempered pure
AEthereal, who all pleasures else despise,
All treasures and all gain esteem as dross,
And dignities and powers, all but the highest?
Thy years are ripe, and over-ripe. The son
Of Macedonian Philip had ere these
Won Asia, and the throne of Cyrus held
At his dispose; young Scipio had brought down
The Carthaginian pride; young Pompey quelled
The Pontic king, and in triumph had rode.
Yet years, and to ripe years judgment mature,
Quench not the thirst of glory, but augment.
Great Julius, whom now all the world admires,
The more he grew in years, the more inflamed
With glory, wept that he had lived so long
Ingloroious. But thou yet art not too late."
To whom our Saviour calmly thus replied:—
"Thou neither dost persuade me to seek wealth
For empire's sake, nor empire to affect
For glory's sake, by all thy argument.
For what is glory but the blaze of fame,
The people's praise, if always praise unmixed?
And what the people but a herd confused,
A miscellaneous rabble, who extol
Things vulgar, and, well weighed, scarce worth the praise?
They praise and they admire they know not what,
And know not whom, but as one leads the other;
And what delight to be by such extolled,
To live upon their tongues, and be their talk?
Of whom to be dispraised were no small praise—
His lot who dares be singularly good.
The intelligent among them and the wise

Are few, and glory scarce of few is raised.
This is true glory and renown—when God,
Looking on the Earth, with approbation marks
The just man, and divulges him through Heaven
To all his Angels, who with true applause
Recount his praises. Thus he did to Job,
When, to extend his fame through Heaven and Earth,
As thou to thy reproach may'st well remember,
He asked thee, 'Hast thou seen my servant Job?'
Famous he was in Heaven; on Earth less known,
Where glory is false glory, attributed
To things not glorious, men not worthy of fame.
They err who count it glorious to subdue
By conquest far and wide, to overrun
Large countries, and in field great battles win,
Great cities by assault. What do these worthies
But rob and spoil, burn, slaughter, and enslave
Peaceable nations, neighbouring or remote,
Made captive, yet deserving freedom more
Than those their conquerors, who leave behind
Nothing but ruin wheresoe'er they rove,
And all the flourishing works of peace destroy;
Then swell with pride, and must be titled Gods,
Great benefactors of mankind, Deliverers,
Worshipped with temple, priest, and sacrifice?
One is the son of Jove, of Mars the other;
Till conqueror Death discover them scarce men,
Rowling in brutish vices, and deformed,
Violent or shameful death their due reward.
But, if there be in glory aught of good;
It may be means far different be attained,
Without ambition, war, or violence—
By deeds of peace, by wisdom eminent,
By patience, temperance. I mention still
Him whom thy wrongs, with saintly patience borne,

Made famous in a land and times obscure;
Who names not now with honour patient Job?
Poor Socrates, (who next more memorable?)
By what he taught and suffered for so doing,
For truth's sake suffering death unjust, lives now
Equal in fame to proudest conquerors.
Yet, if for fame and glory aught be done,
Aught suffered—if young African for fame
His wasted country freed from Punic rage—
The deed becomes unpraised, the man at least,
And loses, though but verbal, his reward.
Shall I seek glory, then, as vain men seek,
Oft not deserved? I seek not mine, but His
Who sent me, and thereby witness whence I am."
To whom the Tempter, murmuring, thus replied:—
"Think not so slight of glory, therein least
Resembling thy great Father. He seeks glory,
And for his glory all things made, all things
Orders and governs; nor content in Heaven,
By all his Angels glorified, requires
Glory from men, from all men, good or bad,
Wise or unwise, no difference, no exemption.
Above all sacrifice, or hallowed gift,
Glory he requires, and glory he receives,
Promiscuous from all nations, Jew, or Greek,
Or Barbarous, nor exception hath declared;
From us, his foes pronounced, glory he exacts."
To whom our Saviour fervently replied:
"And reason; since his Word all things produced,
Though chiefly not for glory as prime end,
But to shew forth his goodness, and impart
His good communicable to every soul
Freely; of whom what could He less expect
Than glory and benediction—that is, thanks—
The slightest, easiest, readiest recompense

From them who could return him nothing else,
And, not returning that, would likeliest render
Contempt instead, dishonour, obloquy?
Hard recompense, unsuitable return
For so much good, so much beneficence!
But why should man seek glory, who of his own
Hath nothing, and to whom nothing belongs
But condemnation, ignominy, and shame—
Who, for so many benefits received,
Turned recreant to God, ingrate and false,
And so of all true good himself despoiled;
Yet, sacrilegious, to himself would take
That which to God alone of right belongs?
Yet so much bounty is in God, such grace,
That who advances his glory, not their own,
Them he himself to glory will advance."
So spake the Son of God; and here again
Satan had not to answer, but stood struck
With guilt of his own sin—for he himself,
Insatiable of glory, had lost all;
Yet of another plea bethought him soon:—
"Of glory, as thou wilt," said he, "so deem;
Worth or not worth the seeking, let it pass.
But to a Kingdom thou art born—ordained
To sit upon thy father David's throne,
By mother's side thy father, though thy right
Be now in powerful hands, that will not part
Easily from possession won with arms.
Judaea now and all the Promised Land,
Reduced a province under Roman yoke,
Obeys Tiberius, nor is always ruled
With temperate sway: oft have they violated
The Temple, oft the Law, with foul affronts,
Abominations rather, as did once
Antiochus. And think'st thou to regain

Thy right by sitting still, or thus retiring?
So did not Machabeus. He indeed
Retired unto the Desert, but with arms;
And o'er a mighty king so oft prevailed
That by strong hand his family obtained,
Though priests, the crown, and David's throne usurped,
With Modin and her suburbs once content.
If kingdom move thee not, let move thee zeal
And duty—zeal and duty are not slow,
But on Occasion's forelock watchful wait:
They themselves rather are occasion best—
Zeal of thy Father's house, duty to free
Thy country from her heathen servitude.
So shalt thou best fulfil, best verify,
The Prophets old, who sung thy endless reign—
The happier reign the sooner it begins.
Reign then; what canst thou better do the while?"
To whom our Saviour answer thus returned:—
"All things are best fulfilled in their due time;
And time there is for all things, Truth hath said.
If of my reign Prophetic Writ hath told
That it shall never end, so, when begin
The Father in his purpose hath decreed—
He in whose hand all times and seasons rowl.
What if he hath decreed that I shall first
Be tried in humble state, and things adverse,
By tribulations, injuries, insults,
Contempts, and scorns, and snares, and violence,
Suffering, abstaining, quietly expecting
Without distrust or doubt, that He may know
What I can suffer, how obey? Who best
Can suffer best can do, best reign who first
Well hath obeyed—just trial ere I merit
My exaltation without change or end.
But what concerns it thee when I begin

My everlasting Kingdom? Why art thou
Solicitous? What moves thy inquisition?
Know'st thou not that my rising is thy fall,
And my promotion will be thy destruction?"
To whom the Tempter, inly racked, replied:—
"Let that come when it comes. All hope is lost
Of my reception into grace; what worse?
For where no hope is left is left no fear.
If there be worse, the expectation more
Of worse torments me than the feeling can.
I would be at the worst; worst is my port,
My harbour, and my ultimate repose,
The end I would attain, my final good.
My error was my error, and my crime
My crime; whatever, for itself condemned,
And will alike be punished, whether thou
Reign or reign not—though to that gentle brow
Willingly I could fly, and hope thy reign,
From that placid aspect and meek regard,
Rather than aggravate my evil state,
Would stand between me and thy Father's ire
(Whose ire I dread more than the fire of Hell)
A shelter and a kind of shading cool
Interposition, as a summer's cloud.
If I, then, to the worst that can be haste,
Why move thy feet so slow to what is best?
Happiest, both to thyself and all the world,
That thou, who worthiest art, shouldst be their King!
Perhaps thou linger'st in deep thoughts detained
Of the enterprise so hazardous and high!
No wonder; for, though in thee be united
What of perfection can in Man be found,
Or human nature can receive, consider
Thy life hath yet been private, most part spent
At home, scarce viewed the Galilean towns,

And once a year Jerusalem, few days'
Short sojourn; and what thence couldst thou observe?
The world thou hast not seen, much less her glory,
Empires, and monarchs, and their radiant courts—
Best school of best experience, quickest in sight
In all things that to greatest actions lead.
The wisest, unexperienced, will be ever
Timorous, and loth, with novice modesty
(As he who, seeking asses, found a kingdom)
Irresolute, unhardy, unadventrous.
But I will bring thee where thou soon shalt quit
Those rudiments, and see before thine eyes
The monarchies of the Earth, their pomp and state—
Sufficient introduction to inform
Thee, of thyself so apt, in regal arts,
And regal mysteries; that thou may'st know
How best their opposition to withstand."
With that (such power was given him then), he took
The Son of God up to a mountain high.
It was a mountain at whose verdant feet
A spacious plain outstretched in circuit wide
Lay pleasant; from his side two rivers flowed,
The one winding, the other straight, and left between
Fair champaign, with less rivers interveined,
Then meeting joined their tribute to the sea.
Fertile of corn the glebe, of oil, and wine;
With herds the pasture thronged, with flocks the hills;
Huge cities and high-towered, that well might seem
The seats of mightiest monarchs; and so large
The prospect was that here and there was room
For barren desert, fountainless and dry.
To this high mountain-top the Tempter brought
Our Saviour, and new train of words began:—
"Well have we speeded, and o'er hill and dale,
Forest, and field, and flood, temples and towers,

Cut shorter many a league. Here thou behold'st
Assyria, and her empire's ancient bounds,
Araxes and the Caspian lake; thence on
As far as Indus east, Euphrates west,
And oft beyond; to south the Persian bay,
And, inaccessible, the Arabian drouth:
Here, Nineveh, of length within her wall
Several days' journey, built by Ninus old,
Of that first golden monarchy the seat,
And seat of Salmanassar, whose success
Israel in long captivity still mourns;
There Babylon, the wonder of all tongues,
As ancient, but rebuilt by him who twice
Judah and all thy father David's house
Led captive, and Jerusalem laid waste,
Till Cyrus set them free; Persepolis,
His city, there thou seest, and Bactra there;
Ecbatana her structure vast there shews,
And Hecatompylos her hunderd gates;
There Susa by Choaspes, amber stream,
The drink of none but kings; of later fame,
Built by Emathian or by Parthian hands,
The great Seleucia, Nisibis, and there
Artaxata, Teredon, Ctesiphon,
Turning with easy eye, thou may'st behold.
All these the Parthian (now some ages past
By great Arsaces led, who founded first
That empire) under his dominion holds,
From the luxurious kings of Antioch won.
And just in time thou com'st to have a view
Of his great power; for now the Parthian king
In Ctesiphon hath gathered all his host
Against the Scythian, whose incursions wild
Have wasted Sogdiana; to her aid
He marches now in haste. See, though from far,

His thousands, in what martial equipage
They issue forth, steel bows and shafts their arms,
Of equal dread in flight or in pursuit—
All horsemen, in which fight they most excel;
See how in warlike muster they appear,
In rhombs, and wedges, and half-moons, and wings."
He looked, and saw what numbers numberless
The city gates outpoured, light-armed troops
In coats of mail and military pride.
In mail their horses clad, yet fleet and strong,
Prancing their riders bore, the flower and choice
Of many provinces from bound to bound—
From Arachosia, from Candaor east,
And Margiana, to the Hyrcanian cliffs
Of Caucasus, and dark Iberian dales;
From Atropatia, and the neighbouring plains
Of Adiabene, Media, and the south
Of Susiana, to Balsara's haven.
He saw them in their forms of battle ranged,
How quick they wheeled, and flying behind them shot
Sharp sleet of arrowy showers against the face
Of their pursuers, and overcame by flight;
The field all iron cast a gleaming brown.
Nor wanted clouds of foot, nor, on each horn,
Cuirassiers all in steel for standing fight,
Chariots, or elephants indorsed with towers
Of archers; nor of labouring pioners
A multitude, with spades and axes armed,
To lay hills plain, fell woods, or valleys fill,
Or where plain was raise hill, or overlay
With bridges rivers proud, as with a yoke:
Mules after these, camels and dromedaries,
And waggons fraught with utensils of war.
Such forces met not, nor so wide a camp,
When Agrican, with all his northern powers,

Besieged Albracea, as romances tell,
The city of Gallaphrone, from thence to win
The fairest of her sex, Angelica,
His daughter, sought by many prowest knights,
Both Paynim and the peers of Charlemane.
Such and so numerous was their chivalry;
At sight whereof the Fiend yet more presumed,
And to our Saviour thus his words renewed:—
"That thou may'st know I seek not to engage
Thy virtue, and not every way secure
On no slight grounds thy safety, hear and mark
To what end I have brought thee hither, and shew
All this fair sight. Thy kingdom, though foretold
By Prophet or by Angel, unless thou
Endeavour, as thy father David did,
Thou never shalt obtain: prediction still
In all things, and all men, supposes means;
Without means used, what it predicts revokes.
But say thou wert possessed of David's throne
By free consent of all, none opposite,
Samaritan or Jew; how couldst thou hope
Long to enjoy it quiet and secure
Between two such enclosing enemies,
Roman and Parthian? Therefore one of these
Thou must make sure thy own: the Parthian first,
By my advice, as nearer, and of late
Found able by invasion to annoy
Thy country, and captive lead away her kings,
Antigonus and old Hyrcanus, bound,
Maugre the Roman. It shall be my task
To render thee the Parthian at dispose,
Choose which thou wilt, by conquest or by league.
By him thou shalt regain, without him not,
That which alone can truly reinstall thee
In David's royal seat, his true successor—

Deliverance of thy brethren, those Ten Tribes
Whose offspring in his territory yet serve
In Habor, and among the Medes dispersed:
The sons of Jacob, two of Joseph, lost
Thus long from Israel, serving, as of old
Their fathers in the land of Egypt served,
This offer sets before thee to deliver.
These if from servitude thou shalt restore
To their inheritance, then, nor till then,
Thou on the throne of David in full glory,
From Egypt to Euphrates and beyond,
Shalt reign, and Rome or Caesar not need fear."
To whom our Saviour answered thus, unmoved:—
"Much ostentation vain of fleshly arm
And fragile arms, much instrument of war,
Long in preparing, soon to nothing brought,
Before mine eyes thou hast set, and in my ear
Vented much policy, and projects deep
Of enemies, of aids, battles, and leagues,
Plausible to the world, to me worth naught.
Means I must use, thou say'st; prediction else
Will unpredict, and fail me of the throne!
My time, I told thee (and that time for thee
Were better farthest off), is not yet come.
When that comes, think not thou to find me slack
On my part aught endeavouring, or to need
Thy politic maxims, or that cumbersome
Luggage of war there shewn me—argument
Of human weakness rather than of strength.
My brethren, as thou call'st them, those Ten Tribes,
I must deliver, if I mean to reign
David's true heir, and his full sceptre sway
To just extent over all Israel's sons!
But whence to thee this zeal? Where was it then
For Israel, or for David, or his throne,

When thou stood'st up his tempter to the pride
Of numbering Israel—which cost the lives
of threescore and ten thousand Israelites
By three days' pestilence? Such was thy zeal
To Israel then, the same that now to me.
As for those captive tribes, themselves were they
Who wrought their own captivity, fell off
From God to worship calves, the deities
Of Egypt, Baal next and Ashtaroth,
And all the idolatries of heathen round,
Besides their other worse than heathenish crimes;
Nor in the land of their captivity
Humbled themselves, or penitent besought
The God of their forefathers, but so died
Impenitent, and left a race behind
Like to themselves, distinguishable scarce
From Gentiles, but by circumcision vain,
And God with idols in their worship joined.
Should I of these the liberty regard,
Who, freed, as to their ancient patrimony,
Unhumbled, unrepentant, unreformed,
Headlong would follow, and to their gods perhaps
Of Bethel and of Dan? No; let them serve
Their enemies who serve idols with God.
Yet He at length, time to himself best known,
Remembering Abraham, by some wondrous call
May bring them back, repentant and sincere,
And at their passing cleave the Assyrian flood,
While to their native land with joy they haste,
As the Red Sea and Jordan once he cleft,
When to the Promised Land their fathers passed.
To his due time and providence I leave them."
So spake Israel's true King, and to the Fiend
Made answer meet, that made void all his wiles.
So fares it when with truth falsehood contends.

THE FOURTH BOOK

Perplexed and troubled at his bad success
The Tempter stood, nor had what to reply,
Discovered in his fraud, thrown from his hope
So oft, and the persuasive rhetoric
That sleeked his tongue, and won so much on Eve,
So little here, nay lost. But Eve was Eve;
This far his over-match, who, self-deceived
And rash, beforehand had no better weighed
The strength he was to cope with, or his own.
But—as a man who had been matchless held
In cunning, over-reached where least he thought,
To salve his credit, and for very spite,
Still will be tempting him who foils him still,
And never cease, though to his shame the more;
Or as a swarm of flies in vintage-time,
About the wine-press where sweet must is poured,
Beat off, returns as oft with humming sound;
Or surging waves against a solid rock,
Though all to shivers dashed, the assault renew,
(Vain battery!) and in froth or bubbles end—
So Satan, whom repulse upon repulse
Met ever, and to shameful silence brought,

Yet gives not o'er, though desperate of success,
And his vain importunity pursues.
He brought our Saviour to the western side
Of that high mountain, whence he might behold
Another plain, long, but in breadth not wide,
Washed by the southern sea, and on the north
To equal length backed with a ridge of hills
That screened the fruits of the earth and seats of men
From cold Septentrion blasts; thence in the midst
Divided by a river, off whose banks
On each side an Imperial City stood,
With towers and temples proudly elevate
On seven small hills, with palaces adorned,
Porches and theatres, baths, aqueducts,
Statues and trophies, and triumphal arcs,
Gardens and groves, presented to his eyes
Above the hight of mountains interposed—
By what strange parallax, or optic skill
Of vision, multiplied through air, or glass
Of telescope, were curious to enquire.
And now the Tempter thus his silence broke:—
"The city which thou seest no other deem
Than great and glorious Rome, Queen of the Earth
So far renowned, and with the spoils enriched
Of nations. There the Capitol thou seest,
Above the rest lifting his stately head
On the Tarpeian rock, her citadel
Impregnable; and there Mount Palatine,
The imperial palace, compass huge, and high
The structure, skill of noblest architects,
With gilded battlements, conspicuous far,
Turrets, and terraces, and glittering spires.
Many a fair edifice besides, more like
Houses of gods—so well I have disposed
My aerie microscope—thou may'st behold,

Outside and inside both, pillars and roofs
Carved work, the hand of famed artificers
In cedar, marble, ivory, or gold.
Thence to the gates cast round thine eye, and see
What conflux issuing forth, or entering in:
Praetors, proconsuls to their provinces
Hasting, or on return, in robes of state;
Lictors and rods, the ensigns of their power,
Legions and cohorts, turms of horse and wings;
Or embassies from regions far remote,
In various habits, on the Appian road,
Or on the AEmilian—some from farthest south,
Syene, and where the shadow both way falls,
Meroe, Nilotic isle, and, more to west,
The realm of Bocchus to the Blackmoor sea;
From the Asian kings (and Parthian among these),
From India and the Golden Chersoness,
And utmost Indian isle Taprobane,
Dusk faces with white silken turbans wreathed;
From Gallia, Gades, and the British west;
Germans, and Scythians, and Sarmatians north
Beyond Danubius to the Tauric pool.
All nations now to Rome obedience pay—
To Rome's great Emperor, whose wide domain,
In ample territory, wealth and power,
Civility of manners, arts and arms,
And long renown, thou justly may'st prefer
Before the Parthian. These two thrones except,
The rest are barbarous, and scarce worth the sight,
Shared among petty kings too far removed;
These having shewn thee, I have shewn thee all
The kingdoms of the world, and all their glory.
This Emperor hath no son, and now is old,
Old and lascivious, and from Rome retired
To Capreae, an island small but strong

On the Campanian shore, with purpose there
His horrid lusts in private to enjoy;
Committing to a wicked favourite
All public cares, and yet of him suspicious;
Hated of all, and hating. With what ease,
Endued with regal virtues as thou art,
Appearing, and beginning noble deeds,
Might'st thou expel this monster from his throne,
Now made a sty, and, in his place ascending,
A victor-people free from servile yoke!
And with my help thou may'st; to me the power
Is given, and by that right I give it thee.
Aim, therefore, at no less than all the world;
Aim at the highest; without the highest attained,
Will be for thee no sitting, or not long,
On David's throne, be prophesied what will."
To whom the Son of God, unmoved, replied:—
"Nor doth this grandeur and majestic shew
Of luxury, though called magnificence,
More than of arms before, allure mine eye,
Much less my mind; though thou should'st add to tell
Their sumptuous gluttonies, and gorgeous feasts
On citron tables or Atlantic stone
(For I have also heard, perhaps have read),
Their wines of Setia, Cales, and Falerne,
Chios and Crete, and how they quaff in gold,
Crystal, and myrrhine cups, imbossed with gems
And studs of pearl—to me should'st tell, who thirst
And hunger still. Then embassies thou shew'st
From nations far and nigh! What honour that,
But tedious waste of time, to sit and hear
So many hollow compliments and lies,
Outlandish flatteries? Then proceed'st to talk
Of the Emperor, how easily subdued,
How gloriously. I shall, thou say'st, expel

A brutish monster: what if I withal
Expel a Devil who first made him such?
Let his tormentor, Conscience, find him out;
For him I was not sent, nor yet to free
That people, victor once, now vile and base,
Deservedly made vassal—who, once just,
Frugal, and mild, and temperate, conquered well,
But govern ill the nations under yoke,
Peeling their provinces, exhausted all
By lust and rapine; first ambitious grown
Of triumph, that insulting vanity;
Then cruel, by their sports to blood inured
Of fighting beasts, and men to beasts exposed;
Luxurious by their wealth, and greedier still,
And from the daily Scene effeminate.
What wise and valiant man would seek to free
These, thus degenerate, by themselves enslaved,
Or could of inward slaves make outward free?
Know, therefore, when my season comes to sit
On David's throne, it shall be like a tree
Spreading and overshadowing all the earth,
Or as a stone that shall to pieces dash
All monarchies besides throughout the world;
And of my Kingdom there shall be no end.
Means there shall be to this; but what the means
Is not for thee to know, nor me to tell."
To whom the Tempter, impudent, replied:—
"I see all offers made by me how slight
Thou valuest, because offered, and reject'st.
Nothing will please the difficult and nice,
Or nothing more than still to contradict.
On the other side know also thou that I
On what I offer set as high esteem,
Nor what I part with mean to give for naught,
All these, which in a moment thou behold'st,

The kingdoms of the world, to thee I give
(For, given to me, I give to whom I please),
No trifle; yet with this reserve, not else—
On this condition, if thou wilt fall down,
And worship me as thy superior Lord
(Easily done), and hold them all of me;
For what can less so great a gift deserve?"
Whom thus our Saviour answered with disdain:—
"I never liked thy talk, thy offers less;
Now both abhor, since thou hast dared to utter
The abominable terms, impious condition.
But I endure the time, till which expired
Thou hast permission on me. It is written,
The first of all commandments, 'Thou shalt worship
The Lord thy God, and only Him shalt serve.'
And dar'st thou to the Son of God propound
To worship thee, accursed? now more accursed
For this attempt, bolder than that on Eve,
And more blasphemous; which expect to rue.
The kingdoms of the world to thee were given!
Permitted rather, and by thee usurped;
Other donation none thou canst produce.
If given, by whom but by the King of kings,
God over all supreme? If given to thee,
By thee how fairly is the Giver now
Repaid! But gratitude in thee is lost
Long since. Wert thou so void of fear or shame
As offer them to me, the Son of God—
To me my own, on such abhorred pact,
That I fall down and worship thee as God?
Get thee behind me! Plain thou now appear'st
That Evil One, Satan for ever damned."
To whom the Fiend, with fear abashed, replied:—
"Be not so sore offended, Son of God—
Though Sons of God both Angels are and Men—

If I, to try whether in higher sort
Than these thou bear'st that title, have proposed
What both from Men and Angels I receive,
Tetrarchs of Fire, Air, Flood, and on the Earth
Nations besides from all the quartered winds—
God of this World invoked, and World beneath.
Who then thou art, whose coming is foretold
To me most fatal, me it most concerns.
The trial hath indamaged thee no way,
Rather more honour left and more esteem;
Me naught advantaged, missing what I aimed.
Therefore let pass, as they are transitory,
The kingdoms of this world; I shall no more
Advise thee; gain them as thou canst, or not.
And thou thyself seem'st otherwise inclined
Than to a worldly crown, addicted more
To contemplation and profound dispute;
As by that early action may be judged,
When, slipping from thy mother's eye, thou went'st
Alone into the Temple, there wast found
Among the gravest Rabbies, disputant
On points and questions fitting Moses' chair,
Teaching, not taught. The childhood shews the man,
As morning shews the day. Be famous, then,
By wisdom; as thy empire must extend,
So let extend thy mind o'er all the world
In knowledge; all things in it comprehend.
All knowledge is not couched in Moses' law,
The Pentateuch, or what the Prophets wrote;
The Gentiles also know, and write, and teach
To admiration, led by Nature's light;
And with the Gentiles much thou must converse,
Ruling them by persuasion, as thou mean'st.
Without their learning, how wilt thou with them,
Or they with thee, hold conversation meet?

How wilt thou reason with them, how refute
Their idolisms, traditions, paradoxes?
Error by his own arms is best evinced.
Look once more, ere we leave this specular mount,
Westward, much nearer by south-west; behold
Where on the AEgean shore a city stands,
Built nobly, pure the air and light the soil—
Athens, the eye of Greece, mother of arts
And Eloquence, native to famous wits
Or hospitable, in her sweet recess,
City or suburban, studious walks and shades.
See there the olive-grove of Academe,
Plato's retirement, where the Attic bird
Trills her thick-warbled notes the summer long;
There, flowery hill, Hymettus, with the sound
Of bees' industrious murmur, oft invites
To studious musing; there Ilissus rowls
His whispering stream. Within the walls then view
The schools of ancient sages—his who bred
Great Alexander to subdue the world,
Lyceum there; and painted Stoa next.
There thou shalt hear and learn the secret power
Of harmony, in tones and numbers hit
By voice or hand, and various-measured verse,
AEolian charms and Dorian lyric odes,
And his who gave them breath, but higher sung,
Blind Melesigenes, thence Homer called,
Whose poem Phoebus challenged for his own.
Thence what the lofty grave Tragedians taught
In chorus or iambic, teachers best
Of moral prudence, with delight received
In brief sententious precepts, while they treat
Of fate, and chance, and change in human life,
High actions and high passions best describing.
Thence to the famous Orators repair,

Those ancient whose resistless eloquence
Wielded at will that fierce democraty,
Shook the Arsenal, and fulmined over Greece
To Macedon and Artaxerxes' throne.
To sage Philosophy next lend thine ear,
From heaven descended to the low-roofed house
Of Socrates—see there his tenement—
Whom, well inspired, the Oracle pronounced
Wisest of men; from whose mouth issued forth
Mellifluous streams, that watered all the schools
Of Academics old and new, with those
Surnamed Peripatetics, and the sect
Epicurean, and the Stoic severe.
These here revolve, or, as thou likest, at home,
Till time mature thee to a kingdom's weight;
These rules will render thee a king complete
Within thyself, much more with empire joined."
To whom our Saviour sagely thus replied:—
"Think not but that I know these things; or, think
I know them not, not therefore am I short
Of knowing what I ought. He who receives
Light from above, from the Fountain of Light,
No other doctrine needs, though granted true;
But these are false, or little else but dreams,
Conjectures, fancies, built on nothing firm.
The first and wisest of them all professed
To know this only, that he nothing knew;
The next to fabling fell and smooth conceits;
A third sort doubted all things, though plain sense;
Others in virtue placed felicity,
But virtue joined with riches and long life;
In corporal pleasure he, and careless ease;
The Stoic last in philosophic pride,
By him called virtue, and his virtuous man,
Wise, perfect in himself, and all possessing,

Equal to God, oft shames not to prefer,
As fearing God nor man, contemning all
Wealth, pleasure, pain or torment, death and life—
Which, when he lists, he leaves, or boasts he can;
For all his tedious talk is but vain boast,
Or subtle shifts conviction to evade.
Alas! what can they teach, and not mislead,
Ignorant of themselves, of God much more,
And how the World began, and how Man fell,
Degraded by himself, on grace depending?
Much of the Soul they talk, but all awry;
And in themselves seek virtue; and to themselves
All glory arrogate, to God give none;
Rather accuse him under usual names,
Fortune and Fate, as one regardless quite
Of mortal things. Who, therefore, seeks in these
True wisdom finds her not, or, by delusion
Far worse, her false resemblance only meets,
An empty cloud. However, many books,
Wise men have said, are wearisome; who reads
Incessantly, and to his reading brings not
A spirit and judgment equal or superior,
(And what he brings what needs he elsewhere seek?)
Uncertain and unsettled still remains,
Deep-versed in books and shallow in himself,
Crude or intoxicate, collecting toys
And trifles for choice matters, worth a sponge,
As children gathering pebbles on the shore.
Or, if I would delight my private hours
With music or with poem, where so soon
As in our native language can I find
That solace? All our Law and Story strewed
With hymns, our Psalms with artful terms inscribed,
Our Hebrew songs and harps, in Babylon
That pleased so well our victor's ear, declare

That rather Greece from us these arts derived—
Ill imitated while they loudest sing
The vices of their deities, and their own,
In fable, hymn, or song, so personating
Their gods ridiculous, and themselves past shame.
Remove their swelling epithetes, thick-laid
As varnish on a harlot's cheek, the rest,
Thin-sown with aught of profit or delight,
Will far be found unworthy to compare
With Sion's songs, to all true tastes excelling,
Where God is praised aright and godlike men,
The Holiest of Holies and his Saints
(Such are from God inspired, not such from thee);
Unless where moral virtue is expressed
By light of Nature, not in all quite lost.
Their orators thou then extoll'st as those
The top of eloquence—statists indeed,
And lovers of their country, as may seem;
But herein to our Prophets far beneath,
As men divinely taught, and better teaching
The solid rules of civil government,
In their majestic, unaffected style,
Than all the oratory of Greece and Rome.
In them is plainest taught, and easiest learnt,
What makes a nation happy, and keeps it so,
What ruins kingdoms, and lays cities flat;
These only, with our Law, best form a king."
So spake the Son of God; but Satan, now
Quite at a loss (for all his darts were spent),
Thus to our Saviour, with stern brow, replied:—
"Since neither wealth nor honour, arms nor arts,
Kingdom nor empire, pleases thee, nor aught
By me proposed in life contemplative
Or active, tended on by glory or fame,
What dost thou in this world? The Wilderness

For thee is fittest place: I found thee there,
And thither will return thee. Yet remember
What I foretell thee; soon thou shalt have cause
To wish thou never hadst rejected, thus
Nicely or cautiously, my offered aid,
Which would have set thee in short time with ease
On David's throne, or throne of all the world,
Now at full age, fulness of time, thy season,
When prophecies of thee are best fulfilled.
Now, contrary—if I read aught in heaven,
Or heaven write aught of fate—by what the stars
Voluminous, or single characters
In their conjunction met, give me to spell,
Sorrows and labours, opposition, hate,
Attends thee; scorns, reproaches, injuries,
Violence and stripes, and, lastly, cruel death.
A kingdom they portend thee, but what kingdom,
Real or allegoric, I discern not;
Nor when: eternal sure—as without end,
Without beginning; for no date prefixed
Directs me in the starry rubric set."
So saying, he took (for still he knew his power
Not yet expired), and to the Wilderness
Brought back, the Son of God, and left him there,
Feigning to disappear. Darkness now rose,
As daylight sunk, and brought in louring Night,
Her shadowy offspring, unsubstantial both,
Privation mere of light and absent day.
Our Saviour, meek, and with untroubled mind
After his aerie jaunt, though hurried sore,
Hungry and cold, betook him to his rest,
Wherever, under some concourse of shades,
Whose branching arms thick intertwined might shield
From dews and damps of night his sheltered head;
But, sheltered, slept in vain; for at his head

The Tempter watched, and soon with ugly dreams
Disturbed his sleep. And either tropic now
'Gan thunder, and both ends of heaven; the clouds
From many a horrid rift abortive poured
Fierce rain with lightning mixed, water with fire,
In ruin reconciled; nor slept the winds
Within their stony caves, but rushed abroad
From the four hinges of the world, and fell
On the vexed wilderness, whose tallest pines,
Though rooted deep as high, and sturdiest oaks,
Bowed their stiff necks, loaden with stormy blasts,
Or torn up sheer. Ill wast thou shrouded then,
O patient Son of God, yet only stood'st
Unshaken! Nor yet staid the terror there:
Infernal ghosts and hellish furies round
Environed thee; some howled, some yelled, some shrieked,
Some bent at thee their fiery darts, while thou
Sat'st unappalled in calm and sinless peace.
Thus passed the night so foul, till Morning fair
Came forth with pilgrim steps, in amice grey,
Who with her radiant finger stilled the roar
Of thunder, chased the clouds, and laid the winds,
And griesly spectres, which the Fiend had raised
To tempt the Son of God with terrors dire.
And now the sun with more effectual beams
Had cheered the face of earth, and dried the wet
From drooping plant, or dropping tree; the birds,
Who all things now behold more fresh and green,
After a night of storm so ruinous,
Cleared up their choicest notes in bush and spray,
To gratulate the sweet return of morn.
Nor yet, amidst this joy and brightest morn,
Was absent, after all his mischief done,
The Prince of Darkness; glad would also seem
Of this fair change, and to our Saviour came;

Yet with no new device (they all were spent),
Rather by this his last affront resolved,
Desperate of better course, to vent his rage
And mad despite to be so oft repelled.
Him walking on a sunny hill he found,
Backed on the north and west by a thick wood;
Out of the wood he starts in wonted shape,
And in a careless mood thus to him said:—
"Fair morning yet betides thee, Son of God,
After a dismal night. I heard the wrack,
As earth and sky would mingle; but myself
Was distant; and these flaws, though mortals fear them,
As dangerous to the pillared frame of Heaven,
Or to the Earth's dark basis underneath,
Are to the main as inconsiderable
And harmless, if not wholesome, as a sneeze
To man's less universe, and soon are gone.
Yet, as being ofttimes noxious where they light
On man, beast, plant, wasteful and turbulent,
Like turbulencies in the affairs of men,
Over whose heads they roar, and seem to point,
They oft fore-signify and threaten ill.
This tempest at this desert most was bent;
Of men at thee, for only thou here dwell'st.
Did I not tell thee, if thou didst reject
The perfect season offered with my aid
To win thy destined seat, but wilt prolong
All to the push of fate, pursue thy way
Of gaining David's throne no man knows when
(For both the when and how is nowhere told),
Thou shalt be what thou art ordained, no doubt;
For Angels have proclaimed it, but concealing
The time and means? Each act is rightliest done
Not when it must, but when it may be best.
If thou observe not this, be sure to find

What I foretold thee—many a hard assay
Of dangers, and adversities, and pains,
Ere thou of Israel's sceptre get fast hold;
Whereof this ominous night that closed thee round,
So many terrors, voices, prodigies,
May warn thee, as a sure foregoing sign."
So talked he, while the Son of God went on,
And staid not, but in brief him answered thus:—
"Me worse than wet thou find'st not; other harm
Those terrors which thou speak'st of did me none.
I never feared they could, though noising loud
And threatening nigh: what they can do as signs
Betokening or ill-boding I contemn
As false portents, not sent from God, but thee;
Who, knowing I shall reign past thy preventing,
Obtrud'st thy offered aid, that I, accepting,
At least might seem to hold all power of thee,
Ambitious Spirit! and would'st be thought my God;
And storm'st, refused, thinking to terrify
Me to thy will! Desist (thou art discerned,
And toil'st in vain), nor me in vain molest."
To whom the Fiend, now swoln with rage, replied:—
"Then hear, O Son of David, virgin-born!
For Son of God to me is yet in doubt.
Of the Messiah I have heard foretold
By all the Prophets; of thy birth, at length
Announced by Gabriel, with the first I knew,
And of the angelic song in Bethlehem field,
On thy birth-night, that sung thee Saviour born.
From that time seldom have I ceased to eye
Thy infancy, thy childhood, and thy youth,
Thy manhood last, though yet in private bred;
Till, at the ford of Jordan, whither all
Flocked to the Baptist, I among the rest
(Though not to be baptized), by voice from Heaven

Heard thee pronounced the Son of God beloved.
Thenceforth I thought thee worth my nearer view
And narrower scrutiny, that I might learn
In what degree or meaning thou art called
The Son of God, which bears no single sense.
The Son of God I also am, or was;
And, if I was, I am; relation stands:
All men are Sons of God; yet thee I thought
In some respect far higher so declared.
Therefore I watched thy footsteps from that hour,
And followed thee still on to this waste wild,
Where, by all best conjectures, I collect
Thou art to be my fatal enemy.
Good reason, then, if I beforehand seek
To understand my adversary, who
And what he is; his wisdom, power, intent;
By parle or composition, truce or league,
To win him, or win from him what I can.
And opportunity I here have had
To try thee, sift thee, and confess have found thee
Proof against all temptation, as a rock
Of adamant and as a centre, firm
To the utmost of mere man both wise and good,
Not more; for honours, riches, kingdoms, glory,
Have been before contemned, and may again.
Therefore, to know what more thou art than man,
Worth naming the Son of God by voice from Heaven,
Another method I must now begin."
So saying, he caught him up, and, without wing
Of hippogrif, bore through the air sublime,
Over the wilderness and o'er the plain,
Till underneath them fair Jerusalem,
The Holy City, lifted high her towers,
And higher yet the glorious Temple reared
Her pile, far off appearing like a mount

Of alablaster, topt with golden spires:
There, on the highest pinnacle, he set
The Son of God, and added thus in scorn:—
"There stand, if thou wilt stand; to stand upright
Will ask thee skill. I to thy Father's house
Have brought thee, and highest placed: highest is best.
Now shew thy progeny; if not to stand,
Cast thyself down. Safely, if Son of God;
For it is written, 'He will give command
Concerning thee to his Angels; in their hands
They shall uplift thee, lest at any time
Thou chance to dash thy foot against a stone.'"
To whom thus Jesus: "Also it is written,
'Tempt not the Lord thy God.'" He said, and stood;
But Satan, smitten with amazement, fell.
As when Earth's son, Antaeus (to compare
Small things with greatest), in Irassa strove
With Jove's Alcides, and, oft foiled, still rose,
Receiving from his mother Earth new strength,
Fresh from his fall, and fiercer grapple joined,
Throttled at length in the air expired and fell,
So, after many a foil, the Tempter proud,
Renewing fresh assaults, amidst his pride
Fell whence he stood to see his victor fall;
And, as that Theban monster that proposed
Her riddle, and him who solved it not devoured,
That once found out and solved, for grief and spite
Cast herself headlong from the Ismenian steep,
So, strook with dread and anguish, fell the Fiend,
And to his crew, that sat consulting, brought
Joyless triumphals of his hoped success,
Ruin, and desperation, and dismay,
Who durst so proudly tempt the Son of God.
So Satan fell; and straight a fiery globe
Of Angels on full sail of wing flew nigh,

Who on their plumy vans received Him soft
From his uneasy station, and upbore,
As on a floating couch, through the blithe air;
Then, in a flowery valley, set him down
On a green bank, and set before him spread
A table of celestial food, divine
Ambrosial fruits fetched from the Tree of Life,
And from the Fount of Life ambrosial drink,
That soon refreshed him wearied, and repaired
What hunger, if aught hunger, had impaired,
Or thirst; and, as he fed, Angelic quires
Sung heavenly anthems of his victory
Over temptation and the Tempter proud:—
"True Image of the Father, whether throned
In the bosom of bliss, and light of light
Conceiving, or, remote from Heaven, enshrined
In fleshly tabernacle and human form,
Wandering the wilderness—whatever place,
Habit, or state, or motion, still expressing
The Son of God, with Godlike force endued
Against the attempter of thy Father's throne
And thief of Paradise! Him long of old
Thou didst rebel, and down from Heaven cast
With all his army; now thou hast avenged
Supplanted Adam, and, by vanquishing
Temptation, hast regained lost Paradise,
And frustrated the conquest fraudulent.
He never more henceforth will dare set foot
In paradise to tempt; his snares are broke.
For, though that seat of earthly bliss be failed,
A fairer Paradise is founded now
For Adam and his chosen sons, whom thou,
A Saviour, art come down to reinstall;
Where they shall dwell secure, when time shall be,
Of tempter and temptation without fear.

But thou, Infernal Serpent! shalt not long
Rule in the clouds. Like an autumnal star,
Or lightning, thou shalt fall from Heaven, trod down
Under his feet. For proof, ere this thou feel'st
Thy wound (yet not thy last and deadliest wound)
By this repulse received, and hold'st in Hell
No triumph; in all her gates Abaddon rues
Thy bold attempt. Hereafter learn with awe
To dread the Son of God. He, all unarmed,
Shall chase thee, with the terror of his voice,
From thy demoniac holds, possession foul—
Thee and thy legions; yelling they shall fly,
And beg to hide them in a herd of swine,
Lest he command them down into the Deep,
Bound, and to torment sent before their time.
Hail, Son of the Most High, heir of both Worlds,
Queller of Satan! On thy glorious work
Now enter, and begin to save Mankind."
Thus they the Son of God, our Saviour meek,
Sung victor, and, from heavenly feast refreshed,
Brought on his way with joy. He, unobserved,
Home to his mother's house private returned.

CLASSIC LITERATURE: WORDS AND PHRASES
adapted from the *Collins English Dictionary*

Accoucheur NOUN a male midwife or doctor ❑ *I think my sister must have had some general idea that I was a young offender whom an Accoucheur Policemen had taken up (on my birthday) and delivered over to her* (*Great Expectations* by Charles Dickens)

addled ADJ confused and unable to think properly ❑ *But she counted and counted till she got that addled* (*The Adventures of Huckleberry Finn* by Mark Twain)

admiration NOUN amazement or wonder ❑ *lifting up his hands and eyes by way of admiration* (*Gulliver's Travels* by Jonathan Swift)

afeard ADJ afeard means afraid ❑ *shake it – and don't be afeard* (*The Adventures of Huckleberry Finn* by Mark Twain)

affected VERB affected means followed ❑ *Hadst thou affected sweet divinity* (*Doctor Faustus 5.2* by Christopher Marlowe)

aground ADV when a boat runs aground, it touches the ground in a shallow part of the water and gets stuck ❑ *what kep' you? – boat get aground?* (*The Adventures of Huckleberry Finn* by Mark Twain)

ague NOUN a fever in which the patient has alternate hot and cold shivering fits ❑ *his exposure to the wet and cold had brought on fever and ague* (*Oliver Twist* by Charles Dickens)

alchemy ADJ false or worthless ❑ *all wealth alchemy* (*The Sun Rising* by John Donne)

all alike PHRASE the same all the time ❑ *Love, all alike* (*The Sun Rising* by John Donne)

alow and aloft PHRASE alow means in the lower part or bottom, and aloft means on the top, so alow and aloft means on the top and in the bottom or throughout ❑ *Someone's turned the chest out alow and aloft* (*Treasure Island* by Robert Louis Stevenson)

ambuscade NOUN ambuscade is not a proper word. Tom means an ambush, which is when a group of people attack their enemies, after hiding and waiting for them ❑ *and so we would lie in ambuscade, as he called it* (*The Adventures of Huckleberry Finn* by Mark Twain)

amiable ADJ likeable or pleasant ❑ *Such amiable qualities must speak for themselves* (*Pride and Prejudice* by Jane Austen)

amulet NOUN an amulet is a charm thought to drive away evil spirits. ❑ *uttered phrases at once occult and familiar, like the amulet worn on the heart* (*Silas Marner* by George Eliot)

amusement NOUN here amusement means a strange and disturbing puzzle ❑ *this was an amusement the other way* (*Robinson Crusoe* by Daniel Defoe)

ancient NOUN an ancient was the flag displayed on a ship to show which country it belongs to. It is also called the ensign ❑ *her ancient and pendants out* (*Robinson Crusoe* by Daniel Defoe)

antic ADJ here antic means horrible or grotesque ❑ *armed and dressed after a very antic manner* (*Gulliver's Travels* by Jonathan Swift)

antics NOUN antics is an old word meaning clowns, or people who do silly things to make other people laugh ❑ *And point like antics at his triple crown* (*Doctor Faustus 3.2* by Christopher Marlowe)

appanage NOUN an appanage is a living allowance ❏ *As if loveliness were not the special prerogative of woman – her legitimate appanage and heritage!* (*Jane Eyre* by Charlotte Brontë)

appended VERB appended means attached or added to ❏ *and these words appended* (*Treasure Island* by Robert Louis Stevenson)

approver NOUN an approver is someone who gives evidence against someone he used to work with ❏ *Mr. Noah Claypole: receiving a free pardon from the Crown in consequence of being admitted approver against Fagin* (*Oliver Twist* by Charles Dickens)

areas NOUN the areas is the space, below street level, in front of the basement of a house ❏ *The Dodger had a vicious propensity, too, of pulling the caps from the heads of small boys and tossing them down areas* (*Oliver Twist* by Charles Dickens)

argument NOUN theme or important idea or subject which runs through a piece of writing ❏ *Thrice needful to the argument which now* (*The Prelude* by William Wordsworth) .

artificially ADJ artfully or cleverly ❏ *and he with a sharp flint sharpened very artificially* (*Gulliver's Travels* by Jonathan Swift)

artist NOUN here artist means a skilled workman ❏ *This man was a most ingenious artist* (*Gulliver's Travels* by Jonathan Swift)

assizes NOUN assizes were regular court sessions which a visiting judge was in charge of ❏ *you shall hang at the next assizes* (*Treasure Island* by Robert Louis Stevenson)

attraction NOUN gravitation, or Newton's theory of gravitation ❏ *he predicted the same fate to attraction* (*Gulliver's Travels* by Jonathan Swift)

aver VERB to aver is to claim something strongly ❏ *for Jem Rodney, the mole catcher, averred that one evening as he was returning homeward* (*Silas Marner* by George Eliot)

baby NOUN here baby means doll, which is a child's toy that looks like a small person ❏ *and skilful dressing her baby* (*Gulliver's Travels* by Jonathan Swift)

bagatelle NOUN bagatelle is a game rather like billiards and pool ❏ *Breakfast had been ordered at a pleasant little tavern, a mile or so away upon the rising ground beyond the green; and there was a bagatelle board in the room, in case we should desire to unbend our minds after the solemnity.* (*Great Expectations* by Charles Dickens)

bah EXCLAM Bah is an exclamation of frustration or anger ❏ *"Bah," said Scrooge.* (*A Christmas Carol* by Charles Dickens)

bairn NOUN a northern word for child ❏ *Who has taught you those fine words, my bairn?* (*Wuthering Heights* by Emily Brontë)

bait VERB to bait means to stop on a journey to take refreshment ❏ *So, when they stopped to bait the horse, and ate and drank and enjoyed themselves, I could touch nothing that they touched, but kept my fast unbroken.* (*David Copperfield* by Charles Dickens)

balustrade NOUN a balustrade is a row of vertical columns that form railings ❏ *but I mean to say you might have got a hearse up that staircase, and taken it broadwise, with the splinter-bar towards the wall, and the door towards the balustrades: and done it easy* (*A Christmas Carol* by Charles Dickens)

bandbox NOUN a large lightweight box for carrying bonnets or hats ❏ *I am glad I bought my bonnet, if it is only for the fun of having another bandbox* (*Pride and Prejudice* by Jane Austen)

barren NOUN a barren here is a stretch or expanse of barren land ❏ *a line* *of upright stones, continued the length of the barren* (*Wuthering Heights* by Emily Brontë)

basin NOUN a basin was a cup without a handle ❑ *who is drinking his tea out of a basin* (*Wuthering Heights* by Emily Brontë)

battalia NOUN the order of battle ❑ *till I saw part of his army in battalia* (*Gulliver's Travels* by Jonathan Swift)

battery NOUN a Battery is a fort or a place where guns are positioned ❑ *You bring the lot to me, at that old Battery over yonder* (*Great Expectations* by Charles Dickens)

battledore and shuttlecock NOUN The game battledore and shuttlecock was an early version of the game now known as badminton. The aim of the early game was simply to keep the shuttlecock from hitting the ground. ❑ *Battledore and shuttlecock's a wery good game vhen you an't the shuttlecock and two lawyers the battledores, in which case it gets too excitin' to be pleasant* (*Pickwick Papers* by Charles Dickens)

beadle NOUN a beadle was a local official who had power over the poor ❑ *But these impertinences were speedily checked by the evidence of the surgeon, and the testimony of the beadle* (*Oliver Twist* by Charles Dickens)

bearings NOUN the bearings of a place are the measurements or directions that are used to find or locate it ❑ *the bearings of the island* (*Treasure Island* by Robert Louis Stevenson)

beaufet NOUN a beaufet was a sideboard ❑ *and sweet-cake from the beaufet* (*Emma* by Jane Austen)

beck NOUN a beck is a small stream ❑ *a beck which follows the bend of the glen* (*Wuthering Heights* by Emily Brontë)

bedight VERB decorated ❑ *and bedight with Christmas holly stuck into the top.* (*A Christmas Carol* by Charles Dickens)

Bedlam NOUN Bedlam was a lunatic asylum in London which had statues carved by Caius Gabriel Cibber at its entrance ❑ *Bedlam, and those carved maniacs at the gates* (*The Prelude* by William Wordsworth)

beeves NOUN oxen or castrated bulls which are animals used for pulling vehicles or carrying things ❑ *to deliver in every morning six beeves* (*Gulliver's Travels* by Jonathan Swift)

begot VERB created or caused ❑ *Begot in thee* (*On His Mistress* by John Donne)

behoof NOUN behoof means benefit ❑ *"Yes, young man," said he, releasing the handle of the article in question, retiring a step or two from my table, and speaking for the behoof of the landlord and waiter at the door* (*Great Expectations* by Charles Dickens)

berth NOUN a berth is a bed on a boat ❑ *this is the berth for me* (*Treasure Island* by Robert Louis Stevenson)

bevers NOUN a bever was a snack, or small portion of food, eaten between main meals ❑ *that buys me thirty meals a day and ten bevers* (*Doctor Faustus 2.1* by Christopher Marlowe)

bilge water NOUN the bilge is the widest part of a ship's bottom, and the bilge water is the dirty water that collects there ❑ *no gush of bilge-water had turned it to fetid puddle* (*Jane Eyre* by Charlotte Brontë)

bills NOUN bills is an old term meaning prescription. A prescription is the piece of paper on which your doctor writes an order for medicine and which you give to a chemist to get the medicine ❑ *Are not thy bills hung up as monuments* (*Doctor Faustus 1.1* by Christopher Marlowe)

black cap NOUN a judge wore a black cap when he was about to sentence a prisoner to death ❑ *The judge* assumed the black cap, and the prisoner still stood with the same air and gesture. (*Oliver Twist* by Charles Dickens)

boot-jack NOUN a wooden device to help take boots off ❏ *The speaker appeared to throw a boot-jack, or some such article, at the person he addressed* (*Oliver Twist* by Charles Dickens)

booty NOUN booty means treasure or prizes ❏ *would be inclined to give up their booty in payment of the dead man's debts* (*Treasure Island* by Robert Louis Stevenson)

Bow Street runner PHRASE Bow Street runners were the first British police force, set up by the author Henry Fielding in the eighteenth century ❏ *as would have convinced a judge or a Bow Street runner* (*Treasure Island* by Robert Louis Stevenson)

brawn NOUN brawn is a dish of meat which is set in jelly ❏ *Heaped up upon the floor, to form a kind of throne, were turkeys, geese, game, poultry, brawn, great joints of meat, sucking-pigs* (*A Christmas Carol* by Charles Dickens)

bray VERB when a donkey brays, it makes a loud, harsh sound ❏ *and she doesn't bray like a jackass* (*The Adventures of Huckleberry Finn* by Mark Twain)

break VERB in order to train a horse you first have to break it ❏ *"If a high-mettled creature like this," said he, "can't be broken by fair means, she will never be good for anything"* (*Black Beauty* by Anna Sewell)

bullyragging VERB bullyragging is an old word which means bullying. To bullyrag someone is to threaten or force someone to do something they don't want to do ❏ *and a lot of loafers bullyragging him for sport* (*The Adventures of Huckleberry Finn* by Mark Twain)

but PREP except for (this) ❏ *but this, all pleasures fancies be* (*The Good-Morrow* by John Donne)

by hand PHRASE by hand was a common expression of the time meaning that baby had been fed either using a spoon or a bottle rather than by breast-feeding ❏ *My sister, Mrs. Joe Gargery, was more than twenty years older than I, and had established a great reputation with herself . . . because she had bought me up 'by hand'* (*Great Expectations* by Charles Dickens)

bye-spots NOUN bye-spots are lonely places ❏ *and bye-spots of tales rich with indigenous produce* (*The Prelude* by William Wordsworth)

calico NOUN calico is plain white fabric made from cotton ❏ *There was two old dirty calico dresses* (*The Adventures of Huckleberry Finn* by Mark Twain)

camp-fever NOUN camp-fever was another word for the disease typhus ❏ *during a severe camp-fever* (*Emma* by Jane Austen)

cant NOUN cant is insincere or empty talk ❏ *"Man," said the Ghost, "if man you be in heart, not adamant, forbear that wicked cant until you have discovered What the surplus is, and Where it is."* (*A Christmas Carol* by Charles Dickens)

canty ADJ canty means lively, full of life ❏ *My mother lived til eighty, a canty dame to the last* (*Wuthering Heights* by Emily Brontë)

canvas VERB to canvas to is to discuss ❏ *We think so very differently on this point Mr Knightley, that there can be no use in canvassing it* (*Emma* by Jane Austen)

capital ADJ capital means excellent or extremely good ❏ *for it's capital, so shady, light, and big* (*Little Women* by Louisa May Alcott)

capstan NOUN a capstan is a device used on a ship to lift sails and anchors ❏ *capstans going, ships going out to sea, and unintelligible sea creatures roaring curses over the bulwarks at respondent lightermen* (*Great Expectations* by Charles Dickens)

case-bottle NOUN a square bottle designed to fit with others into a case ❑ *The spirit being set before him in a huge case-bottle, which had originally come out of some ship's locker* (*The Old Curiosity Shop* by Charles Dickens)

casement NOUN casement is a word meaning window. The teacher in Nicholas Nickleby misspells window showing what a bad teacher he is ❑ *W-i-n, win, d-e-r, der, winder, a casement.'* (*Nicholas Nickleby* by Charles Dickens)

cataleptic ADJ a cataleptic fit is one in which the victim goes into a trancelike state and remains still for a long time ❑ *It was at this point in their history that Silas's cataleptic fit occurred during the prayer-meeting* (*Silas Marner* by George Eliot)

cauldron NOUN a cauldron is a large cooking pot made of metal ❑ *stirring a large cauldron which seemed to be full of soup* (*Alice's Adventures in Wonderland* by Lewis Carroll)

cephalic ADJ cephalic means to do with the head ❑ *with ink composed of a cephalic tincture* (*Gulliver's Travels* by Jonathan Swift)

chaise and four NOUN a closed four-wheel carriage pulled by four horses ❑ *he came down on Monday in a chaise and four to see the place* (*Pride and Prejudice* by Jane Austen)

chamberlain NOUN the main servant in a household ❑ *In those times a bed was always to be got there at any hour of the night, and the chamberlain, letting me in at his ready wicket, lighted the candle next in order on his shelf* (*Great Expectations* by Charles Dickens)

characters NOUN distinguishing marks ❑ *Impressed upon all forms the characters* (*The Prelude* by William Wordsworth)

chary ADJ cautious ❑ *I should have been chary of discussing my guardian too freely even with her* (*Great Expectations* by Charles Dickens)

cherishes VERB here cherishes means cheers or brightens ❑ *some philosophic song of Truth that cherishes our daily life* (*The Prelude* by William Wordsworth)

chickens' meat PHRASE chickens' meat is an old term which means chickens' feed or food ❑ *I had shook a bag of chickens' meat out in that place* (*Robinson Crusoe* by Daniel Defoe)

chimeras NOUN a chimera is an unrealistic idea or a wish which is unlikely to be fulfilled ❑ *with many other wild impossible chimeras* (*Gulliver's Travels* by Jonathan Swift)

chines NOUN chine is a cut of meat that includes part or all of the backbone of the animal ❑ *and they found hams and chines uncut* (*Silas Marner* by George Eliot)

chits NOUN chits is a slang word which means girls ❑ *I hate affected, niminy-piminy chits!* (*Little Women* by Louisa May Alcott)

chopped VERB chopped means come suddenly or accidentally ❑ *if I had chopped upon them* (*Robinson Crusoe* by Daniel Defoe)

chute NOUN a narrow channel ❑ *One morning about day-break, I found a canoe and crossed over a chute to the main shore* (*The Adventures of Huckleberry Finn* by Mark Twain)

circumspection NOUN careful observation of events and circumstances; caution ❑ *I honour your circumspection* (*Pride and Prejudice* by Jane Austen)

clambered VERB clambered means to climb somewhere with difficulty, usually using your hands and your feet ❑ *he clambered up and down stairs* (*Treasure Island* by Robert Louis Stevenson)

clime NOUN climate ❑ *no season knows nor clime* (*The Sun Rising* by John Donne)

clinched VERB clenched ❑ *the tops whereof I could but just reach with my fist clinched* (*Gulliver's Travels* by Jonathan Swift)

close chair NOUN a close chair is a sedan chair, which is an covered chair which has room for one person. The sedan chair is carried on two poles by two men, one in front and one behind ❑ *persuaded even the Empress herself to let me hold her in her close chair* (*Gulliver's Travels* by Jonathan Swift)

clown NOUN clown here means peasant or person who lives off the land ❑ *In ancient days by emperor and clown* (*Ode on a Nightingale* by John Keats)

coalheaver NOUN a coalheaver loaded coal onto ships using a spade ❑ *Good, strong, wholesome medicine, as was given with great success to two Irish labourers and a coalheaver* (*Oliver Twist* by Charles Dickens)

coal-whippers NOUN men who worked at docks using machines to load coal onto ships ❑ *here, were colliers by the score and score, with the coal-whippers plunging off stages on deck* (*Great Expectations* by Charles Dickens)

cobweb NOUN a cobweb is the net which a spider makes for catching insects ❑ *the walls and ceilings were all hung round with cobwebs* (*Gulliver's Travels* by Jonathan Swift)

coddling VERB coddling means to treat someone too kindly or protect them too much ❑ *and I've been coddling the fellow as if I'd been his grand-mother* (*Little Women* by Louisa May Alcott)

coil NOUN coil means noise or fuss or disturbance ❑ *What a coil is there?* (*Doctor Faustus 4.7* by Christopher Marlowe)

collared VERB to collar something is a slang term which means to capture.

In this sentence, it means he stole it [the money] ❑ *he collared it* (*The Adventures of Huckleberry Finn* by Mark Twain)

colling VERB colling is an old word which means to embrace and kiss ❑ *and no clasping and colling at all* (*Tess of the D'Urbervilles* by Thomas Hardy)

colloquies NOUN colloquy is a formal conversation or dialogue ❑ *Such colloquies have occupied many a pair of pale-faced weavers* (*Silas Marner* by George Eliot)

comfit NOUN sugar-covered pieces of fruit or nut eaten as sweets ❑ *and pulled out a box of comfits* (*Alice's Adventures in Wonderland* by Lewis Carroll)

coming out VERB when a girl came out in society it meant she was of marriageable age. In order to 'come out' girls were expecting to attend balls and other parties during a season ❑ *The younger girls formed hopes of coming out a year or two sooner than they might otherwise have done* (*Pride and Prejudice* by Jane Austen)

commit VERB commit means arrest or stop ❑ *Commit the rascals* (*Doctor Faustus 4.7* by Christopher Marlowe)

commodious ADJ commodious means convenient ❑ *the most commodious and effectual ways* (*Gulliver's Travels* by Jonathan Swift)

commons NOUN commons is an old term meaning food shared with others ❑ *his pauper assistants ranged themselves behind him; the gruel was served out; and a long grace was said over the short commons.* (*Oliver Twist* by Charles Dickens)

complacency NOUN here complacency means a desire to please others. Today complacency means feeling pleased with oneself without good reason. ❑ *'Twas thy power that raised the first complacency in me* (*The Prelude* by William Wordsworth)

complaisance NOUN complaisance was eagerness to please ❑ *we cannot wonder at his complaisance* (*Pride and Prejudice* by Jane Austen)

complaisant ADJ complaisant means polite ❑ *extremely cheerful and complaisant to their guest* (*Gulliver's Travels* by Jonathan Swift)

conning VERB conning means learning by heart ❑ *Or conning more* (*The Prelude* by William Wordsworth)

consequent NOUN consequence ❑ *as avarice is the necessary consequent of old age* (*Gulliver's Travels* by Jonathan Swift)

consorts NOUN concerts ❑ *The King, who delighted in music, had frequent consorts at Court* (*Gulliver's Travels* by Jonathan Swift)

conversible ADJ conversible meant easy to talk to, companionable ❑ *He can be a conversible companion* (*Pride and Prejudice* by Jane Austen)

copper NOUN a copper is a large pot that can be heated directly over a fire ❑ *He gazed in stupefied astonishment on the small rebel for some seconds, and then clung for support to the copper* (*Oliver Twist* by Charles Dickens)

copper-stick NOUN a copper-stick is the long piece of wood used to stir washing in the copper (or boiler) which was usually the biggest cooking pot in the house ❑ *It was Christmas Eve, and I had to stir the pudding for next day, with a copper-stick, from seven to eight by the Dutch clock* (*Great Expectations* by Charles Dickens)

counting-house NOUN a counting house is a place where accountants work ❑ *Once upon a time – of all the good days in the year, on Christmas Eve – old Scrooge sat busy in his countinghouse* (*A Christmas Carol* by Charles Dickens)

courtier NOUN a courtier is someone who attends the king or queen – a member of the court ❑ *next the ten courtiers;* (*Alice's Adventures in Wonderland* by Lewis Carroll)

covies NOUN covies were flocks of partridges ❑ *and will save all of the best covies for you* (*Pride and Prejudice* by Jane Austen)

cowed VERB cowed means frightened or intimidated ❑ *it cowed me more than the pain* (*Treasure Island* by Robert Louis Stevenson)

cozened VERB cozened means tricked or deceived ❑ *Do you remember, sir, how you cozened me* (*Doctor Faustus* 4.7 by Christopher Marlowe)

cravats NOUN a cravat is a folded cloth that a man wears wrapped around his neck as a decorative item of clothing ❑ *we'd a' slept in our cravats to-night* (*The Adventures of Huckleberry Finn* by Mark Twain)

crock and dirt PHRASE crock and dirt is an old expression meaning soot and dirt ❑ *and the mare catching cold at the door, and the boy grimed with crock and dirt* (*Great Expectations* by Charles Dickens)

crockery NOUN here crockery means pottery ❑ *By one of the parrots was a cat made of crockery* (*The Adventures of Huckleberry Finn* by Mark Twain)

crooked sixpence PHRASE it was considered unlucky to have a bent sixpence ❑ *You've got the beauty, you see, and I've got the luck, so you must keep me by you for your crooked sixpence* (*Silas Marner* by George Eliot)

croquet NOUN croquet is a traditional English summer game in which players try to hit wooden balls through hoops ❑ *and once she remembered trying to box her own ears for having cheated herself in a game of croquet* (*Alice's Adventures in Wonderland* by Lewis Carroll)

cross PREP across ❑ *The two great streets, which run cross and divide it into four quarters* (*Gulliver's Travels* by Jonathan Swift)

culpable ADJ if you are culpable for something it means you are to blame ❏ *deep are the sorrows that spring from false ideas for which no man is culpable.* (*Silas Marner* by George Eliot)

cultured ADJ cultivated ❏ *Nor less when spring had warmed the cultured Vale* (*The Prelude* by William Wordsworth)

cupidity NOUN cupidity is greed ❏ *These people hated me with the hatred of cupidity and disappointment.* (*Great Expectations* by Charles Dickens)

curricle NOUN an open two-wheeled carriage with one seat for the driver and space for a single passenger ❏ *and they saw a lady and a gentleman in a curricle* (*Pride and Prejudice* by Jane Austen)

cynosure NOUN a cynosure is something that strongly attracts attention or admiration ❏ *Then I thought of Eliza and Georgiana; I beheld one the cynosure of a ballroom, the other the inmate of a convent cell* (*Jane Eyre* by Charlotte Brontë)

dalliance NOUN someone's dalliance with something is a brief involvement with it ❏ *nor sporting in the dalliance of love* (*Doctor Faustus Chorus* by Christopher Marlowe)

darkling ADV darkling is an archaic way of saying in the dark ❏ *Darkling I listen* (*Ode on a Nightingale* by John Keats)

delf-case NOUN a sideboard for holding dishes and crockery ❏ *at the pewter dishes and delf-case* (*Wuthering Heights* by Emily Brontë)

determined ■ VERB here determined means ended ❏ *and be out of vogue when that was determined* (*Gulliver's Travels* by Jonathan Swift) ■ VERB determined can mean to have been learned or found especially by investigation or experience ❏ *All the sensitive feelings it wounded so cruelly, all the shame and misery it kept alive within my breast, became more poignant as I thought of this; and I determined that the life was unendurable* (*David Copperfield* by Charles Dickens)

Deuce NOUN a slang term for the Devil ❏ *Ah, I dare say I did. Deuce take me, he added suddenly, I know I did. I find I am not quite unscrewed yet.* (*Great Expectations* by Charles Dickens)

diabolical ADJ diabolical means devilish or evil ❏ *and with a thousand diabolical expressions* (*Treasure Island* by Robert Louis Stevenson)

direction NOUN here direction means address ❏ *Elizabeth was not surprised at it, as Jane had written the direction remarkably ill* (*Pride and Prejudice* by Jane Austen)

discover VERB to make known or announce ❏ *the Emperor would discover the secret while I was out of his power* (*Gulliver's Travels* by Jonathan Swift)

dissemble VERB hide or conceal ❏ *Dissemble nothing* (*On His Mistress* by John Donne)

dissolve VERB dissolve here means to release from life, to die ❏ *Fade far away, dissolve, and quite forget* (*Ode on a Nightingale* by John Keats)

distrain VERB to distrain is to seize the property of someone who is in debt in compensation for the money owed ❏ *for he's threatening to distrain for it* (*Silas Marner* by George Eliot)

Divan NOUN a Divan was originally a Turkish council of state – the name was transferred to the couches they sat on and is used to mean this in English ❏ *Mr Brass applauded this picture very much, and the bed being soft and comfortable, Mr Quilp determined to use it, both as a sleeping place by night and as a kind of Divan by day.* (*The Old Curiosity Shop* by Charles Dickens)

divorcement NOUN separation ❏ *By all pains which want and* *divorcement hath* (*On His Mistress* by John Donne)

dog in the manger, PHRASE this phrase describes someone who prevents you from enjoying something that they themselves have no need for ❑ *You are a dog in the manger, Cathy, and desire no one to be loved but yourself* (*Wuthering Heights* by Emily Brontë)

dolorifuge NOUN dolorifuge is a word which Thomas Hardy invented. It means pain-killer or comfort ❑ *as a species of dolorifuge* (*Tess of the D'Urbervilles* by Thomas Hardy)

dome NOUN building ❑ *that river and that mouldering dome* (*The Prelude* by William Wordsworth)

domestic PHRASE here domestic means a person's management of the house ❑ *to give some account of my domestic* (*Gulliver's Travels* by Jonathan Swift)

dunce NOUN a dunce is another word for idiot ❑ *Do you take me for a dunce? Go on?* (*Alice's Adventures in Wonderland* by Lewis Carroll)

Ecod EXCLAM a slang exclamation meaning 'oh God!' ❑ *"Ecod," replied Wemmick, shaking his head, "that's not my trade."* (*Great Expectations* by Charles Dickens)

egg-hot NOUN an egg-hot (see also 'flip' and 'negus') was a hot drink made from beer and eggs, sweetened with nutmeg ❑ *She fainted when she saw me return, and made a little jug of egg-hot afterwards to console us while we talked it over.* (*David Copperfield* by Charles Dickens)

encores NOUN an encore is a short extra performance at the end of a longer one, which the entertainer gives because the audience has enthusiastically asked for it ❑ *we want a little something to answer encores with, anyway* (*The Adventures of Huckleberry Finn* by Mark Twain)

equipage NOUN an elegant and impressive carriage ❑ *and besides, the equipage did not answer to any of*

their neighbours (*Pride and Prejudice* by Jane Austen)

exordium NOUN an exordium is the opening part of a speech ❑ *"Now, Handel," as if it were the grave beginning of a portentous business exordium, he had suddenly given up that tone* (*Great Expectations* by Charles Dickens)

expect VERB here expect means to wait for ❑ *to expect his farther commands* (*Gulliver's Travels* by Jonathan Swift)

familiars NOUN familiars means spirits or devils who come to someone when they are called ❑ *I'll turn all the lice about thee into familiars* (*Doctor Faustus 1.4* by Christopher Marlowe)

fantods NOUN a fantod is a person who fidgets or can't stop moving nervously ❑ *It most give me the fantods* (*The Adventures of Huckleberry Finn* by Mark Twain)

farthing NOUN a farthing is an old unit of British currency which was worth a quarter of a penny ❑ *Not a farthing less. A great many back-payments are included in it, I assure you.* (*A Christmas Carol* by Charles Dickens)

farthingale NOUN a hoop worn under a skirt to extend it ❑ *A bell with an old voice – which I dare say in its time had often said to the house, Here is the green farthingale* (*Great Expectations* by Charles Dickens)

favours NOUN here favours is an old word which means ribbons ❑ *A group of humble mourners entered the gate: wearing white favours* (*Oliver Twist* by Charles Dickens)

feigned VERB pretend or pretending ❑ *not my feigned page* (*On His Mistress* by John Donne)

fence ■ NOUN a fence is someone who receives and sells stolen goods ❑ *What are you up to? Ill-treating the boys, you covetous, avaricious, in-sa-ti-a-ble old fence?* (*Oliver Twist* by

Charles Dickens) ■ NOUN defence or protection ❑ *but honesty hath no fence against superior cunning* (*Gulliver's Travels* by Jonathan Swift)

fess ADJ fess is an old word which means pleased or proud ❑ *You'll be fess enough, my poppet* (*Tess of the D'Urbervilles* by Thomas Hardy)

fettered ADJ fettered means bound in chains or chained ❑ *"You are fettered," said Scrooge, trembling. "Tell me why?"* (*A Christmas Carol* by Charles Dickens)

fidges VERB fidges means fidgets, which is to keep moving your hands slightly because you are nervous or excited ❑ *Look, Jim, how my fingers fidges* (*Treasure Island* by Robert Louis Stevenson)

finger-post NOUN a finger-post is a sign-post showing the direction to different places ❑ *"The gallows," continued Fagin, "the gallows, my dear, is an ugly finger-post, which points out a very short and sharp turning that has stopped many a bold fellow's career on the broad highway."* (*Oliver Twist* by Charles Dickens)

fire-irons NOUN fire-irons are tools kept by the side of the fire to either cook with or look after the fire ❑ *the fire-irons came first* (*Alice's Adventures in Wonderland* by Lewis Carroll)

fire-plug NOUN a fire-plug is another word for a fire hydrant ❑ *The pony looked with great attention into a fire-plug, which was near him, and appeared to be quite absorbed in contemplating it* (*The Old Curiosity Shop* by Charles Dickens)

flank NOUN flank is the side of an animal ❑ *And all her silken flanks with garlands dressed* (*Ode on a Grecian Urn* by John Keats)

flip NOUN a flip is a drink made from warmed ale, sugar, spice and beaten egg ❑ *The events of the day, in combination with the twins, if not with the flip, had made Mrs. Micawber hysterical, and she shed tears as she replied* (*David Copperfield* by Charles Dickens)

flit VERB flit means to move quickly ❑ *and if he had meant to flit to Thrushcross Grange* (*Wuthering Heights* by Emily Brontë)

floorcloth NOUN a floorcloth was a hard-wearing piece of canvas used instead of carpet ❑ *This avenging phantom was ordered to be on duty at eight on Tuesday morning in the hall (it was two feet square, as charged for floorcloth)* (*Great Expectations* by Charles Dickens)

fly-driver NOUN a fly-driver is a carriage drawn by a single horse ❑ *The fly-drivers, among whom I inquired next, were equally jocose and equally disrespectful* (*David Copperfield* by Charles Dickens)

fob NOUN a small pocket in which a watch is kept ❑ *"Certain," replied the man, drawing a gold watch from his fob* (*Oliver Twist* by Charles Dickens)

folly NOUN folly means foolishness or stupidity ❑ *the folly of beginning a work* (*Robinson Crusoe* by Daniel Defoe)

fond ADJ fond means foolish ❑ *Fond worldling* (*Doctor Faustus 5.2* by Christopher Marlowe)

fondness NOUN silly or foolish affection ❑ *They have no fondness for their colts or foals* (*Gulliver's Travels* by Jonathan Swift)

for his fancy PHRASE for his fancy means for his liking or as he wanted ❑ *and as I did not obey quick enough for his fancy* (*Treasure Island* by Robert Louis Stevenson)

forlorn ADJ lost or very upset ❑ *you are from that day forlorn* (*Gulliver's Travels* by Jonathan Swift)

foster-sister NOUN a foster-sister was someone brought up by the same nurse or in the same household ❑ *I had been his foster-sister* (*Wuthering Heights* by Emily Brontë)

fox-fire NOUN fox-fire is a weak glow that is given off by decaying, rotten wood ❑ *what we must have was a lot of them rotten chunks* *that's called fox-fire (The Adventures of Huckleberry Finn* by Mark Twain)

frozen sea PHRASE the Arctic Ocean ❑ *into the frozen sea (Gulliver's Travels* by Jonathan Swift)

gainsay VERB to gainsay something is to say it isn't true or to deny it ❑ *"So she had," cried Scrooge. "You're right. I'll not gainsay it, Spirit. God forbid!" (A Christmas Carol* by Charles Dickens)

gaiters NOUN gaiters were leggings made of a cloth or piece of leather which covered the leg from the knee to the ankle ❑ *Mr Knightley was hard at work upon the lower buttons of his thick leather gaiters (Emma* by Jane Austen)

galluses NOUN galluses is an old spelling of gallows, and here means suspenders. Suspenders are straps worn over someone's shoulders and fastened to their trousers to prevent the trousers falling down ❑ *and home-knit galluses (The Adventures of Huckleberry Finn* by Mark Twain)

galoot NOUN a sailor but also a clumsy person ❑ *and maybe a galoot on it chopping (The Adventures of Huckleberry Finn* by Mark Twain)

gayest ADJ gayest means the most lively and bright or merry ❑ *Beth played her gayest march (Little Women* by Louisa May Alcott)

gem NOUN here gem means jewellery ❑ *the mountain shook off turf and flower, had only heath for raiment and crag for gem (Jane Eyre* by Charlotte Brontë)

giddy ADJ giddy means dizzy ❑ *and I wish you wouldn't keep appearing and vanishing so suddenly; you make one quite giddy. (Alice's Adventures in Wonderland* by Lewis Carroll)

gig NOUN a light two-wheeled carriage ❑ *when a gig drove up to the garden gate: out of which there jumped a fat gentleman (Oliver Twist* by Charles Dickens)

gladsome ADJ gladsome is an old word meaning glad or happy ❑ *Nobody ever stopped him in the street to say, with gladsome looks (A Christmas Carol* by Charles Dickens)

glen NOUN a glen is a small valley; the word is used commonly in Scotland ❑ *a beck which follows the bend of the glen (Wuthering Heights* by Emily Brontë)

gravelled VERB gravelled is an old term which means to baffle or defeat someone ❑ *Gravelled the pastors of the German Church (Doctor Faustus 1.1* by Christopher Marlowe)

grinder NOUN a grinder was a private tutor ❑ *but that when he had had the happiness of marrying Mrs Pocket very early in his life, he had impaired his prospects and taken up the calling of a Grinder (Great Expectations* by Charles Dickens)

gruel NOUN gruel is a thin, watery corn-meal or oatmeal soup ❑ *and the little saucepan of gruel (Scrooge had a cold in his head) upon the hob. (A Christmas Carol* by Charles Dickens)

guinea, half a NOUN a half guinea was ten shillings and sixpence ❑ *but lay out half a guinea at Ford's (Emma* by Jane Austen)

gull VERB gull is an old term which means to fool or deceive someone ❑ *Hush, I'll gull him supernaturally (Doctor Faustus 3.4* by Christopher Marlowe)

gunnel NOUN the gunnel, or gunwhale, is the upper edge of a boat's side ❑ *But he put his foot on the gunnel and rocked her (The Adventures of Huckleberry Finn* by Mark Twain)

gunwale NOUN the side of a ship ❑ *He dipped his hand in the water over the boat's gunwale (Great Expectations* by Charles Dickens)

Gytrash NOUN a Gytrash is an omen of misfortune to the superstitious, usually taking the form of a hound ❑ *I remembered certain of Bessie's tales, wherein figured a*

North-of-England spirit, called a 'Gytrash' (Jane Eyre by Charlotte Brontë)

hackney-cabriolet NOUN a two-wheeled carriage with four seats for hire and pulled by a horse ❑ *A hackney-cabriolet was in waiting; with the same vehemence which she had exhibited in addressing Oliver, the girl pulled him in with her, and drew the curtains close.* (Oliver Twist by Charles Dickens)

hackney-coach NOUN a four-wheeled horse-drawn vehicle for hire ❑ *The twilight was beginning to close in, when Mr. Brownlow alighted from a hackney-coach at his own door, and knocked softly.* (Oliver Twist by Charles Dickens)

haggler NOUN a haggler is someone who travels from place to place selling small goods and items ❑ *when I be plain Jack Durbeyfield, the haggler (Tess of the D'Urbervilles* by Thomas Hardy)

halter NOUN a halter is a rope or strap used to lead an animal or to tie it up ❑ *I had of course long been used to a halter and a headstall (Black Beauty* by Anna Sewell)

hamlet NOUN a hamlet is a small village or a group of houses in the countryside ❑ *down from the hamlet (Treasure Island* by Robert Louis Stevenson)

hand-barrow NOUN a hand-barrow is a device for carrying heavy objects. It is like a wheelbarrow except that it has handles, rather than wheels, for moving the barrow ❑ *his sea chest following behind him in a hand-barrow (Treasure Island* by Robert Louis Stevenson)

handspike NOUN a handspike was a stick which was used as a lever ❑ *a bit of stick like a handspike (Treasure Island* by Robert Louis Stevenson)

haply ADV haply means by chance or perhaps ❑ *And haply the Queen-Moon is on her throne (Ode on a Nightingale* by John Keats)

harem NOUN the harem was the part of the house where the women lived ❑ *mostly they hang round the harem (The Adventures of Huckleberry Finn* by Mark Twain)

hautboys NOUN hautboys are oboes ❑ sausages and puddings resembling flutes and hautboys (Gulliver's Travels by Jonathan Swift)

hawker NOUN a hawker is someone who sells goods to people as he travels rather than from a fixed place like a shop ❑ *to buy some stockings from a hawker (Treasure Island* by Robert Louis Stevenson)

hawser NOUN a hawser is a rope used to tie up or tow a ship or boat ❑ *Again among the tiers of shipping, in and out, avoiding rusty chain-cables, frayed hempen hawsers (Great Expectations* by Charles Dickens)

headstall NOUN the headstall is the part of the bridle or halter that goes around a horse's head ❑ *I had of course long been used to a halter and a headstall (Black Beauty* by Anna Sewell)

hearken VERB hearken means to listen ❑ *though we sometimes stopped to lay hold of each other and hearken (Treasure Island* by Robert Louis Stevenson)

heartless ADJ here heartless means without heart or dejected ❑ *I am not heartless (The Prelude* by William Wordsworth)

hebdomadal ADJ hebdomadal means weekly ❑ *It was the hebdomadal treat to which we all looked forward from Sabbath to Sabbath (Jane Eyre* by Charlotte Brontë)

highwaymen NOUN highwaymen were people who stopped travellers and robbed them ❑ *We are highwaymen (The Adventures of Huckleberry Finn* by Mark Twain)

hinds NOUN hinds means farm hands, or people who work on a farm ❑ *He called his hinds about him (Gulliver's Travels* by Jonathan Swift)

histrionic ADJ if you refer to someone's behaviour as histrionic, you are being critical of it because it is dramatic and exaggerated ❑ *But the histrionic muse is the darling* (*The Adventures of Huckleberry Finn* by Mark Twain)

hogs NOUN hogs is another word for pigs ❑ *Tom called the hogs 'ingots'* (*The Adventures of Huckleberry Finn* by Mark Twain)

horrors NOUN the horrors are a fit, called delirium tremens, which is caused by drinking too much alcohol ❑ *I'll have the horrors* (*Treasure Island* by Robert Louis Stevenson)

huffy ADJ huffy means to be obviously annoyed or offended about something ❑ *They will feel that more than angry speeches or huffy actions* (*Little Women* by Louisa May Alcott)

hulks NOUN hulks were prison-ships ❑ *The miserable companion of thieves and ruffians, the fallen outcast of low haunts, the associate of the scourings of the jails and hulks* (*Oliver Twist* by Charles Dickens)

humbug NOUN humbug means nonsense or rubbish ❑ *"Bah," said Scrooge. "Humbug!"* (*A Christmas Carol* by Charles Dickens)

humours NOUN it was believed that there were four fluids in the body called humours which decided the temperament of a person depending on how much of each fluid was present ❑ *other peccant humours* (*Gulliver's Travels* by Jonathan Swift)

husbandry NOUN husbandry is farming animals ❑ *bad husbandry were plentifully anointing their wheels* (*Silas Marner* by George Eliot)

huswife NOUN a huswife was a small sewing kit ❑ *but I had put my huswife on it* (*Emma* by Jane Austen)

ideal ADJ ideal in this context means imaginary ❑ *I discovered the yell was not ideal* (*Wuthering Heights* by Emily Brontë)

If our two PHRASE if both our ❑ *If our two loves be one* (*The Good-Morrow* by John Donne)

ignis-fatuus NOUN ignis-fatuus is the light given out by burning marsh gases, which lead careless travellers into danger ❑ *it is madness in all women to let a secret love kindle within them, which, if unreturned and unknown, must devour the life that feeds it; and, if discovered and responded to, must lead ignis-fatuus-like, into miry wilds whence there is no extrication.* (*Jane Eyre* by Charlotte Brontë)

imaginations NOUN here imaginations means schemes or plans ❑ *soon drove out those imaginations* (*Gulliver's Travels* by Jonathan Swift)

impressible ADJ impressible means open or impressionable ❑ *for Marner had one of those impressible, self-doubting natures* (*Silas Marner* by George Eliot)

in good intelligence PHRASE friendly with each other ❑ *that these two persons were in good intelligence with each other* (*Gulliver's Travels* by Jonathan Swift)

inanity NOUN inanity is sillyness or dull stupidity ❑ *Do we not wile away moments of inanity* (*Silas Marner* by George Eliot)

incivility NOUN incivility means rudeness or impoliteness ❑ *if it's only for a piece of incivility like to-night's* (*Treasure Island* by Robert Louis Stevenson)

indigenae NOUN indigenae means natives or people from that area ❑ *an exotic that the surly indigenae will not recognise for kin* (*Wuthering Heights* by Emily Brontë)

indocible ADJ unteachable ❑ *so they were the most restive and indocible* (*Gulliver's Travels* by Jonathan Swift)

ingenuity NOUN inventiveness ❑ *entreated me to give him something as an encouragement to ingenuity*

(*Gulliver's Travels* by Jonathan Swift)

ingots NOUN an ingot is a lump of a valuable metal like gold, usually shaped like a brick ❑ *Tom called the hogs 'ingots'* (*The Adventures of Huckleberry Finn* by Mark Twain)

inkstand NOUN an inkstand is a pot which was put on a desk to contain either ink or pencils and pens ❑ *throwing an inkstand at the Lizard as she spoke* (*Alice's Adventures in Wonderland* by Lewis Carroll)

inordinate ADJ without order. Today inordinate means 'excessive'. ❑ *Though yet untutored and inordinate* (*The Prelude* by William Wordsworth)

intellectuals NOUN here intellectuals means the minds (of the workmen) ❑ *those instructions they give being too refined for the intellectuals of their workmen* (*Gulliver's Travels* by Jonathan Swift)

interview NOUN meeting ❑ *By our first strange and fatal interview* (*On His Mistress* by John Donne)

jacks NOUN jacks are rods for turning a spit over a fire ❑ It was a small bit of pork suspended from the kettle hanger by a string passed through a large door key, in a *way known to primitive housekeepers unpossessed of jacks* (*Silas Marner* by George Eliot)

jews-harp NOUN a jews-harp is a small, metal, musical instrument that is played by the mouth ❑ *A jews-harp's plenty good enough for a rat* (*The Adventures of Huckleberry Finn* by Mark Twain)

jorum NOUN a large bowl ❑ *while Miss Skiffins brewed such a jorum of tea, that the pig in the back premises became strongly excited* (*Great Expectations* by Charles Dickens)

jostled VERB jostled means bumped or pushed by someone or some people ❑ *being jostled himself into the kennel* (*Gulliver's Travels* by Jonathan Swift)

keepsake NOUN a keepsake is a gift which reminds someone of an event or of the person who gave it to them. ❑ *books and ornaments they had in their boudoirs at home: keepsakes that different relations had presented to them* (*Jane Eyre* by Charlotte Brontë)

kenned VERB kenned means knew ❑ *though little kenned the lamplighter that he had any company but Christmas!* (*A Christmas-Carol* by Charles Dickens)

kennel NOUN kennel means gutter, which is the edge of a road next to the pavement, where rain water collects and flows away ❑ *being jostled himself into the kennel* (*Gulliver's Travels* by Jonathan Swift)

knock-knee ADJ knock-knee means slanted, at an angle. ❑ *LOT 1 was marked in whitewashed knock-knee letters on the brewhouse* (*Great Expectations* by Charles Dickens)

ladylike ADJ to be ladylike is to behave in a polite, dignified and graceful way ❑ *No, winking isn't ladylike* (*Little Women* by Louisa May Alcott)

lapse NOUN flow ❑ *Stealing with silent lapse to join the brook* (*The Prelude* by William Wordsworth)

larry NOUN larry is an old word which means commotion or noisy celebration ❑ *That was all a part of the larry!* (*Tess of the D'Urbervilles* by Thomas Hardy)

laths NOUN laths are strips of wood ❑ *The panels shrunk, the windows cracked; fragments of plaster fell out of the ceiling, and the naked laths were shown instead* (*A Christmas Carol* by Charles Dickens)

leer NOUN a leer is an unpleasant smile ❑ *with a kind of leer* (*Treasure Island* by Robert Louis Stevenson)

lenitives NOUN these are different kinds of drugs or medicines: lenitives and palliatives were pain relievers; aperitives were laxatives;

abstersives caused vomiting; corrosives destroyed human tissue; restringents caused constipation; cephalalgics stopped headaches; icterics were used as medicine for jaundice; apophlegmatics were cough medicine, and acoustics were cures for the loss of hearing ❑ *lenitives, aperitives, abstersives, corrosives, restringents, palliatives, laxatives, cephalalgics, icterics, apophlegmatics, acoustics* (*Gulliver's Travels* by Jonathan Swift)

lest CONJ in case. If you do something lest something (usually) unpleasant happens you do it to try to prevent it happening ❑ *She went in without knocking, and hurried upstairs, in great fear lest she should meet the real Mary Ann* (*Alice's Adventures in Wonderland* by Lewis Carroll)

levee NOUN a levee is an old term for a meeting held in the morning, shortly after the person holding the meeting has got out of bed ❑ *I used to attend the King's levee once or twice a week* (*Gulliver's Travels* by Jonathan Swift)

life-preserver NOUN a club which had lead inside it to make it heavier and therefore more dangerous ❑ *and with no more suspicious articles displayed to view than two or three heavy bludgeons which stood in a corner, and a 'life-preserver' that hung over the chimney-piece.* (*Oliver Twist* by Charles Dickens)

lighterman NOUN a lighterman is another word for sailor ❑ *in and out, hammers going in ship-builders' yards, saws going at timber, clashing engines going at things unknown, pumps going in leaky ships, capstans going, ships going out to sea, and unintelligible sea creatures roaring curses over the bulwarks at respondent lightermen* (*Great Expectations* by Charles Dickens)

livery NOUN servants often wore a uniform known as a livery ❑ *suddenly a footman in livery came running out of the wood* (*Alice's Adventures in Wonderland* by Lewis Carroll)

livid ADJ livid means pale or ash coloured. Livid also means very angry ❑ *a dirty, livid white* (*Treasure Island* by Robert Louis Stevenson)

lottery-tickets NOUN a popular card game ❑ *and Mrs. Philips protested that they would have a nice comfortable noisy game of lottery tickets* (*Pride and Prejudice* by Jane Austen)

lower and upper world PHRASE the earth and the heavens are the lower and upper worlds ❑ *the changes in the lower and upper world* (*Gulliver's Travels* by Jonathan Swift)

lustres NOUN lustres are chandeliers. A chandelier is a large, decorative frame which holds light bulbs or candles and hangs from the ceiling ❑ *the lustres, lights, the carving and the guilding* (*The Prelude* by William Wordsworth)

lynched VERB killed without a criminal trial by a crowd of people ❑ *He'll never know how nigh he come to getting lynched* (*The Adventures of Huckleberry Finn* by Mark Twain)

malingering VERB if someone is malingering they are pretending to be ill to avoid working ❑ *And you stand there malingering* (*Treasure Island* by Robert Louis Stevenson)

managing PHRASE treating with consideration ❑ *to think the honour of my own kind not worth managing* (*Gulliver's Travels* by Jonathan Swift)

manhood PHRASE manhood means human nature ❑ *concerning the nature of manhood* (*Gulliver's Travels* by Jonathan Swift)

man-trap NOUN a man-trap is a set of steel jaws that snap shut when trodden on and trap a person's leg ❑ *"Don't go to him," I called out of the window, "he's an assassin! A* man-trap!" (*Oliver Twist* by Charles Dickens)

maps NOUN charts of the night sky ❑ *Let maps to others, worlds on worlds have shown* (*The Good-Morrow* by John Donne)

mark VERB look at or notice ❑ *Mark but this flea, and mark in this* (*The Flea* by John Donne)

maroons NOUN A maroon is someone who has been left in a place which it is difficult for them to escape from, like a small island ❑ *if schooners, islands, and maroons* (*Treasure Island* by Robert Louis Stevenson)

mast NOUN here mast means the fruit of forest trees ❑ *a quantity of acorns, dates, chestnuts, and other mast* (*Gulliver's Travels* by Jonathan Swift)

mate VERB defeat ❑ *Where Mars did mate the warlike Carthigens* (*Doctor Faustus Chorus* by Christopher Marlowe)

mealy ADJ Mealy when used to describe a face meant palid, pale or colourless ❑ *I only know two sorts of boys. Mealy boys, and beef-faced boys* (*Oliver Twist* by Charles Dickens)

middling ADJ fairly or moderately ❑ *she worked me middling hard for about an hour* (*The Adventures of Huckleberry Finn* by Mark Twain)

mill NOUN a mill, or treadmill, was a device for hard labour or punishment in prison ❑ *Was you never on the mill?* (*Oliver Twist* by Charles Dickens)

milliner's shop NOUN a milliner's sold fabrics, clothing, lace and accessories; as time went on they specialized more and more in hats ❑ *to pay their duty to their aunt and to a milliner's shop just over the way* (*Pride and Prejudice* by Jane Austen)

minching un' munching PHRASE how people in the north of England used to describe the way people from the south speak ❑ *Minching*

un' munching! (*Wuthering Heights* by Emily Brontë)

mine NOUN gold ❑ *Whether both th'Indias of spice and mine* (*The Sun Rising* by John Donne)

mire NOUN mud ❑ *Tis my fate to be always ground into the mire under the iron heel of oppression* (*The Adventures of Huckleberry Finn* by Mark Twain)

miscellany NOUN a miscellany is a collection of many different kinds of things ❑ *under that, the miscellany began* (*Treasure Island* by Robert Louis Stevenson)

mistarshers NOUN mistarshers means moustache, which is the hair that grows on a man's upper lip ❑ *when he put his hand up to his mistarshers* (*Tess of the D'Urbervilles* by Thomas Hardy)

morrow NOUN here good-morrow means tomorrow and a new and better life ❑ *And now good-morrow to our waking souls* (*The Good-Morrow* by John Donne)

mortification NOUN mortification is an old word for gangrene which is when part of the body decays or 'dies' because of disease ❑ *Yes, it was a mortification – that was it* (*The Adventures of Huckleberry Finn* by Mark Twain)

mought PARTICIPLE mought is an old spelling of might ❑ *what you mought call me? You mought call me captain* (*Treasure Island* by Robert Louis Stevenson)

move VERB move me not means do not make me angry ❑ *Move me not, Faustus* (*Doctor Faustus 2.1* by Christopher Marlowe)

muffin-cap NOUN a muffin cap is a flat cap made from wool ❑ *the old one, remained stationary in the muffin-cap and leathers* (*Oliver Twist* by Charles Dickens)

mulatter NOUN a mulatter was another word for mulatto, which is a person with parents who are from different races ❑ *a mulatter, most as white as* a white man (*The Adventures of Huckleberry Finn* by Mark Twain)

mummery NOUN mummery is an old word that meant meaningless (or pretentious) ceremony ❑ *When they were all gone, and when Trabb and his men – but not his boy: I looked for him – had crammed their mummery into bags, and were gone too, the house felt wholesomer.* (*Great Expectations* by Charles Dickens)

nap NOUN the nap is the woolly surface on a new item of clothing. Here the surface has been worn away so it looks bare ❑ *like an old hat with the nap rubbed off* (*The Adventures of Huckleberry Finn* by Mark Twain)

natural ■ NOUN a natural is a person born with learning difficulties ❑ *though he had been left to his particular care by their deceased father, who thought him almost a natural.* (*David Copperfield* by Charles Dickens) ■ ADJ natural meant illegitimate ❑ *Harriet Smith was the natural daughter of somebody* (*Emma* by Jane Austen)

navigator NOUN a navigator was originally someone employed to dig canals. It is the origin of the word 'navvy' meaning a labourer ❑ *She ascertained from me in a few words what it was all about, comforted Dora, and gradually convinced her that I was not a labourer – from my manner of stating the case I believe Dora concluded that I was a navigator, and went balancing myself up and down a plank all day with a wheelbarrow – and so brought us together in peace.* (*David Copperfield* by Charles Dickens)

necromancy NOUN necromancy means a kind of magic where the magician speaks to spirits or ghosts to find out what will happen in the future ❑ *He surfeits upon cursed necromancy* (*Doctor Faustus chorus* by Christopher Marlowe)

negus NOUN a negus is a hot drink made from sweetened wine and water ❑ *He sat placidly perusing the newspaper, with his little head on one side, and a glass of warm sherry negus at his elbow.* (*David Copperfield* by Charles Dickens)

nice ADJ discriminating. Able to make good judgements or choices ❑ *consequently a claim to be nice* (*Emma* by Jane Austen)

nigh ADV nigh means near ❑ *He'll never know how nigh he come to getting lynched* (*The Adventures of Huckleberry Finn* by Mark Twain)

nimbleness NOUN nimbleness means being able to move very quickly or skillfully ❑ *and with incredible accuracy and nimbleness* (*Treasure Island* by Robert Louis Stevenson)

noggin NOUN a noggin is a small mug or a wooden cup ❑ *you'll bring me one noggin of rum* (*Treasure Island* by Robert Louis Stevenson)

none ADJ neither ❑ *none can die* (*The Good-Morrow* by John Donne)

notices NOUN observations ❑ *Arch are his notices* (*The Prelude* by William Wordsworth)

occiput NOUN occiput means the back of the head ❑ *saw off the occiput of each couple* (*Gulliver's Travels* by Jonathan Swift)

officiously ADJ kindly ❑ *the governess who attended Glumdalclitch very officiously lifted me up* (*Gulliver's Travels* by Jonathan Swift)

old salt PHRASE old salt is a slang term for an experienced sailor ❑ *a 'true sea-dog', and a 'real old salt'* (*Treasure Island* by Robert Louis Stevenson)

or ere PHRASE before ❑ *or ere the Hall was built* (*The Prelude* by William Wordsworth)

ostler NOUN one who looks after horses at an inn ❑ *The bill paid, and the waiter remembered, and the ostler not forgotten, and the chambermaid taken into consideration* (*Great Expectations* by Charles Dickens)

ostry NOUN an ostry is an old word for a pub or hotel ❑ *lest I send you into the ostry with a vengeance* (*Doctor Faustus* 2.2 by Christopher Marlowe)

outrunning the constable PHRASE outrunning the constable meant spending more than you earn ❑ *but I shall by this means be able to check your bills and to pull you up if I find you outrunning the constable.* (*Great Expectations* by Charles Dickens)

over ADJ across ❑ *It is in length six yards, and in the thickest part at least three yards over* (*Gulliver's Travels* by Jonathan Swift)

over the broomstick PHRASE this is a phrase meaning 'getting married without a formal ceremony' ❑ *They both led tramping lives, and this woman in Gerrard-street here, had been married very young, over the broomstick (as we say), to a tramping man, and was a perfect fury in point of jealousy.* (*Great Expectations* by Charles Dickens)

own VERB own means to admit or to acknowledge ❑ *It's my old girl that advises. She has the head. But I never own to it before her. Discipline must be maintained* (*Bleak House* by Charles Dickens)

page NOUN here page means a boy employed to run errands ❑ *not my feigned page* (*On His Mistress* by John Donne)

paid pretty dear PHRASE paid pretty dear means paid a high price or suffered quite a lot ❑ *I paid pretty dear for my monthly fourpenny piece* (*Treasure Island* by Robert Louis Stevenson)

pannikins NOUN pannikins were small tin cups ❑ *of lifting light glasses and cups to his lips, as if they were clumsy pannikins* (*Great Expectations* by Charles Dickens)

pards NOUN pards are leopards ❑ *Not charioted by Bacchus and his pards* (*Ode on a Nightingale* by John Keats)

parlour boarder NOUN a pupil who lived with the family ❑ *and somebody had lately raised her from the condition of scholar to parlour boarder* (*Emma* by Jane Austen)

particular, a London PHRASE London in Victorian times and up to the 1950s was famous for having very dense fog – which was a combination of real fog and the smog of pollution from factories ❑ *This is a London particular . . . A fog, miss'* (*Bleak House* by Charles Dickens)

patten NOUN pattens were wooden soles which were fixed to shoes by straps to protect the shoes in wet weather ❑ *carrying a basket like the Great Seal of England in plaited straw, a pair of pattens, a spare shawl, and an umbrella, though it was a fine bright day* (*Great Expectations* by Charles Dickens)

paviour NOUN a paviour was a labourer who worked on the street pavement ❑ *the paviour his pickaxe* (*Oliver Twist* by Charles Dickens)

peccant ADJ peccant means unhealthy ❑ *other peccant humours* (*Gulliver's Travels* by Jonathan Swift)

penetralium NOUN penetralium is a word used to describe the inner rooms of the house ❑ *and I had no desire to aggravate his impatience previous to inspecting the penetralium* (*Wuthering Heights* by Emily Brontë)

pensive ADV pensive means deep in thought or thinking seriously about something ❑ *and she was leaning pensive on a tomb-stone on her right elbow* (*The Adventures of Huckleberry Finn* by Mark Twain)

penury NOUN penury is the state of being extremely poor ❑ *Distress, if not penury, loomed in the distance* (*Tess of the D'Urbervilles* by Thomas Hardy)

perspective NOUN telescope ❑ *a pocket perspective* (*Gulliver's Travels* by Jonathan Swift)

phaeton NOUN a phaeton was an open carriage for four people ❑ *often* condescends to drive by my humble abode in her little phaeton and ponies (*Pride and Prejudice* by Jane Austen)

phantasm NOUN a phantasm is an illusion, something that is not real. It is sometimes used to mean ghost ❑ *Experience had bred no fancies in him that could raise the phantasm of appetite* (*Silas Marner* by George Eliot)

physic NOUN here physic means medicine ❑ *there I studied physic two years and seven months* (*Gulliver's Travels* by Jonathan Swift)

pinioned VERB to pinion is to hold both arms so that a person cannot move them ❑ *But the relentless Ghost pinioned him in both his arms, and forced him to observe what happened next.* (*A Christmas Carol* by Charles Dickens)

piquet NOUN piquet was a popular card game in the C18th ❑ *Mr Hurst and Mr Bingley were at piquet* (*Pride and Prejudice* by Jane Austen)

plaister NOUN a plaister is a piece of cloth on which an apothecary (or pharmacist) would spread ointment. The cloth is then applied to wounds or bruises to treat them ❑ *Then, she gave the knife a final smart wipe on the edge of the plaister, and then sawed a very thick round off the loaf: which she finally, before separating from the loaf, hewed into two halves, of which Joe got one, and I the other.* (*Great Expectations* by Charles Dickens)

plantations NOUN here plantations means colonies, which are countries controlled by a more powerful country ❑ *besides our plantations in America* (*Gulliver's Travels* by Jonathan Swift)

plastic ADV here plastic is an old term meaning shaping or a power that was forming ❑ *A plastic power abode with me* (*The Prelude* by William Wordsworth)

players NOUN actors ❑ *of players which*

upon the world's stage be (*On His Mistress* by John Donne)

plump ADV all at once, suddenly ❑ *But it took a bit of time to get it well round, the change come so uncommon plump, didn't it?* (*Great Expectations* by Charles Dickens)

plundered VERB to plunder is to rob or steal from ❑ *These crosses stand for the names of ships or towns that they sank or plundered* (*Treasure Island* by Robert Louis Stevenson)

pommel ■ VERB to pommel someone is to hit them repeatedly with your fists ❑ *hug him round the neck, pommel his back, and kick his legs in irrepressible affection!* (*A Christmas Carol* by Charles Dickens) ■ NOUN a pommel is the part of a saddle that rises up at the front ❑ *He had his gun across his pommel* (*The Adventures of Huckleberry Finn* by Mark Twain)

poor's rates NOUN poor's rates were property taxes which were used to support the poor ❑ *"Oh!" replied the undertaker; "why, you know, Mr. Bumble, I pay a good deal towards the poor's rates."* (*Oliver Twist* by Charles Dickens)

popular ADJ popular means ruled by the people, or Republican, rather than ruled by a monarch ❑ *With those of Greece compared and popular Rome* (*The Prelude* by William Wordsworth)

porringer NOUN a porringer is a small bowl ❑ *Of this festive composition each boy had one porringer, and no more* (*Oliver Twist* by Charles Dickens)

postboy NOUN a postboy was the driver of a horse-drawn carriage ❑ *He spoke to a postboy who was dozing under the gateway* (*Oliver Twist* by Charles Dickens)

post-chaise NOUN a fast carriage for two or four passengers ❑ *Looking round, he saw that it was a post-chaise, driven at great speed* (*Oliver Twist* by Charles Dickens)

postern NOUN a small gate usually at the back of a building ❏ *The little servant happening to be entering the fortress with two hot rolls, I passed through the postern and crossed the drawbridge, in her company* (*Great Expectations* by Charles Dickens)

pottle NOUN a pottle was a small basket ❏ *He had a paper-bag under each arm and a pottle of strawberries in one hand . . .* (*Great Expectations* by Charles Dickens)

pounce NOUN pounce is a fine powder used to prevent ink spreading on untreated paper ❏ *in that grim atmosphere of pounce and parchment, red-tape, dusty wafers, ink-jars, brief and draft paper, law reports, writs, declarations, and bills of costs* (*David Copperfield* by Charles Dickens)

pox NOUN pox means sexually transmitted diseases like syphilis ❏ *how the pox in all its consequences and denominations* (*Gulliver's Travels* by Jonathan Swift)

prelibation NOUN prelibation means a foretaste of or an example of something to come ❏ *A prelibation to the mower's scythe* (*The Prelude* by William Wordsworth)

prentice NOUN an apprentice ❏ *and Joe, sitting on an old gun, had told me that when I was 'prentice to him regularly bound, we would have such Larks there!* (*Great Expectations* by Charles Dickens)

presently ADV immediately ❏ *I presently knew what they meant* (*Gulliver's Travels* by Jonathan Swift)

pumpion NOUN pumpkin ❏ *for it was almost as large as a small pumpion* (*Gulliver's Travels* by Jonathan Swift)

punctual ADJ kept in one place ❏ *was not a punctual presence, but a spirit* (*The Prelude* by William Wordsworth)

quadrille ■ NOUN a quadrille is a dance invented in France which is usually performed by four couples ❏ *However, Mr Swiveller had Miss Sophy's hand for the first quadrille (country-dances being low, were utterly proscribed)* (*The Old Curiosity Shop* by Charles Dickens) ■ NOUN quadrille was a card game for four people ❏ *to make up her pool of quadrille in the evening* (*Pride and Prejudice* by Jane Austen)

quality NOUN gentry or upper-class people ❏ *if you are with the quality* (*The Adventures of Huckleberry Finn* by Mark Twain)

quick parts PHRASE quick-witted ❏ *Mr Bennet was so odd a mixture of quick parts* (*Pride and Prejudice* by Jane Austen)

quid NOUN a quid is something chewed or kept in the mouth, like a piece of tobacco ❏ *rolling his quid* (*Treasure Island* by Robert Louis Stevenson)

quit VERB quit means to avenge or to make even ❏ *But Faustus's death shall quit my infamy* (*Doctor Faustus 4.3* by Christopher Marlowe)

rags NOUN divisions ❏ *Nor hours, days, months, which are the rags of time* (*The Sun Rising* by John Donne)

raiment NOUN raiment means clothing ❏ *the mountain shook off turf and flower, had only heath for raiment and crag for gem* (*Jane Eyre* by Charlotte Brontë)

rain cats and dogs PHRASE an expression meaning rain heavily. The origin of the expression is unclear ❏ *But it'll perhaps rain cats and dogs to-morrow* (*Silas Marner* by George Eliot)

raised Cain PHRASE raised Cain means caused a lot of trouble. Cain is a character in the Bible who killed his brother Abel ❏ *and every time he got drunk he raised Cain around town* (*The Adventures of Huckleberry Finn* by Mark Twain)

rambling ADJ rambling means confused and not very clear ❏ *my* head began to be filled very early with rambling thoughts (*Robinson Crusoe* by Daniel Defoe)

raree-show NOUN a raree-show is an old term for a peep-show or a fairground entertainment ❑ *A raree-show is here, with children gathered round* (*The Prelude* by William Wordsworth)

recusants NOUN people who resisted authority ❑ *hardy recusants* (*The Prelude* by William Wordsworth)

redounding VERB eddying. An eddy is a movement in water or air which goes round and round instead of flowing in one direction ❑ *mists and steam-like fogs redounding everywhere* (*The Prelude* by William Wordsworth)

redundant ADJ here redundant means overflowing but Wordsworth also uses it to mean excessively large or too big ❑ *A tempest, a redundant energy* (*The Prelude* by William Wordsworth)

reflex NOUN reflex is a shortened version of reflexion, which is an alternative spelling of reflection ❑ *To cut across the reflex of a star* (*The Prelude* by William Wordsworth)

Reformatory NOUN a prison for young offenders/criminals ❑ *Even when I was taken to have a new suit of clothes, the tailor had orders to make them like a kind of Reformatory, and on no account to let me have the free use of my limbs.* (*Great Expectations* by Charles Dickens)

remorse NOUN pity or compassion ❑ *by that remorse* (*On His Mistress* by John Donne)

render VERB in this context render means give. ❑ *and Sarah could render no reason that would be sanctioned by the feeling of the community.* (*Silas Marner* by George Eliot)

repeater NOUN a repeater was a watch that chimed the last hour when a button was pressed – as a result it

was useful in the dark ❑ *And his watch is a gold repeater, and worth a hundred pound if it's worth a penny.* (*Great Expectations* by Charles Dickens)

repugnance NOUN repugnance means a strong dislike of something or someone ❑ *overcoming a strong repugnance* (*Treasure Island* by Robert Louis Stevenson)

reverence NOUN reverence means bow. When you bow to someone, you briefly bend your body towards them as a formal way of showing them respect ❑ *made my reverence* (*Gulliver's Travels* by Jonathan Swift)

reverie NOUN a reverie is a day dream ❑ *I can guess the subject of your reverie* (*Pride and Prejudice* by Jane Austen)

revival NOUN a religious meeting held in public ❑ *well I'd ben a-running' a little temperance revival thar' bout a week* (*The Adventures of Huckleberry Finn* by Mark Twain)

revolt VERB revolt means turn back or stop your present course of action and go back to what you were doing before ❑ *Revolt, or I'll in piecemeal tear thy flesh* (*Doctor Faustus 5.1* by Christopher Marlowe)

rheumatics/rheumatism NOUN rheumatics [rheumatism] is an illness that makes your joints or muscles stiff and painful ❑ *a new cure for the rheumatics* (*Treasure Island* by Robert Louis Stevenson)

riddance NOUN riddance is usually used in the form good riddance which you say when you are pleased that something has gone or been left behind ❑ *I'd better go into the house, and die and be a riddance* (*David Copperfield* by Charles Dickens)

rimy ADJ rimy is an ADJECTIVE which means covered in ice or frost ❑ *It was a rimy morning, and very damp* (*Great Expectations* by Charles Dickens)

riper ADJ riper means more mature or older ❏ *At riper years to Wittenberg he went* (*Doctor Faustus chorus* by Christopher Marlowe)

rubber NOUN a set of games in whist or backgammon ❏ *her father was sure of his rubber* (*Emma* by Jane Austen)

ruffian NOUN a ruffian is a person who behaves violently ❏ *and when the ruffian had told him* (*Treasure Island* by Robert Louis Stevenson)

sadness NOUN sadness is an old term meaning seriousness ❏ *But I prithee tell me, in good sadness* (*Doctor Faustus 2.2* by Christopher Marlowe)

sailed before the mast PHRASE this phrase meant someone who did not look like a sailor ❏ *he had none of the appearance of a man that sailed before the mast* (*Treasure Island* by Robert Louis Stevenson)

scabbard NOUN a scabbard is the covering for a sword or dagger ❏ *Girded round its middle was an antique scabbard; but no sword was in it, and the ancient sheath was eaten up with rust* (*A Christmas Carol* by Charles Dickens)

schooners NOUN A schooner is a fast, medium-sized sailing ship ❏ *if schooners, islands, and maroons* (*Treasure Island* by Robert Louis Stevenson)

science NOUN learning or knowledge ❏ *Even Science, too, at hand* (*The Prelude* by William Wordsworth)

scrouge VERB scrouge means to squeeze or to crowd ❏ *to scrouge in and get a sight* (*The Adventures of Huckleberry Finn* by Mark Twain)

scrutore NOUN a scrutore, or escritoire, was a writing table ❏ *set me gently on my feet upon the scrutore* (*Gulliver's Travels* by Jonathan Swift)

scutcheon/escutcheon NOUN an escutcheon is a shield with a coat of arms, or the symbols of a family name, engraved on it ❏ *On the*

scutcheon we'll have a bend (*The Adventures of Huckleberry Finn* by Mark Twain)

sea-dog PHRASE sea-dog is a slang term for an experienced sailor or pirate ❏ *a 'true sea-dog', and a 'real old salt,'* (*Treasure Island* by Robert Louis Stevenson)

see the lions PHRASE to see the lions was to go and see the sights of London. Originally the phrase referred to the menagerie in the Tower of London and later in Regent's Park ❏ *We will go and see the lions for an hour or two – it's something to have a fresh fellow like you to show them to, Copperfield* (*David Copperfield* by Charles Dickens)

self-conceit NOUN self-conceit is an old term which means having too high an opinion of oneself, or deceiving yourself ❏ *Till swollen with cunning, of a self-conceit* (*Doctor Faustus chorus* by Christopher Marlowe)

seneschal NOUN a steward ❏ *where a grey-headed seneschal sings a funny chorus with a funnier body of vassals* (*Oliver Twist* by Charles Dickens)

sensible ADJ if you were sensible of something you are aware or conscious of something ❏ *If my children are silly I must hope to be always sensible of it* (*Pride and Prejudice* by Jane Austen)

sessions NOUN court cases were heard at specific times of the year called sessions ❏ *He lay in prison very ill, during the whole interval between his committal for trial, and the coming round of the Sessions.* (*Great Expectations* by Charles Dickens)

shabby ADJ shabby places look old and in bad condition ❏ *a little bit of a shabby village named Pikesville* (*The Adventures of Huckleberry Finn* by Mark Twain)

shay-cart NOUN a shay-cart was a small cart drawn by one horse ❏ *"I were at the Bargemen t'other night, Pip;"*

whenever he subsided into affection, he called me Pip, and whenever he relapsed into politeness he called me Sir; "when there come up in his shay-cart Pumblechook." (Great Expectations by Charles Dickens)

shilling NOUN a shilling is an old unit of currency. There were twenty shillings in every British pound ❑ *"Ten shillings too much," said the gentleman in the white waistcoat.* (*Oliver Twist* by Charles Dickens)

shines NOUN tricks or games ❑ *well, it would make a cow laugh to see the shines that old idiot cut* (*The Adventures of Huckleberry Finn* by Mark Twain)

shirking VERB shirking means not doing what you are meant to be doing, or evading your duties ❑ *some of you shirking lubbers* (*Treasure Island* by Robert Louis Stevenson)

shiver my timbers PHRASE shiver my timbers is an expression which was used by sailors and pirates to express surprise ❑ *why, shiver my timbers, if I hadn't forgotten my score!* (*Treasure Island* by Robert Louis Stevenson)

shoe-roses NOUN shoe-roses were roses made from ribbons which were stuck on to shoes as decoration ❑ *the very shoe-roses for Netherfield were got by proxy* (*Pride and Prejudice* by Jane Austen)

singular ADJ singular means very great and remarkable or strange ❑ *"Singular dream," he says* (*The Adventures of Huckleberry Finn* by Mark Twain)

sire NOUN sire is an old word which means lord or master or elder ❑ *She also defied her sire* (*Little Women* by Louisa May Alcott)

sixpence NOUN a sixpence was half of a shilling ❑ *if she had only a shilling in the world, she would be very lilkely to give away sixpence of it* (*Emma* by Jane Austen)

slavey NOUN the word slavey was used when there was only one servant in

a house or boarding-house – so she had to perform all the duties of a larger staff ❑ *Two distinct knocks, sir, will produce the slavey at any time* (*The Old Curiosity Shop* by Charles Dickens)

slender ADJ weak ❑ *In slender accents of sweet verse* (*The Prelude* by William Wordsworth)

slop-shops NOUN slop-shops were shops where cheap ready-made clothes were sold. They mainly sold clothes to sailors ❑ *Accordingly, I took the jacket off, that I might learn to do without it; and carrying it under my arm, began a tour of inspection of the various slop-shops.* (*David Copperfield* by Charles Dickens)

sluggard NOUN a lazy person ❑ *"Stand up and repeat 'Tis the voice of the sluggard,'" said the Gryphon.* (*Alice's Adventures in Wonderland* by Lewis Carroll)

smallpox NOUN smallpox is a serious infectious disease ❑ *by telling the men we had smallpox aboard* (*The Adventures of Huckleberry Finn* by Mark Twain)

smalls NOUN smalls are short trousers ❑ *It is difficult for a large-headed, small-eyed youth, of lumbering make and heavy countenance, to look dignified under any circumstances; but it is more especially so, when superadded to these personal attractions are a red nose and yellow smalls* (*Oliver Twist* by Charles Dickens)

sneeze-box NOUN a box for snuff was called a sneeze-box because sniffing snuff makes the user sneeze ❑ *To think of Jack Dawkins — lummy Jack — the Dodger — the Artful Dodger — going abroad for a common twopenny-halfpenny sneeze-box!* (*Oliver Twist* by Charles Dickens)

snorted VERB slept ❑ *Or snorted we in the Seven Sleepers' den?* (*The Good-Morrow* by John Donne)

snuff NOUN snuff is tobacco in powder form which is taken by sniffing ❑

as he thrust his thumb and fore-finger into the proffered snuff-box of the undertaker: which was an ingenious little model of a patent coffin. (*Oliver Twist* by Charles Dickens)

soliloquized VERB to soliloquize is when an actor in a play speaks to himself or herself rather than to another actor ❑ *"A new servitude! There is something in that," I soliloquized (mentally, be it understood; I did not talk aloud)* (*Jane Eyre* by Charlotte Brontë)

sough NOUN a sough is a drain or a ditch ❑ *as you may have noticed the sough that runs from the marshes* (*Wuthering Heights* by Emily Brontë)

spirits NOUN a spirit is the nonphysical part of a person which is believed to remain alive after their death ❑ *that I might raise up spirits when I please* (*Doctor Faustus 1.5* by Christopher Marlowe)

spleen ■ NOUN here spleen means a type of sadness or depression which was thought to only affect the wealthy ❑ *yet here I could plainly discover the true seeds of spleen* (*Gulliver's Travels* by Jonathan Swift) ■ NOUN irritability and low spirits ❑ *Adieu to disappointment and spleen* (*Pride and Prejudice* by Jane Austen)

spondulicks NOUN spondulicks is a slang word which means money ❑ *not for all his spondulicks and as much more on top of it* (*The Adventures of Huckleberry Finn* by Mark Twain)

stalled of VERB to be stalled of something is to be bored with it ❑ *I'm stalled of doing naught* (*Wuthering Heights* by Emily Brontë)

stanchion NOUN a stanchion is a pole or bar that stands upright and is used as a buidling support ❑ *and slid down a stanchion* (*The Adventures of Huckleberry Finn* by Mark Twain)

stang NOUN stang is another word for pole which was an old measurement ❑ *These fields were intermingled*

with woods of half a stang (*Gulliver's Travels* by Jonathan Swift)

starlings NOUN a starling is a wall built around the pillars that support a bridge to protect the pillars ❑ *There were states of the tide when, having been down the river, I could not get back through the eddy-chafed arches and starlings of old London Bridge* (*Great Expectations* by Charles Dickens)

startings NOUN twitching or night-time movements of the body ❑ *with midnight's startings* (*On His Mistress* by John Donne)

stomacher NOUN a panel at the front of a dress ❑ *but send her aunt the pattern of a stomacher* (*Emma* by Jane Austen)

stoop VERB swoop ❑ *Once a kite hovering over the garden made a swoop at me* (*Gulliver's Travels* by Jonathan Swift)

succedaneum NOUN a succedaneum is a substitute ❑ *But as a succedaneum* (*The Prelude* by William Wordsworth)

suet NOUN a hard animal fat used in cooking ❑ *and your jaws are too weak For anything tougher than suet* (*Alice's Adventures in Wonderland* by Lewis Carroll)

sultry ADJ sultry weather is hot and damp. Here sultry means unpleasant or risky ❑ *for it was getting pretty sultry for us* (*The Adventures of Huckleberry Finn* by Mark Twain)

summerset NOUN summerset is an old spelling of somersault. If someone does a somersault, they turn over completely in the air ❑ *I have seen him do the summerset* (*Gulliver's Travels* by Jonathan Swift)

supper NOUN supper was a light meal taken late in the evening. The main meal was dinner which was eaten at four or five in the afternoon ❑ *and the supper table was all set out* (*Emma* by Jane Austen)

surfeits VERB to surfeit in something is to have far too much of it, or to overindulge in it to an unhealthy degree ❑ *He surfeits upon cursed necromancy* (*Doctor Faustus chorus* by Christopher Marlowe)

surtout NOUN a surtout is a long close-fitting overcoat ❑ *He wore a long black surtout reaching nearly to his ankles* (*The Old Curiosity Shop* by Charles Dickens)

swath NOUN swath is the width of corn cut by a scythe ❑ *while thy hook Spares the next swath* (*Ode to Autumn* by John Keats)

sylvan ADJ sylvan means belonging to the woods ❑ *Sylvan historian* (*Ode on a Grecian Urn* by John Keats)

taction NOUN taction means touch. This means that the people had to be touched on the mouth or the ears to get their attention ❑ *without being roused by some external taction upon the organs of speech and hearing* (*Gulliver's Travels* by Jonathan Swift)

Tag and Rag and Bobtail PHRASE the riff-raff, or lower classes. Used in an insulting way ❑ *"No," said he; "not till it got about that there was no protection on the premises, and it come to be considered dangerous, with convicts and Tag and Rag and Bobtail going up and down."* (*Great Expectations* by Charles Dickens)

tallow NOUN tallow is hard animal fat that is used to make candles and soap ❑ *and a lot of tallow candles* (*The Adventures of Huckleberry Finn* by Mark Twain)

tan VERB to tan means to beat or whip ❑ *and if I catch you about that school I'll tan you good* (*The Adventures of Huckleberry Finn* by Mark Twain)

tanyard NOUN the tanyard is part of a tannery, which is a place where leather is made from animal skins ❑ *hid in the old tanyard* (*The Adventures of Huckleberry Finn* by Mark Twain)

tarry ADJ tarry means the colour of tar or black ❑ *his tarry pig-tail* (*Treasure Island* by Robert Louis Stevenson)

thereof PHRASE from there ❑ *By all desires which thereof did ensue* (*On His Mistress* by John Donne)

thick with, be PHRASE if you are 'thick with someone' you are very close, sharing secrets – it is often used to describe people who are planning something secret ❑ *Hasn't he been thick with Mr Heathcliff lately?* (*Wuthering Heights* by Emily Brontë)

thimble NOUN a thimble is a small cover used to protect the finger while sewing ❑ *The paper had been sealed in several places by a thimble* (*Treasure Island* by Robert Louis Stevenson)

thirtover ADJ thirtover is an old word which means obstinate or that someone is very determined to do want they want and can not be persuaded to do something in another way ❑ *I have been living on in a thirtover, lackadaisical way* (*Tess of the D'Urbervilles* by Thomas Hardy)

timbrel NOUN timbrel is a tambourine ❑ *What pipes and timbrels?* (*Ode on a Grecian Urn* by John Keats)

tin NOUN tin is slang for money/cash ❑ *Then the plain question is, an't it a pity that this state of things should continue, and how much better would it be for the old gentleman to hand over a reasonable amount of tin, and make it all right and comfortable* (*The Old Curiosity Shop* by Charles Dickens)

tincture NOUN a tincture is a medicine made with alcohol and a small amount of a drug ❑ *with ink composed of a cephalic tincture* (*Gulliver's Travels* by Jonathan Swift)

tithe NOUN a tithe is a tax paid to the church ❑ *and held farms which, speaking from a spiritual point of view, paid highly-desirable tithes* (*Silas Marner* by George Eliot)

towardly ADJ a towardly child is dutiful or obedient ❑ *and a towardly child* (*Gulliver's Travels* by Jonathan Swift)

toys NOUN trifles are things which are considered to have little importance, value, or significance ❑ *purchase my life from them bysome bracelets, glass rings, and other toys* (*Gulliver's Travels* by Jonathan Swift)

tract NOUN a tract is a religious pamphlet or leaflet ❑ *and Joe Harper got a hymn-book and a tract* (*The Adventures of Huckleberry Finn* by Mark Twain)

train-oil NOUN train-oil is oil from whale blubber ❑ *The train-oil and gunpowder were shoved out of sight in a minute* (*Wuthering Heights* by Emily Brontë)

tribulation NOUN tribulation means the suffering or difficulty you experience in a particular situation ❑ *Amy was learning this distinction through much tribulation* (*Little Women* by Louisa May Alcott)

trivet NOUN a trivet is a three-legged stand for resting a pot or kettle ❑ *a pocket-knife in his right; and a pewter pot on the trivet* (*Oliver Twist* by Charles Dickens)

trot line NOUN a trot line is a fishing line to which a row of smaller fishing lines are attached ❑ *when he got along I was hard at it taking up a trot line* (*The Adventures of Huckleberry Finn* by Mark Twain)

troth NOUN oath or pledge ❑ *I wonder, by my troth* (*The Good-Morrow* by John Donne)

truckle NOUN a truckle bedstead is a bed that is on wheels and can be slid under another bed to save space ❑ *It rose under my hand, and the door yielded. Looking in, I saw a lighted candle on a table, a bench, and a mattress on a truckle bedstead.* (*Great Expectations* by Charles Dickens)

trump NOUN a trump is a good, reliable person wo can be trusted ❑ *This lad Hawkins is a trump, I perceive* (*Treasure Island* by Robert Louis Stevenson)

tucker NOUN a tucker is a frilly lace collar which is worn around the neck ❑ *Whereat Scrooge's niece's sister¯the plump one with the lace tucker: not the one with the roses¯blushed.* (*A Christmas Carol* by Charles Dickens)

tureen NOUN a large bowl with a lid from which soup or vegetables are served ❑ *Waiting in a hot tureen!* (*Alice's Adventures in Wonderland* by Lewis Carroll)

turnkey NOUN a prison officer; jailer ❑ *As we came out of the prison through the lodge, I found that the great importance of my guardian was appreciated by the turnkeys, no less than by those whom they held in charge.* (*Great Expectations* by Charles Dickens)

turnpike NOUN the upkeep of many roads of the time was paid for by tolls (fees) collected at posts along the road. There was a gate to prevent people travelling further along the road until the toll had been paid. ❑ *Traddles, whom I have taken up by appointment at the turnpike, presents a dazzling combination of cream colour and light blue; and both he and Mr. Dick have a general effect about them of being all gloves.* (*David Copperfield* by Charles Dickens)

twas PHRASE it was ❑ *twas but a dream of thee* (*The Good-Morrow* by John Donne)

tyrannized VERB tyrannized means bullied or forced to do things against their will ❑ *for people would soon cease coming there to be tyrannized over and put down* (*Treasure Island* by Robert Louis Stevenson)

'un NOUN 'un is a slang term for one – usually used to refer to a person ❑ *She's been thinking the old 'un* (*David Copperfield* by Charles Dickens)

undistinguished ADJ undiscriminating or incapable of making a distinction between good and bad things ❏ *their undistinguished appetite to devour everything* (*Gulliver's Travels* by Jonathan Swift)

use NOUN habit ❏ *Though use make you apt to kill me* (*The Flea* by John Donne)

vacant ADJ vacant usually means empty, but here Wordsworth uses it to mean carefree ❏ *To vacant musing, unreproved neglect* (*The Prelude* by William Wordsworth)

valetudinarian NOUN one too concerned with his or her own health. ❏ *for having been a valetudinarian all his life* (*Emma* by Jane Austen)

vamp VERB vamp means to walk or tramp to somewhere ❏ *Well, vamp on to Marlott, will 'ee* (*Tess of the D'Urbervilles* by Thomas Hardy)

vapours NOUN the vapours is an old term which means unpleasant and strange thoughts, which make the person feel nervous and unhappy ❏ *and my head was full of vapours* (*Robinson Crusoe* by Daniel Defoe)

vegetables NOUN here vegetables means plants ❏ *the other vegetables are in the same proportion* (*Gulliver's Travels* by Jonathan Swift)

venturesome ADJ if you are venturesome you are willing to take risks ❏ *he must be either hopelessly stupid or a venturesome fool* (*Wuthering Heights* by Emily Brontë)

verily ADJ verily means really or truly ❏ *though I believe verily* (*Robinson Crusoe* by Daniel Defoe)

vicinage NOUN vicinage is an area or the residents of an area ❏ *and to his thought the whole vicinage was haunted by her.* (*Silas Marner* by George Eliot)

victuals NOUN victuals means food ❏ *grumble a little over the victuals* (*The Adventures of Huckleberry Finn* by Mark Twain)

vintage NOUN vintage in this context means wine ❏ *Oh, for a draught of vintage!* (*Ode on a Nightingale* by John Keats)

virtual ADJ here virtual means powerful or strong ❏ *had virtual faith* (*The Prelude* by William Wordsworth)

vittles NOUN vittles is a slang word which means food ❏ *There never was such a woman for givin' away vittles and drink* (*Little Women* by Louisa May Alcott)

voided straight PHRASE voided straight is an old expression which means emptied immediately ❏ *see the rooms be voided straight* (*Doctor Faustus 4.1* by Christopher Marlowe)

wainscot NOUN wainscot is wood panel lining in a room so wainscoted means a room lined with wooden panels ❏ *in the dark wainscoted parlor* (*Silas Marner* by George Eliot)

walking the plank PHRASE walking the plank was a punishment in which a prisoner would be made to walk along a plank on the side of the ship and fall into the sea, where they would be abandoned ❏ *about hanging, and walking the plank* (*Treasure Island* by Robert Louis Stevenson)

want VERB want means to be lacking or short of ❏ *The next thing wanted was to get the picture framed* (*Emma* by Jane Austen)

wanting ADJ wanting means lacking or missing ❏ *wanting two fingers of the left hand* (*Treasure Island* by Robert Louis Stevenson)

wanting, I was not PHRASE I was not wanting means I did not fail ❏ *I was not wanting to lay a foundation of religious knowledge in his mind* (*Robinson Crusoe* by Daniel Defoe)

ward NOUN a ward is, usually, a child who has been put under the protection of the court or a guardian for his or her protection ❏ *I call the Wards in Jarndcye. The*

are caged up with all the others.
(*Bleak House* by Charles Dickens)

waylay VERB to waylay someone is to lie in wait for them or to intercept them ❑ *I must go up the road and waylay him* (*The Adventures of Huckleberry Finn* by Mark Twain)

weazen NOUN weazen is a slang word for throat. It actually means shrivelled ❑ *You with a uncle too! Why, I knowed you at Gargery's when you was so small a wolf that I could have took your weazen betwixt this finger and thumb and chucked you away dead* (*Great Expectations* by Charles Dickens)

wery ■ ADV very ❑ *Be wery careful o' vidders all your life* (*Pickwick Papers* by Charles Dickens) ■ *See* wibrated

wherry NOUN wherry is a small swift rowing boat for one person ❑ *It was flood tide when Daniel Quilp sat himself down in the wherry to cross to the opposite shore.* (*The Old Curiosity Shop* by Charles Dickens)

whether PREP whether means which of the two in this example ❑ *we came in full view of a great island or continent (for we knew not whether)* (*Gulliver's Travels* by Jonathan Swift)

whetstone NOUN a whetstone is a stone used to sharpen knives and other tools ❑ *I dropped pap's whetstone there too* (*The Adventures of Huckleberry Finn* by Mark Twain)

wibrated VERB in Dickens's use of the English language 'w' often replaces 'v' when he is reporting speech. So here 'wibrated' means 'vibrated'. In Pickwick Papers a judge asks Sam Weller (who constantly confuses the two letters) 'Do you spell is with a 'v' or a 'w'?' to which Weller replies 'That depends upon the taste and fancy of the speller, my Lord' ❑ *There are strings . . . in the human heart that had better not be wibrated*' (*Barnaby Rudge* by Charles Dickens)

wicket NOUN a wicket is a little door in a larger entrance ❑ *Having rested here, for a minute or so, to collect a good burst of sobs and an imposing show of tears and terror, he knocked loudly at the wicket;* (*Oliver Twist* by Charles Dickens)

without CONJ without means unless ❑ *You don't know about me, without you have read a book by the name of The Adventures of Tom Sawyer* (*The Adventures of Huckleberry Finn* by Mark Twain)

wittles ■ NOUN vittles is a slang word which means food ❑ *I live on broken wittles – and I sleep on the coals* (*David Copperfield* by Charles Dickens) ■ *See* wibrated

woo VERB courts or forms a proper relationship with ❑ *before it woo* (*The Flea* by John Donne)

words, to have PHRASE if you have words with someone you have a disagreement or an argument ❑ *I do not want to have words with a young thing like you.* (*Black Beauty* by Anna Sewell)

workhouse NOUN workhouses were places where the homeless were given food and a place to live in return for doing very hard work ❑ *And the Union workhouses? demanded Scrooge. Are they still in operation?* (*A Christmas Carol* by Charles Dickens)

yawl NOUN a yawl is a small boat kept on a bigger boat for short trips. Yawl is also the name for a small fishing boat ❑ *She sent out her yawl, and we went aboard* (*The Adventures of Huckleberry Finn* by Mark Twain)

yeomanry NOUN the yeomanry was a collective term for the middle classes involved in agriculture ❑ *The yeomanry are precisely the order of people with whom I feel I can have nothing to do* (*Emma* by Jane Austen)

yonder ADV yonder means over there ❑ *all in the same second we seem to hear low voices in yonder!* (*The Adventures of Huckleberry Finn* by Mark Twain)